HICCUPS

A love story with a difference

I0564556

HARSH PANDE

JAICO PUBLISHING HOUSE

Ahmedabad Bangalore Bhopal Bhubaneswar Chennai
Delhi Hyderabad Kolkata Lucknow Mumbai

Published by Jaico Publishing House
A-2 Jash Chambers, 7-A Sir Phirozshah Mehta Road
Fort, Mumbai - 400 001
jaicopub@jaicobooks.com
www.jaicobooks.com

HICCUPS
ISBN 978-81-8495-414-2

First Jaico Impression: 2013

Page design and layouts: Special Effects, Mumbai

Printed by

"No one has a monopoly on ideas!"
"No matter how severe the storm is, you can still smile!"

– Harsh Pande

Contents

Foreword

It gives me great pleasure and immense happiness to write the foreword for this book *HICCUPS* by Harsh Pande (Harshvardhan Lalit Pande).

I have been fortunate to be associated with Harsh since his childhood as a treating orthopaedic surgeon. Since childhood he has shown a sense of humour and a sharp wit which belied his age. He always smiled no matter what phase of treatment he was undergoing and encouraged his treating team to perform better.

Harsh displayed exceptionally admirable spirit and intelligence which helped him to achieve excellent results in academics and other endeavours, despite suffering from complicated orthopaedic disorder by birth. As an orthopaedic surgeon, I will always be fascinated by his indomitable cheerful attitude towards life.

He was very well guided and supported by his family in all his efforts.

His entrepreneurship and sagacity is evident from his literary effort so vividly put forth in his novel *HICCUPS*.

I extend my wishes to Harsh, his family, friends and the readers. I am sure this book will be a very valuable gift to all those who were closely associated with him.

—Dr. K. H. Sancheti
Chief Orthopaedic Surgeon
Recipient of Padma Awards

Acknowledgements

Deeply acknowledge the contributions of:

Digvijay Pande, for encouraging his younger brother in the creation of Hiccups and the subsequent follow up thereafter.

Profoundly – All the Vincentians, COEPeans, corporate associates, friends and relatives who always loved and supported Harsh Pande.

And above all

Harsh's parents who always encouraged Harsh to follow his dreams.

PROLOGUE

The Monologue with God

He buried his face in his palms. There was no one to look up to for help. He was all alone. There was light all around him and yet darkness filled his heart. Though the walls displayed pictures of smiling patients and doctors, he felt nothing but dread. The verdict had been delivered, she wasn't going to return. All the medical jargon that the men in white coats threw around was irrelevant. They couldn't bring his mother back.

He felt a tear flow down his index finger, leaving a moist trace as it trickled down his right hand. He did not know why, but he wanted to hold onto the tear, he didn't want to let it flow right through his hand. He commanded it to stop flowing, it didn't heed his call. There, in that silent corridor of a large hospital, a young man felt the deepest sense of helplessness.

He got up, numb, barely able to command his feet to move towards the glass panel on the ICU door. Every step he took towards the small window made him nervous. He could not bear to watch his mother in that state, but he knew that he had to. He peered through the glass, which was immediately covered with a shroud of moisture from the teary air he exhaled. He observed the way she was breathing; short gasps of inhaling followed by slow breathing out, almost as if she was sighing. At the point where she exhaled completely, his heart skipped a beat as he did not see her breathe in again. He stopped breathing too. His heart despaired for a brief moment, until he saw the white hospital sheet covering her, rise again. It took him nearly half a minute to realize that he was still to take in his next breath. Another tear-drop made its way down his face.

He stood there for what seemed like an eternity, barely blinking, afraid that if he did not oversee every breath of hers, she would stop breathing. He wished he could stop the tears from welling up in his eyes, they were blurring his vision. He had never felt so alone in his life before. His hand reached for the *rudraksh* his mother had given to him. She had told him it would protect him from all harm. How he wished, that it would've protected its original owner. As he kissed the sacred bead and placed it back on his chest, he felt the envelope that was kept in his shirt pocket. It contained a cheque, given to him by his uncle. The amount on the cheque was all that a brother's love for his sister had come down to. He looked at it with resentment but decided that the time to think about finances would come later. Dawn was a few hours away, and he knew he wasn't going to move from the spot where he stood. He knew that the first sight of sunlight would lift his spirit. He made up his mind, to stand guard all night, in front of the ICU door. No angel of death would be allowed to pass through during his watch.

The stars faded away as dawn approached, replacing the dark night sky with hints of the early morning hue. The night shift employees at the hospital were the only ones moving around. A few of them stopped to look at the man standing in front of the ICU door, but no one bothered to talk to him. It was just the end of another night of work for them, they were preparing to leave for their homes and get back to their families.

For the young man, the only family he had was battling death a few feet away and he could do little but wait and hope. His eyes were tired, his tears had dried up over the course of the night and his feet were numb. But his resolve to stand guard until he saw the morning sun was firm. From the corner of his eye he looked towards the window at the end of the corridor, the sun was just an hour away; hope was just an hour away. That thought gave him the strength to continue his vigil with renewed determination.

The morning signalled the start of yet another day at the hospital. The regular shift doctors and nurses replaced their night shift counterparts. The young man wondered why the emergency ward of the hospital followed the norms of the rest of the hospital wards, with the diluted staffing at night. Pain and death did not differentiate between night and day. He shrugged off such musings from his mind and tried to focus on what was important.

The real reason why he was waiting for the morning was because it would bring back the neurologist in charge of his mother's case. There were a lot of questions he had in his mind. Things that the doctor had told him yesterday which he had not fully registered because of the state of mind he was in. Not in his worst nightmare did he imagine that he'd have to see a day like the one that had just gone by. He wanted to speak to the doctor again and get some answers.

His chain of thought was disturbed by some movements he saw from the corner of his eye. A few doctors were making their way from down the corridor towards the ICU. Dr. Roy, the neurologist, was leading the way while a couple of other doctors followed closely. He had a file in his hand and a worried look on his face. As the doctors came closer to the ICU, they put on their surgical masks; they had already donned their gloves. The young man was about to say something, when the neurologist raised his hand in a calming gesture and walked past him to enter the ICU.

He peered through the glass panel once again; disappointed by the fact that he couldn't hear what the doctors were discussing inside. Dr. Roy seemed to be very animated in his discussions with the other doctors, one of whom was a cardiologist. The third man in a white coat was a junior doctor. *His* mother's case was probably some kind of a case study for the junior doctor. He shook his head as he thought about it for a second. After a ten minute discussion the doctors were out of the ICU. Dr. Roy tried to feign a smile as he looked at the anxious youngster standing near the glass panel, but couldn't conceal the hopelessness behind the smile. The neurologist asked the youngster, who was the patient's son, to follow him. The son looked at his mother through the glass panel and silently promised that he'd return very soon.

He walked briskly, the numbness in his feet receding with each step. As he passed by the window at the end of the corridor, he looked towards the sun. Despite it being too bright, he gazed directly at it, asking the sun to protect his mother while he was away. They entered the elevator and made their way to the floor below where Dr. Roy's office was located. Not a word was spoken during the interim. Finally they reached his office; the junior doctor pulled out a few X-rays from the file and put them up on the display board. The mix of black and deathly grey on an X-ray made the young man feel uncomfortable. Dr. Roy stood next to the display panel and took in a deep breath before starting off with what he had to say.

Half an hour later, the young man walked out of the doctor's office. His shoulders were drooping and his steps were unsure. He found it hard to breathe. What Dr. Roy had to say was devastating: *his* mother's life was in grave danger. Prior to the meeting, he was under the impression that the major point of concern was whether or not she would come out of the coma. He had just been informed that things were so bad that they did not know if she would survive the day. As he made his way back towards the elevator, his cell phone started to vibrate; it was a call from his uncle. He rejected the call, pressing the red button on his phone as hard as he could, out of frustration. On what could be the last day of his mother's life, his uncle was probably getting ready for office. The phone call to check on her state was probably an afterthought. He clenched his fists together as he felt a surge of anger from within. But he realized that now was not the time to get riled up. Calm down, he told himself. He blanked out all thoughts from his mind and rushed back to the ICU corridor.

He looked through the glass panel once again, she was still breathing. He heaved a sigh of relief. As long as she's breathing, she s fighting. As long as she's fighting, she's winning. He looked at his mother, speaking to her in his mind as if she could hear him telepathically. He told her, that everything was fine and that it was a matter of time before she'd be back on her feet. He looked at his watch; it was nine in the morning. Exactly two days ago, he was having breakfast at home with her. He wanted to rush through his breakfast and get out of the house to meet his friends for the matinee show. She was telling him to have his breakfast slowly, to chew his food properly. I'm not a child anymore, he remembered telling her. You are to me; she had said. A tear started to form in his eye again; he flicked it off with his finger. This is not how it ends, he told himself. No matter what the men in white coats say, this is not how it ends; he kept repeating the words to himself. You have been through too much in life and so have I. Better days and better times will come, they have to, and you and I will see them together *maa*, I promise; he said to her in unspoken words. He looked at his watch again. He had a meeting with the dean of the hospital in fifteen minutes. He took one more look at her before moving away.

He was back on the floor below, and turned right to an extended corridor. The senior members of the hospital staff had their offices spread through the corridor. He passed by Dr. Roy's office and the cardiologist's office, up next was the Dean's office followed by a fair amount of empty space with a small temple at the end of the corridor. He was not in a state to laugh, but he found the location of the temple amusing. After one crossed all the senior-most doctors offices and some space beyond, then, after everything else, you could finally come to God for help. He couldn't say whether the architect of the hospital was a believer or an atheist with a sense of humour.

After he waited for a few minutes in front of the Dean's office, a secretary walked up to him and asked him to enter. The meeting lasted barely ten minutes, but to him it seemed like an eternity. The Dean informed him about the financial requirements of *his* mother's treatment. He asked the Dean how much money he needed to pay and how much time he had to arrange the funds. He did not panic when he heard the massive amount and the short time he had to pay up. The Dean wanted to comfort the young man, he was used to people breaking down in such situations; but he noticed a calm determination about the eighteen year old sitting in front of him. The young man thanked him for the time and walked towards the door. *He* stepped out of the office and walked straight to the temple. It was time for a monologue with God.

He stood in front of the temple and looked at the idol adorned with flowers and jewels. He looked over his shoulder; he saw a couple, probably married, waiting for their meeting with the dean. No one else stood in the entire corridor; it was safe for him to speak aloud without being noticed. He concentrated on the idol and tried to blank out all other thoughts from his mind. He took a deep breath and began praying with folded hands and a bowed head.

"Over the years I have prayed to You for a lot of things, right from toys to high scores in exams. Today when I think of it, I wasted all those prayers, they involved things that were so trivial. I could have lived without that toy; life would've gone on fine had I scored a little lesser in those exams. But today I have come to pray for what matters the most to me – my mother's life. She is the only light in my world. Do not let that one flame go out. Please... I know that at this moment, there are probably millions of people praying to you. Why should You pay attention to my prayer? Well... this is the last time I will pray to you in this lifetime; regardless of my prayer being answered or not. If it is answered, I will have nothing more to ask of you; if my prayer falls on deaf ears, there will be nothing left to pray for.

From hereon, I forfeit my right to pray to You. For the rest of my life, I will bear every hardship in silence, suffer every misfortune without complaint and strive to achieve every goal all by myself. I promise. Just spare my mother's life. That's all I have to ask of You. That's all I will ever ask of You."

He closed his eyes and fought back a tear before taking a few steps back, turning around and moving towards the elevator to get back to the ICU. He found himself standing in front of the ICU glass panel once again. He looked through the glass panel and watched his mother breathe. This time he wasn't nervous or afraid. He knew what he had to do. He pulled out the envelope with the cheque from his pocket. Without batting an eyelid, he tore it into pieces and threw it into the dustbin kept in the corridor. He needed no favours to save his mother's life. He walked to the elevator and soon he was out of the hospital premises. He was going to make sure that he provided his mother with everything she could possibly need to win her battle. He had no idea how long this struggle would last; all he knew was that he wasn't going to give up. He would fight and fight until he won; he would fight until a mother was returned to her son.

Music and the Flashing Lights

Two years later she woke up from her afternoon nap feeling a little light-headed. She had a notion that there was something important about the afternoon, but she simply couldn't remember what it was. She walked towards the bathroom with her eyes half-closed. She splashed some water on her face to get over the grogginess. Out of nowhere it struck her; it was the annual prize distribution day at college. She stepped out of the bathroom, water dripping down her chin, and took a look at the wall clock. Half past five. She muttered a few expletives under her breath and rushed towards her bed. She found her cell phone next to the pillow. It showed five missed calls from Suparna, her best friend. She dialled Suparna's number:

"I can't believe I overslept" she said to Suparna in a state of panic.

"Forget all that now, get ready quickly. The ceremony starts in half an hour. I'll come pick you up; you'll make it on time. I'll be there in fifteen. Don't worry!" Suparna said, trying to calm her best friend.

"Okay, thanks!" she said hurriedly and hung up.

She looked at her wardrobe and decided to go with a simple grey *kurta* and blue jeans combo. The college prize distribution ceremony was not the ideal place for a fashion statement. Besides, she didn't have the time to put on anything fancy. She got dressed in ten minutes flat, a personal record, and stepped out of the apartment.

As per plan, she saw Suparna arrive in fifteen minutes. Suparna treated her Activa like it was some superbike, zip zapping across the streets, causing near-accidents every once in a while. She knew Suparna loved riding fast, taking sharp turns and cutting across lanes. They weren't best friends for no reason; she had a tendency to procrastinate while Suparna loved haste.

They reached the college parking lot and then ran towards the auditorium. They entered as discreetly as they could. She looked around and realized that the ceremony had barely started, since the audience looked pretty fresh. She sat alongside Suparna on the nearest empty seats they could find. The Director of the college had just started his speech and she got a feeling that it would be a long one. Half-way through the speech, she was nearing her personal best score in the all-time hit cell phone game – *Snake*.

The applause from the audience at the end of the Director's speech broke her concentration and forced her to pause the game. The moment the Chief Guest, an ex-student and entrepreneur, started his speech; she regained her focus and continued the game. She could never understand why the college authorities felt the need for delivering long drawn speeches about doing well in life to students during the prize distribution day. The prize winners were doing pretty well in life as it is.

After delivering a verbose speech, the Chief Guest finally uttered the words 'thank you' which got the audience to respond with a resounding applause of relief. The prize distribution ceremony then reached its business end. The Chief Guest stood up as the Director called out each topper, by batch, branch and rank. As soon as the names of the students who had topped in their Second Year of engineering began to be called out, she started to feel a little excited. Mid-way through her engineering course, she had managed to make it to the podium. It didn't really matter to her as much as it did to her father who had specifically requested that she send him photos from the ceremony. Suparna was in charge of making sure that a high resolution photograph would be secured as *she* went on stage to receive her prize for standing second in the Computer Sciences batch.

The student who stood third was called on stage. He was a nerdy looking guy who didn't speak much to anyone but the professors. He went on stage and collected a bronze medal, a certificate along with a cheque. She hadn't realized that money was involved until she saw him come down the stage and pass by her seat. She was glad that she didn't know the amount on the cheque, it added to the excitement.

The moment arrived at last, she heard her name being announced, causing Suparna to yell at the top of her shrill voice. She made her way to the stage while Suparna readied the camera. As soon as she walked onto the stage, a number of male students from the audience started hooting – a development that she had expected and pretended to ignore. She smiled and shook hands with the Chief Guest, who was making a lot of effort to seem genuinely interested while saying the customary 'Congratulations, well done. All the best for the future!' line. 'Thank you, thanks a lot' was all she could manage in reply.

Things were moving along too fast. She wanted to savour the moment, with the spotlight on her and the attention of hundreds of people in the audience, but she simply couldn't register everything in her memory. She realized that time went by a lot quicker on stage than off it. Before she knew it, she was walking back to her seat amongst the audience.

Meanwhile the first prize was being given away for her batch. She turned around and looked at the stage; she saw *him* collecting his prize. He was wearing his trademark attire – a cotton shirt, white with blue horizontal stripes, along with a pair of faded black jeans. He wasn't smiling much, as if he didn't really care; she thought it was discourteous. She took her seat and looked on as he walked towards his seat. He was seated a small distance away to her right on the same row. As soon as he sat down, he opened the envelope with the cheque in it. That reminded her to find out how much money she'd earned herself. She practically ripped through the envelope and saw the amount. It was substantial; it'd take care of a couple of months of expenditure for her and still leave enough for giving a treat to her friends. She handed over the cheque to Suparna, who demanded a look at the silver medal as well. The rest of the ceremony got over in a hurry. The final bit of 'torture' she had to endure was the 'vote of thanks'.

Tea and snacks had been arranged at the lawn adjacent to the auditorium. She was quite hungry and decided to enjoy every freebie the college was offering. Soon enough, she was enjoying some hot tea and pretty delightful biscuits on the lawn while conversing with Suparna and some of the other prize winners. She took off her slip-on shoes and felt the soft grass caress her feet with every step she took. She took Suparna's help to avoid the unwanted male attention she was getting. Guys were coming up to her and trying to use 'Congratulations' as a pick-up line. She didn't find any of the guys present at the lawn party interesting. She tried looking for *him* amongst the crowd at the lawn but he was nowhere to be seen.

She always rued the lack of quality guys in engineering colleges. College had turned out to be filled with stereotypes. There were a lot of nerds with whom she hated conversing, and then came the overtly macho types who were obviously interested in just one thing when they looked at her. The girls were a bit too timid for her liking. The few guys whom she liked were already dating or were too busy drinking and getting wasted. But for some reason she felt that *he* was different, even though, despite spending more than two years in the same class she barely knew a thing about him. He didn't fall into any of her defined stereotypes, but then again, she thought, she didn't know him well enough to know for sure. Just as she was discussing the topic with Suparna, she saw him walk out of the auditorium along with the HoD of their department. That's why I didn't see him at the lawn, she thought.

"That's it, I m going to talk to him today to find out some more about what kind of a guy he is" she declared her intent to her best friend."

OK. May I ask why this interest in him all of a sudden?" asked Suparna.

"It s not all of a sudden. I just realized that this is the first time in two years that I am seeing him outside of any lecture or practical. Isn't that weird? I just want to know what his deal is?" she clarified.

"And how do you plan to approach him" questioned Suparna.

"As I've learnt from my male counterparts today; 'Congratulations' is a decent ice-breaker" she replied with a wink.

She followed him with her eyes as he stood and spoke to the HoD for a few minutes; she thought that he'd join the tea party as soon as the HoD was done. She was wrong. The moment the HoD finished the talk with him, he started walking towards the parking lot. "Damn it!" she muttered as she put on her slip-ons and made a dash for the parking. She caught up with him as he was making room to get his bicycle out of the parking lot. She had a tendency to over-think when she was nervous and hence decided not to pass judgment on the fact that he commuted by bicycle. Maybe he's one of those environmental types; I hope he is not poor. What if he is? That'll make him cuter. Thoughts like that ran through her mind.

He saw her; the eye contact broke her chain of thought. "Hey. Congratulations" he said to her. Damn it! There goes my ice-breaker, she thought. "Thanks and congrats to you too" she said, flashing her smile with her head tilted a little to the right; a pose that she had mastered over the years. She saw him notice the beauty spot on the left of her chin. The pose had worked its magic yet again. He sensed that she had taken note of him looking at her beauty spot. He immediately looked away from her and started to focus on undoing the lock on his cycle. He used an old fashioned chain-lock on his cycle.

"Ummm, so you're not planning to attend the tea party?" she asked him.

"No, I have to go somewhere; I'm already late" he said to her as he managed to get his cycle out of the maze that had been created in the overcrowded college parking lot.

She wanted to ask him where he was going or what plans he had for the upcoming weekend, just so she could form an opinion about him from his answers. But there was something that stopped her from asking those questions; the way he looked at things around him, the way he moved, the way he spoke, it gave her a feeling as if he was detached from what was going on. Before she knew it, he got onto his cycle, waved goodbye to her and was off. She walked back disappointed to the lawn.

Suparna could read the dejection on *her* face. "Did he leave before you reached?" Suparna asked. "No. I just couldn't get the conversation going" she said with a shrug and took off her slip-ons once again to feel the soft grass below her feet. It made her feel better. She discussed with Suparna in surprising detail, the short conversation *she* had with *him* at the parking lot.

They dissected each word he spoke and analysed every movement of his. Suparna thought it was rude of him to ride off the way he did. He should've realized that *she* had walked all the way just to talk to him. But *she* didn't believe that he was being deliberately rude. She felt that there was a genuineness in the way he said that he needed to go somewhere. They then decided that the conversation was too short to come to a conclusion about him.

It was getting close to sundown and the two of them felt that it was the right time to leave the tea party and get to a real party. It was Saturday evening and the city was full of places to celebrate and she had more than enough reason to let her hair down. They went back to their respective homes and planned to meet after an hour at Hiccups, a popular nightclub.

She got back to the apartment pretty quickly. She stayed at her paternal uncle's place ever since she had shifted to the city for her engineering studies. They had made life pretty comfortable for her, she could go wherever she liked as long as she kept them informed about her whereabouts. She handed over the medal to her aunt who asked her to keep it in the '*puja*' room for the night. She complied with the request and then snuck into her room to get ready for the party. Her room was in the same state as she had left it.

Over the past couple of years, the room she occupied in the apartment had become her sanctuary, no one ever intruded upon her privacy. She had put up a poster of Clint Eastwood on one wall and on another wall was a large poster of the Atlas statue in New York. Her bed was kept alongside one wall and on the other side of her room she had an old dysfunctional treadmill, the sole item in the room that she hated. A dartboard was pinned to the back of the door to her room.

She lay down on the bed, closed her eyes and relived the moment on the stage. She thought about the hooting that had started as soon as she went up on the stage. She had felt a bit embarrassed back then but it brought a slight smile to her face as she thought how even the simple *kurta* she had worn elicited such a response from the college guys. She then thought about what she'd wear to the party. A shimmering black top, her most recent wardrobe acquisition came to her mind. She got up and looked inside her cupboard; the top was neatly pressed and ready to wear. She then chose her favourite dark blue jeans to go with the top. As she waited for her bath water to fill up, she played some party music and started to dance. It helped her get into the mood for all the dancing she planned to do later at Hiccups. She had a feeling that the night would turn out to be a lot of fun, she also planned to have a couple of drinks there.

Soon she was on her way to the club with Suparna and a couple of other friends; it was an all-girl gang. They reached the club, which offered 'free entry for women' that night, at least for well dressed women; for the rest of the world they just offered, as the term went, 'couples entry'. She preferred that rule; it drastically reduced the number of single male lechers that were on the prowl at night-clubs on most occasions. Even then, as she made her way inside the club she noticed a few guys standing around the bar, doing little apart from eying women from a distance.

They were probably friends of the owners or just guys who were cashing in on favours that the ushers owed them. As a rule, she avoided making eye-contact with such elements. She and her friends sat down on a table and ordered a round of drinks. The music was so inviting that she didn't wait for her drink and the moment her eyes had adjusted to the disco lights, she made her way to the dance floor and started dancing.

She loved it, the whole party atmosphere; to her it was the best way to celebrate an occasion, listening to some awesome, loud music and dancing the night away. The transformation from the world outside to the dance-floor was what she admired the most: the way the powerful beats shut out all the noise of the rest of the world, the way the flashing lights made everyone look so different, the ability to shout out loud without being heard and sway to the rhythm along with unknown faces and become one with the crowd. She danced tirelessly; the music itself was her food and drink. For that brief period, she was in heaven.

She walked out of the club a few memorable hours later. Even though the music had stopped and the flashing lights were gone, somewhere in her mind, she saved that feeling of pure freedom and joy to reminisce about later. As she got back home late at night and lay down on her bed, she closed her eyes and for a second, thought about the dance-floor and the moments that had just gone by. She felt like it was a dream that she was trying to hold onto, despite having woken up. The only way to make it last longer was to go back to sleep.

2

Brainstorming

He entered the hall, it was filled with students from several city colleges and some working professionals had also made it for the quiz. He took a seat and waited for the customary five minute welcome talk. The quiz master hurried through the sponsor credits and asked the organizers to start distributing the elimination round questionnaires. He looked at the elimination questions. They were simply too easy, he didn't even feel like writing the answers down, but he knew he had to. He decided to get it over with quickly.

Q1: What do the initials JRR stand for in the writer JRR Tolkien's name?

Q2: *Mahabharat* – Name the only son of *Dhritarashtra* who survived the *Kurukshetra* war?

Q3: In which Indian state did the game of Polo originate?

He wrote down the answers without having to think too much – *John Ronald Reuel, Yuyutsu* and *Manipur*. The remaining questions weren't very difficult and he was done with the whole question set in half the stipulated time. One of the questions cracked him up a bit –

Q. What was Hitler's first name?

A – Andrew
B – Leonard
C – Adolf
D – Heil

He was sure some dumbasses would choose Heil. It was one of the questions that the quiz masters had put in to have some fun. The elimination round was the second biggest money spinner for the quiz organizers after sponsorship. They priced the entry fee at a level that attracted many people who didn't actually stand a chance against the seasoned campaigners, but it helped create a buzz around the quiz. The audience prizes added to the interest and helped ensure a full house. The quizzing season lasted all year and he had earmarked all the quizzes which offered cash prizes. He didn't care about the contests that offered gift vouchers and other sponsored products like cell phones and cameras as prizes. For him, quiz competitions were a way to ease his financial burden, not just something he did for fun, although he did enjoy the challenge. Winning a quiz, to him was the ultimate victory; it was the equivalent of topping an exam where the syllabus could cover any subject on Earth.

The results of the elimination round were out after a short break. He always wondered how the organizers managed to correct so many entries in very quick time. He had made it to the top six; the scores of the finalists were never disclosed. The quiz master declared that a fair number of people believed that Hitler's full name was Heil Hitler. The remark had the desired effect and the audience laughed. Everyone looked around the hall giving each other the what-dumbasses-exist-in-the-world look; including the ones who had given that particular incorrect answer.

He made his way to the stage, and sat down on the designated seat. The Q&A started, the initial rounds were easy pickings. He had the lead in the first round itself. The next round focused more on movie trivia. "What was Clint Eastwood's character name in the movie 'The Good, The Bad and The Ugly'?" asked the quiz master, in the hurried tone that all quiz masters used.

"Trick question. His character had no name but was referred to as Blondie" he answered swiftly.

"Correct. Ten bonus points for the catch" said the quiz master and continued with the questions.

The questions for the quiz were framed in a way that kept the audience interested. He was enjoying the quiz and paid attention to the questions meant for the other contestants as well. The most interesting question that he had to answer was of the 'connect the dots' variety. An image was displayed using a projector. It had three smaller pictures:

- A quote on the top-left corner that said "... this is my finest sword. If on your journey, you should encounter God, God will be cut."
- A photo of George Michael and an alarm clock.
- A poster of Rajesh Khanna and Sharmila Tagore.

The question was to decipher the name of the Bollywood movie which could be derived by connecting the dots. He had a minute to give the answer. His brain started to work on it furiously.

60 seconds to go...

He read the quote and remembered that he had heard it in a movie. Think... which movie? He repeated the quote once more in his head. Got it, Kill Bill Vol. 1. 53...

He looked at the next image – George Michael and an alarm clock. For the first time in his life he rued not listening to any George Michael music. He thought really hard, sifted through his mental play-list; it came to him in a flash. Without a shadow of doubt he knew the song had to be 'Wake me up before you go go'. He couldn't remember where he had heard the song, but that wasn't important any more, he knew he had the right song in mind. 40...

What is common between Kill Bill and that song? He thought of various connections and rejected each one of them. Each time he rejected a connection, another one popped into his head, but each time it was the wrong one, he knew it. 30...

Half the time was up. The question was for thirty points; if he got it wrong his lead would come under threat. Think!

'Wake me up before you go go' and Kill Bill. Of course, how dumb could I get, it's so evident, he thought to himself as he connected the first two dots. Time to move on to the third. 21...

Rajesh Khanna + Sharmila Tagore = ?

He had the answer. With a smile on his face he looked at the quiz master and said, "*Andaaz Apna Apna*"

"What's the logic?" asked the quiz master.

"The quote in the first image is from Kill Bill Vol. 1, the second picture refers to the George Michael song 'Wake me up before you go go'. The two pictures point towards the female assassin Gogo from Kill Bill Vol 1. Whereas the third image shows Rajesh Khanna and Sharmila Tagore; they starred together in a movie called Amar Prem. The dots connect to three characters from the movie Andaaz Apna Apna – Amar, Prem and Crime Master Gogo."

The audience burst into applause and laughter. The quiz master barely managed to conceal a smile, the event was turning out to be a major success. The quiz master looked at him and said, "Thirty points" and moved onto the next contestant.

He sailed through the next round and had an unassailable lead of fifty points by the time the final round began. He completed the formalities of answering the questions in the final round. There was no prize distribution ceremony for that particular quiz. As soon as the quiz was over, the organizers got the top three contestants together to take a bow in front of the audience and handed over to each one of them an envelope with a cheque along with a nicely packaged box, which contained some gift vouchers and other sponsored give-aways. He did not hang around for a second longer than required and got onto his bicycle to head off towards the bank.

It was a hot afternoon and the bank was a fair distance away from the hall. He braced himself to face the heat and made his way around the jam packed traffic. With his face dripping with sweat, he finally reached the bank to deposit the cheque. It was the third cheque he was depositing that month. He got his pass book updated and felt a sense of pride as he saw the balance amount. Over the past two years, he had built up his reserves with a lot of hard-work and some luck. No one knew how he had managed to survive those early months after his mother's accident: the cheque from his uncle which he had torn and how many times he had wondered whether his impulsive outburst would come back to haunt him; it hadn't.

Those nights that he had stayed hungry, simply because there wasn't any money left. He had been through far too much, far too early in his life. It'll all be worth it, he thought to himself, when she returns. He waited for a few minutes at the bank reception and got some rest before starting the journey to the hospital.

It was lunch time when he reached the hospital; he passed by the canteen entrance where he saw a serpentine queue of people, a mix of hospital staff and visitors. He made his way to the private ward where his mother lay in a comatose state. Each time he entered the ward, the first thing he did was look at her breathe. He did not care about the stats on the monitors next to her bed. The only evidence he sought of her being alive was her breath. He sat down on the chair kept beside the hospital bed and said, "Look *maa*, I won today". He held the gift box aloft even though he knew she wouldn't see it. "It was brilliant. You know, there was this really interesting question..." he began narrating the highlights of the quiz. He spoke to her as if they were having a lunch time discussion together on a regular Saturday afternoon. For some reason he felt that she could hear him and he always wanted to keep her spirits up and make the fight worth it. Every day he wanted to make her proud so that when she returned, he would have a mountain of achievements for her to marvel at. He knew he couldn't allow himself to feel dejected. A little over two years had gone by and there had been no improvement in her condition. But he was steadfast in his resolve to see this through. He believed that somehow she would return and he would wait till that day came.

After he had finished the narration of his victory at the quiz, he decided to step out for lunch. He made his way to the hospital canteen; post-lunch lull was the best time to grab a bite. The waiters were in a hurry to wrap things up and delivered very prompt service. Even though the food wasn't particularly tasty, it was cheap and safe; a rare and much sought after combination. As he got busy having his lunch, he thought about the weeks gone by and how he had won all five quiz competitions which he had entered as a contestant. It was turning out to be his best season yet. The previous year, he had won just three of the seven quiz competitions that he contested. Fortune was favouring him and he was making the most of it. Over the past year the total prize money in most competitions had shot up with a surge in corporate sponsorships.

Another win this season and I'll probably have to pay taxes this year, he thought to himself and chuckled. The winnings had taken a lot of pressure off him. He had enough money to see things through for the rest of the academic year, unless something unforeseen was to take place. He was done with his lunch and in a flash he was back in the private ward that had become his second home for the past couple of years.

Sharp at six in the evening, the door opened; he saw a nurse enter the ward. She was there to ensure things were in order before Dr. Roy's daily round at half past six. She checked the stats on the monitor and made some notes in the case file. She gave him a polite smile, which he returned. She admired his dedication towards his mother and indulged in some small talk with him before continuing to the next ward. Soon enough Dr. Roy made his way to the ward, along with an entourage of junior doctors. He examined the notes that the nurse had just made and discussed the case details with his team. Dr. Roy then asked them to move on to the next ward and wait. He wanted to speak with the patient's son.

"How did your competition turn out today?" Dr. Roy asked the young man.

"I managed to win it" he replied.

Dr. Roy smiled at him and gave him a pat on the back. "Well done. You're on a roll aren't you?" the doctor said, with genuine happiness in his voice.

"One more quiz to go" the young man replied and then queried "anything from the reports?"

Dr. Roy sighed and shook his head to signal that there was no change in her state. There had been no change at all for the past two years, but he kept asking the doctor on each visit. *He* knew how much patience Dr. Roy had shown in his mother's case and he was grateful for that. The doctor chit-chatted with him for a few minutes and then left for the next ward.

The young man sat down disappointed. Every evening when the doctor arrived for his daily round, he hoped that something positive would come out of it. Something that he could build his hopes on. But that breakthrough was yet to come. He hid the disappointment in his voice and started his end of day talk with his mother. Each evening before he left the hospital, he would do a short *puja* by reciting the few *mantras* that he knew. As per his oath, he never prayed during the *puja*, he just recited the *mantras* since it was something his mother would do every evening before her accident. He wanted to continue that tradition until she recovered.

After sun-down, he packed some dinner for himself from the hospital canteen and cycled to a boys hostel which was mid-way between his college and the hospital. He had been living there since the start of his engineering course. It wasn't the college hostel, it was a private one. He hadn't taken up the college accommodation because it was too far away from the hospital and during the initial phases of his mother's treatment, he had to travel very frequently to the hospital. He was well settled at the private hostel, where they rented out single rooms at very affordable rates, with some bare essentials like a bed, table, one tubelight and a ceiling fan. He hadn't ever spoken to anyone else who lived in that hostel; most of the folks didn't occupy rooms for more than a few weeks. He had spent close to two years there. He paid the rent on time and never created any trouble for the owners. To them he was the ideal tenant.

As the day came to a close, he settled down on the study table and worked on some notes he had been preparing for his college studies. Once he was done with the notes, he had his dinner, after which his eyes fell upon the bed and the book he had kept next to his pillow... *Atlas Shrugged*. He had won it as a prize for one of the quizzes. From the first page, he was hooked.

He loved verbose books like that, the ones that took some

time to read. It gave him a sense of security; it made him feel that even though the world was moving faster every day, with some people surging ahead while others fell behind; he still had that book to finish. That it would wait for him and unfold at his pace; that the next page wasn't going to change until he picked up the book and continued reading.

He read the book until the wee hours of the morning. The city was completely silent just before the first light of dawn. He walked to the window and looked out. He breathed in the cool wind and stared at the city. It was his favourite time of the day; it gave him a sense of stillness and calm. He wondered how many people were awake at that time. He could spot just one light far away in the distance coming from one of the high rise buildings.

"What's your story?" he asked in a whisper that got lost in the wind. He felt like writing a few lines in his diary; he moved to his study table, picked up a pen and the diary and returned to the window.

Why do you wake while the world is asleep?
Why do you await the light of day?
Does the night fill your heart with fear and make you weep?
When the light pierces the darkness, are the tears of the night driven away?

He shut the diary the moment he penned his thoughts and returned to his bed. A tinge of sadness had started to enter his emotions, which he had tried very hard to stay away from; but whenever he put pen to paper and the words began to flow, they were always sad. He thought about how happy a person he was until that fateful morning, two years ago.

Ever since then, he had fought valiantly, but time was taking a toll on him. Nothing seemed to cure his sadness; winning the quizzes didn't do much for him, neither did the academic success. In his heart of hearts, he knew that the only thing that could cure him was his mother's recovery. He was tired of putting up a brave face in front of the world and acting mature. He was afraid that someday his strength would break. What then? Who would he turn to? Who would rescue him? What would happen the day he despaired?

Just as those thoughts were about to take over his mind, he closed his eyes and took a deep breath. The fresh morning air helped him stop the negative chain of thoughts. He lay down on his bed and brought up an image in his head of the good times from a couple of years back. The memories filled him up with warmth that he used as a blanket to protect himself from the cold thoughts of sorrow. He thought of his mother one last time before falling asleep.

3

Teamwork

Five minutes into the lecture and *she* was bored to death, the only saving grace being the fact that she was sitting beside Suparna. It was the second lecture for the day and she knew she'd struggle to get through the long day filled with back to back lectures and a practical.

Prof. Jakhad, aka Jacko, was one of those guys who liked to go on and on about his personal achievements and the worst part was he didn't have too many. A few weeks ago, her class had celebrated the 100th time Jacko had mentioned his University Gold Medal. Jacko also had a problem with pronouncing a few words, like circuit, which always came out as "*sir-cute*". This was a major problem since the subject he taught was – Analog and Digital Circuits.

She looked at her cell phone; her battery was low, which ruled out any chances of playing Snake. Suparna suggested a game of 'cross and noughts', for lack of a better option, she agreed. There they were, two Computer Engineering students, attending an ADC lecture, seeking solace in a game they had probably learnt in primary school. She beat Suparna three games in a row and both the girls were too busy to notice Prof. Jacko approach their bench. Her sixth sense told her something was amiss but it was too late, he had seen them and the notebook page filled with crosses and circles. He quickly picked up the book from their desk and held it aloft for the class to see.

"Look, this is why India is not progressing" he said in a miffed tone. "Is this why you took admission into engineering? There is a lecture on *sir-cutes* going on for the past twenty minutes and here you both are playing cross and *nuts!*" he continued. The entire class was laughing while the two girls suppressed their laughter and put up fake apologetic expressions. "These are not the games that students should be playing at this age!" he said to them. Words that led to another round of rapturous laughter, before he realized the unintentional innuendo in his statement. She heard some student pass a remark about *'jawaani ke khel'* which she decided to ignore.

The two girls apologized repeatedly, but Jacko was adamant that they leave the classroom since they were clearly not interested in the subject. The two girls simply had no argument and decided to leave. They weren't too bothered about Jacko getting upset since ADC did not involve a practical exam. The moment they left the classroom, they were laughing about the whole matter and walked to the library.

She saw him sitting in a corner and reading a book. It didn't look like an engineering book from its size. She walked up to him with Suparna following closely.

"Hey, what are you doing here?" he heard a familiar female voice ask him.

He looked at them and smiled, "Oh, hi. Nothing much... I accidentally attended all of Jacko's lectures so far this sem. It was time to do the right thing and bunk the lecture. What are you two doing here?" he inquired as they took a seat next to him.

"We got caught playing cross and noughts" she said plainly, it brought a smile to his face.

"What are you reading?" asked Suparna. *Shantaram* he said. "Oh, I've heard a lot about it, haven't read it though" Suparna replied.

"If you've not read it yet, you haven't heard enough. It's brilliant!" he replied.

"Give it to me once you're done" Suparna said to him.

"Sure" he said.

There was a short period of silence and no one really had anything to talk about. A couple of students walked into the library with some posters that they put up on the notice board.

"It's here, at last" he said, thinking aloud.

"What?" she asked him.

"Fastermind India" he said.

"What's that?" asked Suparna.

"It's the biggest quiz competition in the country. It started ten years ago as a tribute to a major TV show. But then it became very popular. I'm surprised you haven't heard of it" he answered.

"I'm not into quizzing" Suparna said, losing interest in the topic.

He ignored the dismissive tone in Suparna's voice and walked to the notice board, where the students had finished setting up the poster. The quiz was two weeks away and set to take place at a massive city auditorium. He looked at the prize money; it was the largest amount till date for any quiz that he had heard of.

She stood alongside him as he read the poster while Suparna decided to make her way to the canteen.

"You seem to be quite enthu about this quiz" she said to him.

"I've been waiting for it all year, it's the first time it's being held in our city" he replied.

"Why did they go with a tacky name like Fastermind?" she asked, causing him to chuckle.

"Well, they say that it was started by a couple of college students who were pissed off about the kind of quiz shows that were on air and wanted to pay tribute to Mastermind India; but obviously, there were copyright issues with the name. They also decided to include an element of speed in the quiz, wherein, the faster you answer the question, the more points you are awarded. Hence the 'tacky' name, Fastermind India... the biggest element common between the original and the tribute competition is the 'specialization section'. Where the contestant chooses a topic of his or her specialization and the questions asked are all based on that topic.

There are three rounds, the elims, the specialization round for the top six teams and the final round which is basically a general knowledge round. The level of difficulty in the final round is insane but the prize money is worth it" he said, taking a deep breath after speaking at a stretch.

She looked at the prize money and thought that the cash reward for standing second in her class was peanuts in comparison.

"I think I'll participate, the concept seems interesting" she said to him.

"So does the prize money" he replied with a knowing smile.

"So what topic will you choose as your specialty?" she asked him.

"It'll either be the *Mahabharat* or the *Lord of The Rings* trilogy" he answered.

"Don't you think both the topics are too vast?" she said, raising doubts over his choices.

"Not really. In any case the topic that you choose is subject to their approval, if you choose something very specific then they can reject it and ask you to choose another" he replied.

"Yeah, that makes a lot of sense, or else you'd have people choose easy topics and max out the points in the specialty round" she said.

"You know, way back on the BBC, there was this comedy show where they would spoof popular TV shows. They had this joke about Mastermind, where there's this contestant whose specialty topic is 'questions to which the answer is *two*'. So the quiz master asks him questions like, 'if I hold two fingers of your hand in mine, how many fingers of your hand am I holding?' and follows it up by asking 'what was the answer to the previous question?' and so on" he said beginning to laugh towards the end of the statement. She was laughing as well.

They spoke for a little while longer before he left the library, he passed by Suparna who was making her way back to the library with some snacks for her best friend.

"So, how was it?" Suparna asked her.

"How was what?" she replied with a question of her own.

"Oh come on! Don't tell me you didn't talk to him, I left just so that you could have some privacy" said Suparna, with a hint of irritation.

"*Accha*, that way. It was good. He seems interesting, decent sense of humour too. Quite an enthu cutlet for this quiz. He even got me a little interested in the whole event. I'm actually thinking of participating" she said to Suparna.

"What? But you've never taken part in a quiz before" Suparna said, surprised at the turn of events.

"It's high time I experience my first time" she said to her best friend with a wink.

"Are you sure you're still talking about the quiz?" Suparna replied as they both shared a laugh.

She took a photograph of the poster on her cell phone before leaving the library for the next lecture.

The remainder of the day was mentally tiring for her and when she got back home, she went straight into her room and turned on some music on her computer. After relaxing for a while she was online and chatting. She decided to read up a bit about Fastermind India. She found out that the quiz involved a qualification round wherein all participating colleges conducted an intra-college GK test. The highest scoring male and female student would pair up as a team for the actual competition to be held in two weeks' time. The qualification round was just a week away.

She didn't fancy herself too much as a quizzer, but then she remembered the conversation she had at the library with him. She liked what she heard about the quiz and decided she'd give the quiz a real go. She entered the following search item on Google – *How to prepare for a quiz*. The topmost search result linked to a website that just displayed one line of text '*You can never truly prepare for a quiz*'.

Despite the not-so-great start to her preparation, she did find quite a few resources to prepare and soon she found herself taking online quizzes. Her success ratio wasn't too bad for a beginner. Before she realized it, she was having fun. She continued reading and taking quizzes till late at night.

The next few days were rather uneventful, she didn't get kicked out of any lectures, neither were there any conversations with him, things just went on normally. However on one Friday, she ran into him during a practical and after some small talk she told him about a movie plan that some of their classmates were coming up with. He declined saying he had some 'personal work'. She went for the movie and was totally disappointed by it. As it turned out, the best bits of the movie were all shown in the trailer and the movie was a complete disaster.

Once the movie was done, she went to *Sheesha*, her favourite hookah lounge along with Suparna. She loved the ambience over there, the lighting was dim, and they had very comfortable *divans* to laze around on. The waiters never bothered the patrons until they were called for, no one hurried you to place an order or to pay the bill once the eating and drinking was over. A cloud of sweet smelling smoke always hung above one's head, which in addition to the soft lilting music gave the whole place a dream-like feel. The place was frequented by a lot of *firangs*, who occasionally indulged in some advanced forms of PDA like making out. That had prompted the owners to put up a sign-board requesting patrons not to indulge in any kind of 'objectionable behaviour'; however that didn't have any affect since no one had ever objected to their behaviour. Young Indian couples never indulged in such behaviour, but they weren't going to allow themselves to be branded as prudes who would discourage such acts of displaying affection.

"Aren't you blowing off your prize money a little too quickly?" asked Suparna, watching her drink the second cocktail for the night.

"We've started our Third Year of engineering, which means that we have less than two years of freedom to enjoy. I'm making the most of it, the best part is, this drink is college sponsored" she replied and took another sip.

"What makes you think that after college you'll not be free?"

"Look around you. You see those slightly older people at that corner table. They're the corporate crowd. Just look at their faces, they've come here to escape. They're not free, they keep looking at their watches, and some of them probably have to work over the weekend. Some of them are worried about EMIs, the married ones are worried about their marriage, and the single ones are worried about getting married. Their lives seem caged.

Then look at people like us, the college crowd – sure, we don't have as much money as them; but we have something far more valuable, time. Once in a while when we get some money, we are free to splurge, without thinking about the future. Our future is uncertain but at least it's open ended. But look at them; they know exactly what they'll be doing for the rest of their lives. We don't even know what we'll be doing an hour from now. That's how it should be."

"But how long will this last? Someday even we'll be like them."

"You're right, but that someday is far away. At least two years away. Till then we're free to do what we like" she said before breathing in a lung full of *hookah* and then adding some more smoke to the air.

"Anyway listen, next weekend onwards I don't think I'm going to be able to hang out on weekends; mid sems are coming close and I need to study" said Suparna.

"Are you sure that's the only reason?" she replied with a naughty smile.

"Yeah, obviously!"

"Oh! I thought it was because your boyfriend is coming back from his trip."

"Damn! How do you know that?"

"I went through your inbox."

"How noble of you to confess."

"Your fault, you left it unlocked. But don't worry, I won't disturb you; I'll be busy preparing for that quiz, that is, if I qualify."

"I'm sure you will."

They had a lavish dinner and Suparna dropped *her* off at her uncle's apartment. Her cousin sister let her in and she quietly sneaked off into her bedroom. She was glad that her uncle and aunt were the 'early to bed, early to rise' kind of people. It spared her the effort of having to conceal her moderate alcohol consumption. She took care to never get drunk nor allow Suparna, her designated driver to get sloshed either. They made a good team and took care of each other. That night she fell asleep in a hurry.

The day arrived at last; the elimination of Fastermind India was to take place after college hours at the college auditorium. She saw him sitting in a row that was totally occupied. He looked calm and focused. She found a seat for herself and waited for the announcements to start. Her palms were sweating; she felt surprised about her own nervousness.

She felt a little excited at the prospect of giving her first ever quiz. She didn't really bother about her chances; it was more about the experience. She looked around and counted barely two dozen female contestants in the auditorium and more than a hundred guys. That'll do my chances some good, she thought to herself. I can take on twenty odd chicks, she continued with her self-motivating propaganda.

The quiz sheets were passed around the hall. She had about thirty minutes to answer as many of the fifty questions. Most of them were MCQs, she chose to start answering the questions with no options first.

Q: What was Mickey Mouse's original name?

What the heck is this, she thought to herself. Mickey Mouse had an original name? How the hell am I supposed to know this? She continued grumbling. Negative marking only applied to the MCQ's, she decided to guess an answer. *Michael* was the answer she gave. She moved on to the next question.

Q: Who is the author of the books *Fantastic Beasts and Where to Find Them* and *The Tales of Beetle the Bard*?

Hey, I have a question – which freak of nature prepared this quiz? She thought to herself, getting a very bad feeling about the quiz. She started to regret all the hours she had spent quizzing. The words '*You can never truly prepare for a quiz*' flashed in front of her eyes. She had no clue about the answer to the question and decided to have some fun and write down crazy answers.

Shikari Shambu was the answer she gave.

Q: Which spirit is the base for a Black Russian cocktail?

Finally, a question that I can answer, she thought as she quickly wrote *vodka* on the answer sheet and moved on.

Q: Who wrote the novel *Dracula?*

She knew the answer was *Bram Stoker.* Her confidence was beginning to rise. She wondered how many of the girls would have known the answers to the questions she had just read. Surely she still had a chance.

Q: Which branch of Medicine is concerned with providing artificial limbs to the human body?

Prosthetics, she wrote down without thinking twice.

Q: What drug is named after the Greek God of Dreams?

Damn it! She had no clue and was getting angry at the quiz master. She had learnt things like, names of capital cities of most countries and that sort of trivia. None of that knowledge was turning out to be useful. She decided to throw another one in the face of the quiz master and wrote *Hajmola* as the answer.

Q: What special feature do the languages Arabic, Mandarin and Hebrew have in common?

She felt she had the answer to that one. She knew that Arabic and Mandarin were written right-to-left which was a major differentiating factor from most other languages. She guessed that the same would probably apply to Hebrew as well and decided to go with the answer – *they are all written left to right.*

Q: Which band is credited for the theme song of the hit sitcom Friends?

This one is easy – *The Rembrandts.*

Q: Who was the oldest member of The Beatles?

Who cares about their age? What is wrong with this quiz master? Alright, just focus. Think! Paul McCartney was too handsome to be the oldest, so was George Harrison; it's between

John Lennon and Ringo Starr. Ringo Starr had the bushiest moustache, I'll go with that. *Ringo Starr* was her answer.

Q: What is Michael Jackson's middle name?

Dude! Do you even listen to music or just search for trivia all the time? She had no clue about the answer and decided to go with *Pyaremohan* as the answer.

Then came the MCQs and surprisingly, she felt at ease having options in front of her, compared to the direct questions she had just answered. She used every ounce of intuition and judgment she had and felt good about the MCQ section. She was done just in time and handed over the answer sheet to the organizers when they came around for collecting them.

At the end of the allotted thirty minutes, she had no clue whether she'd qualify. The organizers said that they'd announce the winners along with the answers the following day. After exiting the auditorium, she started to walk towards the parking lot where Suparna was waiting for her. She saw *him* walking right in front of her, with a couple of quick steps she caught up with him.

"Hey, how did the quiz go?" she asked him.

"Oh, hi. It was decent" he replied.

"Some of the questions were insane, like what was Mickey Mouse's original name..."

"Mortimer"

"What?"

"Yeah, Mortimer Mouse was what Walt Disney named the character originally before changing it to Mickey."

"Woah! How the hell did you know that?"

"No clue, I must've read it somewhere... probably Wikipedia."

"OK. And what was that random question – Who wrote *Tales of Beetle the Bard*. I haven't even heard of the damn book!"

"It's J.K. Rowling. She wrote it as a tie-in to *Harry Potter* and *The Deathly Hallows*"

"Damn! And what about the drug named after some Greek God?"

"It's Morphine named after Morpheus"

"Was there a single question that you didn't get?"

He smiled after listening to her question. "Yeah, I didn't have a clue about that Russian cocktail question." She jumped at the opportunity to show off and literally yelled "It was Vodka!"

"Well, it's the first time I've regretted being a teetotaller" he said, making her chuckle.

She didn't want their Q&A session to go on any more, since she had the high ground of knowing something he didn't.

They had reached the parking lot; Suparna pretended not to see the two of them and faked a phone call. She wanted to ask him if he was interested in helping out with the upcoming class trip, but before she could do that, he took a quick look at his watch and quickened his pace. He told her he was getting late... wished her luck for the result and was off in a flash on his bicycle. She was once again left with a feeling of disappointment with the abrupt end to their conversation.

The next day she woke up with a feeling of anxiousness. She was surprised about how desperately she wanted to qualify for the quiz. She reached college early, for the first time in her life and headed straight towards the notice board at the library. The list was out, and she was the only one present there to look at it.

She looked up the list of students who had qualified. She couldn't believe it – her name was on the list. She had gone on to beat the twenty odd girls who had come in for the quiz. She then looked at the other qualifying student's name. *He* had qualified. There is a God, she thought to herself. She dialled Suparna's cell phone and told her the news. Suparna congratulated her and wished her luck for the next round which was to be held in a week's time. She decided to wait in the library for a while; she suspected that he would arrive soon. That's when she had a thought that filled her with excitement. She'd have to team up with him for the remainder of the quiz. She'd finally get an opportunity to spend some time with him and figure him out.

She didn't know what exactly it was about him that she found appealing. He was unlike any guy she had ever met before. He wasn't shy, but avoided interacting with people. Despite being intelligent he didn't come across as nerdy. Though not exceedingly handsome, she found him to be fairly good-looking. He had great hair and a cute smile. He was tall, had broad shoulders and strong arms. He seemed naturally well built but not like the chiselled, gym-frequenting guys. He had a raw strength about himself. But that much was not enough for her to get attracted to him. She wanted to know what sort of a person he was; his likes, dislikes, temperament and other characteristics. Right now she didn't even know if he was single or committed. Just as she was thinking of him, he walked into the library. He didn't notice her sitting across the notice board.

He was panting, sweat dripped from his chin to the floor; he had obviously been rushing on his cycle. She watched closely as he read his name on the board. He punched the air, betraying his normally concealed emotions but then quickly gained composure. He then looked at the other qualifying name, he had a hint of a smile on his face; she felt thrilled. She cleared her throat making an audible sound; he turned around and saw her sitting on a nearby table.

"Oh, hi! Congrats" he said to her with a smile.

"Thank you! Wish you the same" she replied.

"Looks like you did pretty well" he said to her.

"Looks like the other girls messed up" she replied honestly.

"Intelligent and modest, nice!"

"Intelligent and well-mannered, really nice."

"OK. Let's stop the mutual admiration! We need to get to work and plan this out. It's the first time I've qualified for this quiz, so I have no head start on strategies or anything"

"It's the first time I've ever qualified for any quiz, so I have no head start on anything"

"That's good; at least one of us will have an unbiased approach"

"Cool! Let's go to the canteen *naa*, the library is not the best place for a long conversation." "Sure."

They walked together to the canteen, but not before she rushed back to the notice board and checked out what Michael

Jackson's middle name was – it was Joseph. They still had some time left for the first lecture of the day and the canteen was very sparsely populated.

She called for a Sprite; he was content with a glass of water. He started discussing strategies immediately; he wanted to discuss what their strengths were and where they needed to work harder. He also gave her a detailed run-down of each round and the rules. Very quickly she realized that he wasn't interested in small talk or getting to know each other on a personal level. He was quite pumped up about the quiz and she was getting worried about the kind of expectations he had from her and decided to get him on board.

"Ummm... look, sorry to interrupt the planning and all, but I had something to say."

"Yeah sure, go ahead."

"You seem to have a lot of quizzing experience and stuff, I am a total newbie. In fact I'll be honest with you, I have no idea how I qualified. What I mean is, I didn't know half the answers and I'm not being modest this time; just honest! For most of the MCQ's I just did some random guess-work and took my chances because I wasn't under any pressure. Whatever I had prepared, none of that was asked. So, I just got lucky! That's the truth. And I don't want you to think I'm some pro at this. I'll work with whatever strategy we decide, but I'm not really that great at this stuff, I just want to be upfront with you; I probably just had luck on my side."

He looked at her with a blank expression for a brief moment and then smiled. "That's perfect. If there's one thing I lack, it's luck. And, in things like quizzes, luck counts more than knowledge or experience. So it's all good, don't worry about it" he said, much to her relief. She appreciated the way he tried to boost her morale. Nice guy test, check!

"Alright then, let's move onto the strategy" she said to him.

"OK, we have one week to prepare in whatever way we can. Although there is no real way to prepare for a quiz."

"Why does everyone say that?"

"Say what?"

"That there is no real way to prepare for a quiz. I read this on a website also. What is so special about a quiz that you can't prepare for it?"

"It's the unpredictability. You can't possibly know what the quiz master is going to ask you. Sure there are general subjects like history, geography, science, sports, entertainment. But that's simply too vast to prepare for."

"So you don't prepare for quizzes?"

"No, not really. After sometime you realize automatically what your strengths are and where your weaknesses lie. All one can do is try to read more and more about subjects where one is weak and hope that it sticks."

"Hmmm... So what are your strengths?" she asked him.

"Sports, Mythology, Science, History, Politics and Current Affairs, all other topics are my weaknesses. What about you?"

"Music and a bit of Geography" she said, feeling bad about how short her list was.

"Great, no overlaps; two weaknesses of mine are covered. That's a solid start to our preparation" he replied.

Positive attitude, check!

"And another thing, I've decided my topic for my specialty round – *Hindi Movies and Music during the 90s.*"

"Interesting choice."

"Yep, don't really need to prepare much for that" she said with a wink and a smile. "So let's do one thing.

Let's meet every day after college and keep a tab on how we're progressing" she said to him.

He looked like he was thinking a lot about what he was going to say next. "What's the matter?" she asked him. "I can't stay back after college, would it be possible to meet up before college or during lunch?" he said to her, in an apologetic tone. "Yeah sure, I'm not really a morning person, so lunchtime should be fine" she replied and then smiled to make him feel more comfortable. "Thanks!" he said to her and then looked at his watch. "Time's up. We should go attend the lecture now" he said to her. "Whose lecture is it?" she asked him. "Wacko Jacko!" he replied. "Oh man! I hate him" she said. "We're all members of that club" he replied as he got up from the canteen chair. She looked at him closely.

4

Prepair

With just five days to go before the quiz, he rushed to college earlier than usual. Like every morning, he stopped by the hospital to check on his mother, who continued to remain in her stable but comatose state. He was in college even before the lab doors had been unlocked. He waited for the lab assistant to arrive with the keys. As soon as the lab was opened, he settled down in front of a PC kept at a corner of the lab and started to read up on topics that he felt were most likely to come up during the quiz. He got completely engrossed in reading and decided to bunk the first couple of lectures. He finally had to leave the lab when a batch of students from a different class entered for their practical session.

He made his way to the lecture room where the next lecture was scheduled. He saw *her* sitting alongside Suparna. He found an unoccupied bench and sat down to endure the torture of staying awake during an engineering lecture. Since it wasn't one of the back-benches, he didn't risk taking out the copy of *Shantaram* that he carried with him for college reading. Jacko strolled into the lecture room. He looked at the class starting from one corner of the room to the other and then said, "You know in our times, we used to stand up when the professor would enter the class."

"No sir that was in school" said someone loud enough for the class to hear.

The students laughed, Jacko ignored the statement and turned around to draw a circuit diagram. The nerdy crowd was busy discussing the diagram and copying it down, the back-benchers were getting set to fall asleep on the desk or read books under it. *He* was struggling to stay awake; he had no clue about the reason but lecture room benches made him instantly drowsy. He knew that Jacko would get upset if a student sitting on one of the front benches was seen dozing off during the lecture. In all his time at the engineering college, he had never rubbed any professor the wrong way and he didn't want to mess around with Jacko. Considering everything he was going through, he did not want any bad *karma* on him.

Jacko turned around to address the class and explain the details of the circuit he had just drawn on the whiteboard. He hated the fact that Jacko kept looking at him every few seconds. He swore that he'd never sit on a front-bench again. Every time Jacko made eye contact with him, he nodded his head vigorously to show that he was paying attention and because it helped him stay awake. Every word that Jacko uttered made his eyelids come closer towards each other. The classroom lights seemed to fade away, all of a sudden he felt Jacko's eyes on him. With a Herculean effort, he parted his eyelids and nodded his head. He could see Jacko's lips move but the words got lost somewhere as they travelled towards him. Everything happened in slow motion. He could hear himself breathe in a slow rhythm; he wasn't going to last much longer. He shifted his position on the bench; the movement drove away the sleep. But he knew it was a temporary victory, sleep would return with a vengeance. A few yawns later, he could feel the next bout of sleep taking over. He had to bring out the heavy artillery; he reached into his bag and took out the water bottle. One of the only advantages of college over school was that one could drink water during a lecture without seeking any permission. Everything that he had seen in movies or read in fiction novels about college life, turned out to be a bunch of fake fantasies. There were no hot women walking around in designer clothes and the only thing that got laid on Fresher's night was the dinner table.

Damn, this lecture is getting me depressed, he thought to himself. He looked towards his bag again; the book began to call out to him. He couldn't resist. He reached for it and found the perfect angle below the table to conceal it from Jacko's view. Within seconds, all signs of the onset of sleep were gone. Reading the book transported him into another world, a world that was interesting; a world where with each page the story moved along. *Shantaram* was the kind of book where the climax did not matter, the journey of reading the book itself was so rewarding. He did not want the book to end; he wished that it would go on and on.

Every now and then he looked up at Jacko and made eye contact followed by a nod of the head. He had cracked the code, the eye contact and nodding was the key to success in a Jacko lecture. That's all he wanted from his students – silence, eye contact and nodding. Just like a surveillance camera, Jacko's eyes shifted from one corner of the room to the other within a fixed duration. He had figured out the exact time interval it took for Jacko's eyes to return to where he was sitting. The fact that he had figured out Jacko's surveillance path gave him a sense of satisfaction that he had never got from learning the nuances of the most complex Analog or Digital Circuit. After reading a chapter of the book, he heard Jacko utter the magic word that all engineering students looked forward to during a lecture – attendance.

As soon as Jacko had left the lecture room, most of the students rushed off for lunch. He continued reading. She walked towards him, he saw her approach.

"Hi" she said to him with a smile and a wave.

He smiled back at her and gave her the 'eyebrow hi.'

"Are you reading some book?" she asked him.

"Yep, still trying to finish *Shantaram*" he replied.

"Oh, I thought you were preparing for the quiz and reading one of those GK type books."

He laughed.

"I hate those books. I never read them" he replied.

"Why?"

"They're filled with all these names and dates. It's like trying to mug up stuff for an exam."

"That's true, but then how else would you find out a lot of information, like names of capital cities or Presidents etc."

"The thing is, the really good quizzes don't ask those kinds of questions. Like, what is the capital of dash country? That's because it doesn't really test your GK. Even if they do ask you a question like that it'd have to be something special, like maybe if a new country got formed recently, then it makes sense to ask a question like that. Primarily because it surely would've come up in the news and one ought to know it. If you see, most of the times, questions in quiz competitions have some connect with current affairs or things that are really interesting like movies or music or special events. No one will ask you, who was the Fifth President of the United States or the name of the Speaker of the Seventh Lok Sabha. Unless of course, it has something to do with a major event or current affairs."

"Holy crap! You're like some quizzing expert."

"Did I just give too much *gyaan*?"

"Nope, I just realized I have too little *gyaan*. How many quizzes have you participated in?"

"I lost count."

"And how many have you won?"

"Too few to count."

"Enough with the modesty routine. How many?"

"This year or overall?"

"Both!"

"About five this year and twelve overall"

She did a mock fainting routine. They both joked about it and started to make their way out of the lecture hall after one of the peons entered the room with a broom and gave them irritable looks. As they walked towards the canteen, she told him about how she had bought a couple of GK books. He felt bad about his rant against such books and tried to tone down his sharp remarks against books which she had already bought.

As they walked together, they were given the customary stare that all engineering students give when they see a guy and a girl walk together in college premises. If the girl was good looking, the stares would have a hint of leching involved. She ignored it, while he was too focused on the quizzing discussion to notice. They sat down at the canteen, away from the crowd. She showed him some of the books that she had bought; he tried his best to hide his disdain towards them.

She had bought a Year-book, another book titled *101 Most Important GK Questions* and a third book with all kinds of lists – Nobel laureates, Football World Cup Winning Teams, Indian Presidents, Prime Ministers and Speakers of the Indian Parliament.

"How're you doing with the specialty round? You've submitted *The Lord of the Rings* Trilogy *and* the *Mahabharat'* as your specialty topic, right? Isn't that a bit of a risk?" she put forth a string of questions to him as she dug into a burger.

"I was thinking about which of the two topics to take on and I realized that if I take both of them, they will have to focus on both, they won't be able to dig too deep into either of them. At least, that's what I hope. Anyway, I'm reading up as much as I can on the *Mahabharat.*"

"What about preparing for the *Lord of the Rings* part of it?"

"I'm not preparing for that."

"Why?"

"I've read the trilogy, cover to cover, eleven times" he said to her. She choked on the burger she was having, a sip of Coke and she was fine.

"Duuuuude! Are you insane? How can you read it so many times?"

He laughed at her reaction.

"I know it sounds stupid. But I started reading it during the summer holidays after the tenth standard board exams. I fell in love with the book. After that, every vacation I got, I just started reading it again. By the time I entered the twelfth standard, I had read it ten times. The last time I read it was a couple of months ago during the break before Third Year. So it's all fresh in my mind, you can relax, I've got that topic covered."

"After eleven readings, you better get all the answers right! *Naah*, I'm just kidding. At least one of us is well prepared. I'm going nuts with my topic. I'm reading all kinds of things on the net; blogs, IMDB, Wikipedia, anything I can get my hands on. Some of the stuff I've read is just so interesting and nostalgic.

Like I was reading this blog about Rajiv Rai movies..."

"That guy is a legend!" he said, interrupting her.

"Yeah, he had a string of super hits during the 80s and the 90s. *Tridev, Vishwatma, Mohra* and *Gupt*" she continued.

"I had bought the tickets of *Gupt*, in black!" he said to her.

"Seriously!"

"Yeah, I just heard the title track and I had to watch it at any cost. The whole techno music got me hooked. What characters and dialogues his movies had *yaar*, I don't know if you remember that jailer dude in the movie and his '*dandaa kar doonga*' dialogue. Imagine the random state of mind the dialogue writer must have been in, to come up with that kind of insanity. It's just insane. In fact it's epic."

She started laughing the moment he said the jailer's line. He followed it up by humming bits of the title track; she was in splits by the time he sang the '*Ai Yai Yai Yai Yaaah*' bit from the song.

"I'm sorry! Those movies just bring back some awesome memories" he said to her, she was still laughing.

"No that was hilarious."

"Yeah, but I should stop now, people are staring at me" he said to her, feeling a little embarrassed about his antics.

"I know, those movies were just amazing. Total *paisa vasool*, proper Bollywood *masala* movies. My favourite was *Mohra*" she said, continuing the conversation, which she was really enjoying.

"Don't remind me of that movie, please!" he said to her with a genuine sense of dread.

"Why? You didn't like that movie?" she asked him, surprised at his reaction.

"No! I loved it. It's one of my all-time favourites. But I have this really embarrassing memory associated with it, which I want to forget."

"What happened? You have to tell me now!"

"Alright, but you can't tell anyone this story. OK?"

"You have my word" she said to him, pursing her lips to prevent a smile from showing up.

"OK, here goes. I had seen *Mohra* when it had released, some cousins of mine took me along and I loved the movie, even though I was a kid. A few years later, I saw an ad on TV – 'world premiere of *Mohra*, Sat 8 PM.' I was on a family vacation and that day we were staying at my uncle's house. Right from the morning I had been talking about the movie, I told everyone in the family about it. None of them had seen the movie, so they were all looking forward to it. That evening, everyone was sitting in front of the TV. The movie started, ten minutes into the movie, there's one attempted rape scene. Some uncomfortable looks were exchanged amongst my family. Five minutes later, a drug rape sequence. Followed by another attempted rape and then four gruesome murders. That was it! The channel was changed and all hell broke loose. People were looking at me as if I was some kind of pervert. I was asked to explain how I could have recommended such a disgusting film. I told them about the awesome plot twists and begged them to put the movie back on, so that I could resurrect my reputation. The movie was back on again. But I watched aghast as *Tip tip barsa paani's* most raunchy part was playing on the screen. The TV was switched off and I was asked to go to my room. The rest of the memories are so traumatic that I cannot recount them. That was the last time I recommended any movie to my family."

She was tearing up with laughter.

"Oh my God! Stop. I can't breathe" she said, still laughing. He laughed along with her. She finally caught her breath and continued the discussion.

"One question. Why the hell did you recommend the movie to your *entire* family?"

"*Arrey*, I didn't remember that the movie had such a random start. I was too small when I saw it for the first time. I just remembered the kick ass action and Naseeruddin Shah's awesome performance as *Jindal*. The whole plot twist with him and his blindness... it blew my mind! That's all I remembered about the movie. I had no memory of the randomly pervy moments in the movie."

"Unbelievable. That was one of the most insane stories I've

heard" she said, still recovering from the bout of non-stop laughter.

"I'll never forget *Mohra*, one of the most awesome Bollywood movies. Everything about it was epic, right from the first frame, with the whole background score lifted from Terminator, to the random humour shoved in, one of the best ensemble villainous cast you ll ever find. And Raveena at the top of her game. I can go on and on. Anyway, you've chosen a brilliant topic. Even the quiz master will have fun with it" he said.

Soon they were done with lunch and walked towards the lecture hall for the next series of lectures. He made sure he was sitting on one of the back benches. She sat next to Suparna. During the lectures she thought about the discussion she had just had with him at lunch. It brought a smile to her face. Especially when she recollected the way he started to hum the title song of Gupt. The memory of him yelling '*Ai Yai Yai Yai Yaah*' made her laugh all over again. She had never seen him talk so freely ever before. She was under the impression that he was this ultra-serious guy who didn't talk much. But the interaction with him today had shown her an entirely different side of his personality. The more time she spent with him, the further away she got from figuring him out.

She wanted to catch up with him after the last lecture for the day, but as soon as the professor was done with the attendance, he rushed out towards the parking lot. She wondered why he rushed off every day as soon as college got done. He never stayed back to talk to people or hang out with the rest of the class. She went back to the canteen and chit-chatted with Suparna and some of her other friends for a while after the last lecture.

Meanwhile, he had reached the hospital. He waited patiently for Dr. Roy to arrive for his daily round. The same routine followed; there was no change in her state. After the doctor left, he spoke to his mother about his preparation and about how important this quiz was to him. Like every day for the past two years, he searched her face for a hint of an expression. There was none.

He spent some more time with his mother and was back at his hostel room. He did some accounting to ensure that finances were in order for the next few months. The recent spate of quiz winnings had helped, but all those winnings combined wouldn't compare to what Fastermind could do for him. Once he was done with the accounting he realized how tired he was and sat next to the window to get some fresh air. He carried his diary of poems along with himself. He looked at the hustle and bustle on the streets below. It was a new moon night, the contrast between the pitch black sky and the glowing city made him feel like writing a new poem.

The sky is dark, the streets are bright,
A crowd of faces, no one I know in sight.
Everyone's in a tearing hurry,
Everyone's got a different worry.

Will their flames go out in the dark of the night?
Or will they survive and carry on the fight?
Everyone's bothered about the future, fearing their doom,
Not realizing, they're just the entertainment for the stars and the moon!

He sat back on his chair and closed his eyes. He smiled as he reminisced about the lunch discussion he had with her. It had been such a long time since he'd had so much fun. It probably was because their discussion reminded him about a time that held so many beautiful memories; when his family was whole. The events of the past few years had clouded some of those memories, but today when he thought about those days again, the images in his mind were crystal clear.

He opened his eyes, the sight of the bright lights and the dark sky reminded him of his state of mind. The past that was long gone had been so bright; the present was as dark as the night. How badly he wanted to bring back those times. How much he wanted to relive those days. With each passing second after he opened his eyes, the memory of that past was fading, like a dream after waking. He didn't want to live in the past, but he couldn't help the fact that everything which was dear to him and had been lost, and etched deep in his memories.

He fought the desire to think about the past again that night. He knew that he couldn't set everything right, but he wasn't going to give up without trying. He had held on for more than two years. If his mother was to leave him, by now she would have, but she was still alive. Every time he was close to despair, he thought about what she was going through. He was only fighting circumstances, she was battling death. He had to go on; he had to carry on the fight. He felt like writing a few more lines.

Until the darkness gives way to the light,
Until all my dreams take flight,
Until every wrong is set right,
I won't give up, I will fight!

There shall be no retreat; there shall be no surrender,
Until fate gives back everything it took away, in all its splendour!

The next morning he woke up early, and reached the college computer lab; he knew that the rest of the class had planned an outing to a nearby hill station. But he chose to stay away and prepare for the quiz instead. He knew that by evening, when the group was back from the trip, they'd upload photos of the outings and just like all previous outings, he would not feature in any. He had lost the enthusiasm for such activities; he knew that even if he did go out with the rest of the class, his mind would always be clouded with worry. He wasn't free like the rest of his classmates, he had more responsibilities than all of them and he had to face them alone. He was afraid to let himself go and was fine with the restricted life that he had created for himself over the past couple of years. He didn't need the distractions of recreation, his time would come... he hoped.

He sat all day in front of a computer screen, reading furiously, going through quiz topics like his life depended on it. He was so immersed in the preparations that he forgot to have lunch, he just kept on reading. His concentration was broken by a lab assistant who asked him to leave at about six in the evening. The whole day had gone by and he had barely realized it. There were just two more days left to go for Fastermind and he really wanted to win it. He sincerely hoped that she would do her bit at the quiz. He knew he wouldn't be able to win it all by himself, the format of the quiz wouldn't allow him to.

By the time he left the lab, he was too mentally tired and the bicycle ride back to the hospital was a welcome break as the winter evening breeze made the journey a pleasant one. Just like every evening, Dr. Roy told him that there was no improvement or deterioration in his mother's condition. He left the hospital soon after and reached his room. As soon as he was done with his dinner, he went to bed and fell asleep.

The next morning he was back in college. Three lectures back to back were taking a toll on the entire class. Most of the students were mentally still at the hill station they had visited a day ago. As soon as the third lecture came to a halt, he rushed off towards the computer lab to read some more. She followed him for a brief distance and caught up with him before he entered the lab.

"Hey. Why didn't you come for the trip yesterday?" she asked him.

He looked at her and thought for a few seconds before answering.

"I couldn't get up on time" he said to her with a smile.

She knew he was lying, but something about his tone suggested that he didn't want to discuss the matter further.

"Really? Well, that's the third outing you've missed" she said to him.

"So how was it?" he asked her, diverting the topic away from his absence.

"It was quite awesome. Super cold weather and we still had Strawberry shake and ice-cream there and the best part of it is, no throat issues as yet" she replied. "Nice!"

"Hey, you want to go to the canteen? We can grab some quick lunch and then discuss some things about Fastermind?" she suggested. He agreed and soon they were having lunch together at the canteen. She wasn't done discussing the outing and started to tell him how the whole trip was.

He enjoyed listening to her account of the trip and her opinion about each location that the class had visited. She continued her narration about how the class then moved onto a plateau-like area and played cricket for a while before arriving at Sunset point, which in her mind was the most picturesque of all the 'points.'

"The view there was spectacular..." she recalled, "... it was so beautiful that I didn't feel like wasting time in taking any photographs. No buildings blocking the view, no sounds from cars and machines drowning the songs of the birds that were making their way back home before the sunset. You don't get that kind of an atmosphere anywhere close to the city; it's a shame that one has to travel for hours and hours to get to such a place. I'd love to go there every week" she said as she looked at some of the photos she had stored on her cell phone.

He wanted to tell her that he knew of a place like that and that it didn't take hours and hours to get there, but he didn't. He watched her as she browsed through the photographs, smiling every now and then, probably because of some memory that the photos brought up in her mind. He could see why the guys in his class discussed her so often.

She was beautiful. Her smile was angelic, her skin was fair and unblemished, her emerald green eyes added to the allure of her face. He had heard the things some of his male friends had to say about her, their descriptions of her beauty were ranged from the innocuous to the perverse. None of their words could do justice to how truly gifted she was when it came to looks. With each passing day he got evidence of how much more there was to her than just her physical beauty.

She was done looking at the photos and looked at him. He realized that her eyes were on him and looked away. He hoped that she hadn't noticed him watching her. He didn't want her to feel that he was like the other guys, he never thought about her the way they did.

"So you want to discuss Fastermind?" she asked him, realizing that she had spent most of the lunch break talking about the trip which he had skipped.

"Yeah sure!"

"One random question. If we win, just suppose we do. What will you do with the money?"

The moment she asked him the question, a flurry of thoughts entered his mind. He thought about a laptop he wanted to buy and then there was that new bike which had been released recently; but then he thought about the hospital and the medical expenses he was responsible for. Once again he refrained from dreaming about the good things in life, lest he gets tempted.

"I haven't thought about it yet" he said to her.

"Oh! You're the – let's not jump the gun – types *kya*?" she asked him.

"No no... it's just that I haven't given it much thought. What about you?"

"I'm the – let's not jump the gun types!" she said to him with a wink. "*Naah*, I'm kidding, I've been busy making a list of things I can buy with that kind of money. That's all I do during Jacko's lectures, with some help from Suparna" she continued.

"So what's on your list?" he asked her.

"Well, there's a new phone, an iPod, lots of new clothes and the rest is for all the remaining college weekends" she replied.

"It's not like winning the lottery, so you may want to scale down the wish list."

"Are you mad? Never question a shopping list made by Suparna and me. We're like the authorities when it comes to shopping. In fact, considering how poor your spending plan is, I think you should enrol for the Shopping 101 course by Prof Suparna and Prof Me."

"We are so going to regret this conversation if we don't win" he said to her, making her laugh.

"The only way to avoid that situation is by winning the damn thing and getting rich" she replied.

Her enthusiasm made him smile. They walked together for the practical, every step of theirs being watched by the keen eyes of college students who almost made it their duty to look out for future couples. Rumours about the two of them had not spread as yet, primarily because people knew about their quiz preparation and thought that the recent sightings of them together were related to the quiz. Plus his reputation as an aloof slash arrogant guy made it difficult for people to imagine him getting friendly with a girl like her.

Students in TY rarely ever coded during the computer practical, all the assignments that they had to complete were gifted to them by their seniors. No one knew who the original author of the program was, all they did was change the name, roll number and date – *that* was the assignment.

She noticed someone ping her on Gtalk. It was Suparna, wanting to inform *her* that Gaurav was going to be in town for the next few weekends.

She was disappointed by the news that he'd be in town for more than one weekend. Suparna was the only company she had for her weekend plans. She pretended to be happy for Suparna. The last five weekends had been filled with a string of evenings out with Suparna, now the run was going to end.

She looked around and saw *him* sitting and reading his email. She looked at her chat window, he showed up as offline. She decided to talk to him about it after the practical. Looking at him, she was reminded about her quiz preparation and she started reading up some more about Bollywood trivia from the 90s. She was happy that the quiz would take up most of her time over the coming weekend.

As soon as the professor in-charge of the practical started to mark the attendance, she looked at *him*. He was packing his bag in a hurry. She knew that as soon as the attendance was over, he'd rush off towards the parking lot and disappear. The professor finished with the last few roll numbers and the moment the professor left the lab, he got up from his seat and dashed off towards the exit. She got up quickly and asked Suparna to take care of her bag, she wanted to have a word with him before he vanished. She had to jog for a short distance before she caught up with him.

"In a hurry to go somewhere?" she asked him. He stopped walking and nodded. "Why do you disappear every day as soon as college is done?" she asked him.

"So that it builds intrigue in the minds of the girls in college" he said to her cheekily. She stifled a smile.

"And why are you always invisible on Gtalk?" she asked him, continuing her investigation into his behaviour.

"That's the closest I get to my Mr. India fantasy. Plus you know how it is nowadays for a single guy, with all those female stalkers online. The Internet just isn't safe anymore" he said to her and this time she could not help but chuckle.

"OK. Seriously, why are you never in college for a single minute more than necessary? I mean every day you just disappear as soon as the last lecture is done. Why do you do that?" she asked him. She was determined to get an answer.

"I just have some personal work to finish. Let's just leave it at that" he answered in a slightly grim tone. She was surprised by the change in his tone.

"OK. Are you coming to college tomorrow?" she asked him. "Yeah. Why do you ask?"

"No, it's just that since tomorrow is the last day before the quiz, I thought you might take the day off to prepare at home" she said to him.

"*Naah*, I have to come to college. I don't have a net connection at home. I'll just sit in the lab and read some more on the net. Probably won't attend any lectures" he said to her, his tone was friendly once again.

He looked at his watch and told her that he was in a rush. He walked quickly to the parking and once again, she saw him leave college on his cycle. She felt stupid about having asked him all those questions and wondered what he might have thought of her for asking him about his reasons for disappearing after college.

Later that evening he was back in his room having dinner. Right from the evening he was feeling uncomfortable about the conversation with her. No one had ever asked him where he went after college, no one had ever asked him why he stayed invisible on chats. The reason was because he had never become friendly with anyone in college, until now. The moment he saw her name on the list of finalists for Fastermind, he knew that he was going to have trouble in remaining aloof. She was an extrovert and was on friendly terms with a lot of people. He on the other hand kept to himself and never got involved in friendships with his classmates. He did not want to get close to people, he did not want anyone to find out his story. No one could help him with the problems he faced. He knew that. He also knew that if people found out about what he was going through, his personal life would simply become a talking point for people. That was just part of the reason.

For the past two years, he had been fighting too many battles and he was too tired to live the life of a normal college student. The others didn't have the constant worry of a mother whose life hung in the balance every day. They did not have to bother about managing finances for everything; right from hospital bills and college fees to their daily meals. He didn't have the energy in him to add to those worries, the normal aspects of college life like running after girls, playing computer games all night, going for college trips etc.

He had enclosed himself in a wall of priorities, doing well in his studies was paramount, then came making some money on the side by winning quizzes; relaxation was the last thing on his mind. He had grown accustomed to living within that wall. It was just him dealing with his hopes and fears. He also knew that he had paid a personal price for his lifestyle choice. He had cut himself off from his school friends and had spent more than half his college life without making any new ones. He knew that his classmates thought he was arrogant and self-obsessed, but he didn't care. For him those four years were like a penance he had to go through. All he wanted to do was get the highest paying job available and see if more money could get his mother better care.

He was aware that he was missing out on a few things due to his overly austere way of life. He could've gone for the outing with the rest of the class, but he chose not to. After the massive setbacks two years ago, he had worked very hard to bring a sense of status quo in his life and he didn't want to disturb it.

But now, he didn't know what was going to happen. There was something about *her* that made him step out of the boundaries that he had set for himself. Every time they sat together to discuss their preparations for the quiz, they always ended up talking about things like movies and outings etc. Things that tempted him subconsciously to step outside the walls that he had built. And today, he sensed how things would go on in the future. If he kept spending time with her, she would keep questioning him about how he spent his time and he would eventually run out of ways to avoid answering. It didn't make any sense to someone looking at him from the outside: why he chose to remain away from his peers or why he refrained from indulging in any college activity and why he chose not to spend a single minute in college at the end of the day.

The other problem was her looks. During the afternoon, when he was sitting with her at the cafeteria, watching her look at the photos from the outing; he could swear he was getting distracted by her physical beauty. Her eyes, her smile and the way she flicked off the long strands of hair that slipped from behind her ear onto her face – it was poetry in motion. And he hadn't dared to look anywhere else apart from her face. Guys, who used words like 'hot' to describe her, simply missed the point.

Right from the first time he had seen her, he had known she was pretty, but there's a difference between seeing a pretty girl from afar and sitting right next to her for hours. Over the past few weeks, ever since they'd started to spend some time together for Fastermind, she had started to enter his thoughts even when she wasn't around. He had to get a grip on himself. She was just acting friendly, there's nothing more to it; he told himself. He knew that he was in no position to even think about anything beyond friendship with a girl like her. He had heard of the kind of lifestyle she led, with parties and movies and other things that he couldn't afford the money or time for. He then thought about his life, filled with all the pressures and responsibilities and how he had decided to shun all these things until better days came along. And now here he was thinking about a girl who he had met because of a quiz. Was he really so vain, that he'd allow himself to get attracted to a girl who in all likelihood was just spending time with him because of the quiz. Get a grip on yourself, he said to himself. He decided that as soon as the quiz was done he'd keep his distance from her and while the quiz was on, he would ensure that he block out all thoughts of her beauty and wouldn't let it impact him. That was the best way forward.

The next day he reached college and headed straight for the labs, he wasn't bothered about attendance; the biggest quiz in the country was less than a day away. He was also feeling relaxed about the fact that he had taken a decision about how he felt about her and now he could concentrate fully on the quiz and not get distracted with unnecessary thoughts. He started reading trivia about *The Lord of the Rings*. He didn't want to completely ignore the subject just because he had read the books so many times. He had left no stone unturned for the preparation and given that it was the last day to prepare, he wanted to cover all bases.

A few hours into his preparation, he heard the sound of approaching footsteps. He hoped it wasn't some batch of students arriving for their practical; he didn't want to break the rhythm he was in. He turned around to take a look. She was walking towards him. She smiled and waved, once again with the slightly tilted head. He smiled back without looking at her beauty spot.

Discipline: 1…
Beauty: 0…

"Hi. What are you doing here? Isn't there a lecture going on right now?" he asked her as she sat down on the seat next to him.

"Jacko kicked me out... again" she replied.

"Why this time? Cross and Noughts again?"

"No. He caught me sleeping in class."

He tried to stifle a smile.

"Don't laugh. OK. You don't know how it feels, getting kicked out of a class. You miss out on the attendance man! And that sucks!" she said to him.

"Why is it so hot in here? Looks like the AC is off" she said, looking towards the AC ducts on the ceiling.

"It's Friday remember, load shedding day" he replied.

"Oh *haan*. Why doesn't the college put the AC on generator backup. This college sucks" she said and started to undo the zip on her sweatshirt. By the time he looked away she was already halfway done with the zipper.

Discipline: 1...

Beauty: 2...

Damn it! Remember what you've decided to do; he reproached himself for losing focus.

"Someday I am going to kill Jacko" she said to him, placing the sweatshirt in her bag.

"Don't get so worked up about it" he replied, trying to calm her down.

"You know, half the class was asleep; and he only kicked *me* out. I don't know what his problem in life is! Bloody frustrated loser."

"Have you ever apologized to him?"

"I said sorry."

"Not the fake sorry we all say when we're caught. I mean a genuine apology, like talking to him after a lecture for a minute. Have you tried that?"

"One apology is all he gets. He can take it or leave it."

"See that's not going to solve the problem. He'll keep an eye on you in all the remaining lectures and you make one mistake and he'll latch on."

"I don't care, I hate him. And it's not just him kicking me out of lectures. Have you seen the way he's always running our batch down, saying that the previous batches were better and how engineering students are turning into pay package whores. That guy is super frustrated. Such people shouldn't become professors."

"Have you ever put yourself in his shoes and thought about why he's frustrated. Look at us, we're young, we have our whole lives ahead of us. He's lived most of his. He has more or less reached as far as he could. People who he taught earlier on are now MDs and CEOs, but he's still teaching Analog and Digital Circuits. And how many of them do you think come back and say thank you or even remember him. I feel bad for college professors sometimes; they get the least credit for their work. We all remember our school teachers, even the crappy ones. But we'll rarely remember our college professors with the same fondness. Then think about him and what his world looks like. Just imagine, teaching the same kind of subjects for two decades to people who don't even seem to care. Walking into a class filled with people who direct their hate for the subject onto him. We make a big deal out of drawing a circuit diagram that we have to draw just for one semester, he has been drawing the same thing for twenty years and will probably be doing it for the next two decades. When he was our age, he probably used to hate some prof, I bet he didn't think at that time that one day he'd turn into the prof who students hate. And then comes what I think is the worst thing for any professor; year after year, the class room benches remain filled with youth while he keeps aging. Imagine watching young faces each day of your life while you keep fading away into obscurity."

The moment he finished speaking, he noticed her looking at him with her eyes open wider than usual. Neither of them spoke a word for a short while. She was thinking about what he had just said and he was wondering what prompted him to go into monologue mode. Once again she had caused him to open up his thoughts and he hadn't even realized it until he finished speaking.

He quickly changed the topic to the quiz and they spent some time discussing their strategy for the quiz. For each of the rounds, she wanted to go first so that she wouldn't be under pressure and so that he knew exactly how much they needed to score when his turn came around. They went through the rules document.

FASTERMIND INDIA:

Day One: Round 1:

A series of 10 questions will be asked within a time limit of two minutes. Each correct answer will be worth ten points and each incorrect answer will result in five points being deducted. If a team answers all ten questions correctly before the two minutes are over, the number of seconds left will be multiplied by five and added to the total score. Of the five participating teams, the top four go ahead.

Day One: Round 2:

This is an Audio-Visual (A/V) round with two questions (one for each team participant) – each of which include an A/V clip of ten seconds. The quiz master will ask the question prior to the clip being shown; the objective for the team is to answer the question before the ten seconds are over. A team that fails to answer the question in the given ten seconds or a team that gives an incorrect answer will have twenty points deducted from their total score. A correct answer leads to fifty points being awarded and the number of seconds remaining will be multiplied by five and added to the total score. Of the four participating teams, the top three go ahead.

Day Two: Round 3:

Each member of the qualifying teams is asked a maximum of twenty questions on his/her specialty subject within a time frame of five minutes. The same scoring pattern is followed as in Round 1.

Tie-Breakers:

At the end of any round, in case of a tie in scores of participating teams a tie-breaker question will be conducted for the concerned teams. Each team will nominate a member who will be asked to take over the role of quiz master for his own team. The official quiz master will hand over an envelope with three questions. The nominated quiz master will pick one of the three questions and will ask the same to his/her team-mate, who will have ten seconds to give the answer. The other tied team(s) will then repeat the same process with a separate question set. The team that answers the question correctly and the fastest will be declared the winner. In case teams give the correct answers in the same amount of time, the round will be repeated until a clear winner can be declared.

Additional rules:

The quiz master is the final authority in case of any dispute and the quiz master's decision will be final and binding on all participants.

"This tie-breaker stuff seems complicated" she said after she read through the rules put up on the website.

"Don't worry about it. They've never had a tie-breaker in the history of the quiz. The make or break round is the specialty round. Do well in that and you're all set to get rich" he said to her.

"I'll win the damn tie-breaker also if it comes to it. *Main paison ke liye kuch bhi kar sakti hoon... kuch bhi!*" she said in an exaggerated Bollywood movie tone which made him laugh.

"I'm sorry for the extremely sad joke. But this overdose of 90s Bollywood is getting to me. Yesterday I was travelling in a rickshaw and the driver had a smallish radio in it. He had put on All India Radio and the song *'Kya adaa kya jalwe tere paaro'* was on and I actually knew all the lyrics. Without realizing it I started to sing the song and the driver looked at me in the rear-view mirror and gave me a random look. It was super embarrassing. I will so need to detox after the quiz *naa*" she continued with her rant about the quiz preparations.

"Hey, I'm not having a cake walk either. Yesterday I was sitting in the lab and reading up some stuff on the *Mahabharat* and a bunch of juniors walked in for their practical. I vacated the comp I was using and this girl who took over looked at the web-page that I had left open in a hurry; it was about the *Draupadi cheer haran*. She gave me the 'what a pervert' look. I didn't bother to explain" he said, responding with a rant of his own which led to some more laughter.

She looked at her watch; it was time for the next lecture.

"I should go now. I guess you're planning to read some more" she said to him as she dug into her bag to hunt for the sweatshirt. He nodded in reply. He looked on as she pulled out the sweatshirt from her bag and put it on. She ran her fingers through her hair to set them before she left. He couldn't help admire how perfect each tress of her dark hair looked.

Discipline 1…
Beauty 3…

She got up, waved goodbye, again tilting her head to the side. His eyes found their way to the beauty spot.

Discipline 1…
Beauty 4…

As she turned around to walk away, he forced himself to look away. He could hear her footsteps as they faded away into the distance but was glad that he was able to overcome the urge to watch her leave.

Discipline 2…
Beauty 4…

He continued reading until late in the evening when it was time for the lab to close. He got out of the lab and walked towards the parking lot. He saw her standing near his cycle. He wondered what it was that she had to say to him. He waved to her, she smiled in return.

"Hi, what are you doing here?" he asked her once he was close enough for her to hear him.

"I just realized one thing. We haven't exchanged phone numbers."

"Oh!" he said in surprise, more out of the fact that she had actually thought about it than the fact that they were classmates for almost two and a half years, and had been in frequent contact over the past couple of weeks and who still hadn't exchanged cell numbers. She asked him for his number and gave him a missed call. He saved her number immediately.

"Will you do me a favour?" he asked her.

"What?"

"Don't give my number to anyone else, please."

She laughed, thinking that he was joking but then realized that he wasn't after looking at his solemn expression.

"You're serious?"

"Yeah, why?"

"I mean, obviously I won't go around advertising your cell number to the whole college, but you make it sound as if no one in the class has your number."

"That's right."

"What the... you haven't given your number to anyone?" she asked again, completely astounded by what she had heard.

"Well, you don't know how dangerous those female stalkers can get. They keep calling late at night and hanging up" he said as he tried to downplay the phone number revelation. But he realized that it wasn't sufficient.

"Listen, I know this sounds weird and crazy. But there is a reason for it, and I don't want to get into it right now. Let's just say I am not a phone person" he said to her.

"No. It's OK. You don't have to make an excuse. I'm sorry about the way I reacted; I was just a little surprised."

"That's fine. Anyway, I better go now. Get a lot of rest today; it's critical that we're both mentally relaxed for the quiz. See you tomorrow" he said to her.

"Don't worry I won't disturb you with any late night blank

calls" she said to him with a wink. "And I guess now, you'll rush off to whatever mysterious location you head off to every evening."

He smiled and said nothing. He rode away on his cycle and she started to walk away towards the cafeteria, where Suparna was waiting.

She got a lift home with Suparna and it was only after she reached home that she realized that she had no plans for the night. After a long time she was going to be all alone on a Friday night, with nothing to do. She hated it. Suparna had dinner plans with Gaurav. She was tired of reading movie and music trivia all week, she didn't have the kind of patience that she knew he had.

She looked at the Clint Eastwood poster on the wall. She got up and stood in front of it. She loved that poster with her favourite actor giving the rugged, man of steel look. It blew her mind each time. If only I had a time machine, she thought to herself and sighed. She went back to her computer to read the rules of Fastermind once again, just so that she was sure of what to expect the next morning. After having her dinner she decided to go to sleep earlier than usual. She had no clue what would happen in the next two days. All she knew was that it was the first time she was participating in a quiz and that she was going to try and make the most of it.

5

Fastermind

He had a rough night, he barely slept a wink. It was the anxiousness before the quiz. He hoped that at least his quizzing partner had a good night of rest. He got dressed and double checked that he was carrying his ID card for the quiz. The quiz was to be held at the city's biggest auditorium – *The Colossus*. Even though the auditorium was located at the opposite corner of the city, he still rode on his cycle and reached the hospital. He walked into the room and saw his mother. Her peaceful face and slow breathing contrasted his tense expression and heavy breathing from riding his cycle. He sat down on the chair next to her bed to catch his breath.

A couple of years ago, on a day like this, his mother would've done a full-fledged *'aarti'* and prepared some *'panchamrit'* for him, to bless him and pray for his success. He had done the *aarti* himself in the morning at his hostel room, without praying for anything. He had even prepared some *panchamrit*. He brought it along to the hospital in a small plastic box. He took the box and touched her right hand with it. Only once he was sure that her hands had touched the box of *panchamrit* did he feel it was blessed. He drank the sweet mixture of honey, sugar, milk, yoghurt and ghee.

"This is it *maa*... the biggest quiz of my life. I really need to win this" he said to his mother, hoping that his words somehow reached her. He really did need to win the quiz. The money would help ease his mind to a large extent.

He wouldn't need to participate in any more quizzes for the rest of the year if he won Fastermind. He wouldn't need to bother about the rent for his hostel room. He would be free of financial worries for the remainder of his engineering course as long as he kept his scholarship, which his academic record ensured he would.

But he didn't say all these things to his mother. If she was listening, she didn't need to know how much was at stake for him. Had things been normal she would've put her right hand on his head and given him her blessings. Right now however, she had an I.V. drip inserted into her hand. He looked at the point where the I.V. needle was injected into her wrist and could almost feel the pain himself. He followed the I.V. lines backwards from her hand right up to the drip bag which contained the life saving drug that was flowing into his mother's body, one drop at a time. He looked closely and was surprised to see that it took exactly one second for a drop to form and flow into the I.V. line. Every second, a drop of life that time took away. Every second, a drop of hope that kept despair at bay.

He broke his chain of thought, it was making him weak. Just keep fighting *maa*, just keep breathing. I have to go now; I'll be back; hopefully with good news. He left the hospital to get to the auditorium.

Meanwhile, a fair distance away from the auditorium, his quizzing partner was asleep. She was dreaming about a quiz where Clint Eastwood was the quiz master, standing on a stage with a cigar and the trademark poncho from *The Good, The Bad and The Ugly*. He was declaring that she had won the quiz. The audience was giving her a standing ovation. The audience was filled with people who looked like Clint Eastwood. She was in heaven. But something was amiss, instead of hearing applause she could feel the stage vibrating. The stage started to shake as the vibrations went out of control, she was about to fall; just as Clint was about to rescue her, she woke up. Her cell phone was vibrating. She grumbled a few words, angry about her sleep being disturbed. She looked at the cell phone display, it was *him*.

"Hail low" she said in a still-dreamy voice.

"Thank God you're awake. You scared me, I've been calling for the last ten minutes" he said to her in a close to panicky voice.

"What time is it?" she asked, as she struggled to open her eyes.

"It's nine o clock. The quiz starts at ten. Please get up and get ready quick. Most of the other teams are here already" he said to her.

"Holy crap! We have the quiz today!" she said aloud, finally realizing what her weird dream was all about. Her reply made him really worried about her chances of making it on time. She got herself together and assured him that she'd reach *The Colossus* ahead of time. She reached five minutes late.

He was already seated on stage, so were the other teams. The quiz master was nowhere to be seen. Thank God, she thought to herself. As she approached the stage, she could see that he was really tense. She gestured to him to calm down, he responded by pointing to his wristwatch. She quickly sat down next to him, the chair she was given was a bit wobbly.

"I'm sorry" she said to him, apologizing to him in earnest.

"You freaked me out! Why weren't you answering your phone?" he asked her.

"I was driving. I couldn't find a *rickshaw*; I borrowed my uncle's car and drove like mad to get here on time."

"Not on time, you're late."

"Since when did we start considering five minutes late as being late?"

"You're actually going to argue about this. We should thank our stars that the quiz master is letting the auditorium fill up before starting the quiz."

"Alright, I'm sorry."

"It's ok."

"Now you see the value in exchanging cell numbers. If we hadn't, you wouldn't have been able to call me to wake me up."

"Are you actually taking credit for using human beings as your morning alarm?"

"Human beings don't have a snooze button" she replied with a wink. His smile meant that their little panic argument was over.

"OK, here's the deal; we need to think up a team name" he said to her.

"You've been here for an hour and didn't even think up a

team name?" she questioned.

"Uhh... no, because I was constantly on the phone wondering whether half the team was asleep or not."

"Alright, let's not go there again. Team name... hmmm.... what have the others decided" she said to him.

"Well so far the names that have been submitted are along the following lines. You see that team opposite us, they're The Gladiators. The ones to their left are calling themselves Zodiac Zombies. Next to them we have Apoorva Kalyan..."

"What sort of a name is that?"

"I guess the girls name is Apoorva and the guy is Kalyan"

"They should've called themselves Kalyanji-Apoorvaji. As in, the music composers Kalyanji Anandji!"

"What?"

"Sorry, bad joke brought about by stage fright" she said to him and they both laughed nervously.

"And the team next to us call themselves The Ring-wraiths. Obviously *Lord of the Rings* fans. Now that leaves us, the nameless team" he said to her.

"That's perfect!" she said excitedly.

"What's perfect?"

"The Nameless Team... No, let's tweak it, The Nameless Victors. How do you like that?" she asked him. He gave it a thought for a brief while and thought it had a nice ring to it. He agreed and submitted the team name to the organizers.

She looked on as each and every seat at *The Colossus* was filled. The first few rows had members of the press and special invitees seated on them. The college crowd started five rows behind and went on till as far as the eye could see. There were more than three thousand people in the auditorium. She had no idea that quizzing was so popular.

"Check out the awesome crowd. I didn't think so many people would come just to watch a quiz" she said to him, expressing her genuine surprise.

"Quiz competitions always have a lot of people who come and watch. There are lots of audience prizes to be won. Plus this is Fastermind, it's a big deal for the quizzing community of the city" he replied.

"Still, only a handful will win the audience prizes. What about the rest of them, what's in it for them."

"Watching a quiz is like watching porn, you may never be as good as the participants; but it's great fun to watch and one might just learn something at the end of it" he said, immediately realizing the inappropriateness of his statement. He looked at her apologetically. For a split second she looked stunned but then burst out laughing.

"Sorry... bad joke brought about by stage fright" he said, reusing her excuse.

She gave him a light punch on the shoulder and told him not to worry about it. She laughed all over again after she thought about what he just said.

The quiz master finally made his entry on stage. He was fair, tall, really tall and well built. He wore black jeans, a white T-shirt with 'Fastermind' written on it and a black leather jacket over the shirt; he also had put on a pair of black aviators. She wondered why he was wearing sun glasses on stage. Just as she had that thought, the lights over the audience dimmed and all the stage lights came on. She had to squint her eyes for a while to get used to the brightness. She looked at the quiz master's aviator glasses with envy.

"Hello and welcome to this year's edition of Fastermind India. We are very pleased to be in your wonderful city and we're sure this year's competition will be the best one yet. There are lots of audience prizes to be won. Our generous sponsors have wristwatches and laptops lined up for you to take away and the grand prize for the audience is a travel package for one couple to Thailand for three days and two nights. So, for all the couples in the audience, pay attention now so you can have fun later" said the quiz master, using a slightly naughty tone for the last part of his opening, which led to a bit of whistling by some sections of the male community in the audience.

"Looks like he's also showing some effects of stage fright"

she said to her quiz partner. *He* looked at her and smiled.

"OK, so before we start with the first round, let's have a quick recap of the elimination round that we conducted earlier this month. We went to over twenty colleges in the city and conducted the elims simultaneously in all those colleges. A round of applause for the volunteers who helped us out... thank you. We had several hundred applicants and shortlisted the ten that you see here on stage. We received the highest female participation ever for Fastermind in your city... a big round of applause for *naari shakti!* Way to go girls..."

"Come on man, get on with the quiz!" she whispered, each second of the quiz master's rambling was getting on her nerves. *He* could see that she was getting a little tense; she was constantly tapping her right foot on the stage floor. He asked her to relax; the quiz wasn't going to start for at least ten minutes. Her foot tapping increased in speed. He decided to let her be and continued listening to the quiz master.

"Now that we've thanked all our sponsors, let's move onto some of the crazy moments from the elimination rounds. We had a lot of participants who submitted some very creative answers to our quiz questions. I just thought of mentioning a few, three to be exact..." continued the quiz master.

"This should be a lot fun" he said to her, in the hope of easing the pressure that she was feeling. It did not help; she remembered some of the stupid answers that she had written out of frustration during the elimination rounds. She wondered if the quiz master was going to divulge the names of the people responsible for the answers and if any of her answers featured in the list.

"Let's go to the first one. We asked 'Who wrote the novel *Dracula?*' A very enlightened soul came up with the answer 'Count Dracula'." the auditorium was filled with laughter. She was relieved that the quiz master was leaving out names. She now waited for the next dumb answer.

After waiting for the audience to settle down again, he went ahead with the next answer on his list of goofs.

"We then asked: 'What is Michael Jackson's middle name?' to which we got the most unexpected answer – '*Pyaremohan*'! We chose that over the second most creative answer we received, which said – 'He had no middle name'."

The audience loved every minute of this, the quiz master was enjoying hitting the bulls eye. She was stunned at making the list of crazy answers; she chose not to tell her partner about it.

This time, the audience got back into silent mode sooner, as they were eager to hear the next one.

"Now for the third and final gem from the elims. We asked: 'What special feature do the languages Arabic, Mandarin and Hebrew have in common?' to which we were given the brilliant answer 'The special feature about all these languages is that I don't speak, read or write any of them'."

She felt a little more relaxed after the quiz master was done with his humorous opening. She was slowly realizing how much of a role entertainment played in quizzing. It wasn't just about Q&A, the quiz master had to ensure that the audience got some laughs along the way. She looked at her partner. *He* was sitting with his eyes closed and his right hand clutching something near his chest. He could sense that she was looking at him. It broke his concentration. He let go of the *rudraksh* that he was holding onto while going through a few *mantras* – a ritual that he always performed before an exam or a quiz. It helped him ease the nervousness.

"Were you praying?" she asked him.

"Nope. Just getting into the zone."

She gave him a '*whateva*' look. The quiz master took his seat at the centre of the stage.

"Alright folks, let's start off with team introductions. From my left to the right, we have five teams. The first team call themselves The Gladiators...."

For some reason her heartbeat started racing as the quiz master's introduction for her team approached. The convention being followed was of the female participant introducing herself first, followed by the male participant. As soon as The Ring-wraiths were done with their introduction, she felt a thousand pairs of eyes on her. She couldn't hear anything else aside from her own pounding heart. She couldn't speak or move. The microphone was right in front of her but she couldn't bend towards it and speak. Every second that passed seemed like an eternity to her. She knew that she was freezing in front of everyone; she couldn't understand what was happening to her. That's when she heard a whisper. *He* moved in right next to her, under the pretext of adjusting his seat, and whispered "Relax, you'll be fine." In a split second she snapped back into reality. Those eyes that she had imagined upon her were far away in the distance. She grabbed the microphone with one hand and introduced herself without hesitation. He followed it with his introduction.

With the formalities done, the quiz master started the first round with the Zodiac Zombies, which meant that The Nameless Victors would be the last team to get their turn. She didn't like that idea too much, whereas he was pretty happy about it. He told her that, by them being the last team to play the round, they'd know for sure how much they needed to score to qualify. She felt the same thing could increase the pressure they faced, but she did not tell him that.

The Gladiators had a poor start. They did not finish on time and hence lost out on the chance to score extra points. Then came the turn of the Zodiac Zombies, who had a cracker of a round, answering all their questions right and getting an extra fifty points for the time they had remaining on the clock. *She* immediately started to worry. The action shifted focus to Apoorva Kalyan, who got all but two of their answers correct. On one occasion, both Apoorva and Kalyan gave two different answers simultaneously. The quiz master chose to deduct points for it even though Apoorva's answer was correct. This led to a minor argument as Apoorva and Kalyan asked the quiz master to consider the correct answer. The quiz master then got up from his chair, pulled out a piece of paper, which looked like the print out of the rules posted on the Fastermind India website. He

addressed the audience and said, "The last rule of this quiz says –
The quiz master is the final authority in the case of any dispute
and the quiz master's decision will be final and binding on all
participants." He looked at Apoorva Kalyan for a second, smiled
and then turned back towards the audience.

Apoorva Kalyan looked a little confused with the quiz
master's reaction but knew that they had no argument left. The
quizzing resumed soon after that. The Ring-Wraiths were under
the firing line next. They did fairly well, answering all but three
questions correctly. Which meant that it was a straight shootout
between The Gladiators and The Nameless Victors. The quiz
master took a sip of water before starting the questions for them.

"Best of luck" he whispered into her ear. She tried to feign a
confident smile. He took a deep breath. For a second he felt a
shiver of fear pass through his spine. What if they got kicked out
at the end of the two minute round? Instinctively his hand found
its way to the *rudraksh* hanging close to his chest. He thought of
his mother. Immediately he felt a surge of adrenaline rush
through his veins. He opened his eyes, looked at her and said,
"We're going to win this round". She wasn't sure if making such
statements was part of his 'getting into the zone' act.

The quiz master then started to fire the questions in a hurry.
120 seconds to go...

"Cricket – In which country was England's former captain,
Tony Greig born?"

He raised his right hand and gestured to her that he knew the
answer.

"South Africa"

"Correct." 114...

"In the year 1960, who became the world's first female Prime
Minister?"

He again repeated the same gesture.

"Sirimavo Bandaranaike"

"Correct." 106...

"What X-Men character shares his name with the electronic
line judge used in Wimbledon?"

She had no clue about any of the answers thus far and this one was no different. It can't be Wolverine; she thought and then looked at him. He had his eyes closed tight and after a few seconds of thinking, he yelled out the answer.

"Cyclops."

"Correct."

He punched the air with his fist. She realized he had taken a risk and it had paid off. 98...

"Which famous pop singer's real name is Eileena Regina Edwards?"

She knew this one. She raised her hand in the same way as he had done for the first three questions. He didn't know the answer, but held his breath as she opened her mouth to give the answer. An incorrect answer would end their chances of getting any bonus points if they were to finish ahead of the stipulated two minutes.

"Shania Twain"

"Correct."

She was ecstatic. She got up from her seat and high-fived her partner. Her first answer at Fastermind was spot on. Despite the tension of the on-going round, he broke into a smile by seeing her over-the-top reaction. She could hear some hoots and whistles from the audience as well. Those were more for her looks than for her answer, but she didn't really care. She realized that precious seconds were being wasted and got back to her seat. 90...

"Name the two authors of The Communist Manifesto?"

"Karl Marx and Friedrich Engels" he replied without wasting a second.

"Correct." 87...

"What is the common link between Mike Whitney, Tania Zaetta and the British SAS?"

He was stumped by the question. The British SAS were a part of the Special Forces of the United Kingdom. He had no clue about the link. He looked at her. She came closer to his ears and whispered her analysis of the question.

"Mike Whitney and Tania used to host that show on AXN...
Who Dares Wins. You remember that? But I have no clue what
they have in common with the SAS. Who dares wins is the
common link between Mike Whitney and Tania. I'm sure of it"

"Then go for it" he said to her.

"Go for what?" she asked, confused by his response.

"Who dares wins."

"What? Are you sure?" she asked him to confirm. He
nodded.

"Who dares wins" she said out loud to the quiz master.

"Correct."

Both of them were stunned. He moved in to whisper into
her ear again.

"Who dares wins" he said with a wink, making her laugh.
They exchanged another high-five. Now it was the turn of The
Gladiators to get tense. One more correct answer from The
Nameless Victors and they were out. 72...

"Apart from Marlon Brando, which other Hollywood star
played the character of Vito Corleone in Francis Ford Coppola's
Godfather series?"

"Robert De Niro" he replied immediately.

"Correct."

The joy on the faces of The Nameless Victors was in sharp
contrast to the dejection on the face of The Gladiators. He felt a
little sad for them, but the quiz master's next question shut out all
thoughts of compassion in his head. 65...

"Hollywood again – Who was the first director in Hollywood
history to have two films released in the same year nominated for
Best Picture?"

Once again he had no clue about the answer. He looked at
her, she was thinking. His mind was blank. A few seconds later,
she tapped his shoulder; he leaned in close to her to listen to
what she had to say.

"It's either Stanley Kubrick or Alfred Hitchcock"

"Is that a guess or you're sure about it?"

"It's a slightly sure guess" she replied.

He didn't know what a 'slightly sure guess' actually meant. But the more he thought about the two names she brought up, the more confident he felt that they had the right options in mind. But which one was it?

"What are you thinking?" she whispered.

"See, I think it's definitely one of the two. But, Kubrick from whatever I have read about him, used to take a long time to finish one movie. I don't think he ever was in a position where he had two releases in the same Oscar year. Hitchcock, I think was more likely to be the kind of person who would have two movies nominated in the same year. Again, I'm not too sure about my theory..."

"It's logical. Go for Hitchcock" she said, interrupting his theory summary.

"It's your answer."

"I'm too tense to answer" she replied.

"Sure about it?"

"Who dares wins, right?"

"Let's find out."

He took a deep breath and answered.

"Alfred Hitchcock."

"Correct."

She got so excited that she almost gave him a hug. He was punching the air wildly. He knew that they had taken a lot of time to answer that question, but it had kept their hopes alive to top the round. He calmed down soon, as the quiz master read out the second last question. 40...

"Which legendary ruler of an Indian princely state is said to be glorified in a portrait at the NASA headquarters, for his use of rockets in warfare?"

Where have I read this? He thought to himself, closing his eyes and rushing through every single memory he had about articles he'd read on Indian kings of the past.

She thought of Shivaji initially, but wasn't completely sure. She whispered her guess to him. But he shook his head, signalling to her that he felt it was the wrong answer. He thought of names ranging from Chandragupta to Prithviraj Chauhan, but none of them seemed to fit.

"What about Tipu Sultan?" she asked. It struck him like lightning. There was a mention of Tipu Sultan's portrait having been on display at a NASA facility, in former President APJ Abdul Kalam's book, *Wings of Fire.*

"You're a genius" he said to her and then promptly turned towards the microphone to give the answer.

"Tipu Sultan."

"Correct."

"Which famous product's name is a portmanteau of the words 'Durability, Reliability and Excellence?' "

"What the heck is a portmanteau?" she whispered to her partner.

"A portmanteau is a word that is formed by blending the sounds of two or more words" he replied, as he wrote down the words on a piece of paper kept on the table.

He kept trying to make a portmanteau out of the words, but couldn't think of anything meaningful. Time was running out quickly. He looked at her, she had her eyes closed. After a few seconds she opened her eyes, took the paper in her hand and held it in the air. She read the words again and her eyes opened wide. She giggled for a second as the answer popped into her head.

"Dude, I don't believe this!" she said to him.

"What?"

She lifted her hand in the gesture that *he* normally used to indicate that the answer had been figured out. He couldn't take the tension. He shut his eyes and cupped his face in his hands. She bent forward towards the mike and gave the answer.

"DUREX."

"Correct."

"What! Durex?" he said out loud. She laughed at his reaction and moved in closer to him to talk to him.

"Dude, you should've had that question covered" she said to him with a naughty smile, almost teasing him.

He let it go; comeback lines for condom jokes were not his forte.

The points were announced.

The Nameless Victors – 260

Zodiac Zombies – 250

Apoorva Kalyan – 160

Ring-Wraiths – 140

The Gladiators – 120

The quiz master got up from his seat and congratulated all the teams for their performance in the first round. The Nameless Victors were on top. Having finished twelve seconds ahead of time, they added a valuable sixty points to their total. The Gladiators however were on their way out. The quiz master announced a half an hour break, which would be filled up by some of the organizers asking 'audience' questions and giving away some freebies.

A volunteer came up on stage and escorted the participants to a room, back-stage. The quiz master was seated in a corner, sipping some cola. The teams were standing at different corners of the room, confused and waiting for instructions on what to do next.

"Hey, do you have Internet access on your cell phone?" he asked her.

"Yeah" she said, pulling out the cell phone from her purse.

"I just want to check that British SAS answer. I still don't know what the connection was between the SAS and Who Dares Wins" he said to her.

She quickly searched for the term 'British SAS + Who Dares Wins'. The first search result itself gave her the answer. "Hey check this out. The motto of the British SAS is – who dares wins" she said to him, handing over the phone so that he could look at the answer for himself.

"And now we know how we won the quiz" he said to her as they both had a laugh about having guessed the answer without really knowing the actual connection.

After a brief wait, someone from the organization team got

all the five participating teams together. A short, bespectacled girl, with an ID card dangling from her neck informed the teams that they could take a quick break of fifteen minutes and after which they would have to reassemble backstage for the next round.

Before the participants dispersed, she handed out an envelope to each participant. It was an entry pass for a party to be held the next night, as a closing celebration of the quiz. The party was basically part of a promotional campaign of one of the sponsors of the quiz – a hugely popular liquor brand. As soon as she got the envelope, she was extremely excited. She read the details printed on the pass and was thrilled by the mention of one of her favourite DJ's who was going to play at the event. She looked at *him*; he didn't share her enthusiasm for the party. She tried to get him pumped up about the party, but he didn't show much interest despite the hype that she tried to create. She thought that he probably did not want to lose focus from the quiz and decided to tone down the party talk that she had been indulging in for a while.

"Hey, listen. Don't think that I'll get carried away with thoughts about the party. As soon as the next round is about to start, I'll get into 'the zone.'" she said, in a bid to reassure him that she hadn't lost focus.

"That's fine. I'm just surprised to see you so excited about this party. I mean, you sort of have a reputation of being a bit of a party animal"

"What? Seriously!"

"Yeah, as in... from whatever I've heard"

"No way, I'm no party animal. I don't know where people get these ideas from. But yeah, I am excited about this party because it'll save my weekend from getting wasted. The last few weekends, I've been having a blast with Suparna. We've gone out every single night to some place or the other. All expenses courtesy the cash from the second rank prize for SY. But this weekend, Suparna isn't free and apart from the quiz, I didn't think I'd have much to do. But here comes a free party invite and it should be fun. I'll get a chance to continue my unbroken streak of weekends spent dancing at parties. Hence saving my weekend from getting wasted" she said, explaining her reasons for looking forward to the party.

"Why is it so important for you to go out and dance every weekend?" he asked, in a tone that conveyed genuine curiosity.

"Hmmm... well, I have this cousin; he's in his late twenties. Every time I meet him he keeps telling me how jealous he is of the fact that I am in college. He says that it's the best time of one's life. And you know, he's not the only one who says that. Most of the people who are older than us, feel the same way. That their college times were the best. Now look around you. How many people in our college actually realize that they're going through the best phase of their life? There will come a time in their life, when they'll suddenly feel that the best phase of their life got over and they didn't even realize it.

I don't want to be in that group of people. I want to enjoy my college life. For some reason I get a great deal of happiness while dancing at a disco. God knows why! But I love it. And every weekend that I don't dance, it feels like I missed out on a chance to add another night to the best time of my life. I guess that's the reason" she said, explaining a bit of her philosophy to him.

He was amazed by her answer. He had never thought that something which seemed as frivolous as dancing at a disco could have such a deeply thought-out motive behind it. Before he could say anything to her, the bespectacled organizer arrived back on the scene. She asked everyone to huddle around her except The Gladiators who were given some participatory certificates, which meant that their role in the competition was over. The two member team, who had been eliminated, walked away with downcast expressions on their faces.

He felt bad for them. They probably had worked just as hard as him and here they were out of the quiz in the first round itself. He asked his partner to pay attention to what the organizer was announcing and walked away from the huddle, towards The

Gladiators who were making their way to the exit. She turned around to see what he was going to do. She saw him as he caught up with them. He shook hands with both the team-mates and had a quick chat with them. She couldn't hear what he was saying, but she could see the expression on the face of the female team-mate, who clearly was appreciative of whatever he was saying.

A few minutes later, he joined the huddle again. She quickly told him that the organizer was just repeating the rules to all the teams, probably to avoid another on-stage argument with the quiz master. She was curious about his conversation with The Gladiators and decided to ask him.

"What did you say to them?"

"Nothing. I just told them that they did pretty well and wished them luck for the future. They just wished me back, nothing major."

"That was thoughtful of you."

"I don't know, I just felt bad *yaar*. In the end it was us against them, in a way. We were lucky to get questions that we were able to answer. Plus they were the first team who were asked questions. Sometimes the situation just gets to you and hampers your thought process. The other teams had time to adjust. So I just thought that it'll be nice to have a word with them. They were pretty chilled out people actually, I was scared that they might think I'm being pompous, but they understood that I meant well."

"Nice. I thought you were trying to hit on the chic" she said with a naughty smile on her face.

"What? No way."

"Why? Do you have some, no flirting with chics rule while you're in 'the zone'?" she said with a chuckle.

"Relax, I'm just pulling your leg" she then told him.

"How long will you take my case for the 'getting into the zone' statement?" he replied, trying to change the topic.

"At least until the quiz is over."

"And just for the record, I wasn't interested in that chic, she wasn't my type" he replied.

"Why was she not your type?"

"Not hot enough" he said, frankly.

"That is so mean" she said, with fake expressions of getting offended.

"Just a minute ago you said I was thoughtful and now you're calling me mean. Very consistent!"

"Nah, I was just messing around. It was very thoughtful."

"I just didn't want any bad vibes from them. In the end I think a quiz boils down to who has more luck on his side. Good *karma* always counts" he said, explaining further, his reason of having a chat with the first team to be eliminated.

"Well, don't expect too much good *karma* either; I doubt that they'll be rooting for us."

"Yeah, I don't expect that either. *Chalo*, time for the next round" he said to her as the organizer asked the four qualifying teams to proceed to the stage.

She noted how different the stage looked after the break. The table and seats occupied by The Gladiators were gone. The remaining four teams had been spread out wider on the stage. The quiz master's table had a projector kept on it and a very large, white screen was kept at the far end of the stage, located at a vantage point from where all teams and the audience could see the screen without obstruction.

The new, spread out seating arrangement made her feel uncomfortable. She thought it increased the sense of isolation for all the participants. She wondered how much more that feeling would increase if their team made it past the round and came back to play the final round the next day, where only three teams would qualify. She shrugged off such thoughts and tried to focus her attention on the task at hand – the Audio/Visual round.

The A/V round was mostly a solo round. Each team-mate would need to stand next to the quiz master and pick up a chit, based on which an A/V clip would play. As soon as the clip started, the clock would start ticking and the participant was required to answer the question on the screen within ten seconds. There was no scope of team work, something that had helped them win the first round. Despite that, she was feeling a little confident about her chances. She had done a decent job in the first round, answering quite a few questions directly and helping her partner out on a few occasions. It wasn't the one-way traffic that she had feared it'd be, prior to the quiz.

The quiz master was back on stage. He started off by congratulating the members of the audience who had won the freebies. He then explained the rules briefly to the audience and started the A/V round. Beginning with the Zodiac Zombies. The girl got up from her desk and walked over to the quiz master's table. The quiz master asked her to pick up a chit from a bowl filled to the brim with folded pieces of paper. She picked up the uppermost chit and handed it over to the quiz master, who opened up the chit. Everyone on stage and in the audience was keen on finding out what the chit contained. It turned out to be an anti-climax when they found out that the chit simply contained a number.

"Clip number 17 please" he said out loud.

Immediately the screen turned bright. At the top right corner of the screen, a countdown clock was displayed which showed the number '10'. The rest of the screen was blank.

"Your question will be on the screen three seconds after I have finished speaking. The countdown will begin as soon as the A/V is displayed" said the quiz master.

The girl was nervous, *he* could tell from the way her fists were clenched. She was digging her nails into her palms. He could sympathize with her. Standing in front of a few thousand strangers, next to a no-nonsense quiz master; waiting for a question that was to show up on the screen and all one got was ten seconds to get the answer right, with no second chances. It was a tough round. Just as he was having these thoughts, an image formed on the screen, covering nearly two thirds of the space. Along with the image, a line of text was displayed at the bottom of the screen.

There were three faces on the screen – Guru Dutt, Rajendra Kumar and Raaj Kumar. All three were major yesteryear stars from Bollywood. The line of text displayed at the bottom of the screen was the question. It read:

"Of the three actors on the screen, whose real life name was Kulbhushan Pandit?"

The clock started to tick. The girl started to bite her nails. *He* could read her lips; she was repeating Guru Dutt, Rajendra Kumar and Raaj Kumar repeatedly. But that was not what was asked. Everyone knew who those three men were. Five seconds flew by and she had her hand on her head. When just two seconds remained, she yelled out "Guru Dutt".

"Incorrect. You lose twenty points" said the quiz master. The timer stopped. The girl walked back slowly to her seat and put her hands on her head. Her team-mate gently patted her on the back trying to console her. Meanwhile the quiz master gave out the correct answer.

"The three gentlemen on the screen are Guru Dutt, Rajendra Kumar and Raaj Kumar. Guru Dutt's real life name was Vasantkumar Shivshankar Padukone; Rajendra Kumar was of course, Rajendra Kumar. The correct answer is Raaj Kumar, whose real life name was Kulbhushan Pandit. A big hand for these stalwarts of Indian cinema" said the quiz master; leading to a rousing round of applause from the audience.

The quiz master then called the second member of the Zodiac Zombies to take centre stage. He walked with some more confidence than his partner. He stood next to the quiz master and picked up a chit.

"Clip Number 5 please."

An image formed on the screen that everyone recognized. It showed Vinod Kambli walking off the Eden Gardens, at the end of the tragic 1996 Cricket World Cup semifinal. Everyone then looked at the question.

"Name the last batsman to be given out prior to the match being awarded to Sri Lanka?"

The timer started. Everyone was wracking their brains out.

All of them had seen that match as kids, but few knew the answer. The man in the firing line sure did not. He decided to take a guess and named Nayan Mongia.

"Incorrect. You lose twenty points. The right answer is Ashish Kapoor."

The Zodiac Zombies had very sullen expressions on their faces. The questions were so frustrating, giving them the 'so-near-yet-so-far' feeling. The other teams also got a little scared. Zodiac Zombies, who until then were sitting pretty on 250 points, were now down to 210.

Up next were Apoorva Kalyan. They got one of their answers correct, with five seconds to spare; adding 55 points to their overall score. A pretty decent score for the round, considering what happened to the Zodiac Zombies.

Then came The Ring-wraiths. They got both their answers correct and in all added twenty-five bonus points. They surged ahead on the points table.

As soon as The Ring-wraiths were done with their questions, *she* felt the pressure on her reach a crescendo. She hated how her palms were sweating. She got up and walked to the middle of the stage. She could hear the hooting and whistles as she made her way to where the quiz master was sitting. She picked up a chit and handed it over to the quiz master.

"Audience, silence please! This will be an audio clip" said the quiz master.

The auditorium was soon completely silent. The contrast in decibel levels within seconds made her feel disoriented. Plus the fact that she was the first to pick an audio clip added to her discomfort. She had gotten accustomed to how the other participants had gone about things with the video and image based questions. The audio clip hadn't been tried so far during the quiz. Her partner was also visibly tense. But he managed to give her a smile and a thumbs up when she looked at him. She smiled back nervously and then looked away. She looked at the screen even though there was nothing on it apart from the countdown clock displaying the number 10.

"Alright Nameless Victor, be ready. You will hear an audio clip and you need to identify the TV show associated with it. Audio Clip Number 3 please."

She closed her eyes and tried to concentrate. The audio clip started, so did the countdown. It was a familiar tune, something she had heard during her childhood. The music sounded like a peppy jazz waltz tune. Within a couple of seconds, *he* had the answer but it didn't matter, *she* was the one who had to figure it out. From the expression on her face, he could make out that she wasn't clueless. She opened her eyes; she had only five seconds to go. That's when it struck her.

"I Dream of Jeannie" she answered.

"That's correct, with four seconds to spare" the quiz master replied. She jumped in the air and screamed 'wohoo' out loud. She forgot that she was standing in front of a large audience. As she walked back, in addition to the expected hooting and whistles, she heard some shouts of 'wohoo' from the audience, imitating her tone.

"Ignore them" said her partner as soon as she was within earshot. He had a big smile on his face; she had ensured that they would end up with a decent score no matter what, by adding seventy points to their total. He got up to take centre-stage and she gave him a best of luck high-five as he passed by her. He wanted to get it over with quickly.

He stood next to the quiz master, rammed his hand deep into the bowl and picked up the chit that was right at the bottom. He handed it over to the quiz master. The quiz master smiled after looking at the number on the chit. *He* had no idea if that was a good sign or a bad one.

"Clip Number 36" yelled out the quiz master.

Nothing could have prepared anyone in the auditorium for what happened next. The screen showed a video of Pamela Anderson running on a beach in a red swimsuit, clearly a clip from the mega-hit TV show – Baywatch. The audience roared louder than they had ever roared during the entire quiz. He was stunned. He looked at the question at the bottom of the screen.

"Name the character played by the celebrity in the video clip?"

He knew the answer but he didn't want to give it; that would stop the clip from continuing. He looked at the countdown, seven seconds to go. He closed his eyes, apologized to all the Pamela fans in the audience and gave the answer.

"C. J. Parker from Baywatch."

"Correct, with six seconds to go."

He looked at his partner; she had a very embarrassed smile on her face. He walked quickly towards her and gave her a massive high-five. They had just won the second round by a huge margin.

The audience was chanting 'once more' over and over again. Both members of The Nameless Victors were laughing; even the quiz master had a tough time concealing a smile.

"How did you know her character's name?" she asked him.

"I'm insulted. Baywatch was the greatest show ever! I remember everything about it."

"Dude, you were a kid when it ran on TV."

"And even then I knew Pamela was a Goddess... OK, sorry, lost control there. But the moment I read the question I had the answer."

"Then why did you take four seconds to answer?"

"You have to be a guy to understand that" he said to her.

She gave him a mock punch on his shoulder. "Anyway, awesome work. We're nailing this thing" she said to him.

"We can't celebrate yet. One more day to go" he replied.

She wanted to tell him to chill out a bit, but then realized that he was right. They had done all the hard work getting through the GK rounds. Tomorrow they would face a test on subjects of their choice. It would be a different ball game. Today, things were completely out of their control. Tomorrow, they'd be closer to their comfort zone. She, with the Hindi movie/music scene; and he would have his *Mahabharat* and *Lord of the Rings* knowledge tested. But for the moment she wanted to relish the moment. She asked him if he wanted to go to a coffee shop nearby. He agreed since he had nothing to do for the rest of the day.

They occupied a table at the coffee shop, she ordered a double grilled chicken sandwich along with an iced tea; he ordered a hot chocolate and a veg sandwich.

"You don't eat much, do you?" she asked.

"Just not hungry" he replied. The real reason however was that he had ordered the cheaper items on the menu and even then the cost would end up being twice that of his simple lunch at the hospital cafeteria.

They discussed the quiz in detail. She was still very excited about everything that had happened.

"I was so scared when I went for the AV round. It was crazy. Especially after what happened to those Zodiac Zombie people. They got killed in that round *yaar*. Eliminated; Then when those Ring-wraiths got both their answers right, I was damn scared..." she recounted her experience before going to collect her chit for the AV round.

"But, you pulled it off. I wasn't sure if you watched I Dream of Jeannie as a kid" he said, acknowledging his anxiousness when she was about to answer the AV round question.

"Oh dude! It used to be my favourite show, right after Dennis the Menace on Sony, I guess. Every evening. I used to come back home, watch Small Wonder on Star TV, Powerpuff Girls on Cartoon Network, then Dennis The Menace and I Dream of Jeannie on Sony. Those were good times for kids watching television."

"The Powerpuff Girls? Seriously?" he asked.

"Please. It was one of my favourite shows. In fact, it was my favourite cartoon. I loved it, that and Dexter's Lab. I even asked my dad to get me some soft toy versions of Dexter, Dee Dee, Bubbles, Blossom and Buttercup. I still have all of them, except for Buttercup. My cousin had come over for a vacation with his pet dog. And his stupid dog ripped the poor soft toy into shreds" she said, remembering a part of her childhood. He laughed at the bit where she mentioned her Buttercup doll being destroyed by a dog.

"Don't laugh OK. Buttercup was my favourite. I loved that doll, I always thought of getting another one, but then I've never gotten around to it. Someday I'll get a replacement of that soft toy and complete my collection again. There's something about those times *naa*, before they dubbed those shows into Hindi and messed them up. Although Small Wonder was pretty cool in Hindi as well" she said.

"Yeah, Small Wonder and even I dream of Jeannie were awesome in Hindi" he said in agreement.

"One question I have to ask you. How the hell did you manage to watch Baywatch as a kid?" she asked him.

"It's a guy thing. We always manage to watch the important shows in life" he replied with a naughty look on his face.

"Alright. Keep your dirty little secrets."

"What Dirty secrets? Baywatch was a prime time show on Star World! The whole country watched it. It was a brilliant show; I learnt how to swim because of that show. Baywatch saved lives" he said to her and his speech on the merits of watching Baywatch was cut short by her laughter.

"All right, fine. God! You guys are so defensive about your guilty pleasures."

"I don't know about guilty, but watching Baywatch was a pleasure" he said and both of them burst out laughing again.

"What happened during that Tipu Sultan question? One second you didn't know the answer and as soon I mentioned the name, you just grabbed the microphone and gave the answer" she said regarding one of the tougher questions that they had faced.

"What happened was... I had read about the 'rockets being used by an Indian king' stuff before. I just couldn't remember the name. I thought of all the kings I had read about, you know, like Chandragupta, Prithviraj Chauhan etc. For some reason Tipu Sultan's name just didn't strike me. The moment you mentioned it, I just knew it had to be him. There was no doubt in my mind. He did use rockets, they probably didn't exist in the times of Chandragupta or Prithviraj Chauhan" he replied.

"I've not heard much about Prithviraj Chauhan. Isn't he that king who had some epic love story?" she asked.

"I can't believe you just said that. He wasn't just *some king who had some epic love story*. There are so many legends about him that it would take all day for me to narrate them and we'd not even get done with half of them" he told her.

"Really? Well, let's hear a few of them."

"OK. I'll tell you two stories that I know. The first one, you may have some idea about – his love story with Princess Samyukta. Now, I am no historian, so I'm just telling you whatever I have gathered about the king, but even if this stuff is partially true, it makes for a pretty kick ass story.

So here goes... Prithviraj Chauhan was this brave king who had to fight a lot of battles all his life. He was one of the last Hindu kings to rule from the throne in Delhi. He became king at the age of twenty and in a few years expanded his kingdom way beyond Rajasthan. He conquered various parts of Gujarat and stretched the realms of his border to several parts of North India. He did this at a very young age and many of his contemporary kings became jealous and scared of him.

Sometime after he had established himself in Delhi, he heard of a princess called Samyukta. Legend says that she was the most beautiful woman of her times. Her father however had some grudge against Prithviraj Chauhan. Even then, Prithviraj wanted to meet Samyukta. He found out that she visited a particular temple for prayers. So he went to that temple in disguise and saw her. He was immediately smitten. Despite his disguise, she recognized him. The two got friendly and he kept meeting her secretly. They fell in love and wanted to marry each other.

Soon, her villain *baap* heard about this and decided to hold a *swayamvar* for Samyukta. Her dad wanted her to marry anyone but Prithviraj Chauhan, so he invited all the famous kings and princes for her to choose from at the *swayamvar*. He deliberately did not invite Prithviraj. In fact, he decided to mock him, by creating a statue of Prithviraj and used it in place of a doorman. Prithviraj Chauhan heard about this plan and he made one of his own and confided in Samyukta.

On the day of the *swayamvar*, Samyukta entered the venue for the ceremony and found a line of potential suitors standing and waiting for her to choose one of them. She had the *varmaala* in her hand and walked slowly past the suitors, pretending to think about whom she wanted to marry out of them. She kept walking and walking and was close to passing by all the suitors. As she reached the end of the line, she made a run for it towards the door. She put a garland over the statue of Prithviraj Chauhan. Everyone was stunned with her act of defiance. But then came the real twist. From behind the statue emerged the real Prithviraj Chauhan and carried her off in his arms, with the *varmaala* around himself. He got onto his horse and rode away with his bride. No one was able to catch them and they lived a blissful married life" he stopped the narration at this point.

"No wonder she fell for a guy like him. What freaking guts he must've had!" she exclaimed.

He let the effect of the story simmer for a while as she looked at the sky out of the coffee shop window, probably creating images of the story in her mind. She finally looked at him, eager to hear the next story.

"If you want the most beautiful woman on Earth, you have to be something special. But this story hardly touches upon the awesome courage of the man. I'll directly skip to the last of his legendary stories.

After close to twenty years of ruling from his throne in Delhi, he met a fierce enemy in Mohammad Ghauri, from present-day Afghanistan. Ghauri challenged Chauhan at a place called Tarain, which is close to present-day Thanesar in Haryana. After a bloody battle, Chauhan defeated the mighty army of Ghauri. The defeated army fled and left their king behind.

Prithviraj Chauhan took Ghauri prisoner and brought him to his capital city, in chains, to be executed. But Ghauri accepted defeat and begged for mercy, swearing never even to look towards any part of Bharat for the rest of his life.

Against the advice of his ministers, Chauhan forgave Ghauri and set him free. Big mistake.

A year later, Ghauri returned with an even bigger army and challenged Chauhan, once again at Tarain. But this time, Ghauri had a secret weapon.

While in captivity, Ghauri learnt a bit about the dynamics of Chauhan's kingdom. He found out that there was a minister in Chauhan's inner circle who harboured thoughts of overthrowing Chauhan. Ghauri conspired with the minister and learnt intricate details of Chauhan's battle tactics and strategies. Armed with those secrets, he fought against Chauhan and having advance knowledge of all the moves that Chauhan's generals made in battle, he defeated their army.

Ghauri took Chauhan prisoner along with a few of his minsters, bound him in chains and took him away to Ghaur in Afghanistan. While Ghauri had begged for mercy, Chauhan did not. Ghauri set up a big public meeting in his palace ground to humiliate Prithviraj Chauhan.

In front of all his subjects, Ghauri hurled insults at Prithviraj and ridiculed him for his defeat. Ghauri even brought the captive ministers to witness the humiliation of their king. Prithviraj reminded Ghauri about his own condition a year back when Ghauri was in chains and told Ghauri that his behaviour was unbecoming of a king. Ghauri got very angry and told Chauhan that as a prisoner he had no right to look him in the eye. He threatened Chauhan that if he did not lower his eyes, he would have them gouged out. Prithviraj Chauhan defiantly continued to look Ghauri in the eye.

Ghauri asked his soldiers to gouge out Chauhan's eyes, right there, in front of all the people assembled at the ground. They complied. Chauhan is said to have remained completely silent while enduring the torture. After mocking Chauhan about being blind, Ghauri decided to execute Chauhan right then and there.

Now comes the kick ass part of the story. Prithviraj Chauhan told Ghauri that all great kings offer one last wish to a dying man. Ghauri asked him what his wish was. Prithviraj Chauhan asked him for a bow and arrow.

"What for?" asked Ghauri.

"To kill you." replied Prithviraj Chauhan.

Ghauri laughed at this. He applauded Chauhan for his defiance but then reminded him about his blindness and that he wouldn't even be able to aim correctly at Ghauri.

"Then you have nothing to fear" responded Prithviraj Chauhan.

Ghauri had to comply with Chauhan's request, for fear of coming across as a coward. He knew that Chauhan was an ace with the bow and arrow. But he was convinced that Prithviraj Chauhan couldn't possibly get his aim right, being blind. He asked for Prithviraj's own bow and arrow to be given to him.

Because of all the words that had been exchanged, Prithviraj Chauhan could judge the direction where Ghauri was seated. But he wasn't able to figure out the exact distance. He started to pull at the bow-string. Ghauri saw that Chauhan had the direction right, he could have changed his location silently to avoid any chance of getting shot, but that would've been seen as a sign of cowardice. He trusted his luck and believed that Chauhan had no chance of getting the distance right.

Chauhan knew that one way or another; this would be the last act of his life. He took his time, the crowd started to murmur. He pulled the string tight and then loosened it a bit, wondering how far Ghauri was located.

Just then, one of Chauhan's ministers yelled out the following couplet at the top of his voice.

Char baans, chaubis gaj, angul ashta praman,
Ta upar Sultan hai, mat chuko Chauhan.

Prithviraj Chauhan recognized the voice of his loyal minister, who had given him the exact distance to strike Ghauri. Chauhan shot his arrow, which flew towards Ghauri at a speed that struck him down before he could blink. Ghauri was dead and the crowd was stunned into silence. The only sound that could be heard was of Chauhan laughing, who knew he had killed his treacherous enemy. The guards then beheaded Chauhan and the ministers. But Chauhan ensured his legend would live on forever" he said, ending his narration on Prithviraj Chauhan.

She was speechless for a few seconds. She couldn't believe that she hadn't heard this story until now. "This was one of the greatest stories I've ever heard" was all she could say.

He smiled, glad that she had found the tale interesting.

"So one thing, that minister who told him the distance with the couplet... what was that couplet again and what does it mean exactly?" she inquired.

"*Char baans, chaubis gaj, angul ashta praman* – roughly means four measures of a bamboo stick, twenty-four yards and an eight finger span. Measurement units from the old times.

Ta upar Sultan hai, mat chuko Chauhan – that's the distance to the Sultan, don't you miss your target Chauhan" he said, translating the remainder of the couplet.

"The archery acumen of Chauhan was so great that despite being blind, he was able to judge the exact distance and location of his target based solely on the utterance of his minister. That is why Prithviraj Chauhan is remembered even today as a legend" he said to her.

"Why the hell don't they teach this stuff to us in school? This is way more interesting than the crappy history lessons we're taught" she said. He nodded in agreement.

"How do *you* know this story in so much detail?" she asked him.

"My dad told me this story when I was a kid" he replied.

"Oh, cool. What does your dad do?" she asked him, just as a conversational point.

"My dad was a lecturer at the state university" he answered.

"And what does he do now?" she asked again.

"He passed away when I was eleven of a brain aneurysm" he replied in a low voice.

She felt like killing herself. He had told her that his dad *was* a lecturer, she should've guessed that he was no more. Why the hell did she ask that question? She didn't even care about what his dad did, she was just trying to start a discussion.

"I am really sorry, I didn't realize... I'm so sorry" she said, frantically apologizing for unintentionally bringing up the topic of his father's death.

"Don't worry about it. How would you have known? It's alright" he told her, trying to make the situation a little less awkward. Nevertheless, she apologized again and then excused herself to go to the washroom.

After she left the table, he felt a little bad. They were having such a good conversation, why did he have to tell her that his father had told him the story. He could have just said that he had read it somewhere. It wasn't really her fault that she asked him about his dad, she wouldn't have known that his dad had expired. He cursed himself for spoiling the relaxed mood they were in.

Meanwhile, she was in the washroom, cursing herself for the same thing. What's wrong with you? She said to herself. Stop asking stupid questions about people's parents. How do you care what they're doing? This is the most idiotic thing you could have done. He must be feeling so bad right now. He's probably thinking about his father now and how he died. You fool! Lesson learnt, never talk about parents, ever! She chastised herself and then looked into the mirror and quickly set her hair right. Before leaving the washroom, she took a quick glance at herself to make sure she was looking fine.

While she was in the washroom thinking about how he felt, he was lost in thoughts from a distant past. He had just returned from school that day, when he saw his uncle standing at the bus stop to receive him instead of his mother. His uncle was dressed in a white *kurta*. He thought it was pretty odd, but he was glad to see him. He waved to his uncle with enthusiasm, but his uncle responded with just a half-hearted smile.

He sensed that something was wrong; he asked his uncle why his mother hadn't come to pick him up at the bus stop. His uncle did not give him a clear answer. As they walked the distance between the bus stop and the apartment where he lived, his uncle did not say a word to him.

When they were closer to the apartment, he noticed a few

cars and scooters parked below their apartment. There were more people gathered there, dressed in white. That's when he felt a sense of fear. The kind that almost stopped his heart. He knew what the congregation of people in white *kurtas* meant. He let go of his uncle's hand and ran towards the apartment and climbed the three floors instead of waiting for the elevator. The apartment door was open, there were more people standing inside, he heard weeping sounds from the apartment.

He saw his mother sitting in a white sari, next to her was a framed photograph of his father with a sandalwood garland on it. He could not believe it. He rushed towards his mother but stopped a few feet away. His eyes fell upon a white sheet of cloth that covered a body. His father's dead body. His heart sank, he felt like he could not breathe. He fell onto his knees, a tear dropped onto the floor. His mother saw him, he looked into her eyes. No words were exchanged, but he knew what she wanted to tell him. Be brave, don't cry. He'd never forget that moment for his whole life. That one moment, where he was on his knees, looking at his mother who was mourning her dead husband. There were so many people around him, but the only person he could see was his mother. She walked towards him and picked him up and gave him a hug.

He couldn't stop the tears but he did not wail or make a sound. She carried him near his father's body and put him down next to it, he saw his father's face. He tapped his shoulder, he wanted to wake him up. But his father wasn't asleep. His father had gone away, never to return. Where have you gone? He wanted to ask him. His father was right in front of him and yet he was gone.

"What happened to him?" he asked his mother. She knew that he wouldn't understand what a brain aneurysm was. He was too young. She held him in a tight embrace and whispered in his ears a simple command that he followed ever since – Be brave.

"I'll be brave *maa*" he said with tears in his eyes. His mother wiped them off with her hands. Don't cry, she told him. That was the first time he learnt how to stop crying. He sat down on a chair, looking at his father's photograph and then at the white sheet that covered his dead body. The elders in his family along with a few neighbours were constantly shuttling in and out of the room; every once in a while whispering something to his mother. He remembered how everyone was in a hurry to get to the crematorium before sundown. He did not understand the rituals that he was asked to follow by a *pundit* whom he hadn't ever seen before.

The *pundit* kept referring to his father as a *shav*, the Hindi term for a dead body; it upset him but he did not say anything. He dutifully performed all the tasks he was asked to. The final task being setting fire to his own father's body. Later, he wondered why it was the son's duty to perform the painful task. Why couldn't his mother do the same thing? After all she was probably the one with the most right over her husband. Why then did she lose the right to even attend his funeral? He remembered watching the funeral pyre and standing there as the sun began to set. The others were relieved that the task was done before sunset, he didn't really care. He had just lost his father. There wouldn't be any more dinner table discussions at night. No more stories about kings and princes of times long gone by; no one to tell him anecdotes about cricket or politics. The third seat on the dinner table would be empty. What about his mother? What would happen to her? What was he supposed to do now? Be brave?

Be brave. That's all he had been doing ever since. A few years later, he had his first brush with the Internet. The first thing he searched for on Google was the term 'brain aneurysm'. He was pretty sure that in the whole world, he was probably the only guy to have that term as his first Google search query. That day, when he read the result; he found out how his father had died.

An aneurysm is the medical name for the weakening of the walls of a blood vessel. In a layman's term blood vessels, like the arteries and veins, are tubes. An aneurysm is when the wall in a section of those tubes becomes weak. The weakened section of the tube bulges out due to the pressure of the flowing blood.

This eventually leads to the rupturing of the artery. The underlying cause was the cholesterol in the arteries. The only symptoms his father had shown were fatigue and occasional bouts of double vision. Those weren't alarming symptoms. He was advised to take rest by the doctor he had visited. Lots of people suffer from fatigue and bouts of double vision, which usually gets cured over time, with adequate rest. The chances of an aneurysm were, one in a million. No one knew that his father was going to be unfortunate enough to be that one person amongst a million. He was probably walking around with the aneurysm for weeks before his death. That day, when he was sitting in the university library, preparing for his next lecture, he just fell over onto the table while reading. The aneurysm had caused the artery to rupture. By the time the university staff brought him to the hospital he had passed away. Ever since that day, things had been going downhill for his family.

Just as he was thinking about that dark part of his past, he saw her return to the coffee table; watching her smile, made him feel better. As soon as she sat down on the table, she steered the conversation towards the other memorable moments from the quiz. Time flew by and when he looked at his watch, it was nearly five in the evening. He realized that he had to leave in a hurry if he wanted to make it to the hospital on time for Dr. Roy's daily round. She also thought that it was time they left. She wanted to get back home and prepare for the next day. He asked her not to overdo the preparation. They called for the bill.

"We'll split it" he said as the waiter placed the bill on the table.

"No way. You're stuff was way cheaper than what I ordered. I won't let my quizzing partner suffer a loss on my account" she said and insisted with him till he agreed. She emptied her entire purse to find the smaller purse in which she carried cash. He had an amused look on his face, which she did not find amusing.

"Hey, just watch my stuff. I think I'll buy some muffins for people back home to celebrate the successful day at the quiz" she said, referring to all the items she had emptied onto their table, as she got up and walked to the display shelf of the shop.

Amongst all the things she had emptied out on the table, he noticed the envelope which had the invite to the Fastermind party. He knew he wouldn't attend that party. It was part of the decision he had taken about his equation with her. Already today he had done something he had refrained from all through his college life. He had told her about his father. No one apart from his school friends knew about that. She had again somehow made him forget the barriers of privacy that he had carefully built for the past couple of years. It was best that he skipped the party, even if they somehow managed to win the quiz.

He looked at her; she was busy deciding which muffins to choose. He pulled out the envelope he had been given and took out the pass for the party. He quickly put his own pass inside her envelope which was lying on the table. She returned to the table with a bag full of muffins and packed all the things she had emptied out on the table, back into her purse. They got up and walked out; it was a pleasant winter evening. He felt that he'd have a good time cycling back to the hospital, even though it was a fair distance to cover. "Hey listen... about tomorrow's party..." Just as he started to tell her about his intention of skipping the party, her cell phone started to ring. Suparna was calling.

"Loser, you were supposed to wake me up. I almost missed the quiz.... We won both the rounds... Wassup with you? How was your party with Gaurav?" she went on and on and on.

Her conversation with Suparna just refused to end. He hung around for quite a while, but their call refused to come to an end. He was getting late. He gestured to her that he was leaving. She asked Suparna to hold the line.

"Hey, Sorry. This will take some more time. You go ahead, I'll see you tomorrow!" she said to him. He waved good bye to her and was on his way. She got back to her conversation with Suparna. He cycled as fast as he could, filled with excitement as he got closer to the hospital. He wanted to tell his mother the good news as soon as he could.

He reached the hospital and rushed to her ward.

"We won *maa*; both the rounds. My quiz partner was amazing. She really did a brilliant job today. I couldn't have asked for a better partner. Now for one more round tomorrow and if we can somehow pull it off, it'll be a dream come true. I don't know what's going to happen tomorrow, but today was simply mind blowing stuff. The organizers have recorded the whole thing. I'll get a copy from them. One day we'll watch it together" he said to his mother excitedly.

He sat down next to her bed and narrated the entire sequence of events. Just like every other day for the past two and a half years, there was no response from her side. He waited for Dr. Roy to arrive and just like every day, the neurologist informed him that there was no change in his mother's condition. He hung around for a while after Dr. Roy left and then headed off to his hostel room.

Meanwhile, Suparna and her best friend were still on the phone. She had just finished narrating the highlights of the quiz to Suparna. She raved on and on about how knowledgeable her partner was. She also repeatedly mentioned how calm he was and actually used the term 'nerves of steel' for the first time in her life during a conversation.

"So you've finally decided what sort of a guy he is?" asked Suparna.

"Um... not totally. I just saw one side of him at the quiz. But you know, you find out a lot about people when they're under pressure. And he was just amazing. He never got flustered or tense, at least he didn't show it" she replied.

"So that's it? He's intelligent and calm, that's all you could figure out?" asked Suparna, forcing her best friend to think harder about the personality traits *he* had demonstrated during the day.

"No. There's more. He's very interesting"

"How did you come to that conclusion?"

"I don't know how to explain this, but you know after the quiz, I thought of hanging out for a while. And believe it or not, we were sitting and chatting at a coffee shop for five hours non-stop. It was incredible; I didn't even realize we had spent such a lot of time together. He had so many things to talk about. He told me this awesome story which I will discuss with you when we meet next in person. It was just great."

"Cool. I am happy for you, may the love blossom."

"Eww... what's wrong with you? You're a total drama queen. I'm just trying to figure out what sort of a guy he is. There's nothing more to it, OK! May the love blossom... what trash" she said.

"OK. Fine. I get it. You just wanna have a *fraansheep* with him" said Suparna and the two girls shared a laugh.

That night, when she was back in her room, she read about Prithviraj Chauhan and after reading about him from several different sources, she finally was able to confirm the story that *he* had narrated to her in the afternoon. She liked how he had narrated the whole story. The stuff that she read on the Internet was just a set of historical facts, but he had strung them together into a very interesting story. She thought about how great it'd feel if the two of them won the quiz the next day. She also started thinking about the party. That filled her with a lot of excitement. Irrespective of what was to happen in the quiz, the party was on! She'd finally get to hang out with him in the kind of environment she enjoyed the most. She was really looking forward to celebrating with him at the party.

That night she had mixed dreams, of sitting on the stage and answering questions, then all of a sudden she dreamt about a princess at a *swayamvar* and running away with a king and finally she dreamt about dancing at the greatest party ever.

Far away from her apartment, a young man lay down on his bed, unable to sleep for the second night in a row. He couldn't get his mind to stop thinking. Even after ensuring that he had done all the revision he wanted to, he still couldn't get his mind to switch off. He finally gave up and headed towards his window. It was a Saturday night and there was a lot more traffic on the road below as compared to the weekdays. He looked on as he saw young guys and girls travelling to and from places like discos, restaurants and karaoke bars.

He thought about his choice of abstaining from the Fastermind party. He wondered if he was doing the right thing. He had all the right to go to the party. Only the finalists of Fastermind had been invited from amongst all his peers. Admission to the party was by invitation only. He had read about the parties in earlier editions of Fastermind. It had been a major event when the competition had been held at Mumbai and Bangalore, making it to 'page three' of various newspapers. But then he thought about the other side of the story. He hadn't been to any party in a long time. He lived a very simple life and indulging in parties would certainly distract him. He had a lot of responsibilities on his shoulders. He couldn't afford to get bedazzled by events like these, only to lose focus on what was important. He hadn't tested himself against such diversions and there was no need to start now.

He had done everything right, so far. His grades were high, he had no *pangas* with any professors and he was building up his resume for the placement season that was fast approaching. As soon as Fastermind was done, he needed to get back to work on studying hard for the semester-end exams. That was just as crucial to him, as winning Fastermind was.

Just as he was thinking about all these things, his mind went back to his conversation with her at the coffee shop. He recollected her expression after he had narrated the story of Prithviraj Chauhan. He smiled as he thought about it; he probably must have had the same expression on his face when his father had narrated the story to him all those years back.

They had gone for an overnight trip to a nearby hill resort. His father had lit a bonfire for him. He loved bonfires; they gave him a mixed feeling of thrill and safety. He could still picture it in his mind. His father sitting across the bonfire, telling him stories late into the night. His mother kept reminding his father that it was getting late, but then his father would beg her for more time telling her that he'd narrate just one more story. His mother would agree even though she knew that the father and son duo would never stop at just one more story. On one occasion, to stop the story telling session which had gone on way past midnight, she had thrown a bucket of water on the bonfire. That memory brought another smile to his face.

Ever since his mother's accident, he had so many responsibilities and duties to take care of that he barely got time to think of his father. He felt guilty about that. But then, he didn't have too many memories of his father in any case. His father had been snatched away from him and his mother when he was barely eleven years old. His mother had struggled a lot to bring him up without his father. It hadn't been easy on her but she had never let him see all the troubles she went through in her day to day life. Back then, he felt that he'd do all he could to make his father proud, as his mother had said. He had thought that by excelling in his academics, he could also make his mother feel that all her struggle had been worth it. And then like a bolt of lightning, tragedy struck his family again. His mother was caught somewhere between life and death for days which stretched on to months and now years.

He wanted to make her proud. His engineering entrance results had been declared days after her accident. He had made it to one of the finest colleges in the country. He hadn't stopped at that; in each of the four semesters thus far, he had topped his batch. He had been relentless, working day and night just to make sure that he scored high even in subjects that he hated. He had won two gold medals for his efforts. But he was still waiting for the day he could see the glint of those medals in his mother's eyes. Heck, she probably didn't even know that he had become an engineer. What if she never woke up from her sleep? All his achievements would come down to nought. Everything he had accomplished would be in vain. Stop, he said to himself. Get rid of such thoughts, they don't help.

Over the past two and a half years, there had been so many occasions when he felt helpless and wanted to seek some solace in prayer. But he couldn't even do that. He had forfeited his right to pray in exchange for his mother's life. Thus far, God had kept his word. His mother hadn't recovered, but she was alive. He was grateful for that. For the past two and a half years, his hopes had been kept alive. He had to go on. He had fought this battle for too long to give up at this stage. He returned to his bed and closed his eyes even though he knew he'd not get sleep.

The next morning she woke up at eight o clock, she had set an alarm for herself this time. She decided to give a phone call to her quiz partner just to make it clear that she was awake for the quiz and would make it on time.

"Hello" she said as he answered the phone.

"Hi, wassup?" he replied.

"Well, just wanted to tell you that I am wide awake and I'll reach *The Colossus* by nine thirty, half an hour ahead of time."

"Uh... if you reach at nine thirty you'll be there seven and a half hours ahead of time."

"What?"

"Yeah. Read the schedule, Day Two of the quiz is scheduled in the evening, so that soon after the quiz, people can move to the party" he informed her.

She felt stupid about not knowing the schedule properly. She also regretted waking up so early; she could have carried on sleeping for as long as she wanted.

"Damn *yaar*. This sucks" she said. Her tone had such a funny mix of embarrassment and irritation that he couldn't help but laugh. That irritated her even more. He asked her to forget about the goof up and relax.

About half an hour before the event they met at the entrance of *The Colossus*. They walked inside the auditorium and waited near the stage, where the organizers were busy in some last minute preparations. She looked at the scoreboard that was kept near the corner of the stage. As she read their name on top of the list, she felt a great deal of satisfaction. It was only when she saw the scorecard that she realized the massive lead with which they had entered the third round. But today that lead was meaningless. The scores from Round 1 and 2 did not carry forward into Round 3. The Specialty Round was one which would have all three qualifying teams, start from scratch.

The Nameless Victors – 395
The Ring-Wraiths – 265
Apoorva Kalyan – 215
Zodiac Zombies – 210

The same bespectacled organizer from yesterday walked onto the stage and wiped out the name of the Zodiac Zombies from the scorecard. She also reset the scores of all three teams to zero.

He felt a little bad when he saw the 395 turn into a zero in a flash. It was almost as though the organizer had erased all the evidence of their brilliance in the first two rounds. But he also realized that it was a fresh start and neither he nor his partner could rest on the laurels of Day One. He spent the rest of the pre-start time chit chatting and joking around with his partner. The two of them were much more comfortable as compared to the earlier day when she had reached late and he was tense about her arrival. They were also at ease with the large crowd that had turned up on Day Two, to witness the most talked about round of Fastermind India.

The organizers finally got the three teams – The Nameless Victors, The Ring-wraiths and Apoorva Kalyan on stage. The quiz master was in a new avatar when he made his entry on stage. He was wearing a tuxedo and looking really dapper in it, getting a few whistles from the girls in the audience.

"Don't get distracted" *he* whispered into his partner's ear.

"Haha, very funny. I've been in 'the zone', ever since I set foot on stage. I won't get distracted even if he takes off that tuxedo and has a six pack underneath."

"What was that? You're definitely getting distracted" he said to her with a wink. She elbowed him lightly in the ribs.

The quiz master made some sponsor related announcements and then started with the introductions for the final round of the quiz. The introductions were followed by a detailed reading out of the rules for the Specialty Round and the Tie-Breaker Round.

"All right, ladies and gentlemen. The next one hour of quizzing promises to be intense and exciting. I request you all to maintain the excellent discipline you have demonstrated and not to indulge in acts like yelling out answers to questions that you know. There will be a special audience round, after the Specialty Round is done, where you can satisfy the quizzer in you and win that special couple's trip to Thailand.

Without wasting another second, let's get on with the quiz. Let me call out the first team that will play the round. In reverse order of qualifying scores, may I call on to the centre of the stage the first member of team Apoorva Kalyan."

Apoorva, walked to the centre of the stage, where an old wooden chair with armrests was kept. The quiz master sat on a leather sofa about ten feet away from the wooden chair. It was a ploy to make the show seem tougher to the audience and the participant. The rest of the participants sat on benches at the far right of the stage. The active participant had her back towards the rest of them when she sat on the wooden chair. The lights on the stage went off and two spotlights came on. One directed at the quiz master and the other, directed at the active participant.

The Nameless Victors knew that their turn would come right at the end, once again having to face the increased pressure of having to beat the scores of the teams ahead of them. She took some time to get adjusted to the new lighting scheme on stage. It was so different from the previous day. The mental disorientation that the lighting caused made the challenge even greater. Just like every other participant and audience member, her eyes were transfixed on the centre of the stage; her gaze alternating between the quiz master and Apoorva.

"Alright Apoorva, you've chosen 'The Life and Times of Bhagat Singh' as your specialty subject. When you hear the buzzer, the timer will start and so will the questions. You have five minutes to answer a maximum of twenty questions. Should you answer all twenty correct with time to spare, you will be awarded five points for each second left. Is that clear?" the quiz master asked after repeating the rules once again.

"Yes" was Apoorva's reply in a very shaky voice.

What followed were twenty of the most difficult questions about Bhagat Singh's life and struggles during the freedom movement. Apoorva failed to answer two questions correctly:

In Lahore jail, which fellow-inmate of Bhagat Singh died after fasting alongside him for 63 days, while Bhagat Singh carried on the hunger strike for a record breaking 116 days?

Name the newspaper in which Bhagat Singh published articles discussing the concept of anarchism?

The correct answers to the questions were Jatindranath Das and *Kirti*.

Despite the two incorrect answers, she had done a splendid job, securing 170 points for her team. Kalyan then made his way to the wooden chair.

The quiz master announced Kalyan's specialty subject as *Harry Potter and The Goblet of Fire*. Kalyan answered all twenty questions right and added sixty bonus points to the tally for finishing with twelve seconds to spare. It was an astonishing performance; even the quiz master seemed impressed.

"How could he choose a subject which just covers one book? No wonder he got all the answers correct! It's not fair" she whispered in an agitated state to her quiz partner.

"No, it is fair. He took a risk and pulled it off. You saw the level of depth in the questions. Plus that book was one of the most complex in terms of number of characters and sequences. Can't grudge the guy, he just nailed it" he replied.

She knew that he was right, when the quiz master announced the total score that Apoorva Kalyan had managed; there was a collective gasp from the entire audience. The two member team had scored a whopping 430 points. The quiz master announced that it was the highest team score in the history of Fastermind India. The Ring-wraiths and The Nameless Victors weren't as excited as the audience upon hearing that little factoid.

The Ring-wraiths went next. The two team-mates had chosen very interesting subjects – The History of the Taj Mahal and The First Battle of Panipat. Although their choices seemed engaging, both the team-mates stumbled at certain stages and ended up giving a total of five incorrect answers, finishing with a total of 325 points. A good effort but one that meant they wouldn't win the contest.

The expression on the faces of Apoorva Kalyan and The Nameless Victors were almost complete opposites of each other. While the former were confident, the latter team could have defined the word 'tense' with their expressions.

She looked at him before she walked to take her place on the wooden chair. He had a sombre look on his face; he wasn't going to give her any fake optimistic smiles. He just nodded and quietly wished her good luck. It made her realize the gravity of the situation. She sat down on the wooden chair in front of the quiz master. The audience continued the tradition of whistling and hooting, especially now that they could see her walk under a spotlight.

"I hope you know the rules by now. Twenty questions, five minutes, bonus points if you max the round and have time to spare. OK? Your specialty subject is – Hindi movies and music in the 1990's. Your timer and the questions will start as soon as we hear the buzzer. Best of luck" said the quiz master. He hadn't said that to any of the earlier contestants. Once again, she had no clue if that was a good thing or not.

She heard the buzzer, the timer had started.

300 seconds to go...

"The opening lines of this song, when roughly translated into English, go like this – *My name is Fonseca, baby you don't know me*. Name the Filmfare award winning Hindi movie that features this song?"

My name is Fonseca, baby you don't know me! She repeated the words in her mind. She then translated it into Hindi – *mera naam hai Fonseca... naam hai mera Fonseca*. Yes that's it.

"Jo Jeeta Wohi Sikandar" she said quickly and loudly.

"Correct." 285...

"In the movie Raja Hindustani, name the hill station where the female lead goes on a vacation and meets the lead character?"

"Palankhet". Pat came the reply from her. She had read a lot about that movie, since it was one of the highest grossing Hindi movies of the 90s.

"Correct." 277...

"In the famous 3-D movie, Chota Chetan; which actor played the role of a doctor tutoring movie goers on how to use the 3-D goggles?"

"Jeetendra" she replied after thinking about the answer for a second. She was sure about her answer; it was the first 3-D movie she had seen in her life. There was no way she could be wrong about it.

"Correct." 265...

"In the movie Border, Sunny Deol utters the famous monologue, '*Zindagi ka doosra naam problem hai*' to a character played by Sudesh Berry. Give me the full names of both the characters with their ranks?"

She pictured the scene in her mind; she could not recollect any mention of their ranks in that scene. She then thought about the start of the movie where each character is introduced. She remembered both names, but wasn't a hundred percent sure.

"Major Kuldeep Singh Chandpuri and Subedar Mathura Das" she answered, her heart skipped a beat as she waited for the quiz master's response.

"Correct." 240...

The first minute had been excellent – four questions and four answers that were spot on. She had done it in fairly good time as well. She answered the next ten questions right. Hope rose in her mind and even her quiz partner began to believe that she might actually max the round and maybe even collect some bonus points. But then, with two minutes to spare and six questions to answer, she hit her first roadblock.

120 seconds to go...

"In the movie Yes Boss, name the character played by Johnny Lever?"

Her heart sank, she didn't know the answer. She thought of taking a chance and answered "Babulal", which was one of the

most common names for characters played by Johnny Lever.
"Incorrect. His character was named Madhav Advani."

Damn it! She told herself not to lose focus, she could still try and get the five remaining questions right. 110...

"In the year 1995, which Indian artist won the International Billboard Award and the Freddie Mercury Award for Artistic Excellence?"

She was panicking and blanking out. Her mind wasn't able to come up with a single name to start guessing from. She just stared at the stage floor; he saw what was happening to her. Snap out of it, he wanted to tell her. But there was nothing he could do but sit and watch.

"Lata Mangeshkar" she said, half-heartedly.

"Incorrect, the answer is Alisha Chinai." 95...

"Who won the Filmfare award for Best Music Director for the year 1997?"

She knew this one. "Udham Singh."

"Incorrect. The name of the music director was in fact Uttam Singh and not Udham Singh. He won the award for his work on the music for Dil Toh Pagal Hai."

She was stunned, it was a minor error, she had simply mispronounced the name of the music director. She wanted to contest the quiz master's harsh decision, but then realized it would be an exercise in futility. The quiz master would invoke the rules and stick to his decision. How could she have messed up such a simple answer?

By now he was getting very worried. The chances of beating the mammoth Apoorva Kalyan score were getting dimmer by the second. The negative marking at the quiz was going to cost them dearly. She still had three questions left; maybe she could restrict the damage. He took a deep breath and waited for the next three questions to unfold. 50...

She gave the wrong answers for the next two questions as well. That made it five in a row. She braced herself for the final question.

"Of all the songs in the soundtrack of Hum Aapke Hain

Kaun, how many are credited with having Lata Mangeshkar as the singer, solo or in combination with other singers?"

This was turning out to be a disaster. She had read a lot about Hum Aapke Hain Kaun, with it being one the biggest block-busters of all time and the first movie to gross more than a 100 Crore rupees in domestic box office collections. She knew the soundtrack had 14 songs in all, but she didn't know how many of those had been sung by Lata Mangeshkar. She started to count the tracks sung by the legendary Indian singer. Ten was the count she had after going through the songs in her mind, but she had only gone through twelve of the fourteen songs. For some reason her memory was betraying her and she just could not remember the names of the two remaining songs. Time was running out and an unanswered question was treated as an incorrect answer, she decided to go with *ten* as the answer.

"Incorrect. Lata Mangeshkar lent her voice to eleven of the fourteen songs in the soundtrack"

She was distraught. Two minutes ago she was coasting, having answered the first fourteen questions correctly and then she had destroyed all their chances of winning the quiz with her performance in the last six questions. She, alone, had given more incorrect answers than both members of The Ring-wraiths.

She got up slowly from the wooden chair and wondered how let down her partner was probably feeling right now. She didn't know what to say to him. Everything happened so fast, she didn't get a chance to recover after she stumbled on the fifteenth question... and the 'Uddham Singh' mistake was unforgivable. As she walked towards the bench, she saw him walking towards the wooden chair. He stopped as he came face to face with her. She looked at him, disheartened and almost in tears. She looked at the floor so that he wouldn't be able to see the tears forming in her eyes.

"I'm sorry" she said to him, knowing fully well that it would make no difference. The damage had been done.

"We're going to win this thing" he replied in a resolute tone.

She laughed in despair, thinking that he was making a vain attempt to cheer her up.

"I'm serious. We're going to win" that was all he said as he walked past her to make his way to the wooden chair.

The quiz master was taking a quick break to drink some water while wishing that there was a feature to forfeit a round. A damp squib of a round, where the winner had already been decided, wasn't a very good way to end what had promised to be a very exciting edition of the quiz.

Meanwhile, he sat down on the designated chair and quickly went through a few *mantras*, to get his focus back on the quiz and blank out all other thoughts from his mind. He reached inside his shirt and pulled out the *rudraksh,* using the thread that let it hang below his neck. He held it in the palm of his right hand and stared at it. She saw him do this from a distance and wondered what he was up to. She could see his lips move quickly as if he was chanting something.

The quiz master was done with his short break and watched with curiosity as the final participant chanted some silent *mantras* while sitting on the wooden chair. No wonder he chose the *Mahabharat* as one of the topics for his specialty, thought the quiz master. He felt bad for the second member of The Nameless Victor. Not because of the score-lines, but because the poor man actually thought he had a chance and was invoking *mantras* to come to his aid. The quiz master sat down on the seat facing the final participant.

She shifted in her seat to find an angle from which she could get a glimpse of his face. He was done with his set of *mantras* and opened his eyes. He seemed completely calm and had a determined look on his face. It made her feel worse about her performance, she could see how badly he wanted to win. She just hoped he fared better than her so that he could at least blame her and not himself.

"So now we have in front of us, the final participant in this final round of Fastermind India. This is it folks. It all boils down to what happens in the next five minutes. We have the second

member from The Nameless Victors, a name that was so apt
yesterday. Will they live up to the name today? We will soon find
out...." said the quiz master, trying to create a buzz around the
final set of questions.

She didn't like the way the quiz master was building up
pressure on him. No such introduction had been given for any of
the previous participants. She looked at *his* reaction keenly,
hoping that he could somehow ignore the statements made by
the quiz master which were almost half-taunts.

"... so your specialty subject is *The Lord of the Rings Trilogy*
and the *Mahabharat*'. Are you aware of the score you need to get
to beat team Apoorva Kalyan?" the quiz master asked him,
continuing with what she felt was some uncalled for
psychological badgering. He nodded without any change in his
expression.

"Well for the benefit of the audience, let me tell the scores as
of now. Apoorva Kalyan are sitting pretty on 430 points, The
Ring-wraiths are on 325 points, the first participant from The
Nameless Victors scored 110 points. Which means that Apoorva
Kalyan have a 320 point lead over The Nameless Victors.

Five minutes... twenty questions a deficit of 320 points. With
those numbers in mind, let's start off with questions on the
Mahabharat and *The Lord of the Rings*" said the quiz master,
completing the build up.

She thought about those numbers, 320 was the lead. Even if
he answered all the 20 questions correctly, he'd only have 200
points with him. He'd have to make up the additional deficit of
120 points with bonus points. Which meant that not only did he
have to get all the answers right, he had to answer them all with
at least 24 seconds to spare. She knew it was impossible and
hated the fact that the quiz master had spelt out the exact scores
which would've increased the burden on his mind.

He took a deep breath, thought about his mother and then
gently brushed the *rudraksh* against his forehead. The quiz master
took note of the act and signalled to the organizer to wait and
not hit the starting buzzer.

"Excuse me. What is that in your hand?" asked the quiz master.

He held out the *rudraksh* in his palm, looked at the quiz master with a steely determination and said:

"One *rudraksh* to rule them all!"

She was stunned by what she heard. Here was her partner taking on the quiz master in front of the entire audience and the quiz master's response was maniacal laughter. Her partner however did not laugh, he just had a calm smile on his face.

Soon, the quiz master regained composure and asked him if he was ready for the questions. He nodded. The buzzer went off and the questions started.

300 seconds to go...

"Under what name did Eowyn fight in the Battle of the Pellenor fields?"

"Dernhelm" he replied in a split second.

"Correct." 297...

"What was Bheeshma Pitamah's real name?"

"Devavrata" he replied, once again, responding almost immediately once the quiz master finished asking the question.

"Correct." 293...

"*In the Lord of the Rings* what was the name of the horse on which King Theoden rode into his final battle?"

"Snowmane" he replied, once again almost instantaneously.

The quiz master was surprised by the speed at which he was answering the questions. Barely ten seconds into the quiz and he had answered three questions accurately.

Even she was amazed by his speed, she wondered whether he even gave a thought to the answers or just blurted out the first word that came into his mind.

But that phase did not last long, the quiz master managed to slow him down with some really tough questions. *He* took his time to answer them, but all his answers were right. The super fast head start that he had taken ensured that he still had a lot of time left.

By the time he finished answering the sixteenth question, he still had ninety seconds to go. The quiz master was very impressed by this fight-back; he hadn't expected the round to stay alive for this long. The quiz master was almost rooting for him, she was definitely rooting for him and even the audience had gotten into the act, cheering every correct answer that he gave.

Team Apoorva Kalyan, who until the tenth question were fairly relaxed, all of a sudden had tense expressions on their faces. But *she* knew that it was still going to be very difficult and was praying as hard as she could, while also paying close attention to the centre-stage action. 90...

"Who served as the Prime Minister under King Dhritarashtra?"

He had to think a little bit about this, he had a few names in his head. Bheeshma, Dronacharya amongst others. But then he thought of Vyasa and his three sons, Dhritarashtra, Pandu and Vidura. Vidura was considered the most intelligent and balanced minds of all the characters in the *Mahabharat*, but he didn't become king since his mother was a maid. But was he the Prime Minister under Dhritarashtra? He tried to concentrate and figure out what the answer was. He wasted several seconds on the answer and finally went along with his gut instinct.

"Vidura."

"Correct."

The crowd applauded and cheered loudly, he was taking the fight really close. Apoorva Kalyan had one eye on the timer, they feared that *he* still had enough time to do the impossible. She was fighting the will to become hopeful, she did not want to feel letdown, but she was glad that he was giving it his all. She prayed harder. 76...

"According to the Appendices of *The Lord of the Rings*, by what name does Aragorn call Arwen when he first sees her?"

The quiz master flashed a wry smile as soon as he completed reading out the question. The quiz master was sure that *he* wouldn't be able to answer a question that had been conjured from the Appendices of *The Lord of the Rings*. The Appendices were filled with pages and pages of names, dates and genealogies.

That question in particular had been pulled out of the most obscure of all the references of the Appendices.

He closed his eyes in despair. The Appendices were the most difficult part of *The Lord of the Rings* to master. How Tolkien had even kept track of all the different names and dates was a mystery to him. But he did not want to throw it away. Not after coming this close. He thought of all the possible names that he could remember having been used in reference to Arwen. Slowly the different names started to emerge in his thoughts. For some reason the name *'Undomiel'* kept coming up, but he knew that it wasn't the right answer. He kept searching his memory for the right name.

She was looking at him, wondering what was going through his mind. She kept track of the time, fifteen seconds had passed by and his eyes were still closed. Another ten seconds passed by and now she was panicking. Was he also facing the kind of blank out that she had faced when it was her turn? There was no returning from that state, she knew it. She lost all hope and looked at Apoorva Kalyan, who were now beginning to look a little relaxed.

The quiz master was sure that he had gotten the better of the participant. He just felt bad that the poor guy had spent a third of his remaining time on that one question. Instead of struggling with that one, he thought, the participant should have moved on to the next question and tried to secure the second prize with ease. Bad strategist, the quiz master thought to himself.

Meanwhile *he* kept sifting through names that he was considering as the right answer. And then all of a sudden, from nowhere, the name popped into his head. As soon as he thought of it, he knew it was the right one.

"*Tinuviel*" he said out loud.

"Correct" said the quiz master, unable to hide the surprise in his voice.

The crowd yelled at the top of their voices, even they had given up hope before he surprised them all and pulled a rabbit out of the hat. 48...

By now the quiz master had turned into a fan of the young man sitting across him. The quiz master respected the knowledge and spirit that *he* was demonstrating in front of a packed house. It was because of contestants like him that Fastermind had gained a massive following over the years.

"From which character's point of view, did Malayalam writer M.T. Vasudevan Nair's novel *Randamoozham*, narrate the *Mahabharat?*"

She looked at *him*; his eyes were closed once again. For the next sixteen seconds she did not breathe and he did not speak. And then he opened his eyes and gave an answer.

"Bheema."

"Correct."

This time the crowd did not respond with the kind of rapturous applause that the previous answers had received. Everyone was too tense to clap. The quiz master couldn't believe it, *he* was actually taking the fight down to the wire. He had eight seconds left to answer the last question and win the quiz. Without wasting even a fraction of a second, the quiz master asked the final question. 32...

"What was the name of the Persian translation of the *Mahabharat*, written under Akbar's orders?"

She stopped breathing. Apoorva stopped breathing. Kalyan stopped breathing. Every single eyeball in *The Colossus* was on the young man sitting at the centre of the stage.

He had his eyes closed again. He had read this somewhere, he knew it for sure. He clutched the *rudraksh* so tight that his palm began to hurt. The word *rudraksh* flashed in his mind and he immediately remembered the answer.

"Razmnama" he yelled at the top of his voice and then immediately looked at the timer.

"Correct, with 24 seconds to spare" the quiz master said as the questionnaire he held slipped out of his hands. The unthinkable had just happened. The scores of Apoorva Kalyan and The Nameless Victors were level.

He got up from the wooden chair. "BRING IT ON! BRING

IT ON!" he bellowed, over and over again. He knew that a tie-breaker would follow and that they hadn't won the quiz yet. But he had to vent out the pressure he had been under for the past two hundred and seventy six seconds. She ran towards him and in the spur of the moment, gave him the tightest hug she had ever given in her life.

The quiz master emptied an entire bottle of water over his own head. Even he had felt the pressure especially during the last three questions. He waited for the star participants to get some control over their emotions and then shook hands with them.

Apoorva and Kalyan looked like they were experiencing a nightmare and wanted to wake up desperately. The Ring-wraiths were applauding the effort by The Nameless Victors. The audience at *The Colossus* gave the two member team a standing ovation.

When they were finally done with their celebrations, they looked at each other, unable to control their smiles.

"Unbelievable" she said looking at him.

"I told you before going for the final round and I'm telling you again, we're going to win this" he said to her. Calm returning to his voice, which had been filled with overwhelming emotion until a few seconds ago.

"I can't believe what you just did. I just sat there, I didn't breathe, I couldn't breathe. And you were ice cool under pressure" she said, continuing her admiration of his performance.

"Well, I gave away the Mr. Cool image by my caveman act of shouting 'bring it on' at the top of my voice" he said to her as she smiled.

"I think it scared them" she replied, referring to Apoorva Kalyan. The Nameless Victors then moved a little away from each other, both of them becoming conscious about the public embrace that they had shared a little while ago.

The quiz master went berserk with a monologue on how a twist like this had never happened before in the history of Fastermind India.

Meanwhile Apoorva and Kalyan finally came to terms with

what had just happened and tried to brace themselves for the tie-breaker. The Nameless Victors were busy preparing their strategy as well. The quiz master finally got some control over his excitement and got back to doing his job, as he started to explain the rules of the tie-breaker round to the audience.

"Ladies and gentlemen, we will soon get on with the tie-breaker round. Let me go through the rules.

Each team will nominate a member who will be asked to take over the role of the quiz master for his own team. I will then hand over an envelope to the nominee with three questions. The nominated quiz master will pick one of the questions and ask the same to his or her team-mate, who will have ten seconds to give the right answer.

The other tied team will then repeat the same process with a separate question set. The team that gives the right answer in the fastest time will be declared the winner. In case both the teams give the wrong answer or if both the teams give correct answers in the same amount of time, the round shall be repeated until a clear winner can be declared.

The nominated quiz master will be given an envelope which he or she can only open at the sound of a buzzer. The nominee will then have sixty seconds to pick one of the three questions. At the end of the sixty seconds, a second buzzer will be heard after which the nominated quiz master must ask the question.

As soon as the question has been read out, a ten second timer will start counting down and the second participant will have to give the answer within those ten seconds. I hope everyone has understood the rules clearly.

In alphabetical order, Apoorva Kalyan will be the first to go through with the tie-breaker round" said the quiz master in conclusion.

She was upset by this decision, which would once again put all the pressure on her team. She asked her partner if they should request the quiz master to reconsider the order and let them go first for the tie-breaker. *He* refused.

"Never do anything to break the flow in a quiz. It always

works against the team who do that" he said to her. She shrugged her shoulders and accepted his decision.

The two of them had also come to an agreement on who amongst them would go and take up the role of quiz master and who would answer the tie-breaker question. This time she had been the one doing the convincing; he wanted her to take up the role of quiz master so that he could be the one answering. But she disagreed.

She didn't tell him this, but she felt that he had already been under too much pressure and it was time to face some of it herself. Besides, the nominated quiz master too had a very difficult task to perform. He would have to choose one of three questions that he felt she would be able to answer. It was almost like having to hold a gun to a friend in a game of Russian roulette.

The two teams informed the quiz master of their respective nominees for the tie-breaker round. Apoorva was the nominee from team Apoorva Kalyan. The quiz master had two envelopes in his hand, of which he picked one at random and handed it over to Apoorva and asked her not to open it till the buzzer had been sounded.

Apoorva sat down on the quiz master's chair and Kalyan took a seat on the wooden chair. There was pin drop silence in the auditorium. The buzzer sounded, Apoorva opened the envelope and read the questions quickly.

1. Name the covert operation directed by Israel and the Mossad to assassinate individuals alleged to have been directly or indirectly involved in the 1972 Munich Olympics attack?

2. On what date did the Jallianwala Bagh massacre take place?

3. What is the duration of time taken by Uranus to complete one revolution around the Sun?

Apoorva started to think about the question that Kalyan would most likely be able to answer. She herself had no idea about the first two questions but she knew the answer to the third. Science was the subject that Kalyan had chosen to prepare for, but would he have studied such details of the solar system? Apoorva decided to take a chance.

The second buzzer went off. Apoorva read out the question to Kalyan. The timer started as soon as the question was read out. Kalyan looked upwards, as if he was imagining the planets revolving around the Sun and calculating the speed. The seconds ticked away. With three seconds to go, he gave an answer.

"29.5 years."

All eyes were now on the real quiz master; who took a deep breath, purposely increasing the wait and the tension.

"That's incorrect. The answer you gave is the time Saturn takes to revolve around the sun. Uranus takes 84 years to do the same" said the quiz master.

A collective gasp could be heard from the audience. Kalyan bit his lip, immediately realizing that he had allowed the pressure to get to him, which led to him giving the wrong answer.

The pressure, though reduced, was now on The Nameless Victors. They didn't need to give a quick answer; they had the entire ten second duration at their disposal. To make things a little more comfortable, they could even afford an incorrect answer; it would lead to another round of tie-breaker questions. She felt like a football goal keeper during the penalty shootout whose opponent had given away the lead; even if she made a mistake, her team would get another chance.

He looked at her, with the same resolute expression he had on his face when he walked to the wooden chair before pulling off the greatest turnaround in the history of the quiz. She felt some of his confidence rub off onto her. He held up his clenched fist as a sign of his belief that they'd win. She nodded, telling him that she now believed it too. They had made it this far, it was time to pack the final punch.

The quiz master handed over the second envelope to him. He repeated his fixed set of *mantras*, this time the quiz master did not feel like mocking him. The quiz master simply repeated the rules to him and asked him to take the nominated quiz master's seat. She walked towards the wooden chair, only a couple of guys in the audience whistled. She gave them a nasty stare and then sat down. She closed her eyes and said a quick prayer.

The first buzzer sounded, he opened the envelope. The auditorium fell silent once again as he started reading the questions.

1. In which year was Lata Mangeshkar conferred with the Bharat Ratna?
2. Name the footballer who holds the record of being the first to score in the final of two different FIFA World Cups?
3. What is the capital city of the African nation, Burkina Faso?

He knew the answers to the first two questions. Lata Mangeshkar had been conferred with the Bharat Ratna in 2001; he also knew that the first footballer who had scored in two different FIFA World Cup Finals was Vavá from Brazil.

It was the third question that he had no idea about. It was the kind of question he despised. But he had seen her reading a book to prepare for such questions. She had specifically mentioned reading up on the names of capital cities.

Would she have read about Burkina Faso? That was the question he had in his mind. It was the first time he had heard of the country's name. What were the odds of her knowing the name of the capital city?

The sixty seconds were about to come to an end. He had to choose, he pictured himself holding a Russian roulette gun to her head.

Screw it; I'll go with the third question. The buzzer sounded.

"What is the capital city of the African nation, Burkina Faso?" he read out the question, speaking as clearly as he could.

She looked into his eyes, as though searching for the answer inside them. All the while she concentrated on the names that she had read. Burkina Faso was a country whose name had come up in her preparations. It was an uncommon name for a country and even the capital had an unusual name. It started with the letter O.

He looked at her face after asking her the question. She was staring at him as though she was lost in deep thought with her eyes open. For a few seconds there was no change in her expression and then she blinked. A smile made its way to her face; she grabbed the armrests of her chair, bent forward and said...

"Ouagadougou."

"What?" he said, wondering whether he had heard her right. He could swear he heard a lot of 'whats' from the audience as well.

"That's correct! The Nameless Victors win this edition of Fastermind India!" said the quiz master.

She jumped out of the wooden chair and ran towards him and gave him another hug. She screamed "we won" over and over again at the top of her voice. He couldn't believe it. They had actually defeated all the odds and emerged victorious. The audience were on their feet, clapping and cheering. Even the quiz master, stood and applauded the winning team for their efforts.

He made it a point to be aware of everyone's reactions so that he would remember it forever. That particular moment and that particular feeling would make for a great memory. She let go of him after nearly a full minute. He suspected for a second that she had tears of joy in her eyes, but couldn't confirm the fact as she was looking downwards. When she finally looked up, she had the most beautiful smile on her face, one that emanated from a sense of achievement, accomplishment, satisfaction and pure joy.

The quiz master was the first to shake hands with the winners, followed by the runners up – Apoorva Kalyan and The Ring-wraiths. There was no sense of enmity between any of the teams. It had been a hard fought battle and the best team had won. There were no grudges. Kalyan even went to the extent of giving *him* a pat on his back, acknowledging his effort, especially in the Specialty Round. *He* responded with words of praise for

Kalyan's own performance, which had set the benchmark of answering all the twenty questions right.

The organizers then quickly made some arrangements on stage for the presentation ceremony. Each finalist was given a brand new laptop with an enviable configuration and a wrist watch. Then came the real awards. The second runners up were given individual trophies and a cheque for each member of the team. Apoorva Kalyan were then given their trophies which were slightly bigger in size and then their cheques. Finally, The Nameless Victors were presented with gold-plated trophies and their cheques.

The two partners held their trophies aloft and then bowed in front of the audience, who gave them another standing ovation. The organizers then got all the finalists to leave the stage and wait in the room backstage. The quiz master had to complete some formalities like announcing the winners for the Thailand trip and some final sponsor messages.

Backstage, the winners mingled freely with each other, for the first time without the shadow of competition around them. *She* was busy talking to Apoorva about the last two rounds and the tie-breaker questions. *He* was talking to Kalyan and The Ring-wraiths. That's when he remembered that the next move would be for everyone to head out to the party, which they had just been informed was to take place at Hiccups. He looked at the time, it was pretty late. He would have to race through the streets to make it on time for Dr. Roy's daily round. He looked at her once again; she was engrossed in her conversation with the female participants. It was the best time for him to make a quiet exit; he knew she would insist on him attending the party.

He quietly excused himself from the conversation with Kalyan and the other participant from The Ringwraiths. He kept the trophy, the laptop and the cheque safely inside a bag he always carried with him while travelling on his cycle. He slung the bag over his shoulders and made his way to the parking lot. As he began to unlock his cycle, he heard someone yell out his name. He turned around, it was her.

"Where did you disappear? I was looking for you backstage. Are you planning to carry the trophy to the party on your cycle? No way! Keep it in my car and take it after the party" she said as she saw the bag he was carrying.

"No, you don't understand. I'm... not coming to the party" he replied.

Her face clearly expressed her disappointment.

"What? Why?"

"I have to go somewhere and I'm late."

"Can't it wait?"

"Not really" he replied and got onto his cycle. She put her hand on the cycle's handle. She shook her head and now had a slightly angry look on her face.

"What is this obsession with rushing off every evening to whatever place it is that you go to? Huh? And why don't you even tell me where it is that you go?" she said, trying to keep her voice down but failing to hide the fact that she was getting upset.

He sighed; this was getting out of hand. He had always wanted to avoid this very development, thinking that he should've left earlier instead of spending time talking to the others backstage.

"Look. I don't want to lie to you and tell you some made up excuse to get away. But I can't tell you where I go either. It's a very personal matter for me and I don't want to get into it" he replied, keeping his voice calm, even though he was starting to get a little agitated about the fact that she was behaving in a very intrusive manner.

"Alright. Don't tell me where you have to go. I won't ask you again. But for God's sake, why can't you just come to the party?"

"Because I can't! Damn it, why don't you understand?" he said, losing control and letting a bit of anger enter his voice, even though he didn't raise his voice.

"This is unbelievable. You're the one with all the secrets and you're asking me why I don't understand. What is wrong with you?" she said and this time her voice was raised.

It was turning out to be a full-blown fight between the two. Tempers had flared and now even he was very angry.

"Listen. I am sorry but I can't come to this party. You go ahead and have a nice time but I have to be somewhere and I am getting late" he said to her as he put his foot on the cycle paddle. She let go of the handle and took a step back.

"Go on then. But I just want to tell you why I am angry right now. We just pulled off a miracle inside that auditorium. We won the bloody quiz, against all odds; we won that thing together. And now when the time has come to celebrate, you're abandoning me.

Do you know all the other team participants are going to be there at the party? All of them, even those freaking Zodiac Zombies and Gladiators who got kicked out of the quiz yesterday. Even they will be there enjoying themselves. And you? After doing the impossible and levelling the scores, you want to miss out on the real celebrations? Can't you just come to the party tonight and do whatever you have to some other time?" she said, fluctuating between a state of anger and that of almost pleading towards the end.

He looked down and thought for a while, almost getting tempted by the idea of attending the party but then thought of his decision and the reasons behind it. He decided against making an exception.

"I'm sorry, I can't. I absolutely have to go" he said to her, apologetically.

"Then go! Leave!" she said, in a very angry tone.

"Why are you getting so upset? It's just a party *yaar*. Why are you making such a big deal out of this?" he said to her.

"Because you're being selfish. It might not be a big deal for you. You might not care for this party. But I do. It matters to me.

You know how stupid I'll look, going there alone? *Haan*? I'll be the only one there without her team partner. Who will I talk to over there or dance with? Kalyan? That bloody quiz master? Have you thought about me for a second? How I feel right now?

No! You're just acting like some selfish, secretive lunatic. You're leaving me here, without a reason, without telling me where it is that you're going! How do you think that makes me feel? You know what. Everyone in our class says that you're arrogant and aloof. I never believed them, but today you've proved them right. And you've also behaved very selfishly.

Now just go... and congratulations on winning Fastermind! I hope you have a great time celebrating wherever you're off to" she said, in an outburst that he wasn't expecting. She then turned around and stomped off towards the auditorium.

Without saying a word, he disappeared from the premises of *The Colossus*. All the happiness of winning the quiz was gone. He felt pained by her words. He knew that some of the things she said were right and did not feel bad about it. But she had called him arrogant, aloof and selfish. That hurt him a lot.

How could he convey to her that he wasn't being arrogant or aloof and least of all selfish? How could he tell her that he was helpless and he had to stand by some decisions he had taken regarding his life? Decisions that he did not take with the intention of causing her any distress. Decisions that he had to take because of the compulsions of his life. There was no one else to take his place in the hospital and to be there when Dr. Roy came on his rounds. Who would take care of a patient who had no guardian around? He could not risk his mother's treatment getting affected, not for anything or anyone in the world. He was already suffering such a lot; he could do without being called names. He had started to think of her as his friend, spending more time with her than with anyone else in college; how could she say that he was aloof? He hadn't said a word to her when she had performed poorly in the quiz. How could she call him arrogant? And what about being selfish? He had gone to the extent of having given his pass to her...

Wait a minute! He thought to himself, she didn't know that he had given his pass to her. Damn! He exclaimed, as he remembered the events of the last evening. Suparna had called her up just as he was going to tell her that he wasn't planning to attend the party. She probably hadn't opened her envelope and did not know about the extra pass she had with her. He stopped cycling and pulled out his mobile phone.

Meanwhile, she went back to the auditorium and collected her gifts and put them inside her car. She didn't want to be around the other participants; she was still too upset to converse with people. She sat down inside the car and rested her head on the steering wheel. She felt a mix of anger and regret. Anger because she would be stuck alone at the party and regret because as she recollected some of the things she had said in anger, she felt that she had gone a bit overboard. Just as she thought about these things, she received a message on her cell phone. It was from him. She read the text – *Check your party invite envelope. Take some friend along.*

P.S. – Not selfish.

She didn't understand the message completely. She opened the dashboard where she had kept the envelope. She took out the envelope and looked inside it. She was astonished. There were two passes inside. How was it possible? Everyone had been given just one pass... unless... he had put his own pass inside her envelope somehow. That's when she remembered what had happened at the coffee shop. She had strewn her purse contents all over the table. Had he slipped in his pass into her envelope then? Why hadn't he told her?

She read his message all over again and uttered a few expletives under her breath. She felt very bad about how she had treated him. Obviously he was hurt. She called his cell phone, it was switched off. Damn it. She wanted to apologize. She tried his number again, to no avail. It was clear that he did not want to speak to her. She didn't know what to do. There was only one person who could help her now.

Suparna heard her cell phone ringing; it was her best friend calling.

"Hello" said Suparna.

"I'm in trouble" she said in a slightly tense voice.

"What happened? How did your quiz go?" asked Suparna, wondering if her friend needed some help regarding the quiz.

"We won. But that's not important..." she replied and then narrated what had happened after the quiz victory. Suparna listened to her friend patiently and attentively, thinking about the best way to go forward.

"Do you know where he stays?" asked Suparna.

"No."

"OK, so the situation is something like this, you don't know where he stays, he has switched off his cell and you don't know where he's gone... as I see it there's only one thing you can do. Pack the guilt and the apology until tomorrow. Apologize to him when you see him in college tomorrow. Tonight, just try and enjoy the celebrations. And take me to the party with the extra pass" suggested Suparna.

"This is no time for kidding *yaar*."

"I'm not kidding. Look, there's nothing you can do about it tonight. Even if you speak to him, it's very unlikely that he'll come for the party. Right? So all you can do is apologize when you meet him. Which will probably happen tomorrow and enjoy yourself tonight. I'm free tonight and if you don't take me along for the party, then you'll have another very pissed off friend to deal with" said Suparna to her best friend.

She couldn't find any fault with Suparna's logic. She was feeling bad about what had happened but then there was nothing she could do to make things better. After giving the matter some thought, she reluctantly agreed with what Suparna had suggested. She then headed off towards Hiccups, hoping that she could have a good time despite what had happened.

The last part of his message kept flashing in her head – *P.S. Not Selfish*.

Far away, a tired young man reached the premises of the hospital where his mother lay in a state of coma.

6

Hiccups

He walked into the ward where his mother was being treated. He shrugged off all thoughts about the heated argument with his quizzing partner. The person who mattered the most to him, for whom he had won the trophy was there right in front of his eyes. He placed the gold-plated trophy on the table next to her bed.

"Look *maa*, this is what I won!" he said, holding the trophy in his hands. He then recounted the entire quiz and enjoyed the process of reliving the moments of victory. Even though he knew that there would be no reaction from her, he still looked at her as he narrated each twist and turn from the quiz his team had just won. He mentioned every detail barring the hugs from his partner and the post-quiz fight.

Just as he was done with his narration, Dr. Roy walked in for his daily round. As soon as he walked into the ward, he noticed the big gold-plated trophy.

"Well, well, well. What do we have here? Am I right in guessing that you won that big quiz you had been preparing for?" asked Dr. Roy.

"Yeah, it'll be in the local newspapers tomorrow. I'll get a copy to show you" he replied with a smile. Dr. Roy walked up to him and gave him a pat on the back.

The neurologist then looked at the patient's stats and gave a familiar answer to the patient's son, telling him that there was no change in her condition. The doctor then walked towards the door but stopped before exiting and turned around to face the young son of the comatose patient.

"You know what. You're giving your mother a lot of reasons to be proud of you when she recovers" Dr. Roy said to him.

"Thanks... for saying *when* and not *if*" he replied, with a lump in his throat.

Dr. Roy looked at him with admiration for his unwavering dedication to his mother. After the doctor had left, he spent another hour talking to his mother and showing her the laptop, turning it on for the first time and explaining all the features to her. He did not show her the cheque; he never discussed finances in his mother's ward. But he did speak about how his mind was more at ease after the victory at the quiz.

He finally got back to his hostel room and had his dinner. The empty Fastermind party invitation envelop was lying on his bed. The moment he looked at it, he was reminded of his fight with her. While he was at the hospital, he had forgotten all about it. But now, all her harsh words came flooding back to his mind. He felt a surge of anger as he looked at the envelope. He tore it to shreds and flung the pieces out of the window. If it weren't for the party, the fight wouldn't have taken place. He would've been feeling a sense of satisfaction at that moment, instead of anger and pain. He didn't know why her words had hurt him so much? But they had. How cruel she had been with her words, calling him aloof, arrogant and a secretive lunatic. Her outburst had crushed him.

The greatest irony was that she had called him selfish, when he had in fact given away his own party invite to her. Even if he hadn't done that, she had no right to call him selfish. Even he could have said a lot of unkind things to her. But he controlled his anger. Why hadn't she shown him the same courtesy? Why did he get punished for being the nice guy and not raising his voice?

He then thought about what he had done after returning from the quiz and what she probably was up to at that exact moment. He had spent the evening talking to a mother who probably did not hear a word he said. She probably was dancing the night away with some friend and the rest of the quiz participants.

The party was really important to her, that's what she had told him; his feelings and sentiments probably did not feature in her priority list. Tonight he did not stop himself from having negative thoughts. The pure happiness he had felt on winning Fastermind had been replaced with a feeling of dejection. A triumph that he had been working to achieve for weeks and had earned through sheer brilliance and determination had been destroyed by her words and the heartlessness with which they had been uttered. His spirit was broken tonight. He fell down on his knees and wept as he felt overcome by sorrow. Even his greatest achievement could not dispel the darkness in his life. Somehow, fate always robbed him of his moment of triumph.

For the past two and a half years, he had no one to celebrate his victories with; he had no memories of celebrations to cherish. Tears streamed down his face as he realized the implications of that thought. The words that *she* had said to him the previous day came to his mind. She had spoken about this being the best time of one's life.

Was *this* the best time of his life? Surely it couldn't be! Struggling every single day with no ray of hope in sight, convincing himself every day that tomorrow would bring better news which never came. Fighting so many battles alone, without complaint and getting nothing in return but scorn and more troubles to overcome.

His spirit was tiring and he knew it. He looked at his diary and thought of writing something to help him put to words the absolute hopelessness that he was experiencing. He wrote another poem that night.

When will I be forgiven, for sins I haven't committed?
When will I cease to be punished, for crimes I haven't committed?

Will all my efforts go down in vain?
Will there be no relief? Will no one ease my pain?
Will adversity not relent? Or will it strike until all my hopes are slain?
Will destiny continue to turn every blessing into a bane?

Why do the victories feel like defeats?
Why has the joy been replaced by sorrow?
How much longer will fate fill anguish into my story?
Will I ever witness the sunshine of redemption, in all its glory?

After writing the poem, he sat down next to the window and spent the entire night awake and lost deep in thought; sleep finally came to him when dawn arrived.

She woke up late on the morning after the party. The first thing she did after waking up was give him a phone call. His phone was still switched off. She looked at the time, it was nearly afternoon. He probably is in a lecture, she thought.

When she reached college, without entering the lecture room, she searched for him amongst all her classmates; he was nowhere to be seen. She then skipped the lecture and rushed towards the labs, with the hope of finding him there. He wasn't to be found in the labs either. As a last resort she headed towards the library and then to the cafeteria, but she found no sign of him. She decided to hang around at the cafeteria and wait there for Suparna, who was attending lectures. After a brief wait, Suparna entered the cafeteria and sat down next to her.

"I don't think he's going to come to college today" she said to Suparna.

"Too bad, the apology will have to wait another day then. Unless he decides to switch on his phone."

"You think he didn't come to college because of me?" she asked Suparna.

"I don't think so. He probably decided to take a break, you're thinking too much about this. Even last night at the party, half the time you were trying to call his cell. Forget about it till you can do something about it. By the way, your photograph featured in today's newspaper. Page two, middle section" Suparna said as she handed over a copy of the local daily to her best friend.

She opened the paper and saw the photograph of herself and her quiz partner lifting their individual trophies. The article was titled "Dazzling Duo Win City's Maiden Fastermind Tryst." She read the entire article, which heaped praises on her team. She was particularly interested in reading a short interview of the quiz master:

"This edition of Fastermind was by far the most exciting and engaging of all. Each and every team performed extremely well. But the nail biting finish which enthralled the audience was courtesy The Nameless Victors. Not only were they involved in an astonishing comeback, they also won the tie breaker round with ease. That required great skill, ability and teamwork. Which is what Fastermind is all about..."

As she read the remainder of the article and took a look at the photograph again, she felt worse about how she had behaved with him. In her heart of hearts, she knew that he hadn't come to college because of her. He probably was feeling hurt and each time she read the sms that he had sent to her, it reinforced that belief.

Suparna tried to get her best friend into a positive frame of mind and forget about what had happened.

"Time heals everything" Suparna said to her best friend.

"Not everything. Some things get worse with time" she replied.

He made his first appearance in college, three days after the quiz victory. He tried to avoid her all day, but when he was walking towards the lab for a practical, she finally caught up with him.

"Hey, can we talk? Please" she said to him, as the rest of their batch made their way to the laboratory. He looked at her and after a short pause, nodded and walked away from the lab building and approached a *peepal* tree, under the shade of which they stopped to talk.

"Look, I am really sorry about what happened that evening. I was going through such a roller-coaster ride of emotions all through the quiz that I sort of lost it when I found out that you weren't coming for the party. I was just really keen on the party and you know the reason for that right? We had spoken about why such things matter a lot to me. But I'm drifting away from the point.

There's no justification for the way I behaved. I don't know how hurt you felt, but I felt horrible about it, the moment you left that place. When I read your message and realized what had happened, you cannot imagine the guilt I went through. And I tried calling you up as soon as I read your sms but your phone was switched off. All through that evening I kept trying your number, but it was no use. Even the past three days, I've been waiting to talk to you so that I could apologize. Now that you finally showed up, you've been avoiding me. Which sort of makes me think you are still very upset and rightly so.

Now, I can't take back what I said, but here I am, telling you that I can't possibly convey to you how sorry I am and how bad I've felt about what happened. Please can you forgive me and forget the whole episode ever happened?" she said in a long drawn out apology.

She looked at him; he had a troubled expression on his face, as though he was debating something in his mind. He wasn't even looking at her; he was staring at the base of the tree.

"So what do you say? Are we cool?" she said, urging him to accept her apology. He finally made eye contact with her. She waited for his response.

"Yeah, we're cool" he said and started to turn around, but she caught his arm and stopped him.

"Look, don't do this, please. Believe me; I am very sorry about what I said. How can I possibly convey that to you, so you'd believe me" she replied, pleading with him to forgive her.

"I believe you" he said and started to walk towards the lab.

She walked ahead of him and stood in his way.

"Just let it go *naa*? I'm sorry, really. Just tell me what I can do to make things better?" she asked him, desperate to resolve the matter. He took a deep breath, his mind was filled with conflicting thoughts, on one hand he knew that her apology was genuine, but on the other hand, he was still hurt. After another period of silence, he finally decided to tell her what he felt.

"Listen. I believe you, believe me. And it's OK; I know that it wasn't completely your fault. I know that my rushing off after the quiz seemed inexplicable. But I had my reasons... and... you know what.... there's another side to the story and why I am upset.

There is a reason why I stay away from people in college and keep a distance. I have some things to look after that don't allow me to mingle with everyone else. I simply do not have that kind of time.

You think I like staying away from the good things in life? I really did want to go to that party, believe me. But I couldn't have gone for it, for reasons I'd rather keep to myself. And I did feel bad about what you said. But it wasn't just that. It's one thing knowing that the whole class thinks I suck, but it's another thing altogether when someone like you says it to me.

In anger we do say a lot of things that we shouldn't, but there is an element of truth in it. And no matter what you say today, we both know that to some extent you do think I am an arrogant, aloof, selfish, secretive lunatic. Isn't it?

That's why I don't make friends in class. Because friendship comes with its own responsibilities and duties. Things which I cannot take up right now in my life. You were completely right in expecting me to be there with you at that party and that's why I understand why you got so upset. But the fact of the matter is, I cannot live up to the expectations that people have of me as a friend. And I would rather be alone and go through college life by myself and have people think whatever they want than become friends with someone like you and reach a stage where you begin to hate me.

So, I don't want you to torture yourself about this. It's fine, we're cool. But I just want to be left alone, I'm better off that way.

One more thing, even I want to apologize to you; for not telling you the reason why I had to leave that day. But I haven't told anyone and I want to keep it that way. I hope you can understand that" he said to her.

She couldn't forget the expression on his face as he finished speaking his piece. It was as though he was battling with himself. Each sentence he spoke had been laboured, with a lot of thought behind it. Where she had expected an outburst of anger from him, she had received a calm, straight from the heart response about his state of mind. She marvelled at how measured and balanced he had been in conveying to her that she had hurt him without going overboard and criticising her behaviour that evening. She knew what she had to tell him.

"Since I know you don't want to talk about it, I will not ask you what it is that you are going through. But just remember, if you ever need a friend to talk to, I will always be there" she said to him.

He responded with a smile and for a second she thought that things had been mended. But then he turned around and walked away; the smile was gone and he had the same troubled expression on his face. He made his way to the lab for the practical and even though she was present for the same practical, she did not make an effort to talk to him. She left him alone as he had requested.

Later that evening she looked on from a distance as he, like always, rushed off on his cycle. She hoped that in a few days or weeks he'd be able to get over what he was going through and then she would try and resume their friendship. They had barely become friends for a month and she had already started to miss his company, his stories and cheeky sense of humour. She decided to wait.

That wait carried on for weeks that turned into months, until the semester exams were over and done with. On the last day, when everyone was celebrating the end of the fifth semester of engineering and taking photographs outside the exam hall, she saw him slip away towards the parking. She followed him and he saw her just as he was about to get on his cycle.

"Hey, how was the exam?" he asked her.

"It was fine. I'll pass" she said.

"And by that you mean, you'll probably end up amongst the toppers" he replied with a smile.

"If only you'd allow someone else to top for a change" she said with a wink. He laughed.

"Hey, you want to grab some lunch? It's been a long time since we caught up *and* it's not evening time right now, so I don't think you need to rush off to your secret lair" she said to him, cheekily.

He couldn't help but chuckle at her 'secret lair' statement. But he looked at her and thought about what had happened when they had gotten close to each other the last time as friends. He didn't want to go through another episode where he'd have his feelings hurt.

"No. I'll skip; you have fun with the others. I think there's a movie plan being made. You should go for that. I'll be fine" he said to her. Something about his expression reminded her of the expression he had on his face the day she had apologized to him. Which meant that he still hadn't gotten over the incident completely.

"OK" she said with a hint of dejection and turned around to walk away.

"Hey, listen..." he said as she stopped in her tracks and looked at him.

"What?" she asked.

"Thanks for being so nice to me. Don't think I'm ungrateful, I am glad that I have a friend like you" he said to her. She did not fail to notice the emotion in his voice when he said those words. She was glad; she knew he had finally forgiven her.

"You're welcome. By the way, I'm off to Bangalore for the vacations; I'll be back in a month. Anytime in between if you feel like talking, you have my number" she replied, smiled at him and then walked away. He watched her leave, her words making him feel better.

That night when she was on the train to Bangalore, she thought about the entire semester, how the thread of her friendship with him had added so much to her life during the six months she had spent in the city. What had started off as curiosity about the class topper, had started turning into a really nice friendship before going through a major upheaval and finally settling into a relationship that threatened to fizzle out but was still alive.

It had been close to a month since the semester vacations had started and that night he was busy surfing the web when he saw

her come online on his chat list. He was invisible as always, but
her status showed up as 'Available'.

India... u der? She wrote in a chat message to him that brought
a smile to his face. Despite the fact that he felt like replying to
her chat, he chose not to. It was the third time during the month
that she had pinged him. Like the previous two occasions, he
decided to drop her an email late into the night, so that she didn't
think he was avoiding her. But he wanted to keep his distance
from her. He closed his laptop and looked at the gold-plated
trophy on his study table. It reminded him of the best moments
of the semester that had just gone by. He was now well and truly
over the incident that had occurred after the quiz. However he
was still adamant to stick to the decision he had taken regarding
his friendship with her. Right now they were neither at
loggerheads, nor strangers to each other and they surely weren't
as close as they had become during the quiz.

As he walked to the trophy to touch it and hold it in his
hands he had a thought. Maybe, that was the purpose of their
friendship; to win that trophy. They became friends thanks to the
quiz, their friendship deepened during the preparation and
peaked during the two days of the main event. The moment they
had won the trophy, their friendship unravelled in a fight that was
triggered by a fairly trivial reason. He didn't know if that theory
was correct, but it helped him avoid thoughts of getting close to
her again.

The time that they had spent had been such a mixed bag for
him. He felt free and relaxed while he was with her; she just had
that effect on him. At times he felt so at ease with her that he
shared stories of his past. Somehow she reminded him of the
times when he was genuinely happy and it made him feel like
those days could still return. But that was when he spent time
talking to her, which wasn't enough; she wanted more. She
wanted him to go for college outings and movies and parties,
things that he did not want to indulge in. Their fight had been
triggered due to these expectations she had. Why couldn't they

just restrict their friendship to spending time in college? Why wasn't that enough for her?

Maybe it wasn't about her, maybe it was his fault. He was the one who did not want to go for outings and movies and parties. He wanted to restrict their friendship to just spending time talking to each other. Maybe that's not how it worked. With time, friendship always progressed. It wasn't stationary unlike the way he lived his life. There was no status quo in friendship. The more time you spent together, the deeper it got. And the lesser time you spent together, the weaker it got. But it somehow never ceased to exist. That was what he hoped; he did not want his friendship with her to end. Maybe a time would come when he could be completely free, maybe someday his mother would recover and he would no longer have the immense burden of responsibilities that he carried right now. Would he then be able to have normalcy in his relationship with a friend like her? Time will tell, he thought to himself.

A month after the fifth semester exams were done, she was back from her vacation in Bangalore. It had been a refreshing change, meeting her parents and all her childhood friends. Despite the fact that she had stayed at her real home, she probably spoke lesser to her parents than she did while staying away for her studies. All her time in Bangalore had been spent meeting relatives and cousins. The fun parts were the night outs with her school friends. She felt a little guilty about not spending enough time with her parents, she decided to make up for it the next time she visited the city.

The worst part had been meeting the relatives; all the conversations started the same way. With an aunt or an uncle exclaiming how little she was when they had first seen her and how much she had grown. That was followed by questions on what she was doing right now. Within the first week she had told her college name and engineering branch to a dozen different relatives, who, she knew did not give a damn about what college she studied in. The discussion then soon shifted to her having reached the 'marriageable age'. She hated those discussions. It was almost as if all those aunts, who seemed pretty unhappy with their own marriages, wanted her to join the bandwagon of suffering as soon as possible. The disappointment on their faces was evident when her parents informed them that she wanted to work for a few years after marriage and that they were fine with it. She was glad that her parents had given her a fair amount of freedom to live her life the way she wanted to.

As she lay down in her room, at her uncle's house in the city; she had just one thought on her mind – her upcoming birthday celebrations. For the first time she had a major pile of money in the bank and she wanted to have the best birthday celebration yet. She also thought it would be a good occasion to resume her friendship with him. He was the one person she always thought of during her time at Bangalore. The more she thought about the way he had responded with restraint all through the time she was yelling at him after the quiz, the more she admired him.

Even when she apologized to him, the way he reacted was so measured and composed. She had begun to think very highly of him. Then those two days during the quiz, where she had really started to see him open up. She could never forget the determination on his face, when he had wrenched victory from the grip of defeat. She also remembered how he still believed in himself when all hope had been lost. The incredible fightback by him during the Specialty Round, still gave her goosebumps. She felt a little embarrassed about the hugs she had given him on stage. But even during those moments, he never took advantage of the situation; he did not try to cop a feel under the garb of the excitement of winning the quiz. He was a genuinely decent guy.

Although she admired him for all these qualities, she disliked the fact that he held himself back and covered himself in layers of secrecy and isolation. Maybe if he shared what he was going through, she could help him out. But as of now, she had no clue what it was that troubled him and she did not want to risk asking him again. That's when she thought of inviting him for her birthday party on the very first day of the new semester. Even though it would be a week ahead of her birthday, it would give them time to get some of their lost chemistry back as friends and ensure that they have fun together on her birthday. It would also make up for the Fastermind party that he had skipped. With those thoughts in mind, she fell asleep, waiting for college to resume.

When she reached college that day, she was late and Jacko had already entered the classroom. Damn, she thought to herself, now she'd have to wait for three back-to-back lectures before getting a chance to talk to *him*. But while she walked into the lecture hall, he did acknowledge her presence when their eyes met. That was an encouraging sign from the days when he had been avoiding her towards the end of the previous semester. She switched off her brain for the next three hours and was lost in thoughts of the birthday party she had planned on Saturday night at Hiccups.

As soon as the third lecture was done, she walked towards him to have a conversation. He saw her approach and waited outside the lecture room. He greeted her with a smile.

"Hey, how was your vacation in Bangalore?" he asked her.

"It was fun, late night parties, lavish lunches and dinners every day. I even managed to escape the clutches of the *rishtaa* hawks" she replied.

"What are *rishtaa* hawks?"

"You know, those aunties who just find out you're above eighteen and want to get you married. So they walk around as unsolicited marriage agents, mouthing off resumes of candidates the moment they see you" she replied as he laughed.

"Anyway, I don't know if you know this, but it's my birthday, this coming Saturday. I am giving a party at Hiccups and you have to come" she said, finally telling him what she wanted to all day.

"What time is it?" he asked, even though he knew he would not attend it no matter what time it was to be held.

"It's in the evening, anytime after seven and I'm inviting you a week in advance, so that you can finish off whatever you have to do in the evening quickly and come to the party" she replied.

"I'll try my best to make it" he replied.

She did not find his reply very reassuring.

"Are you still angry about what happened?" she asked.

"No. Not at all. Just forget about whatever happened. It's just that I am not cent percent sure of being able to make it there, I'll let you know by Friday" he replied.

He tried his best to sound convincing. It worked, she let go of the topic and despite wanting to ask him to have lunch together, decided to go and meet Suparna. He walked away towards the lab.

Meanwhile, she was busy discussing her birthday party with Suparna. She told her best friend about the discussion she had with him. Suparna was of the opinion that he was still hungover about the fight and that he was probably not going to attend her party. She did not believe that. She knew that he wouldn't lie to her and he did tell her that he'd confirm by Friday. She decided not to give up hope.

"When are we going to do the pre-birthday shopping?" asked Suparna.

"Thursday, it's a holiday. We can make good use of the time" she replied.

The next two days flew by without much happening. On Thursday, she spent hours and a lot of money with Suparna at a mall, shopping for clothes and shoes. Her birthday was just an excuse, she had a lot of money to spend, courtesy the earnings from Fastermind. While she was driving back home she noticed someone riding a cycle at a distance. The rider looked very similar to *him*. She squinted her eyes to confirm, it really was him. She checked the time, it was just past five thirty in the evening, close to the time that he usually left college.

Was he on his way to his secret lair? She thought to herself. She decided to follow him for a while to see where he went. This is exciting, she said to herself. She felt like a character in some detective novel. Driving slowly and maintaining a safe distance from the person she was following. He was riding at a fair pace for a cyclist. She almost lost his trail on one occasion, when she got stuck at a traffic signal that he had managed to cross in time. But she caught up with him; he was one of the few cyclists on that road.

After spending close to half an hour following him, she was tiring. She wondered how he had the stamina to ride the cycle for such a long time and distance. Finally he started to slow down and move to the left of the road. It was the entrance to a hospital. She stopped the car by the side of the road, a short distance ahead of the hospital entrance. She got out of the car and started to walk towards the hospital. When she got closer to the entrance, she stopped. What are you doing? She asked herself. Get back in the car and leave; you've let this game go on far too long. She turned around and walked to her car and got in. She had come so close to finding out what it was that he did every evening and what pressing task made him rush off and skip events like the Fastermind party. She had come so close. Why turn back now? What were the odds of something like this happening? Maybe she was meant to have spotted him on the road and to have followed him. Damn it! Why is this so hard?

She got out of the car and decided to go through with what she had started. She entered the hospital premises and could see his cycle in the parking lot. She walked to the reception and darted her eyes around the hospital to see if she could spot him. She did, he was on the second floor talking to a nurse and walking towards some room. What if he sees you? She asked herself. Hey, I was just passing by and saw you walk into the hospital, thought of saying hi! That will not work, she said to herself after thinking up a lame excuse.

Alright, this is what you'll do – go to the second floor, see if you can find out anything and then get out before he sees you. She formulated a plan and convinced herself that it would work. Once again she felt an element of thrill in what she was about to do. She saw him enter the room he was walking towards and then made her way to the elevator. By the time she reached the second floor, her heart was pounding. She took a couple of deep breaths to calm herself down a bit. She slowly stepped out of the elevator and checked to see if the coast was clear. There was no sign of him. She looked in the direction of the room towards which he was walking. 'Neurology Ward 7' said a board on top of the door to the room. Interesting, she thought to herself.

Just then, she saw the nurse who he was talking to a brief while ago. The nurse was walking straight towards her. "Excuse me, are you looking for someone?" the nurse asked her. She almost panicked and thought of turning around and bolting towards the staircase on her right. But she decided to stick to her plan. She introduced herself as a friend of *his*, the moment she did that, the nurse had a big smile on her face.

"You're here to visit the patient?" asked the nurse.

"Yes" she said. She didn't know who the nurse was referring to as the patient.

"That is so nice of you. I think you are the first visitor I've ever seen that he's brought along. I keep telling him to take a break, but he's such a devoted son that he makes it a point to come see his mother everyday" said the nurse.

Alright, so his mom is unwell. Time to go. Or maybe I could slip in one more question.

"Uh, so how long will his mother remain admitted?" she asked. The nurse had a slightly surprised look on her face after she heard the question.

"No one can say, she's in a coma. Didn't you know that?" asked the nurse.

"Well, he doesn't talk much about it" she replied honestly.

"That's understandable, he is very optimistic, he comes here every day and waits for the doctor's report. He still thinks she'll recover, he's hoping for a miracle. Initially I used to pity him, but now for his sake, even I've started praying that she comes back. He's put in his heart and soul to see that she recovers and he refuses to give up. God has been very cruel to him, it's about time He showed him some kindness..." said the nurse.

"How long has his mother been here?" she asked.

"Ever since her accident, it's been what, almost three years now" replied the nurse.

"And he's been coming here every day for the past three years?" she inquired.

"Yes. You ask too many questions. I have to go now, you can find him in that room ahead, ward seven" the nurse said and walked to the staircase.

She did not know why, but her feet started moving towards the room. The door had a small square window, as she got closer to the door, she could see a little bit of what was happening inside the room. She could see him talk to someone, after she took another step, she saw a frail woman lying on a bed. He was talking to his mother, even though she was in a coma. That didn't make any sense. She got closer to get a better look; the woman on the bed was clearly unconscious. She heard approaching footsteps, fear ran through her veins. It was time to go. She walked quickly towards the steps and with hurried steps made her way towards the exit.

The nurse who was returning to the neurology ward with reports of some of the patients, saw the young woman hurry towards the exit. The nurse found it a little odd and decided to ask him what had happened.

The ward door opened, he wasn't expecting Dr. Roy for another fifteen minutes, but it wasn't the neurologist at the door, it was the nurse who tended to his mother.

"I just saw your friend leave in a hurry. Is everything OK?" asked the nurse.

"What friend?" he asked, confused with the nurse's query.

"The girl who arrived just after you came here. She asked for you, so I assumed she was your friend" replied the nurse, now it was her turn to get confused.

"Wait, who are you talking about? I came here alone. There was no one along with me" he replied.

"Yes there was. I just saw her leave... pretty girl, fair with a beauty spot right here" the nurse said, pointing to her chin.

He couldn't believe it. Was it really *her*? What was she doing here?

"When did you see her leave?" he asked her with urgency.

"Just a minute ago" said the nurse.

He rushed out of the room and ran down the stairs towards the exit. After reaching the reception, he looked around to see if he could spot her. He looked towards the parking lot, she wasn't there; he walked towards the exit. He couldn't believe his eyes; she was on the phone, walking towards a car. He jogged towards her, his mind had gone blank, he had no idea what she was up to and why she was even there. As he neared her, he could hear what she was saying.

"No, he didn't see me... I ran away after talking to the nurse, I couldn't stay there, what would I have told him... No I don't know what happened to his mother..." was what she was saying, he could bet that it was Suparna on the other end of the line. He was furious.

"I'll tell you what happened to my mother" he said aloud, his voice shaking with anger. She turned around and was stunned to see him. She immediately regretted calling up Suparna instead of making a quick exit from the area. She hung up the phone and decided to speak to him to clear the air.

"I know this looks bad, but just listen to me..." she said trying to explain her presence.

"No! You listen to me. I can't believe you came here to snoop on me and then discuss what you found out with Suparna! Is that why you came here? To find some material for gossip..."

"Please hear me out. It's not what you think. I just saw you on your cycle while I was driving and all I wanted to do was to see where you go..."

"So you followed me to the hospital and then stalked me and got talking with a nurse to find out my story? Huh? I can't believe what you've just done. What right do you have to intrude into my personal life like this? What perverse sense of achievement will you get by finding out where I go and what I do? How is it any of your business?" he asked her. His face was a picture of torment and anger.

"Listen, I didn't mean to intrude into your personal life. I just wanted to find out..."

"Don't try and come up with a reason. What you have done is inexcusable! I asked you several times to let it go. Didn't you realize that I did not want you or anyone else to know where I go to after college? Well congrats, now you know. What did you achieve by doing this?

You want to know what happened to my mother? I'll tell you, three years ago she had an accident. For the past three years, she has been in a coma. I come here every evening when the doctor comes for his round to find out if there's any chance of her coming back.

Now you know my secret. This is my secret lair! This hospital, where my mother is fighting for her life. Anything else you want to find out? Please ask me, it'll save you the effort of following me around to get your story" he said with his temper still running high but controlling himself from yelling at her.

She was crying. It did not make a difference to him, he was too angry to care about her tears.

"You just broke all our bonds of friendship. You followed me, then spied on me and then were busy gossiping about me with your best friend. You have no idea how much you've hurt me today!

Now you know why I stayed away from everyone in college? Because I did not want people to find out that my mother is in a coma. I don't need the others to give me that look you're just giving me. It's called pity and I hate it.

If you have any sense of decency and respect for my personal life, please keep this matter between you and Suparna. You have no idea what I will do if people in general find out details of my personal life..."

"No one will find out. I promise..."

"That is so kind of you" he said sarcastically.

"Now please leave. Leave, before I say something in anger that I will regret" he said to her and walked back.

She sat down in her car and drove off with tears in her eyes. She cried not just because of his words, but because she had lost respect for herself after what she had done. This was *his* life that she had intruded into. She felt ashamed of herself when she thought about how thrilled she had felt while following him to the hospital. At any point of time, she could have turned back, but she chose to follow him right up to his mother's ward. When he was talking to his mother, she had looked on for minutes, as if it was some reality show on TV. She had encouraged the nurse to divulge details of his mother's case.

This was the worst thing she had ever done to a friend in her life. No apology would suffice for her shameful behaviour. Treating his personal life like a mystery novel was a juvenile thing to do with very serious consequences. How could she have behaved in such a thoughtless manner? Just when things between them were getting better. It was all over and she knew it. She was astonished that even today he had refrained from hurling even a single word of abuse at her. She would have felt a little less guilty if he would've yelled at her, instead of admonishing her with a sense of restraint. She stopped the car on the side of the road; she was a fair distance away from the hospital. She called Suparna and explained what had happened.

"This is bad" said Suparna.

"I know, listen. Just don't tell anyone what I told you about his mother. Please" she requested.

"Don't worry. No one will know. I swear" Suparna reassured her friend.

They spoke for a long time, Suparna tried to console her but *she* kept crying all through the phone call. Suparna finally got her to calm down and drive back home. As soon as she got back home, she locked herself in her room and wept inconsolably on her bed. There was nothing she could say to defend her actions; they were so incredibly insensitive and thoughtless. She skipped dinner that night, claiming a stomach ache; she wanted to be left alone.

He cycled back to his hostel room. He could not fathom the reason for her actions. Why had she followed him? He did not even know where she followed him from. Why was she doing this? His impulse accusation was wrong; he knew she hadn't come there to hunt for gossip. But no matter what her intent was, it had done him a lot of damage. For five semesters he had been able to keep his personal tragedy a secret, now he was at her mercy. He was also upset at the nurse for divulging his mother's case history to someone who the nurse had just met.

Was that the state of medical institutions, that anyone who claimed to know the patient had the right to know the case details? It was unfair. But he had not raised the matter with the authorities, it wouldn't help. The damage had been done. Besides, he did not want to offend the nursing staff at the hospital; they had taken very good care of his mother, at times going beyond the call of duty to tend to her. He would have to let this incident go.

He had no control over what *she* would do in college and whom she spoke to. He just hoped that for the sake of the friendship they once had, she'd respect his request for privacy. But he no longer wanted to have anything to do with her. She had blown it, destroyed the remaining friendship that they had. Along with the anger he felt about her actions, he was also upset about the fact that their friendship was over. He really had started to hope that with time they would settle into a comfortable friendship without any more hassles. But that was not to be.

That night, both of them got very little sleep. Their tired minds were pondering about the series of events that had taken place between them. Going through their past and present and wondering what would happen in the future. She now understood some of his actions over the course of their time together, why he abstained from class trips and activities and why he did not come to the Fastermind party. She remembered snatches of conversations that they had during and after the post-quiz spat.

"I don't want to lie to you and tell you some made up excuse to get away. But I can not tell you where I go either. It's a very personal matter for me and I don't want to get into it."

That was what he had told her. Why didn't she just turn away after reaching the hospital entrance? If only she had remembered these words at that time. But she wasn't thinking straight at the time. She had given in to her curiosity. As she thought about the conversation they had on the day she had apologized to him, she remembered another snippet that she should've taken cognizance of.

"... friendship comes with its own responsibilities and duties. Things which I cannot take up right now in my life... I cannot live up to the expectations that people have of me as a friend. And I would rather be alone and go through college life by myself and have people think whatever they want than get close to someone like you and reach a stage where you begin to hate me."

Well, now he's the one who is going to hate me, she thought to herself.

Meanwhile he too was going through all their past interactions. Should he have confided his secret in her?

Would that have avoided all the bitter experiences? He remembered the night when he had cried, it was after her outburst regarding the Fastermind party. And today, she had been crying. He hated himself for letting things reach such a stage. He did not want to see her that way. There was something about watching a girl cry that made him feel miserable.

He knew it was her fault and that he had managed to control himself and had avoided an outburst like she had inflicted on him; but even then he felt bad about the fact that he had something to do with the tears that fell from her eyes. He felt like giving her a call to talk to her. But just as he was about to dial her number, he stopped. Maybe the end of their friendship would also mean the end of any more such incidents, things that ended up hurting both of them. He knew that she did not get any joy out of causing him trouble; it was just that their personality types were such that she could not resist a chance to discover what his secrets were and he was a guy who preferred facing his problems alone and keeping them to himself.

With these thoughts in mind, both of them stayed awake till

the wee hours of the morning and finally went to sleep out of sheer exhaustion.

The next morning he debated whether he should go to college or not, but then he remembered that Jacko had setup a class test, the only professor to do so in the first week of the semester. He visited the hospital first and then made his way to college. He saw her sitting in the lecture room waiting like the rest of the class for Jacko to unleash hell. He avoided making eye contact with her. All through the test, he was distracted by what would happen if they came face to face. Had they reached the stage where they'd deny each other's existence and move on? She had similar thoughts on her mind. The whole day went by without them crossing paths.

After all the lectures were over, he made his way to the parking; he saw her standing beside his cycle. Oh no, here we go! He thought to himself anticipating another apology. Their eyes met, neither of them smiled. He walked slowly towards her and stopped when he was close enough to hear what she had to say.

"Hi" she said to him.

"Hi" he replied.

"I am not here to apologize. What I did was unforgivable and I know that no apology can undo what I did. What I did was immature and unbelievably inconsiderate. But I want you to know the reasons that drove me to follow you. Firstly it was just pure curiosity, but there was more to it. I wanted to know what it was that bothered you so much that you decided to keep away from any kind of friendship in college. It wasn't so that I could gossip about it after finding out. I wanted to know the reason so that I could find out if there was some way by which I could help out.

Obviously, now that I know your reasons, I realize there is nothing I can do about it. So rest assured I will stay away from you and your personal life. I also have sworn Suparna to secrecy, no one will find out about this. I promise. But before I let you go, there is something I have to say to you.

This is probably the last time we'll be speaking as friends, but for the sake of that very friendship I ask you to please give some thought to what I have to say.

While we spent some time together courtesy Fastermind, I realized a few things about you. You are brilliant and amazingly talented. You're also extremely interesting in ways that you may not realize. You have a great sense of humour and it's always fun spending time with you. The best part is... you have all these qualities despite everything you're going through.

When I unfairly called you names after the quiz victory, you showed such a lot of maturity and did not fight back. Even yesterday, I bet you were extremely angry with me, but you showed tremendous self-restraint once again. Unlike me, you did not lose control, saying things that you come to regret later. That is a gift.

But there is a difference between self-restraint and curbing your natural self. Somehow I get a feeling that you're always holding yourself back from unleashing your full potential. Right now, you top exams at will and win quizzes from positions where anyone else would've given up. But you are capable of so much more. You are denying yourself those opportunities with your self-enforced exile.

I don't know the full extent of your troubles and I swear I will make no more effort to find out. But all I am telling you is this, I had a great time when we were friends and I am sure it wasn't too bad an experience for you too, until I went and messed things up. Forget whatever happened with me, it's not important. But don't let this one experience define the remainder of your college life.

Life ensures that we experience a lot of pain; it is for us to find ways to experience happiness. If you can face all the challenges you're facing alone; I bet you can find a way to make the journey have some memorable moments as well.

You're doing all this for your mother, but ask yourself this question – is this the kind of life your mother would want you to live? Would she want you to live in a state of isolation and self-exile? Wouldn't she want you to enjoy your success after all the efforts you put in?

That's all I wanted to say. Once again, I promise you no one will find out about your personal life. I also swear not to interfere in any way. I admire you for what you are and I hope someday you can understand that my intentions were never to hurt you. Take care" she said to him and walked away without looking back at him.

He stood there for a few minutes; once again she had said something completely unexpected that had stunned him. He did not know how to react to her words. He was still grasping everything that she had just said. The only reason he forced himself to get on his cycle and leave was because he was getting late to get to the hospital. He decided to think about what she had said after he reached his hostel room.

Meanwhile, *she* felt a little at ease having told him what she wanted to. She was glad that just like him, she had been able to restrain herself from going overboard, and she had not said a single thing which could've hurt his sentiments. She felt that even if he did not forgive her for what she had done, even if it he gave some thought to her words and if it somehow ended up helping him, it would suffice. She would feel content with the knowledge that she had been able to help him in some way.

She reached home and lay down on her bed. Suparna called asking her whether or not she had booked the lounge at Hiccups. That was when she remembered that in a few hours she'd be celebrating her birthday. The thought of her birthday party distracted her for a while.

Soon the clock struck twelve, the phone calls started flooding in. As always, her parents were the first to wish her on her birthday. Then her friends from Bangalore and her college friends called. She had a quick cake cutting ceremony with her cousin, uncle and aunt; after which she got back to answering phone calls.

Each time she received a call, she hoped it would be him. She hoped that he'd at least wish her via sms, just as a sign that he wasn't angry with her. She waited till 3 am, long after she had received her last birthday wish for the night; but he neither called nor messaged to wish her. She felt a little disheartened and went to sleep, with the hope that a good night's sleep would get her in the mood to celebrate her birthday.

She woke up just before noon. The first thing she did was to check her cell phone, there were several messages and a dozen missed calls. None of them were from him. She spoke to Suparna who asked her to get over thinking about him and get on with enjoying her birthday. She realized that her best friend was saying the right thing and as the evening approached; her mind started getting diverted towards the party at Hiccups. It was going to be an expensive affair, she had been offered a package of four drinks and a buffet per person at a fairly steep price; but she had accepted it for the music and ambience, it was her favourite disco. She had bargained and secured an exclusive lounge for the fifteen odd friends she had invited to the party, she expected them all to arrive; no one would pass over an opportunity to spend an evening on the house at Hiccups.

Suparna picked up her best friend at seven in the evening. In no time, they were inside Hiccups at their exclusive lounge. The dance-floor at the lounge was made of glass squares with lights underneath them, which changed colour when someone stepped on each square. As her friends started to trickle in and the party really kicked off, she got onto the dance floor made up of those glass squares and got all her friends to dance along. The colour changing floor along with the flashing disco lights gave a surreal effect to the ambience. She grooved to the music and let all her worries disappear into the din of the music. A little while later, when the starters began to arrive, the group of friends sat down together and cut the cake that Suparna had brought along. Her friends then handed over a bunch of gifts, things like t-shirts, books and a couple of friends, who couldn't think of anything to gift, gave her shopping vouchers. She was happy with all her gifts.

Just as they were about to settle down for dinner, she saw someone enter the lounge, she couldn't clearly see who it was because of the lights, until that person was very close to her. She couldn't believe it, it was *him*! He saw her sitting on the edge of a couch, two other girls whom he did not recognize were sitting alongside her on the same couch. Across her was Suparna, who had a surprised look on her face as she saw him. He smiled at Suparna and then looked at the birthday girl. She got up and greeted him with a friendly hug.

"Happy Birthday. I took a chance that the invite you gave me, still applied" he said to her as she looked at him, flashing her beautiful smile.

"Of course the invite was still on. Thanks for coming, it means a lot, really" she said to him and then introduced him to her friends.

None of the people whom she had invited to the party were from their college, barring Suparna and him. A couple of people at the party were her school friends who happened to be in the city, the rest were her friends from outside college. He was surprised by the number of friends she had outside of her college and school group. After a bit of small talk with her friends, he dug into the food being served as part of the buffet. It was the first time in years that he was eating out. She insisted that he try all the items on the menu. He found the food to be delicious, but ensured that he did not overeat.

Once all the guests at the party were done with their dinner, she got everyone to the dance floor. He did not trust his dancing skills too much and stuck to some base moves, especially one that went by the name of The Bus Stop – all that it involved was to step to the side with the right foot, and then to bring in the left foot so they touch; he continued to repeat this, and then switch directions. He could clearly see that she was a fairly sophisticated dancer, her moves were smooth and graceful, she was always in sync with the rhythm and never missed a beat when dancing. While dancing he couldn't help but notice how beautiful she looked. She was wearing a silver brocade dress, which glittered with different hues under the ever changing disco lights, along with black corduroy pants and shiny black suede shoes while her

flowing dark hair added to the radiance of her fair skin. Suparna
noticed him noticing her best friend and had a smirk on her face.

After a few songs of non-stop dancing, she tapped him on
the shoulder and asked him to come with her and rest on the
couch in the lounge. Suparna made sure that none of the other
friends disturbed the two.

"You dance really well" he said to her.

"What? Can't hear you" she replied.

"I said, you dance really well" he repeated, raising his voice
so that she could hear him over the loud music.

"Thanks, you're not too bad yourself" she said to him with a
smile.

"Don't mock me" he said to her.

"What?"

"I said, don't mock me. M-O-C-K" he said out loud, ensuring
that she wouldn't assume that he had used some other word that
rhymed with mock.

"No, I'm not M-O-C-King you. You're pretty decent. You
stick to your safety zone" she said to him.

"Believe it or not, this is the first time I've danced since my
junior college farewell in the twelfth standard" he said to her.

"I can't live without dancing for a month, how could you not
dance for three years?" she asked and then immediately wished
she hadn't said that.

She was afraid that he'd get offended by her insensitive
question, but he allayed her fears by just raising his hand in a
reassuring gesture. She mimed the words – I'm sorry – he
responded by miming – it's OK.

She had the last of her four allotted drinks and then asked
him to join her again on the dance floor. For the next half an
hour, he forgot about all his worries and fears and got lost in the
music and the beats. He realized that enjoyment was a contagious
feeling; just dancing there in the midst of a bunch of youngsters
who were carefree and relaxed made him feel like he had been
taken away to a different world altogether – a world of blissful
faces and never-ending energy.

Each time he felt like he was tiring, a new song would begin playing, a cheer would ring all over the disco and he'd feel a surge of energy flow through him. Where that energy came from he did not know, but he felt it and used it to the fullest degree. The DJ finally announced that the last three songs of the night were about to be played. That got everyone onto the dance floor, even those who until then were busy eating or drinking. More and more people joined until he thought that no more could be accommodated, but people kept coming in, everyone kept getting closer to each other until he could no longer differentiate between individuals on the dance-floor – the bunch of people had now become one whole entity – gyrating, leaping and bouncing together. And even more people kept coming in as the last song began playing – the dance floor always seemed to have room for more.

The last song came to an end and the crowd dispersed to their respective tables and lounges, the tiles stopped changing colour and the loud beats were replaced by some breezy instrumental tunes for the guests to listen to as they wrapped up their dinners and conversations. As he sat down in the lounge, one by one her friends began to leave for the night. He waited for the rest to leave, he wanted to speak to her in private. Suparna got the drift of what was going on and as soon as there were only the three of them remaining, she went away under the pretence of visiting the washroom.

"Hey, listen. I just wanted to say Thank You" he said to her, looking into her eyes.

"I wanted to tell you the same thing. You have no idea how relieved I felt when I saw you tonight. Over the past few months I've been so upset with myself for ruining our friendship and last week I thought it was all over. But here you are and I'm glad about that" she replied.

"Yesterday, after you spoke to me near the parking lot; I kept thinking about what you said. I just couldn't get your words out of my head. I guess it was something I should've been telling myself all this while; but when you said it, it just resonated and I could not ignore any of the things that you mentioned. Even today, when I woke up, I kept debating, whether I should stick to what I had decided for the past three years or whether time had come to change things a bit. By evening I saw people on the streets heading off to enjoy their Saturday night and I knew it was time. I visited my mother during the time the doctor comes for his round and then I was off. I knew I had to come for your party. Even if you didn't want me to come, I would've come here just to say thank you" he said to her.

She just looked at him and smiled. He then remembered that he hadn't given her the gift he had bought for her. He reached into the bag he always carried with him and pulled out a gift-wrapped box. He looked at all the other gifts she had received and wondered if she would like what he had brought for her. She had a surprised look on her face as he held out the gift for her.

"Happy Birthday" he said as he handed over the gift.

"Wow. I wasn't expecting a gift."

"Why?"

"The fact that you came for the party itself was enough" she said to him.

She unwrapped the gift box, it contained a soft toy. She was stunned when she saw what it was. A soft toy version of Buttercup from the Powerpuff Girls. She ripped apart the box and gave a tight hug to the soft toy. He couldn't help but smile as he saw her reacting like a small child.

"Oh my God! This is the sweetest gift ever. Thank you thank you thank you" she said in a purring voice.

"Where did you get this?" she asked him.

"At some random gift shop that I found after hunting all over the city. I'm glad you liked it, when I saw some of the other gifts I was seriously doubting my choice of gifts" he said to her.

"Why?"

"Well... honestly, the soft toy is not as expensive as some of these other gifts" he replied.

She smiled, put her hand on his shoulder and said –

"The true value of a gift is the thought behind it."

Their conversation was interrupted when Suparna returned. After some more chit chat, they decided it was getting late and they should get home. They walked out of Hiccups together and Suparna asked the two to stand near the exit while she brought her Activa out of the parking space.

He looked at her under the moonlight. The silver rays of the moon added to the glow of her dress, accentuating her beauty even further. She saw him as he admired her beauty and felt a little embarrassed. He noticed her getting a little conscious of the fact that he was staring at her.

"I'm sorry, but it's not my fault. You're just looking too beautiful" he said to her cheekily.

That made her blush, she gave him a mock punch and jokingly asked him to look away. They both had a small laugh about it. Soon Suparna arrived on the Activa and she hopped on.

He thanked her for the party and she thanked him for coming to it. She then thanked him for the gift and he thanked her for giving him the talk the other day. Suparna revved the engine loudly to put a stop to all the thanking. The two girls were off on the Activa. He watched them disappear into the distance.

He turned back to look at Hiccups once again and closed his eyes to enshrine the past few hours in his memory forever. After a really long time, he had felt a sense of pure joy within him during the party that had just gotten over. He was glad that she had made him change his decision. He did not know why she had come over to have a word with him the previous day, but it had changed his mindset. For the first time in the past three years, he felt like he wasn't alone. She was there for him. She could help him tide through the tough times. She was his friend.

He closed his eyes to picture her standing next to him under the moonlight.

"She's my friend..." he whispered into the night, "... and she is beautiful."

7

Pessimistic Optimism

He woke up the next morning with the kind of pleasant hangover that one can only feel the morning after an incredible night. When he had taken the decision to leave for the party, he hadn't imagined that the night would be so exciting. He checked the time, it was nearly afternoon. He picked up his cell with the intent to give her a call but before calling her, he had second thoughts.

Should I give her a call? Would she think I'm getting a little over friendly? What if she gets conscious about the way I was looking at her last night? Damn! Why did I generally start staring at her like that? Jackass! But damn, she was looking smokin hot! Stop it. She's your friend. Forget about her looks. Give her a call, talk to her and thank her again.

He dialled her number.

"Hail low" he heard her say in her trademark, 'I'm sleepy' voice.

"Hi, I hope I didn't wake you up" he said to her. She had answered the phone without checking who had called, the moment she recognized his voice, she got up with a start.

"Hi, wassup?" she asked him, shrugging off the sleepiness in her voice.

"Hey if you're still sleepy, just get back to sleep. I'll call later."

"No dude. I was wide awake when you called" she lied.

"Well, I just called to ask if you were free to catch up sometime today?"

What? Where did that come from? He thought to himself, surprised by the impromptu invite he had given her.

She was also taken by surprise with his suggestion of meeting up. She looked at the wall clock, lunch time would be perfect.

"How about lunch?" she asked him.

"Sure. Where?"

"You know that place, Cafe Goodluck, just ahead of college?"

"Yep" "Let's meet there" she said.

"Alright. What time?" he asked.

"I can get there in an hour."

"Same here."

"OK. I'll see you in an hour then."

"Cool. See you."

"Buh bye" she said.

He loved the way she said that, he kept looking at his phone for a while after the call was over. He wondered what power she had over him that made him break all his rules of not thinking of her as more than a friend. Each time he closed his eyes, he pictured her standing under the moonlight wearing the clothes she had put on the previous night. He found it impossible to remove that one image from his thoughts. After spending some more time marvelling about her beauty and other attributes, he forced himself to get ready.

He reached well ahead of time, so that he could cool down from all the effort it took to cycle to the cafe. At five past one, he saw her driving a car and approach the parking lot. As soon as she got out of the car, she saw him. She greeted him with her signature look – a smile with her head tilted to the side. Her beauty spot got him yet again.

"Sorry, I got a bit late" she said to him as they made their way to a vacant table.

"Five minutes late, isn't late" he replied, it made her smile.

They sat down and ordered some starters and shared a soup - one by two – style. While munching on some delicious *kebabs* and *tikkas*, they discussed the birthday party.

"So who were all those people at the party? The ones who weren't from Bangalore" he asked.

"They were some friends from a dance workshop I attended during First Year" she replied.

"No wonder everyone there was dancing sort of professionally."

"As I told you last night, you were pretty decent yourself."

"You don't have to be nice" he said, asking her to stop with what he thought was false praise.

"No really. If you don't believe me, I'll explain what I mean. You were pretty good with following the beats and the rhythm, but the most important quality you showed was expression..."

"Expression?" he asked, interrupting her explanation.

"Yeah. Expression. Have you ever noticed the people who have these God awful expressions on their faces when they dance? Almost as if they're about to punch someone in anger, biting their lips and their eyes popping out. They contort their faces as though they're in pain or something. It's kinda scary when you're dancing next to some of them. They dance like serial killers or something, even their moves are stupid, they're either punching or stabbing imaginary victims" she went on, he was laughing.

"Thank God I didn't do any serial killer moves last night" he said.

"That's why I'm saying. You were pretty good. With some practice you can turn pro" she replied.

"Where *yaar*? People like you have actually learnt dancing, I can't compete with expertise like that" he said to her.

"No way! I haven't learnt dancing. I just went for that workshop for a month and stopped going because they weren't teaching me anything new" she said.

"So how did you learn how to dance?" he asked.

"I didn't. You don't have to *learn* how to dance. You just need to observe a little and then use your imagination. It's only for stuff like the salsa, flamenco and such things that you need to learn properly. And I don't want to do that. I want to have fun right now, maybe sometime later I'll learn those dance forms" she said to him with a tone that told him how much important dancing was to her.

They discussed several things during the afternoon and

eventually they were back to discussing their Fastermind win.

"So what have you done with your prize money?" she asked him.

"I've put in half of it into Fixed Deposits. Spent the rest" he replied.

"What? You spent half of it already? What did you buy, a bike or something?"

"No, I bought something different."

"What?"

"I won't tell you today. But I can show it to you next weekend, if you're free" he said to her.

He was enjoying the inquisitive look she had on her face.

"Dude, this is so not fair. Building up the suspense for a week!" she complained.

"I'll try and make sure it's worth the wait" he said to her.

"OK. I will wait but at least give me some hint *naa*" she begged.

"Alright. All I will say is that for you to be able to see it, you have to go to a place outside the city" he said, dropping as much of a hint as he could without giving it away. But the hint did not help her too much, confusing her even more.

"So what you're saying is we have to travel to someplace outside the city to see what you bought yourself?" she asked.

"Yep."

"OK. So here's the deal, I will go with you to see this surprise under the condition that this coming Saturday night, you agree to come with me to Hiccups" she said to him.

"What? No way. You just want to have fun laughing at me while I dance like a fool" he replied.

"No. It's not that. The thing is, Suparna's boyfriend is in town and she won't have time to hang out and you know how much I hate wasting my weekends" she explained.

"Alright. It's a deal" he said, offering a hand shake. They shook hands in a business-like manner and then had a chuckle about it.

The fact was that he would've agreed to go to Hiccups even

if it wasn't for the pretend deal that they had. He had a great time there the previous night and was looking forward to a chance to party with her again. They hung out together for a little while longer until it was time for him to head off to the hospital.

Once Dr. Roy was gone after the daily round, he sat down next to his mother to talk to her.

"Last night I went to a disco. Weird name it has. Hiccups. It was for her birthday party. It was an excellent party. I've never seen a place like that. Lights on top and lights on the floor, all of them changing colours all the time. The music was incredibly good. Even I was dancing. Imagine, me, dancing. All thanks to her.

Next weekend she's taking me there again, just like that. And on Sunday, I'll be taking her to the hill. She doesn't know where I'll be taking her, so it should be a fun surprise" he spoke to his mother in an excited tone.

He spoke at length about her and how good a friend she had been to him. He skipped the parts about how she had visited the hospital and their fight after that, but he did mention how she encouraged him to have a bit of fun in his life.

"But don't worry *maa*. I won't get carried away with all this. I won't become complacent" he said, speaking more to himself than his mother.

It was a fear that was constantly on his mind over the past few months, ever since he had become friendly with her. He had used it as an excuse to convince himself that he had to stay away from her. But now, he had decided to enjoy his friendship with her while making sure that he worked just as hard for his studies as he used to.

Late into the night as he stood near the window, he did not feel sad looking at the hustle and bustle of people on the street. He was no longer just watching other people living their lives; he was busy living his own. That feeling gave him a sense of happiness that was unmatched. It had barely been two days since he had buried the hatchet with her and she had already done so much for him. He wasn't living every day just to make it to the hospital on time for the doctor's round. He had other things on his mind as well.

The weekdays passed by in a hurry. On Friday she asked him if he wanted to watch a movie the next day. It was Jodha Akbar. She was a fan of Hrithik Roshan and he had high hopes from Ashutosh Gowariker. He agreed to go for the movie. They decided to go for the afternoon show, so they could have lunch before the movie and coffee after the show.

The next day, he waited for her outside the multiplex cum shopping mall. She reached exactly five minutes late once again. As they walked inside the complex, she saw him look at all the shops and showrooms with a half-smile on his face.

"Why are you smiling like that?" she asked him.

"I'm just wondering how much this place has changed since I last came here" he replied.

"When was the last time you came here?"

"Believe it or not, three years ago" he said to her as she responded with a wide-eyed look of surprise that he expected.

"This is the first time you've come to this multiplex in three years?" she asked.

"This is the first time I've come to *any* multiplex in three years!" he replied.

"Holy crap! How did you manage to watch movies the past three years?"

"Holy crap is your preferred non-expletive phrase *naa*?" he remarked. She responded with a mock punch.

"Answer the question. Movies, three years, how?" she asked.

"Two words – hostel, LAN" he replied.

"Oh man! But still *yaar*, watching a movie in theatre has its own charm" she said.

"Yep, even the bad movies seem OK because of the jokes that people crack in the theatre" he replied.

They occupied a table at a Chinese restaurant. He had the same look of partial amusement on his face while reading the menu.

"Please don't tell me this is the first time you're having

Chinese food in three years!" she remarked.

"No. It's the first time I'll be having Chinese food in my life" he responded.

She let out a gasp of shock that made him laugh.

"Relax. First time in three years!" he replied.

"Thank God! Just for a second I actually thought you were serious" she said.

"I'm going to have a lot of fun today" he said, which irritated her further.

They had a good time conversing with each other during lunch and then made their way to the movie hall. The seats were choc-a-bloc full. There were a lot of married couples and senior folks in the theatre. Youngsters were a minority. They sat down on a row close to the top. Next to them sat an elderly couple. He smiled at them and nodded, they did the same. She did not like the fact that the theatre was filled with such a senior crowd.

As they waited through the movie trailers and advertisements, the elderly couple ordered some cold drinks. The waiter handed over the bottles to the aged man, who took a sip and then kept the bottle on the floor instead of in the holder on the arm rest of the theatre seat. He saw that and asked the aged man if he wanted to put the bottle in the holder, the old man agreed and thanked him.

After he put the bottle in the holder, he felt her tap his shoulder. He leaned closer towards her as she whispered into his ear.

"I think even they've come to a multiplex after three years" she said and then started to giggle.

He stifled a smile and then reprimanded her for mocking older people.

"I wonder if they even remember the name of the movie they've come to watch!" she said. He asked her to stop.

"Ask them what year it is, I bet you fifty bucks they won't know" she continued with him struggling to pretend that he wasn't amused with her one liners.

"They're old *yaar*, please. *Thoda* respect" he said to her.

"OK. OK. Chill. Just because I'm making fun of them doesn't mean I don't respect them" she replied.

"I think you need to read the dictionary meaning of respect once again" he retorted.

"Old people are on this earth only for three things, to crib about the new generation, to give *aashirwaad* and to serve as material for jokes" she said to him.

"That is such a rude thing to say."

"It's the truth, have you seen old people do anything else apart from the three things I mentioned?" she asked.

He shrugged his shoulders and shook his head in disagreement.

"Alright, fine. I'm sorry. No more old people jokes. OK?"

"OK. Hey the movie's about to start" he said to her.

They watched as the movie unfolded. She was visibly impressed by her favourite actor's Mughal Emperor look. During the scene where they show the Emperor practicing his sword fighting skills without any clothing on the top half of his body, he observed her reactions closely. She was totally in awe of the actor on screen. He wondered why female audience members didn't whistle, if there would have been a scene where the female lead was scorching the screen with her looks, the male audience would've surely displayed their emotions more vociferously.

"Are you OK?" he whispered into her ear.

"Shh..." was her response, she clearly did not want to be disturbed from the visual treat she was enjoying.

"Stop visually molesting the poor guy. He's a married man for God's sake!" he said, continuing to tease her about her pretty obvious infatuation with the actor on screen.

She responded with a punch on his arm. This time it wasn't a mock punch. It was the real deal. He wanted to rub the spot where he had felt the impact, but his male ego stopped him from doing so. After the topless sword fighting practice scene was done, he noted the change in her expression, she was almost feeling let down that the scene got over so fast. He couldn't help but smile while observing her reactions.

Half-way into the movie and it had already been *paisa vasool* for both of them, although for different reasons. Then came a segment in the movie which made the two friends face the wrath of the old brigade.

In a scene, the Queen writes down the Emperor's name in Arabic and shows it to him, as a sign of their love. The Emperor tells the Queen that he doesn't know how to read.

For some reason, she found this revelation a little humourous and exclaimed aloud, "*Bechara*, he's not had any education."

A few minutes later, when the Emperor and the Queen professed their love for each other, face-to-face, for the first time in the movie; a very romantic cum passionate track began to play in the background. For most part of the track, the Emperor and the Queen are shown in several romantic poses, hinting at getting physically intimate with each other but never sealing the deal.

Every now and then the Emperor would begin planting kisses on the Queen's cheeks and then decide to go North and kiss her eyes and forehead. This process kept repeating right through the song until it had almost ended, causing a lot of frustration amongst the younger members in the audience. After the fourth such instance, he just couldn't hold himself back.

"Looks like he's not had any sex education either" he said out loud. She laughed, so did a few youngsters within hearing range. But the elderly couple gave him a very stern look and then mumbled a crib about, '*Aaj kal ke youngsters...*'

She gave him the 'I told you so' look. He felt bad about spoiling his image in the minds of the aged couple but then forgot all about it as the movie went on. After the climactic battle between the Emperor and a rebel prince, the audience was more than satisfied with the movie. People came out of the theatre having seen one of the best looking on-screen couples of all time in a movie that was fairly well made despite the longer than usual duration.

After they got out of the movie theatre, they made their way to a cafe in the mall. There they began discussing the movie.

"So what did you think?" she asked.

"It was good" he replied.

"Better than good, I thought it was great."

"I thought you'd say that, given how you were busy leching at your favourite actor" he said to her with a naughty smile.

"I was not leching at him..."

"I think staring shamelessly at a guy's abs and biting your lips while doing so, qualifies as leching."

"Oh my God! That's the height of exaggeration, I was so not staring and where the hell did you come up with the biting my lips part!" she said, defending herself as he laughed.

"Alright fine. I was exaggerating. And you're right, the movie was better than good. Would've been great if it had some memorable dialogues. Historical movies need great lines, so do fantasy movies. Like Gladiator, no one can forget the line by Russel Crowe, 'father to a murdered son, husband to a murdered wife and I will have my vengeance in this life or the next'" he said, with an accent that she found amusing.

"Pretty good stuff Maximus. What lines were there in the *Lord of the Rings?*" she asked.

"Loads. The book is filled with classic lines, but the movies had some pretty good ones too. Like before the battle, a legendary character tells the self-exiled king – 'become who you were born to be'" he said.

"Yeah. But I guess Hindi movies don't have the whole legendary dialogues culture" she remarked.

"No way. Maybe in recent movies. But during the Salim Javed era and even before that, one had some brilliant dialogues and punch lines..."

"*Mere paas maa hai* and all that stuff" she said, interrupting him.

"Yeah. See the point is, the phrase '*mere paas maa hai*' is not the reason for the dialogue being legendary. It's the timing. Words do not make a dialogue great, moments do. That scene from Deewar builds up to a crescendo and then Salim-Javed hit the audience with the punch line and everyone gets knocked out.

In fact Deewar is one of the greatest pieces of writing in the history of Hindi cinema. You remember the movie?" he asked.

"Yeah I do, but not like scene by scene" she replied.

"I remember it frame by frame. There's another scene that blows me away, somehow it hasn't been given the same kind of hype as some of the others from the movie. It's the *'main phaike hue paise nahi uthaata'* scene. That scene has no major consequence on the story, but it s a masterpiece of writing. They actually have a background build up scene just for that one punch line.

In the beginning of the movie, they show a young Vijay, polishing boots on the street and delivering the line in front of a city don when his henchman throws change at the kid who just polished their shoes. Showcasing the kid's self respect, something that the don appreciates and comments to his henchman that the kid will rise to great heights.

Decades later, the don hires a brave dock worker who hammered the hell out of his rival's gang members. When he throws a wad of cash at the young man, he is reminded about that incident with the boot polish kid. The don wonders how the young man knows about the incident. The young man tells the don, *'main aaj bhi phaike hue paise nahi uthaata'*. That is a memorable moment created out of thin air by pure writing skill" he spoke at length about one of his favourite movies.

"Holy crap! I need to watch that movie again. *Waise*, another movie that had awesome lines was *Sholay*" she said to him.

"Yet another Salim Javed script. I envy the people watching movies in 1975. Imagine a year with two movie releases that changed Hindi cinema forever. Such a large proportion of Indian cultural references come from just those two movies. It's incredible. No two movies have made that kind of an impact ever since" "I wonder why?" she asked.

"Lack of brave writers" he replied.

"Brave?"

"Yeah. You need to be brave to create a character called *'Soorma Bhopali'* and expect it to work. Forget about the risks in *Sholay*, I read somewhere that when Mr. India was being made,

Shekhar Kapur was not too happy with the line *'Mogambo khush hua'* and it was only when Salim Javed insisted on using the line that the director went ahead with it. Just think about it, creating a villain called Mogambo and then backing a dialogue like *'Mogambo khush hua'*. You need to be brave to remain unconcerned about what the audience would think and to believe in yourself."

"Dude. You should've been the one giving the Hindi movie quiz at Fastermind instead of me. Why did you choose Lord of the Rings and Mahabharata?" she said.

"Whatever we did was perfect. It worked. We won. Nothing else matters" he replied.

She smiled.

"So the conclusion of our discussion is that old movies had awesome dialogues and new movies have none" she said.

"No. That's not entirely true. Some dialogues are totally meaningless. Like *'mard ko dard nahi hota'*. Every time we men put on the shaving lotion after a shave, we know we've been lied to" he replied, making her laugh.

"You're crazy you know that!" she said and continued laughing.

"Let me add that to the wonderful list of adjectives you've used to describe my personality – aloof, arrogant, secretive, lunatic, selfish and now crazy! This just keeps getting better and better" he said to her with a smile.

"Shut up! When will you forget about what I said that day?"

"The day my lunacy turns into amnesia" he said to her, both of them smiled. Glad about the fact that they could now joke about what had happened.

They spent some more time together at the multiplex before heading out to their respective abodes. As soon as he was back in his room, he started to watch a few Michael Jackson dance videos, with the hope that it would inspire him to dance a little. He wasn't intimidated by her superior dancing prowess, but didn't want to come across as a 'serial killer' on the dance floor either.

Meanwhile, she was busy selecting her wardrobe for the night. She felt thrilled about how much of an effect her birthday party dress had on him. Even before he had arrived at the party that night, she had received a lot of approving male glances at Hiccups; but it was the look on his face that she felt most content about. She knew that he had tried his best, not to get caught looking at her; as he had always done in all their interactions. But that night, he was at her mercy.

She could not forget the look of awe he had on his face. She wanted to get a similar reaction from him again. That was when she laid her hands on exactly the kind of top she wanted to wear for the night. She had a smile on her face as she imagined his reaction on seeing her in that combination dress. She started to get ready.

He was done talking to his mother and waited for Dr. Roy to come into the ward. Dr. Roy made an entry right on time and was surprised to see him in party wear.

"Where's the party tonight?" asked the neurologist.

"Somewhere down the road" he replied, bringing a smile to the doctor's face.

"Significant change in wardrobe, increased usage of deodorant and immaculately combed hair. Tell tale signs that there's a beautiful girl involved. Am I right?" asked the doctor with a naughty smile on his face.

"Shh... Dr. Roy!" he exclaimed, pointing towards his mother with a tense expression on his face; as though he did not want his mother to find out he was going to meet a girl in the evening, and Dr. Roy had just blown his cover. Dr. Roy had a good laugh about the situation and then put his hand on the young man's shoulder.

"Remember, always try and maintain eye contact; no matter how beautiful she looks. Don't let her think that you've surrendered to her looks. Make her feel like she needs to do more to get your attention, it drives women crazy" said the neurologist in a hushed tone.

"Will keep that in mind. Thanks" he replied.

The doctor then went ahead with monitoring the patient's stats and concluding that there had been no change whatsoever.

But this time the patient's son did not feel as disheartened as usual. The young man was in a positive frame of mind and the doctor was happy for him.

The doctor called the young man outside the ward.

"Have a good time and remember. Always use protection" said the neurologist, just to have some fun at the expense of the youngster.

"I always ride with a helmet on" replied the young man, as both the men started laughing.

"But on a serious note. There's nothing like that going on. We're just *good friends* and I don't mean it in the Bollywood way" he said, making the doctor laugh again.

"I was just making sure I do my duty. Anyway, I better get going to the next ward. But have a lot of fun, you deserve it" said the neurologist.

He nodded and then returned to the ward, spent some time talking to his mother and then was on his way to Hiccups. Once again, he reached well ahead of time, ensured that he was looking his best and then calmly waited for her to arrive. After a brief wait, he saw her getting out of a *rickshaw*. As he saw her walk towards him, he noticed what she was wearing.

She had a dark blue, off shoulder top that shone like velvet. Her hair fell over her right shoulder, covering her fair skin, exposed by the off shoulder top. She had also put on metal gray ear rings that looked perfect against her dark hair. On her left shoulder she carried a black leather purse that matched her black jeans and heels.

He thought of the advice Dr. Roy had given him and maintained eye contact with her. But as she came closer to him, she flicked the strands of hair that covered her exposed shoulder, to reveal her flawless and radiant skin.

Focus, maintain eye contact. Remember what Dr. Roy said. She ran her right hand through her hair, tilted her head to the side and flashed her smile. I've never seen so much of her before, he thought to himself as she took the final few steps towards him. Balls to the eye contact and screw Dr. Roy's advice! I surrender.

She smiled as she saw the look on his face. He had been blown away yet again. She was thrilled.

"Hi" she said to him.

"You look stunning" he said to her, completing his surrender. She smiled.

"You're quite the handsome man tonight. Never seen you in party wear before. Even last week, you weren't wearing this stuff. Looking good" she said as she grabbed him by the arm and took him into the discotheque. The usher inked their hands as they paid the "couples entry" fee. They wandered across the crowded disco, finally spotting a vacant table.

He noticed subtle changes in her behaviour once she entered Hiccups, every step she took as she walked to the table, matched the beats of the song that was playing. Even when she sat on her chair, she was always attuned to the music that was playing. Her shoulders gently swung side to side with the rhythm and every once in a while she'd tap the table with her fingers when the drum beats got louder. Things like that made him realize how much she loved music and dancing.

"Hey, check out that guy in the corner" he said to her. She looked at a meek looking man, sitting alone in a corner, staring at his mobile phone.

"What about him?" she asked.

"I think he's somehow managed to come in here alone, in the hope that he'll manage to meet some girl. But he won't" he said to her.

"Hmm... and how do you know that?" she asked him again.

"A guy who can't impress a girl in the outside world will never be able to impress a girl inside a disco" he replied.

"Then why do you think he's come here?" she inquired.

"Because he's the kind of guy who has read some fiction books and seen some movies and believed the unreal stuff that they sell. Which is why he probably spent a lot of money on his clothes, acquired an expensive cell phone; which he uses to try and act busy while he's actually trying to spot any girl who doesn't have a guy around. But, even if he does manage to spot a girl like that, he won't have the courage to talk to her. He'll keep sitting, watching other people dance and drink until he reaches his spending limit before walking out, frustrated" he said.

"And you know this for sure?" she asked him.

"Yep. He looks like he's the kind of guy whose cell phone is smarter than him" he remarked.

"You're being mean" she said before having a chuckle.

"No, I'm being honest. See, there are three kinds of guys at any disco. Those who actually like music and dancing. Those who come here because of their girlfriends and those who come here in the hope of *pataoing* women" he said.

"And what category do you fall into?" she asked.

"Obviously the ones who've come here in the hope of *pataoing* women. But I've got one thing going my way."

"What?" she asked.

"I'm smarter than my cell phone" he replied, she laughed.

"If you're done with your analysis of lame disco guys, let's order some drinks and then hit the dance floor" she said to him. He agreed.

A waiter came across to their table and asked them what they'd like to have.

"I'll have some nachos and a 'sex on the beach'" she said.

He was a little amused by her choice of cocktail and had a smirk on his face.

"What? It's an awesome drink, I didn't choose the name" she said to him.

"Get me a non-veg platter and a coke" he said to the waiter, who left after taking the order.

"You don't have drinks?" she asked him.

"Of course I have drinks... they're just non-alcoholic" he replied.

"If it's non-alcoholic, it's not a drink" she remarked with a smirk. Just then the waiter arrived with their drinks and starters.

"Cheers" he said to her as they lightly tapped their glasses against each other.

She finished her cocktail in no time and called for the waiter, who attended to their table in no time.

"I'd like to have another cocktail. Do you have Strawberry Daiquiri?" she asked the waiter.

"Yes ma'am, we do" replied the waiter.

"Alright. I'll have one please" she said.

"And what about you sir?" the waiter asked him.

"Nothing for me as of now. Thank you" he replied.

"Did you just order a different cocktail?" he asked her, once the waiter left.

"Yeah. Why do you ask?"

"I was just wondering why you ordered a different one; not satisfied with sex on the beach?" he asked her with a naughty smile on his face.

"How will you understand? You've never had sex on the beach!" she replied with a wink and an even naughtier smile.

"Touché!" he replied as the waiter returned with her second cocktail for the night. They finished their respective drinks and the starters and she suggested they head out to the dance floor. He stuck to his safe dance moves, while watching her groove to the music. He was amazed by her ability to dance in a crowded space without banging into anyone. Whereas he had collided with at least half a dozen people in a matter of minutes. He hated the green laser lights which weren't steady and the blinking lights made it too dark for brief periods of time for him to see her. Finally the usual disco lights came back on and he could watch her without interruptions.

He noticed that her moves were different from the ones she was using the night of her birthday party. Tonight her dance was a lot more sensuous. Every now and then she'd close her eyes and run her hands through her hair, slowly and deliberately; accentuating the beauty of her slender hands and her jet black long hair. Or she'd swing her hips from side to side, making it very hard for him to ignore her slender waist and her shapely legs. She was looking so attractive that he was having trouble focusing on dancing.

"Dude, why don't you loosen up a bit" she said to him, screaming into his ear so that he could hear her voice over the music.

"What do you mean?" he asked.

"You're just moving your feet. Do something with your shoulders, it'll help you loosen up and it's fun" she said to him.

After a couple of failed attempts at moving his shoulders in sync with the beat, he gave up, it made her laugh.

"Wait I'll help you" she said as she put her arms around him to make sure his shoulders moved along with hers. As soon as he felt her arms on his shoulders, he froze and had a very tense look on his face, but then recovered quickly. She however, noticed his discomfort.

"Relax, I won't molest you" she said to him, making him smile.

"Damn it! I was so hoping that would happen tonight" he said to her.

She laughed and then gave him a light punch on his shoulder.

"Keep dreaming" she said to him.

"Now that I have your permission, I will" he replied with a wink.

The banter helped him relax and he was soon moving a lot freely than earlier. As the night wore on, the music got better and better and the dance-floor kept getting smaller and smaller as more people poured in. They got so close that their hands touched each other while dancing, he kept apologizing to her each time he ended up touching her due to someone pushing him. After a while, she asked him to forget about the apologies and grabbed his hands, resting them on her shoulders as she rested her hands on his shoulders and they danced together like that for the rest of the evening.

When he touched her bare shoulder, he could not believe how soft her skin was; her shoulders were so slender he was afraid of resting the weight of his hands on them. It was the first time he had been involved in a fair degree of physical contact with her and it was an incredible experience for him. After a brief period of being extremely conscious of that fact, he started to relax and enjoy himself. When the song 'Let The Music Play' by Shamur was played, a cheer rang out from the crowd on the dance floor.

It was one of her favourite numbers and it was the first time she was dancing with a guy on that song. That thought gave her a rush which resulted in her dancing with a lot of vibrance. Even he loved that song and she could feel him move with the kind of confidence a person gets when he's lost in the music.

After a marathon dance session lasting more than an hour, they got back to their table – to catch their breath and have dinner. While having dinner, she gave a call to Suparna. He could not hear what she was saying because of the loud music, but when the call was over, she looked a little worried.

"What's the matter?" he asked her.

"*Arrey yaar*, Suparna was supposed to pick me up and take me home. But she's saying her bike has a puncture and she won't be able to make it. It's already quite late now, I won't get a *rickshaw*" she said to him.

"Don't worry. I'll get a *rickshaw* for you. Relax and have your food *aaraam se*" he said, trying to comfort her.

She thought about the best way that she could resolve her transport hassle and had an idea.

"Hey, I know this old shortcut, it's not too far away from this place; it leads straight to M G Road, where I can easily get a late night bus for home. Can you just walk with me till the bus stop?" she asked him.

"Of course. Or if you want I can give you a ride on my cycle, 1970s Bollywood style!" he said to her in jest.

"Dude, I'm not that drunk" she said to him as the two friends shared a laugh. She was happy that she had thought of the shortcut, it would give them a chance to talk a while longer and she wouldn't have to bother about transport issues.

After dinner they danced for a while and left the disco much before the final song. She knew that despite the shortcut to the bus station, she'd still have to walk for some time and she didn't want to go home too late into the night.

He pushed his cycle along as he walked beside her. According to her the shortcut was about a kilometer away from Hiccups, where a narrow alley, that passed between a bunch of buildings, cut across a part of the city and finished up another kilometer away from the bus station. She thought about twenty minutes would suffice to make the journey. They walked briskly and were making good time.

"Hey, so what's the plan for tomorrow? You're supposed to show me what you bought for yourself with the quiz money" she said to him.

"Oh *haan*, I almost forgot about that."

"I didn't. What's the plan?"

"Well, we need to travel a fair distance, it's away from the city as I told you..." he said before she interrupted him.

"That's fine. I can get hold of my uncle's car. Where is this place exactly?" she asked him.

"Patience! Everything shall be revealed in time. Can you pick me up from college, sometime around ten in the morning. We can get some rest also before the trip. From college I will tell you the way" he said to her.

She nodded in agreement with his suggested plan.

"Hey, you see that alley on the left. We need to take that, if I remember correctly" she said to him, pointing to a dark alley.

He took a few quick steps ahead of her and had a look at the alley. It seemed to be pitch dark and the only light seemed to emanate for afar and it was dim. He guessed that the light was coming from the other end of the alley. The alley seemed to be quite long and there were old residential buildings on both sides. Taking a closer look, he noticed that the alley was littered with garbage and filth on the sides. He could see remnants of stolen street lamps on the sides of the alley. For some reason, he did not get a very good feel about the idea of walking through the fairly long alley in the dark.

"Are you sure this is the right way?" he asked her.

"Yeah it is. Last time I came here, there were proper lights and all. But then that was quite sometime ago. I wonder what happened to this place" she said.

Despite his apprehension about the shortcut, he led the way into the alley, pulling out his cell phone and using the light from it to see their path. It was strewn with all kinds of trash and broken beer bottles. The initial few steps were easy, because of the light that reached the alley from the main road they were walking on before entering the alley. But as they journeyed deeper into the alley, their eyes were wide open as they used the cell phone light to find their way. She took support of the cycle as she found the alley slippery, she rued the fact that she was wearing heels.

When they reached the middle of the alley, he heard sounds of breathing. It wasn't coming from her, he moved his cell phone from left to right, surveying the area that got illuminated by the grey cell phone light. He was startled when he saw two large burly men lying down on the side alley road against a massive garbage bin. He noticed an empty rum bottle next to one of the men. They seemed to be asleep. He looked at her and held his finger against his lip, signalling to her to remain silent. She had a tense look on her face. He switched off the cell phone light and grabbed her left hand as they passed by the two sleeping men. She walked as gently and quickly as she could, now regretting her decision of using the shortcut.

As they crossed the two sleeping men, she heaved a sigh of relief. But a few seconds later, she felt like she heard some movement behind her. She strained her ears and could hear footsteps approaching them. He held her hand tightly and whispered, "Don't worry."

With each step he increased his pace and pulled at her hand, making her walk fast as well. Even though they were walking for quite a while, the other end of the alley did not seem to get any closer. All of a sudden, the dark alley was filled with a broad beam of light. It came from behind them. He turned around to look, the same two men were walking towards them. One of them had a torch in his hand. The two men looked scary, both of them walked with drunken steps. She looked over her shoulder and was filled with dread when she saw the two drunkards following them. She grabbed his arm and looked at him. He saw the fear in her eyes. He was very worried himself. The two men were huge compared to him, there was no way he could challenge them physically; despite their drunken state. They had a torch, it was quite likely they carried a knife as well. It was too risky.

"*Oye heroine*" shouted one of the drunkards.

"*Cycle chodh, aaja meri gaadi mein baith jaa*" yelled the other drunkard as the two goons shared a laugh.

Her heart was pounding very hard. She could feel a cold sweat develop on her forehead. What should I do? She thought to herself. She looked over her shoulder again, the goons were closer than the last time she had looked. They had quickened their pace. She looked ahead, the end of the alley was still not in sight. There was no one else around to call for help. She pulled out her cell phone to dial 100, but there was zero connectivity. Damn it, she thought to herself. She looked at him, he had a worried look on his face but it seemed like he was thinking of something.

He pushed her ahead of himself and the two youngsters walked even faster. But the sounds of the goons laughing and yelling seemed to be getting closer and closer. He realized that the goons would catch up with them well before they had any chance of reaching the end of the alley, even after that, there was no guarantee of finding help. He had to do something right away.

"Get ready to run" he whispered to her. She started jogging and after a few steps, noticed that he had stopped. She turned around to look at what was happening.

He was standing his ground as the goons got closer. When they were fairly close to him, the goons also stopped moving; she guessed that the goons were wondering what he was going to do. For a few seconds there was complete silence, even she stood still. The two goons had their gaze fixed on him and he was looking towards them, without batting an eyelid despite the bright torch light hitting him directly in the eyes.

All of a sudden, in a swift move, he lifted his cycle over his head and flung it towards the goons with all his might. One of the goons got hit on the head with the cycle handle, while the other was struck by the rear tyre. The torch fell down and rolled on the floor. He could see the goon, who had taken a hit on the head, groan with agony. The second goon had lost his balance and was on the ground but wasn't visibly hurt.

"Run" he yelled as he made a dash towards the alley end. Within a few steps he had caught up with her. He caught her by the hand and made her run as fast as she could as they made their way towards the exit. When they were about to reach the end of the alley, they were thankful for the improved light that helped them see the path better.

"Left" she shouted as they could see the beginning of the main road. He turned left as the alley ended and they hit the main road. There were a few vehicles driving on the road at a distance. Even though they couldn't hear the goons following them, they kept running. They ran and ran until they reached the bus station. All the while, she kept looking back to see if they were being followed. There was no sign of the goons.

They stopped close to a bus stand, where along with some men a few women stood waiting for a bus. Probably night shift employees of some office, he thought to himself.

She looked at him, he was catching his breath and looking at the people waiting at the bus stand. He finally looked at her, she was breathing normally now.

"Are you OK?" he asked. She nodded.

"What about you?" she inquired.

"I'm alright" he said to her.

Just then, he saw a bus approaching.

"This bus will stop right next to my society" she said to him.

"Wait" he said to her. She wondered why he asked her to stop.

He saw two of the women present at the bus station get onto the bus.

"It's fine now, you can get on the bus, it s safe. Give me a call once you reach home" he said to her.

After she climbed onto the bus, she turned around and looked at him. The bus started to move, but she kept standing near the bus door, watching him as the bus increased the distance between the two. He raised his hand and waved slowly at her. But she did not wave back. She just stood there and looked at him. She did not blink her eyes as he kept fading into the distance. Neither of them moved until the other became a tiny speck barely visible from afar.

He waited for a while at the bus stand until a bus arrived that would drop him off right in front of his hostel. When he was half way home, he received an sms from her.

Reached home safe and sound. See you in the morning at college.
Ten o'clock sharp. A deal is a deal.

He smiled after reading the message. Despite what had happened, she wanted to go ahead with the outing they had planned for the morning.

Once he reached his room, he fell onto his bed out of exhaustion. The party itself had been draining and then the escape from the dark alley. He closed his eyes and remembered each second of the incident. A shiver of fear passed down his spine as he pictured their faces once again but then felt a rush of excitement as he thought of the moment when he heaved his cycle towards the two goons. It was an impulse decision. Fortunately it had worked. He knew the injuries to either of the thugs were not serious. The alley was dark and the goons were quite drunk; they wouldn't remember his face or hers. They were safe. There would be no repercussions in the future. He thought about the bad feeling he had experienced before entering the alley. Lesson learnt, always follow your gut instinct. He told himself.

Then he remembered the look she had on her face after she had gotten onto the bus. There was something special about the way she was looking at him. Something about her eyes. They said so much to him, without her uttering a word. That one look portrayed gratitude and admiration in equal measure. He had a smile of contentment on his face as he brought up an image in his mind of the look that she gave him.

He got up from his bed, walked to the study table and opened up a new section of his diary.

Thoughts about *Her* – was the title he gave to it.

He closed his eyes and once again pictured her moving away from him, fading into the distance, leaving behind the memory of that look on her face that said so much. He penned down the first line in his diary that would be dedicated to her.

She needs to say no words... her eyes speak a language of their own.

The next morning, she woke up feeling tired from all the strain of the previous night – running for her life, on heels, was not part of her plans when she had left home for the party. She felt like cancelling the outing, but then realized that he had been looking forward to it and did not want to let him down. She got ready, choosing to wear a combination of simple denim jeans and a black t-shirt for the trip. Since it was a Sunday, she borrowed her uncle's car and left for college.

She saw him waiting near the parking lot, he stood next to a black sports bicycle. She immediately felt a little embarrassed about the incident last night, which was the reason why, she guessed, he had to buy a new bicycle.

She got out of the car and waved to him as he walked towards her.

"You look tired" he said to her.

"Not really, I'm very used to having goons chase me in the middle of the night. It happens very often" she replied, making him laugh.

"Well it was a lesson learnt in life" he said to her.

"Absolutely, never walk into a dark alley. That's the lesson I learnt" she said to him.

"I learnt a different lesson" he said.

"What?" she asked, with curiosity.

"Bicycles have become expensive" he replied with a smile. As they both shared a laugh.

"I still can't believe you threw the bicycle at them. Thanks" she said to him.

"For what?" he asked.

"You know, for saving me from those goons" she replied.

"That is so presumptive. How do you know both of them were after you? In fact, I believe the one on the left was after me. The one who said '*aaja meri gaadi main baith jaa*'. I saw him giving me the *havas* look" he said to her.

"What is the *havas* look?" she asked.

"I'm sorry I can't show you right now, I only give that look to women at night" he replied, making her laugh.

"You're crazy!" she said to him.

"I know, you've told me that before!" he replied.

"When did you buy that new cycle?" she asked.

"An hour ago. Yet another acquisition courtesy Fastermind money."

"Can I ask you something? Why do you always travel by cycle? This would've been a good time to buy a proper bike or something" she said.

"I thought about it. But there is a reason for it, which I will tell you later."

"There you go again... with your secrets" she replied, rolling her eyes.

"Well, the secrets help in getting beautiful girls to stalk me" he replied with a wink.

"Shut up!" she said and punched him on his right shoulder.

"Ow. That hurt. I think I needlessly threw away my cycle last night. Your punches would've done the trick. Damn these Bollywood movies and their 'rescue the damsel in distress' agenda" he said in an over-the-top tone.

"Shut up and get into the car or else you get another punch" she said to him in a fake stern tone.

"You sound a lot more menacing right now than the drunk

goon who said '*aaja meri gaadi main baith jaa.*'"

"Get in" she said, stifling a smile.

"Whose car is this?" he asked after settling down in his seat.

"It's my uncle's car. When he's not using it, it's mine" she replied.

"Nice!"

"So where are we going?" she asked him.

"Do you know the way to the fort outside the city?"

"Yeah. That's like a hundred and fifty kilometers from here" she said to him.

"Don't worry we don't have to go that far. This place is about fifty kilometers from here. But it's on the same road" he replied.

"Alright then. Let's go" she said, turning on the ignition.

While they were on their way, he realized that she was a fairly cautious driver. She insisted that he wear his seat-belt, even when they had gone beyond the city premises. The traffic thinned out as they went further out. After more than an hour and a half of driving on a straight road, he asked her to take a turn to the left of the road. They were now on a mud road, where she drove with even more caution.

As she was driving, she noticed the changes in topography while they moved away from the city. Their city was surrounded on all sides by a series of hills. From the higher buildings in the city, during early mornings, one could see the range of hills on the horizon; before the city's dust and pollution blocked the view. On one such hill was the lone fort of the city, built ages ago by the ruler of the princely state of which the city was the capital. It was a major tourist spot and she had been there a couple of times – once with friends and on one occasion with her parents who had come to visit the city.

"You know I just remembered an incident about the fort" she said to him.

"Tell me."

"There are so many things that we laugh about with our friends when we are together and how those same things can be majorly embarrassing when you are with your parents. So I had gone to the fort, first with friends. We saw all these sculptures and paintings and all the graffitti on the walls and some of those things were damn funny.

You know how it is *naa*? With random people making chalk marks and circling the sculptures at strategic locations. Or when they write some random stuff on the walls. I remember this one thing that we all laughed about. Some lame guy had written this quote on the wall with a pink chalk.

I love you Pammi,
Will you be my children's mummy

I'm serious" she said as they burst out laughing.

"Oh man. That is insane. I bet Pammi said yes, after reading that" he replied.

"God knows, what happened to Pammi, but my Mummy definitely did not find it funny. Everywhere my parents went, they had this 'how disgusting' *waala* look on their faces. And I was having a hard time controlling my laughter" she said as they both laughed and joked about the incident for a while.

The mud road ended at the foot of a small hill range, where there was a signboard – *Welcome to Shringaar Hill Resort.*

"OK. Why are we going to a hill resort?" she asked him.

"We're not going to the hill resort. The front side of the hill is the resort, the other side is where we need to go. Just follow the road going up the hill, after we're half way to the top, there's a road that veers off to the other side of the hill. That's where we're going" he explained to her.

On their way up the hill, they passed by a park, which was part of the hill resort. She was very taken up with the park; it had a lush green lawn, filled with blooming flowers even though it was winter. It had different kinds of swings, some made of large rubber tyres hanging from a pole.

"I want to stop here and see this park. It's so beautiful. Can we stop, please please please" she said to him as she slowed down the car.

"Ummm... if you want to, but we'll get late in reaching the

top and the sun will be up on us in an hour" he said to her.

"Ah, you're right. It may sound stupid, but I so want to get onto those swings" she said, with longing in her voice.

"You like swings a lot?" he asked.

"Yeah. They remind me of my childhood. I still remember the first time I was on a swing, I thought I was flying. Those were the days, now I can't even remember the last time I sat on a swing" she said and wondered why he had a smile on his face.

They hit the road that turned sharply taking them over to the other side of the hill.

"Alright dude. We're on the other side of the hill. Where is the thing you wanted to show me?" she asked.

"You see that flat patch on the far end of the hill top?" he asked her pointing his finger in the direction.

"Yeah."

"Drive up there" he said.

"We've been driving forever and I still have no freaking clue what you're going to show me" she said, cribbing about the increased suspense.

They finally reached the hill top and he asked her to stop the car as soon as the edge was visible at a distance.

"We walk from here" he said to her, removing his seat belt and getting out of the car.

"Where to?" she asked him, but he had already started walking ahead. She looked around, there was no one else in sight.

"Are you scared of heights?" he yelled from afar.

"What? No!" she shouted out in reply.

"Then hurry up and come here" he said to her as he walked closer to the edge.

As she followed him, a pleasant breeze started to blow across the hill top. The air was so pure that it almost had a sweet fragrance to it. There were patches of brown grass and mud all over the hill, but as she got closer to the edge, the grass started to turn green. She walked a few steps ahead and was able to see the view over the edge, it was spectacular. She could see the next hill range at a distance, without any obstruction in sight. Roads, which looked like small threads, wound around the hill. At a distance she could also see the fort. She wondered how people had managed to build the fort at the top of a hill, hundreds of years ago and how it had retained its strength and magnificence ever since.

She then focused on the view closer to her. She could see him standing very close to the edge and looking at the hills beyond. A carpet of lush green grass lay in front of her as the hill top narrowed towards the edge. On her right, a large banyan tree with several roots plunging down from the tall branches, stood a few feet away from the edge. On her left, were three rows of different flowers, leading almost up to the edge. The closest to the edge were a set of carnations of different colours, purple, red and dark blue. Next to the carnations she saw a row of white gladioli, several of which were blooming. A bunch of chrysanthemums flourished at a spot that was closest to where she was standing.

"This is beautiful" she said to him.

He turned around to look at her and smiled.

"I thought you may like it" he said.

"But what was the thing on which you spent half your Fastermind money?" she asked.

"You're standing on it" he replied.

"What? I didn't understand"

"This plot of land, starting five metres behind where you're standing right now and going on right till the edge of the hill; about six hundred square metres, belongs to me" he replied.

"You own this land?" she asked him.

"Just this little patch" he replied.

"Holy crap! How rich are you dude?" she asked, making him laugh.

"I'm not rich. This land is cheap. The whole hill is owned by a local corporator, who converted the front portion of the hill into a resort. This side however is for residential plots. The plots are generally expensive given the view and everything, especially in the middle section of the hill. But as you get higher, it gets difficult to construct, since the upper portions of the hill are made of really hard stone. So the prices of the plots here are very cheap.

The approach road too is a few years away from getting properly done up with tar and all, so no one is in a hurry to buy any land around this area. I bought the plot a year ago on instalments, but then paid the final few instalments in advance using the Fastermind money. So in a way, this is what I bought with half my Fastermind money" he said to her at a stretch.

"Wow! This is amazing" she said, looking at the plot once again.

"There's one more thing I want to show you. Come closer to the tree" he said, asking her to approach the side of the tree that was facing the edge.

She walked closer to the edge and looked in the direction where he was pointing. She felt thrilled by what she saw. Younger roots of the banyan tree, that hung from the branches but were still a few feet above the ground, had been intertwined together to form a swing-like structure. The base of the banyan tree swing was wide enough for an adult to sit on. She rushed towards it and tugged on the roots.

"It's strong enough, don't worry" he said to her.

She sat on the swing, grabbing the roots on the sides for support and used her legs to give an initial push. She followed the path of the roots from the base of the swing to the top, they got thicker as they reached closer to the branches on top.

"This is so much fun" she said as she kept swinging harder, enjoying the feeling of the cool winter breeze brush against her flowing hair.

He smiled as he saw the thrilled look on her face; she was clearly having a great time.

"Did you make this swing?" she asked him.

"Yeah, I made it during the initial days when I had taken possession of the plot. Started it off with wrapping the roots around each other, one monsoon later, nature completed the job for me as the roots grew. All I need to do is twirl the roots as they grow. Once a month is enough to keep things working" he replied.

"I love how far this swing moves, I can almost swing right up to the edge of the hill" she said.

"If you push hard enough you can even get it to swing over the edge of the hill. I've tried it, although I would not recommend it, it scared the daylights out of me when I did it" he said to her.

"But won't the flexibility, I mean, range of the swing reduce as the roots grow?" she asked.

"Not really. The roots grow thick only when they reach the soil. Till then they'll keep growing longer and I'll keep entangling them and make the base broad and more comfy" he replied.

"Hey, how come the grass is green in your plot and gets drier as we move away from the edge?" she asked, observing the grass below her feet.

"I don't know for sure, but my guess is that there's some source of water under this plot. There's a general belief that banyan trees only come up next to perennial water sources. Another thing is that during the rainy season, if you go take a look over the edge, about ten feet below the edge, a spring of water flows out from the side of the hill. Maybe that's the excess water flowing out from wherever the underground source is. But yeah, the grass here is always green, even during summer.

You see those flowers, they don't require any watering. I just make sure no weeds get near the flower beds, that's it" he said to her.

"This is like a small piece of heaven. Feeling the cool wind on your face as you look at the lush green grass, flowers blooming in winter while sitting on a swing under the shade of an evergreen tree" she said to him and then looked at the view over the edge once again.

"This place reminds me of my childhood. My father would get me and my mother to some place like this on a hill and light a bonfire at night. He carried a proper tent and sleeping bags and the works. We'd all sit around the fire and roast different stuff on it and I'd lap it up as soon as my mother handed out some roasted potatoes with salt and pepper on it. It was simple but delicious.

Dad and I would sit late into the night, he'd tell me stories and I'd ask him all kinds of questions. The last time we went out for an outing to the hills at night, he was teaching me how to look at the night sky and find the constellations and the planets that are visible. No better place for star gazing than a hill top.

My mom hated it when he'd discuss these things with me late at night. She'd ask us to go to bed immediately. We both would comply and get into bed for a while. As soon as we were sure that mom was asleep, he'd get up, then pick me up and we'd get back to discussing things till it was close to sunrise. Those were some great times" he said to her, as his eyes searched the horizon for a glimpse of the past that was never to return.

She saw him stare at the wide open spaces beyond the edge of the hill. He did not blink as he was lost in his thoughts. She couldn't figure out whether he was feeling sad contemplating about the past or just reliving old memories.

"Are you OK?" she asked him, after a long period of silence, causing him to snap out of his thoughts.

"Yeah. I'm fine. Sorry, I was just thinking about some stuff" he replied with an apologetic smile.

"You really miss your dad don't you?" she asked him.

"I miss the times that never came to be" he sighed.

"You want to talk about it?" she inquired.

"There's really nothing to talk about" he replied.

"And what about your mom?" she asked him.

"Didn't you find out enough during your investigation" he said to her, with a dismissive tone.

"Look. I don't mean to intrude, but I think you'll feel better if you just share some of these things instead of bottling it up inside. You know I won't tell anyone" she said to him.

"I know you won't. But I didn't bring you here to tell you my sob story. I wanted to show you this place and the view" he said to her.

"Alright, I'll ask some other time" she replied, he had a smile on his face, knowing fully well that she wasn't going to let go of the topic.

"Why do you want to know?" he asked her.

"Because we're friends. Technically I've known you for almost three years, being classmates. We've been friends for a good eight months now, barring a few hiccups here and there. And here I am, on top of a hill far away from the city with a guy who is my friend, but in many ways is someone I hardly know" she said to him.

He thought about what she said for a few seconds and then looked at her to respond.

"Alright. Let's start with one question for today. You can ask me anything, apart from what happened to my mother or father; we'll talk about that some other time. Ask me anything apart from that and I promise you I'll give you a detailed answer" he said to her.

"OK. Why do you always travel on a cycle?" she asked him.

"You want to know why I always travel on a cycle!"

"Yeah and you promised a detailed answer."

"Fine. After my mom met with an accident, I had a bit of a financial crunch to deal with. I got rid of a lot of stuff to generate some cash flow to face the situation, including the vehicle we had. Since I was the only one left who needed transport I started to use my cycle. It's the cheapest means of transport after walking.

After some time I got used to it and even began to enjoy it. There are a lot of benefits to cycling. I don't give a damn about the price of petrol and whether it goes up or down. I don't feel a shred of guilt when I hear reports about global warming. Last but not the least, I don't have to spend time doing exercise, I get all of it when I'm travelling" he explained.

"So what started as a solution to a cash crunch became your preferred mode of transport" she remarked.

"Spot on."

"But what about speed? A cycle surely can't compete with a bike or a car in that department. What if you have to go somewhere and you're getting late?" she asked.

"You can't get late if you have nowhere to go to. Besides I am pretty punctual" he replied.

"Hmm... so your mind is set on sticking to the cycle?" she asked.

"That plan has worked fine for me so far. I don't see the need to waste money on a bike at this stage" he said to her.

"So you're fine with spending money on a plot of land but not on a bike?"

"Everyone should have a place on this Earth that they can call their own. Things like a bike or a car don't appeal so much to me as this place. The time for bikes and cars may come in the future, if better times come along.

This edge on the hill has been around since way before I was born and it'll remain right here for ages, long after I'm gone. But while I'am here, I'd like to call it my own" he said to her. His words brought a thoughtful smile to her face.

"You're the most different guy I've met" she said to him.

"In the good way or the bad way?" he asked.

"In a way that's beyond good or bad" she replied.

"I have no idea whether that works out to be a compliment for me or not" he said to her as she laughed.

"Don't worry, I meant it as a compliment" she said to him.

"Hey have you been to the fort?" she asked him, pointing towards the historical site far away in the horizon.

"Yeah. But my last visit was quite some time back" he replied.

"Did you take the guided tour?" she asked.

"Not really, no. Did you?"

"Yeah I did, on my second visit there. Found out a lot. Did you know that it was the only fort in the state that was never captured by either the Mughals or the British in a battle?"

"Yeah I knew that" he replied.

"OK. Did you know that the king who made it had a separate room just for his personal sword collection that boasted of more than five hundred swords?" she asked.

"No. Did the guide tell you that?" he asked her.

"Yeah" she replied.

"Did he tell any facts that a normal human being would find interesting?" he asked with a smirk.

"Very funny! In fact the guide did tell a fact that you may find interesting. Did you know that the same king had thirty queens?"

"That is interesting" he said with a naughty smile.

"See I told you. Although, I wonder what he achieved by marrying thirty women?" she mused.

"I can think of a few things, which as a gentleman I cannot talk about in front of a lady" he replied.

"Yeah right, the gentleman who watched Baywatch as a kid" she said.

"Only to learn swimming" he replied, making her laugh.

"Anyway, that king died of poisoning. Probably courtesy some jealous 'gentleman'" she said to him.

"That is quite likely, guys getting jealous of him. Imagine, thirty queens. One queen for each day of the month."

"That's sick" she said with mock disgust.

"If you find that sick, I better not raise the question of what would happen on February 28th" he said as they both started to laugh.

"Or what would happen on the months with 31 days" she said, adding on to the joke thread.

They continued laughing about the king and his queens for a brief while.

"But on a serious note. I think that king was a visionary. Imagine meeting a wife just once a month. It'd keep the relationship fresh" he said to her.

"Whatever!" she responded.

"Hey, it's almost lunch time. Feeling hungry?" he asked.

"I wasn't, until you mentioned it. Did you bring something along to eat?"

"No. But there is a restaurant at the resort side of the hill. It's just a quick drive away" he replied.

"Cool. Let's go" she said as she got up from the swing she was on and walked towards her car.

The restaurant was right next to the park that they had crossed earlier that day. It was built with a village theme, with wooden cots in place of chairs. Water was served in earthen pots instead of glasses, it added to the flavour of the place. She liked it there. The food was simple and easy on the stomach and the prices were very reasonable. They discussed several things while eating but then settled down on movies as a major conversation.

"Hey, you remember that day we were discussing movie dialogues?" she said to him, picking up the discussion thread from where they had left it some days ago.

"Yeah, I remember" he replied.

"Well, so I thought about what you said. You know about the quality of scripts in the post Salim-Javed era and I did find a few worthwhile movies. I'm not talking about art movies, I'm talking about blockbusters."

"Such as?" he asked.

"Well, for starters *Baazigar*. That was one killer script and had one of the best ever performances of SRK. The movie justifies every move of the lead character. Even though he does a lot of bad stuff in the film, the writing made sure that the audience will still root for him at the end. It was one of the highest grossing movies of the 90s" she said.

"It had to be, considering the fact that it had superhit songs and a standout SRK performance, along with a tight screenplay" he added.

"Yeah. It was one of the few 'thrillers' that Bollywood pulled off. But I always found that song which is played at the engagement ceremony pretty funny. I can't remember the name."

"*Chupaana bhi nahi aata?*"

"Yeah. That's the one" she said.

"That was one song, which was destined never to be sung by any guy, unless he'd want to publicly acknowledge that he had a screwed up love life" he commented.

"One movie which had the craziest plot point was *Hamraaz*" she said.

"What was so crazy about the plot?" he asked her.

"See the chic and her real lover hatch the most insane plan to rip off money from a business tycoon. She marries the business tycoon and tells him she can't have the *suhaag raat* because of some *vrat* she kept before her marriage. Right?

The second part of the scheme is for her to file for divorce claiming that he is impotent and thus get to his wealth as part of the divorce settlement. You remember this part of the movie *naa*?" she asked to check if he was following.

"Yeah, I remember. What's so crazy about that?"

"Well, what if they actually went to court and the tycoon proved that his... how should I put it... well, what if they went to court and the tycoon proved that his phoenix could rise. End of the stupid scheme. What say?" she asked.

"Hold on. Did you just use the word 'phoenix' for you-know-what?" he said, with a shocked look on his face.

"For lack of better options yes" she replied with an embarrassed look on her face.

He burst out laughing, falling onto the wooden cot. After watching him laugh uncontrollably for a while, even she laughed silently.

"Alright enough" she said to him after he went on laughing for a long time.

"You know something. Considering the revelation by J.K. Rowling that Dumbledore was gay, this gives a whole new spin to the fact that a secret society he founded was called The Order of the Phoenix" he said as he burst out into another fit of laughter.

"That's not funny" she said to him.

"Thanks to you, I will never be able to look at that book again or watch the movie without laughing at the title" he replied.

They carried on talking for a while longer as they had lunch. After which they returned to the hill top. They spent the rest of the afternoon sitting together on the lawn. She took off her shoes and felt the soft grass caress her feet. They discussed the great view that the location of the plot offered and spoke about a lot of other things. The wide open spaces and the warm winter sun on their backs created an atmosphere which helped the conversation flow without a break.

When it was close to five in the evening, he suggested that they head back to the city.

"I need to get to the hospital by..."

"Six thirty. I know!" she said to him with an understanding smile.

"If you don't mind me asking, what exactly happens there at six thirty?" she asked.

"A neurologist, who's been in-charge of my mom's case from the start, comes on his daily round. He checks some stats and reports to see if there has been any change in her condition. Thus far there hasn't been any" he said, with some sadness entering his voice.

"Don't lose hope, things will work out" she said to him, in an upbeat tone.

"I have never lost hope and will never lose hope. It's the one thing that cannot be snatched away or stolen or even lost. There's always more of it, if you look for it. You can have as much hope as you want. That's the beauty of it. Hope is the world's only never ending emotional resource. And right now it's all I have. Hope." he said to her with a pained smile on his face.

"You know I can't tell if you're being a pessimist or an optimist right now" she mentioned.

"I'm an optimist, because I have no choice" he said to her.

"Pessimistic Optimism. I like it" she said to him.

"And now it's time we make a move" he said to her as she turned her car around and headed back to the city.

8

One Thing You Didn't Know about Me

It was the middle of the week but she was still thinking about the weekend gone by. She saw him sitting and writing something during Jacko's lecture. She smiled as she thought about the fact that amongst all the students sitting in the lecture hall, *he* probably was the only one who actually owned a piece of land. She found the laid back Sunday spent at the hill very refreshing and was already looking forward to the next visit.

They had now made it a routine to have lunch together in college and spend some time talking after college until it was time for him to leave for the hospital. He was beginning to open up to her with each passing day. She found out a lot about him and he learnt some more about her. He learnt that she was born and brought up in Bangalore even though her parents were not from the city originally. She was an only child and her father was a nuclear scientist and worked for a couple of government organizations as a consultant. Her mother was a housewife.

She told him that she lived with her paternal uncle in the city and that she loved the freedom she had despite staying with her extended family members. While she shared all kinds of details with him, he only shared stories from his past. He never spoke about what had happened to his mother or what the medical state of the case was. He always avoided speaking about those topics, but despite that they had so much to discuss. They realized that they shared a passion for movies, music and books. They had such a great influence on each other that her love for dancing was resulting in him getting interested in the same. She also was changing a little bit because of him. Earlier, all she cared about was going to malls and multiplexes, she had now started to enjoy visiting places of natural beauty and appreciating the wonders of nature.

"You know, after the visit to the hill when I saw all those flowers, I have started to actually take time out and notice flowers at other places in the city. Like, all these years in the city, I never properly looked at this park that's located between home and college. Yesterday when I was on my way home in the evening, I actually asked Suparna to slow down near the park and look at all the flowers there. I saw some gardeners pulling out the weeds and watering the plants. How much effort those people put in and most of the folks passing by don't even take a second to give a glance to it. I went and spoke to those workers and asked them the names of the flowers. They were so happy to see someone who was interested" she said to him.

"That was nice of you" he replied.

"I don't know about that, but it felt good. And yesterday I spoke to Jacko after college. I was at the cafeteria with Suparna once you left and I saw him having coffee. So I spoke to him and told him that I was sorry about my behaviour at times during his lectures and that I would not repeat those things again" she said.

"Wow, that was unexpected!" he exclaimed.

"Yeah. Even I hadn't planned it. I just felt sorry for him, sitting alone after all the other staff members were gone for the day. I remembered what you said long back about why he acts the way he does and thought, *chalo* let's patch things up."

"I guess this means that you're probably not going to be kicked out of any more of his lectures."

"As long as I don't fall asleep or get caught playing cross and noughts" she said to him.

"Hey, not to raise your expectations or anything, but I have been practicing my dancing skills for Saturday night" he said to her.

"So... about Saturday night. I don't think I'll come to Hiccups" she said to him in an unsure voice.

"Why? Do you have other plans?" he asked her.

"Not really. I'm just not feeling like going there this weekend" she said to him.

"Is it because of what happened last time?" he asked, referring to the incident in the dark alley.

Her silence told him that his guess was correct.

"Oh come on. You can't let that affect you. I was the one who lost his cycle and I still want to go. All we need to do is stay away from the alley" he said to her, appealing to her to change her decision.

"You don't understand, it's not about what happened that night. It's about what could have happened. It's not so easy for me to shrug off the incident as a one-time happening."

"But..."

"You're a guy, you won't understand. Give me some time, I'll get over it" she said to him.

"No, I don't think so. If you lock yourself away, it'll be out of fear of something bad happening. Right? And that fear will keep getting worse with time and there will come a time when you'll say – I'll only go to places that are safe. You'll restrict yourself to places where you feel secure until the next incident. It may not be something that happens to you, it may be some incident you heard of, that took place with a friend of yours. You'll get more worried and will further restrict yourself, until you're locked up in your home after sundown.

There is a constant war going on in every city, a war that women have to fight... for their freedom. You givein to your worries this one time and it'll be one battle lost. The fewer the women on the streets at night, the easier it gets for the likes of those thugs we encountered in the alley.

I'm not saying that one needs to act foolhardy and intentionally walk into dark places, but you need to make sure that you do not curtail your way of life because some anonymous degenerate may be on the prowl somewhere.

Besides you'll be with me and I'll have my new cycle. You'll be safe, I promise you" he said to her, in a bid to change her mind. She smiled as she heard the mention of his cycle.

"I'll think about it. But you're quite the women's lib advocate" she replied.

"I'm not a women's lib advocate, but I do think that our generation has a responsibility to restore some balance when it comes to men and women in society.

There are so many things that are historically wrong in this world when it comes to men and our behaviour towards women. Men aren't going to do much about it. Women have to do everything possible to restore order. I am convinced that women and men are different but equal. But somehow, over the years men figured out a way to take over the reins of society and gain total control over half the world.

The only way to dominate those who are more powerful than you is by convincing them that they are weaker than you.

Men have mastered that art. Right from their birth to their death, across religions and cultures, women are taught to follow and never to lead. There's a constant effort all the time to stamp the notion of male superiority.

Think about it, in a marriage, why do they say 'I now pronounce you man and wife'? Why is it never, 'I now pronounce you woman and husband'? Phrases like 'pati parmeshwar'... or legends like the one of Pandora's box, where Pandora, the first woman on Earth, is blamed for unleashing all the evils on Earth and countless other examples are proof of a persistent effort to subconsciously etch into our minds that somehow men are at a higher pedestal than women. That women make all the mistakes and men are the noble ones undoing all the damage since times immemorial. Then we have traditions and ceremonies the world over where women come across as weak and in need of protection. Whereas the truth is, if it weren't for men ruining the lives of women, they'd probably not need any protection.

The victims are portrayed as the villains, while the aggressors masquerade as the protectors.

Women like you have to stand your ground and refuse to give in. You are educated and independent. If you decide to retreat, what hope do the others have" he said at length.

As he spoke, she felt moved by the sincerity in his voice. He was disclosing a part of his own philosophy, things that he truly believed in.

"Alright. You've successfully convinced me. I'll come to Hiccups this Saturday" she said to him and looked at him as he smiled.

"Great and you don't have to worry about anything" he said to her.

"Speaking of worrying. I wanted to tell you something. I noticed this during Fastermind and even at the alley that night. I have never seen you getting worried. How do you do that?" she asked him.

"There's no use getting worried. We worry because we expect something bad is likely to happen. Right? In my experience the worst things happen when you least expect them to. How many times has something bad actually happened when you've been expecting it? Think about it" he replied.

"You're full on in *gyaan* mode today" she said with a chuckle.

"Nothing like that" he replied.

"You sir, have achieved *nirvana*" she said, having fun as she saw him getting embarrassed.

"I have not achieved *nirvana*. There are things that do worry me. But you have to restrict the number of things one worries about. Otherwise life can get very difficult" he said to her.

"So what is it that worries you?"

"I've managed to restrict my worries to balding, losing my virginity and world peace. That's it" he replied, as she began laughing.

"You're crazy" she said to him.

"That statement has started to sound very familiar" he replied.

They spent the rest of their lunch time together and headed back to the lecture rooms for the remainder of the day.

The rest of the week flew by in a hurry and before he knew it, it was Saturday evening and he was at the hospital, dressed once again for a party. Dr. Roy was surprised to see him in party wear once again. After checking the patient's reports and stats, the neurologist gave the usual answer to the young man. But he was glad to see that the patient's son did not feel morose even for a second.

Dr. Roy called *him* out of the ward to have a chat.

"I see you're ready for another party. What's the occasion?" asked the doctor.

"Saturday night" he replied, bringing a smile to the doctor's face.

"Same girl?" asked Dr. Roy

"Yes. I've been told that being faithful is just as important as using protection" he said in jest as both of them shared a laugh.

"I'm glad you've started to let your hair down a little. You deserve a break. Have fun" said the neurologist and moved on to the next ward.

She wanted to break her streak of arriving five minutes late, but couldn't break it that evening. That night she drove the car to Hiccups and spotted him waiting for her near the entrance with a smile on his face and his hand pointing to the watch.

"Right on time" he said to her as she walked up to him with hurried steps.

"Bad traffic" she mentioned as her excuse.

"The eternal culprit" he replied as they made their way inside Hiccups.

They occupied a table, gave their order and started talking as they waited for the starters and drinks to arrive.

"I was just thinking the other day, you're doing so many things to build up your resume; I feel like I'm doing nothing. In fact sometimes I wonder why I'm even doing engineering" she said to him.

"I think the whole point of doing engineering is to find out why you're doing it" he said, making her laugh.

"Sometimes when I look at the number of students standing in the admission queues each year, I wonder how come people are so eager to get into engineering and end all their chances of leading a normal, happy and easy going life. I see their faces... the guys wearing their best shirts, clean shaven faces and the girls looking so bright and full of life. A month into college and all the guys have depressed looks on their faces..."

"But somehow the girls remain fairly happy. I don't know how you all manage to do it" he said, interrupting her.

"Guys get depressed because of college and girls get depressed because of marriage. Hence girls are usually happy during college life" she said to him.

"*Gyaan* alert!"

"Just think about it. Whenever we have sky high expectations from something, it invariably sucks. Most guys have very high expectations from college life, everyone comes in with dreams of a hot girlfriend and a fat pay package. Few get either of the two. That leads to frustration.

On the other hand, most girls know that college is their window to freedom before marriage, so they make the most of it. However, they do have expectations from their marriage; which again in most cases are not met.

Hence my statement. Reality bites guys in college and girls during marriage" she said, completing her theory.

"Basically what you're saying is we're all either depressed or on the way to depression?" he asked her.

"*Naah*, I was just trying to give *gyaan* like you. I suck at it" she said with a chuckle.

"No, your theory really had me going for a while. All you need to do is add a few case studies and examples to prove it. That's all it takes to sell a theory" he replied.

"I'm sorry I tried to compete" she said raising her right hand in a mock salute.

The waiter arrived with the starters and drinks. Midway through her drink, she excused herself to visit the restroom.

"Don't slip anything into my drink or purse without telling me" she said to him with a wink as she started walking to the restroom.

She left her purse on the table. He wondered why she carried such a large purse with her. He looked around at other women in the club, they all had large purses with them. Just then she returned to the table.

"Can I ask you a question about female accessories?" he asked.

"Sure."

"Why do women carry such massive purses with themselves wherever they go?"

"Firstly they're not massive. Secondly, we carry a lot of stuff. Chap sticks, car keys, house keys, some women carry mirrors and small makeup items..."

"Hold on. Don't chap sticks come under makeup items?" he asked.

"No! A chap stick is not part of makeup. What's wrong with you?"

"I'm sorry, my experience with makeup kits is limited" he replied with an amused smile.

"Anyway, in addition to all that, we have our wallets and cell phones. Hence the need for at least a medium size purse" she said, concluding her explanation on why women carry large purses.

"Why can't you just put the keys, the wallet and the cell phone in your jeans pockets?" he asked her.

"Women's jeans are not like guy jeans. They're tighter, showing fat wallets in our pockets would spoil the look" she replied.

"Why are women's jeans tighter?" he asked.

"To help showcase the figure" she replied.

"Oh" he said as he mulled over what she told him.

He had never thought about it and looked around at all the women clad in jeans at the disco. She was right, their jeans were tighter. His eyes then veered towards *her* legs, visible under the glass table. The fabric of her jeans seemed to cling to her skin. His eyes moved from her ankles upwards. He was amazed at how shapely her legs were and how he had never noticed that before.

"Ahem. Eye contact please" she said to him.

"Sorry. Got distracted" he replied, with a hint of embarrassment.

He was blushing, she found it cute. After that, he kept looking at different corners of the disco, going overboard in trying to prove that he wasn't checking out her legs. It brought a smile to her face.

After they were done with the starters and drinks, they got onto the dance floor. She noticed how much more comfortable he was with dancing. His movements were much smoother and he was gaining in confidence and had increased his repertoire of moves. That night they had so much fun dancing, that they did not take a break for dinner and had their meal only after the last song had been played. While having dinner they struck a conversation about placements.

"Three weeks to go before the first company comes in" she said to him.

"Yeah, but these are just service companies. The real deal will be next year when the dream slot companies come in. That's what I am looking forward to" he replied.

"True, but the service companies will also be fun naa, giving interviews and all. Seeing who all get placed on the first day itself" she said.

"The thing is, service companies come with a mindset that they must hire a few hundred people. So they don't care about how good people are, they just have a lower cut off for intelligence and whoever makes the cut gets selected. Whereas, dream companies want very specific kinds of talent and have a very high benchmark. Getting into those companies would be fun. Even the agenda of service and dream companies is so different.

Service companies come to reject people below a certain threshold, dream companies come to select people above a threshold" he said, explaining his theory of placements.

"*Aap gyaani hai, antaryaami hai*" she said in the tone of a trademark *Andaaz Apna Apna* fan.

They both started laughing.

"So tell me one thing, you've taken some oath never to drink *kya?*" she asked him.

"No oath or anything like that, but it's just that right from childhood we hear people telling us that it's bad to smoke and drink. But then, the moment we grow old enough, almost everyone automatically starts doing both. I've never quite understood it. Smoking is clearly bad for health and drinking... most people say that they don't like the taste of alcohol initially, but they carry on until they 'acquire' a taste for it. I just can't seem to understand it" he replied.

"I don't like the taste of alcohol directly, but cocktails are pretty good. They have different flavors and give you the high of having alcohol as well. Like... Sex On The Beach, it tastes sweet and a little tangy. Strawberry Daiquiri, which is another one of my favourites, that's also sweet and has just a hint of alcohol in it, giving it a unique flavor. You want to try it?" she asked him, handing over her cocktail glass.

"No thank you" he responded with his hand raised in a gesture of refusal.

"Come on. Be a man" she said in an exaggerated tone, making him smile.

"I don't think having a Strawberry cocktail is the test of 'being a man'" he replied.

"Having Sex On The Beach definitely is" she replied with a wink.

"Nice try, but no thanks" he replied.

"Damn *yaar!*" she exclaimed with a hint of disappointment.

"Why are you so hell bent on me having a drink?" he asked.

"Because I want to see how you behave when you're drunk" she replied.

"What?"

"Yeah. I bet, when you're drunk you'll spill out all your secrets and brush aside all your inhibitions"

"I'm already doing that *naa*. Over the last few weeks, I have become more chilled out than I've ever been.

I've told you so many things, I've even started to dance a bit."

"*Haan*, but alcohol will fast track the process" she said excitedly.

"I can't believe you are actually encouraging me to have alcohol" he said to her.

"I'm asking you to try it, not to become a drunkard who stalks women in dark alleys" she replied.

"Maybe I should try the 'drunk stalker in the dark alley' thing. Chances are that some other guy will throw a cycle at me and I can recover my costs" he replied, as they both shared a laugh.

"But you know what. Now that you make me think about it. I really do wonder how I'll behave when I'm drunk" he said to her.

"It's a fun thought *naa*?" she said.

"Yeah. What about you, what do you do when you're drunk?" he asked.

"I don't know, I've never been drunk!" she replied.

"What? Never!"

"Never. I always stick to my quota of two to four cocktails and that too mild ones. It just makes me a little high, never drunk. But yeah, I would like to find out what I do when I'm drunk... Hey, let's make a pact. After we both get placed, we'll get drunk. Somewhere safe. And we'll record what we do with a cam. So we can watch it when we're sober. What say?" she asked.

"Only if you promise not to molest me when you're drunk" he replied.

"Aah damn! You're asking for a lot, but I think I'll control myself" she said to him as they both started laughing.

"So it's a deal?" she asked, stretching her hand out towards him.

"It's a deal" he replied, shaking her hand to seal the pact.

They hung out for a long time at Hiccups and were amongst the last to leave the club. Neither of them had transport worries, she had her car and he had his cycle. They went their separate ways and reached home safe and sound.

Even though he was at his hostel room, his mind was still at the club. He could not stop thinking about dancing with her. It was like being in a dream. The way she moved her hips, the graceful movements of her hands, the way her hair swayed as she grooved to the music, everything about her was flawless. He pulled out his diary to make another post under *Thoughts about Her*:

The night arrives just to watch her dance,
The moon peeks through the clouds, just to get a glance.

She was home and lying down on her bed, thinking about him. She had a quiet laugh as she remembered the way she had caught him admiring her legs and how embarrassed he had felt that time. The entire time after that she saw him make an effort not to look at any part of her except her face. Poor guy, she said to herself, too decent for his own good.

She thought about how much time the two of them had started to spend with each other. He was so different from all the other guys she had met. He was honest in his behaviour towards her, he did not try to act like a different person just to impress her. There were so many layers to his personality. The more she tried to unravel him, the more layers she found underneath. She felt glad that she was spending time with someone like him.

With another night of dancing and laughter behind them, the two of them fell asleep with their minds at ease.

Over the next few weeks, they spent all their free time together, travelling to the hill on Sundays and partying each Saturday night. They even went for the occasional movie together. People around them were beginning to notice how close they had grown. Dr. Roy pointed out how he always seemed to be in high spirits ever since he had started spending time with her. Suparna complained about getting ignored because *she* spent all her time with him. When asked, they denied having feelings for each other. But individually, they both knew that they had started to get attracted to each other.

He did not tell her anything about his feelings for her, because he was afraid that she might not reciprocate his sentiments and that would ruin everything. She had become a beacon of light in his dark life, he did not want to do anything to disturb their equation.

On the other hand, she was afraid that because of all the things he was going through, he may not want to get into a relationship. She knew that he liked her. She could see it in his eyes, every time he looked at her. However, she decided to continue things as they were and wait for a time when he would have lesser worries on his mind.

As placement week drew nearer, they put a temporary stop to their outings and parties. Placements in their college worked in a slightly long drawn out manner. Towards the end of Third Year, service companies like the major Indian IT firms were invited for placement week. Students were allowed to sit for as many interviews as they liked until they got placed in a company. As soon as someone got placed, they would not be permitted to sit for any other service company interview.

Then, towards the end of Final Year, the big guns would join the hunt. All the major global software and consulting firms would hold their interviews. The value of the package offered would decide which company got the first crack at hiring the available talent. The higher the package, the higher the cut-off GPA.

The safety first approach employed by all students was to ensure that they secured a service job as soon as possible and then wait for phase two that took place almost a year later. Phase two for most people was a make or break time, phase one however, was something that students took a little lightly; especially those with a higher GPA. The students with backlogs and low GPAs were the ones who looked the most worried during phase one, while those with GPAs soaring in the high 8s and 9s were relaxed.

The situation got reversed during phase two, when the high scoring students looked tense about which company they'd end up in, while the low GPA folks were at ease, since they didn't make the cut-offs in any case.

During the run up to placement week, students spent time preparing their resumes. Requests were made to seniors to share the 'format' of their resumes. That would be followed by searching their memories for all kinds of 'achievements' that they could list out on sheets of paper meant to sum up their nascent careers.

While some of the gifted students had amazing achievements like having stood first at the NTS exam or winning scholarships every year or having a lot of sporting medals and trophies to boast of; others had to embellish a lot to fill in the two page format. Entries like:

Participated in several National Level C contests and *Shortlisted for a multitude of National level Paper Presentation contest* – were the norm.

Any event, no matter how inconsequential would be billed as a National Level competition.

'Languages spoken' was another extremely abused section – some students would mention German and French as languages they spoke, even though they knew little more than how to say 'Good Morning' and 'Good Night' in those languages. Such students took their chances with the hope that the interviewer would not know the languages they listed.

However, the one place where students used all their creativity was in the 'Hobbies' section.

Most students had entries like – reading, sports, music, movies, cricket (despite having mentioned sports already) and blogging (even if their blog has just one post) on their resume.

A few misguided students added some unintended humour to their resumes –

One resume mentioned the following under 'Languages spoken' – *English, Hindi, Marathi, Gujarati, C,* C++, Java (beginner level).

He had his resume worked out well ahead of Placement week, so did she. They reviewed each other's resume and even prepared for aptitude tests and interviews together.

He despised preparing for service company interviews, they involved a set pattern of questions repeated year after year that were easily available on the Internet. Questions like the one below were the norm:

Write a C program to display the following output on screen:

```
*
**
***
****
*****
```

"How the hell is a question like this applicable to the real world..." he complained to her, "... anyone can mug up the program for this and spill it out. After three years of engineering, is this the sort of question that will get students a job? Shouldn't there be a better way of judging a student's calibre?" he went on.

"Shut up and learn the standard answer!" she said to him plainly.

"I won't!" he replied.

"You want to write some original code in front of the interviewer, then be my guest. Just remember, some of the interviewers themselves don't know how to code for nuts. They ask standard questions so they get standard answers which they can use to select or reject students. It's the wrong time to showcase your brilliance" she said.

"I'd rather remain *berozgaar* than get a job by writing a C program to draw a right angled triangle made up of asterisks!"

"I bet you'll be asked to write this program."

"I won't write it" he replied.

"Sometime you act really silly, you know that" she said to him and ruffled his hair.

He wondered how girls took liberties in making physical contact with guys without thinking twice. She had lovely hair that he wanted to run his fingers through, but if he did, she'd probably think that he was a nut-job and here she was, ruffling his hair and punching his shoulder at will.

What does this mean? Does it have any significance or is it just normal female behaviour with a familiar male friend? Why doesn't someone teach this stuff in a book? Who the hell cares about drawing a triangle in C ? Here's a girl who I like and I don't even know if she likes me or is acting friendly. Damn this world! There's only one man who can help me, Dr. Roy – he thought to himself.

That evening he waited for Dr. Roy to arrive for the daily round. After the doctor was done examining his mother, he asked the doctor to meet him outside the ward.

"I need some advice" he said to Dr. Roy.

"Sure, what is it?"

"It's about a girl" he said.

"The Saturday night girl?" asked the doctor.

"Yeah" he said with a tense expression.

He did not know how to put the question across to Dr. Roy. The neurologist was the closest thing he had to an elder brother, but Dr. Roy was a good twenty years older than him.

"Don't tell me you did something stupid?" Dr. Roy asked, wondering why the youngster was looking so worried.

"No way! We're nowhere close to doing anything remotely stupid" he replied, surprised by the direction in which Dr. Roy was thinking.

"Thank God. So what is it?" asked the relieved doctor.

"The thing is, we've become very close friends. We spend a lot of time together. We go out for movies and parties etc with each other and it's all a lot of fun. But..."

Dr. Roy knew what his question was going to be and was enjoying the build up. Looking at the young man experiencing his first crush woes, reminded him of his own college days.

"... but now I think I've started to like her and I don't know if she likes me. I don't know if I should tell her and it's getting so difficult. Every day I convince myself not to think of her as anything more than a friend.

But the moment I see her, I feel like telling her that I have feelings for her. What do I do?" he asked Dr. Roy.

"Alright, I think I got the picture. So here's one question. Is this girl fairly balanced and rational?"

"Yes" he replied.

"Then you have nothing to fear. Just go ahead and tell her, but tell her nicely. Make it special" said the doctor.

"What happens if she says no?" he asked.

"I don't know. But, I will tell you this; if you do tell her and she says no, you may regret it; but if you don't tell her... you will regret it" said the neurologist.

He knew that Dr. Roy was right, and that he had to confess his feelings to her sometime. He decided to wait for the right moment.

That night as he sat in front of his study table, in the hope of preparing for the placement process that would begin the next day, all he could do was think about her and how all his efforts to prevent himself from getting attracted to her, had been in vain. He wondered how she actually forced his mind to disobey simple instructions like, not looking at her beauty spot or her shapely legs or her stunning figure. She seemed to do that without any effort, all she had to do was stand in front of him. And it wasn't just her looks, he felt attracted to her personality as a whole. She had changed his life for the better. In the face of despair, she had become his one hope for a normal life.

Just as he was thinking about her, he got a call on his cell phone. It was from her.

"Hey, wassup?" he said to her.

"I am home alone... and bored... and not getting sleep" she replied.

"Why are you alone?"

"My aunt's grandmother died. So she, along with my uncle and cousin sister have all dashed off to Bangalore."

"Oh I'm sorry to hear that. Are you feeling sad or something because of that" he said to her.

"No not really. I'm just bored, had they told me earlier that they were going I would've called Suparna over, but now it's too late."

"So you're just bored and not sad that someone died?"

"I'm not happy that someone died, but I'm not going to fake sadness because of it. I haven't even met the person who passed away, I did not exist in her world. I bet her soul would not appreciate fake and insincere demonstrations of sorrow at her death. My uncle and all are actually going there because the old lady's will shall be read out, they've gone to try their luck" she said.

"OK" he said, not knowing how exactly to respond.

"I don't understand why wills are opened up after the person dies. They should open it before, when the person is getting old or something. It'll save everyone all the suspense. Plus the old people can have some fun by giving the finger to the people they dislike by willing to them useless stuff like old socks or torn clothes" she said, making him laugh a bit.

"Why do you hate old people so much?" he asked.

"I don't hate old people. What made you think so?"

"You have a tendency to come across as someone who doesn't really respect old people too much" he answered.

"It's not that I disrespect old people. But I do strongly feel that having white hair should not be considered as a criterion for respecting a person."

"Hmm... I can't really argue with that. So when are your relatives going to return?" he asked.

"Three days later" she replied.

"OK. Anyway, all set for tomorrow?" he asked her.

"I'm not doing any preparation, if that's what you mean. I'm too tired of solving those aptitude test problems..." she said as he interrupted her.

"That stuff is retarded. It's like going back to eight standard *yaar*. Ramesh, Suresh and Rakesh start running at blah speeds, how far will they get in five minutes. What the heck?

Then you have the 'boat moving upstream and downstream' question. Or some question like – a man moves 3 km east, then 5 km north and 7 km west, how far is he from the starting point? Such questions are an insult to one's intelligence. What are they trying to asses? Whether we cheated while passing high school?" he stopped as he heard her laugh.

"Why are you laughing?" he asked.

"It's funny how you get so riled up about such things. I think all these quizzes have spoilt you. You're like some addict looking for tough questions all the time. You don't get a thrill from these standard tests; you want something exciting all the time. Right?" she asked.

"Damn it! You're right" he said to her.

"I think I know you better than you know yourself" she said to him.

Immediately his mind recognized the truth in the innocuous statement she had made. She was right. She did know him better than anyone else, including himself.

"Can I ask you something random?" he asked her.

"Sure."

"Do you have a boyfriend?"

His heart rate increased exponentially as he asked the question and waited for her answer.

She laughed silently when she heard the question. She hadn't expected it, but when he asked the question, she found the hesitancy in his voice quite funny and a little cute.

"That is a random question. And the answer is no. If I did have a boyfriend, you would've known by now" she replied.

He heaved a sigh of relief.

"Why did you ask me that question?"

Now it was her turn to get anxious as she awaited his answer. Was he going to ask her out? Surely he wouldn't do that over the phone? She wanted it to happen face to face.

Meanwhile, he had other questions on his mind. Should I tell her? Would a phone ask-out be too lame? On the plus side, if she rejects me it'll be less awkward. Damn it! This is so hard. Why did she have to call up at this time of the night?

"I just asked, by the way. No reason" he replied, fighting the will to ask her out.

"What about you? Any girlfriend or exes?" she asked him.

"No girlfriend, no exes" he replied.

She had expected that answer from him. Considering the fact that he hadn't been socializing for years, his chances of dating a girl were fairly low. But having her presumption confirmed, made her feel glad.

"What about you, I mean, any exes?" he asked, out of curiosity. His guess was that she did have some ex or exes.

"No exes, but I did have a stalker" she replied.

"A stalker?"

"Yeah. In the eleventh standard. There was this guy in my class, he used to stay close to my house. Every morning, he'd wait somewhere near my house and watch me leave for junior college. Then he'd come to class, wearing a shirt that matched the color of my top."

"That is... weird!"

"I know. It was crazy. The weirdest part was, he never ever spoke to me or tried to approach me. All he did was stalk me in the morning and wear the same color clothes as me" "So what did you do?" he asked.

"What could I do? I just kept as far away as I could from him. That guy ended up failing the eleventh standard and he left the junior college. Never heard from him again and I'm glad about that" she replied.

"I wish I had a female stalker like that, who'd try and copy my clothing. I'd just come out wearing an underwear and *baniyaan*, that would mean she'd have to put on some lingerie" he said.

She burst out laughing.

"You're seriously insane" she said as she continued laughing.

The sound of her laughter was music to his ears. She had the most perfect laugh. It wasn't shrill, or loud, it was graceful and innocent, just like the rest of her traits.

"Can I tell you something? You're the most incredibly amazing girl I've ever met" he said to her as he once again felt a surge of emotion in his mind to tell her how he felt about her.

"Thank you" she replied in broken words as she was taken by surprise by the out of the blue compliment.

"Can I tell you something else?"

"Yeah" she said, holding her breath as she anticipated that he may actually ask her out.

"Best of luck for tomorrow" he said, bailing out at the last moment.

"Thanks" she said, feeling a mixture of relief and disappointment.

Relief because she did not want to be asked out over a phone call and disappointed because she did not know when next he'd feel brave enough to do so.

They spoke for a while longer and then hung up. Long after the call was over, they both were thinking about each other. He had come so close to telling her how he felt. Why is it so difficult? He thought to himself.

Why can't a guy just tell a girl that he likes her, without having the fear of rejection crushing him?

He finally went to sleep, simply because he had to be in college by nine in the morning for the Pre-Placement Talk (PPT) by the biggest IT company in India.

As soon as he woke up, all thoughts of asking her out were gone from his mind. He knew he did not want to prolong phase one of placements by a single day. He wanted to get it over with that day itself. He went to the hospital and touched his mother's feet, seeking her blessings.

He then reached college and sat down at the designated lecture hall, he reserved a seat for her. She walked in, wearing the official college uniform – a dark grey *kurta* with a white *salwaar* and *dupatta*. It was the first time, he saw her in such simple clothing. She still looked hot.

Her eyes searched for him as she entered the lecture hall. She found him and walked towards him. It was the first time she had seen him wearing the college uniform, a white shirt, grey cotton pant and a dark red tie with the college emblem on it. He was dressed immaculately. She wondered how he managed to look so neat and tidy despite travelling on a bicycle.

"Someone is looking really handsome today" she said to him as she took the seat next to him.

"Thanks. I'm hoping I can seduce my way into getting the job. All I need is some luck so that I get a straight female or a gay male interviewer. When I walk in for my interview, I've decided that I'll keep the first two buttons of my shirt open" he said to her, making her laugh.

"Any tips for me?" she asked.

"Yeah. If you don't know the answer to a question, just bite your lips seductively" he replied. She laughed even harder.

A few minutes prior to the start of the PPT, the lecture hall was filled up with students. The college staff made their entry, signalling that the Hiring Team from the company would make their entry very soon. And sure enough, a few minutes later, a team of five corporate executives made their way to the lecture hall. Three men, aged between twenty-five to forty walked in along with two women, one of whom was slightly senior and looked like she was in her late thirties. The last one to enter was an extremely attractive woman – the HR. The HR had sharp features, long hair, full lips and wore a figure hugging top and cotton pants along with heels.

The moment she entered the hall, there was a buzz of murmurs all over, caused mainly by excited male students celebrating the sighting of an angel. Even *he* had an 'I'm impressed' look on his face. He wasn't expecting the HR to be so attractive.

One by one, each member of the hiring team presented slides to the audience of Third Year students. The first part of the talk was about the history of the company. The next segment was about the different domains of work that the company offered. The third segment was about the 'work-life balance' offered by the company and had slides showcasing several office parties and outings. The fourth segment was about the values of the company, it had a lot of management jargon like 'growth opportunities', 'diversity', 'flat organizational structure' and so on. Everyone in the audience knew that it was all a load of corporate bullshit, but they patiently heard all of it.

The final presentation was delivered by the hot HR. Everyone paid extra attention to her talk. The guys in the audience laughed at all her planned jokes and responded eagerly to every question the HR put to them.

"I can't believe how hot she is. Half the guys will fail their interviews because of her" he said.

"She's not *that* hot!" she replied. He could sense a hint of jealousy in her tone.

Just then, the HR dropped a bomb on the audience and mentioned details of the package being offered. The gross component of the salary had been reduced by a small amount, which had been adjusted in the performance based bonus component.

He realized why the company had sent an HR as hot as her. She had been able to distract the audience from the minor but important change in salary structure.

"The smaller the package, the hotter the HR" she said to him with a smile as she saw him get irritated.

"I don't care about the package, I will ensure that I reach the HR round just to get a chance to talk to her. I love her accent, the way she says package... *'pha-kij'*, it's almost seductive" he said to her.

She responded with a punch on his shoulder.

"Focus on what's important, she just told us that the smallish package just got smaller" she said to him.

"I will accept whatever *pha-kij* she gives me" he said to her, the result of which was another punch.

The HR finally wrapped up her presentation and the aptitude test began almost immediately. The students were asked to spread out over the hall and sit with a large gap between adjacent students. Not that copying was too easy in an aptitude test. The tight time line made it into an 'every man for himself' situation.

The questions were just as he had expected. Mathematics problems that he had solved way back in high school along with some probability and logical reasoning problems. Midway through the paper, he came across the exact question he had criticised a day ago when talking to her.

Ramesh, Suresh and Rakesh...

Even the values of speeds at which the fictional characters were travelling had been copied straight from the book of Aptitude Tests that he had gone through. As soon as he read the question, he looked towards her. She read the question a minute later and looked at him. He gave her the 'I told you so' look and they both smiled as he marked the answer out of memory without having to solve the problem. She, being diligent, chose to solve the problem even though she had seen him mime the answer to her.

Both of them finished the aptitude well ahead of time and were confident of clearing the round. They waited at the cafeteria and in an hour, word arrived, that the results had been displayed on the placement cell notice board. The results weren't in any order and they just listed out the names of students who had cleared the aptitude test. As expected, their names featured on the list.

Despite having been sure of her performance in the aptitude test, she felt a hint of nervousness as she hunted for her name on the list. She felt relieved after seeing her name there. On the other hand, he was calm and the only thing odd about his behaviour was that he kept uttering the word '*pha-kij*' every now and then.

"I'm getting nervous" she said to him.

"Why?"

"That's the problem. I don't really know. I guess it's because I'm scared of being rejected" she replied.

Boy, do I know how that feels! He thought to himself.

"Don't worry, you'll sail through."

"How do you know?" she asked him.

"Because you're a class topper, your resume is filled with loads of authentic achievements. You're carrying a newspaper clipping with your photo on it for winning India's biggest quiz...

and last but not the least... you're hotter than the HR" he said to her, with a wink.

"Shut up!" she said to him with another punch on his shoulder.

"You know what, your punches are freaking painful and it's high time someone told you that before you break some poor guy's shoulder. *Mard ko bhi dard hota hai*" he said to her in an exaggerated tone. It made her laugh and distracted her from the thoughts of the interview that was slated to start in a short while.

His name was called out amongst the first lot of students to be interviewed. She wished him good luck and saw him walk in confidently.

Half an hour later, he walked out of the placement cell building and looked around for her. She was nowhere to be seen. He waited for her near the building and spent an hour there wondering when she'd get done with her interview. She finally emerged with a smile on her face as she saw him.

"How did it go?" he asked her.

"It was fun, what about you?"

"It was boring" he replied.

"Let's go to the cafeteria and talk" she suggested as they made their way to their favourite college hang out spot.

"By the way, you lost the bet. I've been told that everyone was asked to draw the asterisk triangle in the technical round" she said to him.

"No, you did not win the bet" he replied.

"What? They didn't ask you that question."

"They did but I refused to write the code."

"What?" she said aloud, with surprise.

"Yeah. So what happened was... I walked in for the technical round. The interviewer started off with the usual questions, what are your favourite subjects etc etc. Then he asks me to write a program for a palindrome, I did that. Then he shows me a piece of paper with the famous asterisk triangle and says, write a program in C to display this output..."

"Then what did you do" she asked impatiently.

"I looked at him and said:

Can I ask you a question?

He says – Sure, go ahead.

From your years of experience in the industry, can you tell me any real life instance when you've actually had to draw any geometric figure made up of asterisks to solve a problem for a client?

He looked at me, stunned, and said – No I went on with the next phase of messing with his head and said – OK.

If I somehow get hired in this company, do you foresee any instance when this particular ability to draw geometric figures out of asterisks will help me serve clients better?

He replies – No, but you are supposed to know how to code this program.

I paused for a brief while and then continued speaking and said – Sure... but before I write this program, I just want to tell you that there are four different solutions to this problem, all of which are available on geekinterview dot com. Three of them involve 'loops', the last one involves 'recursion'. Which approach do you want me to use?

He took a sip of water and said – In the interest of time, let's move on to the next question" he said to her as she had a look of shock on her face.

He enjoyed the look on her face and laughed as she punched him once again on the shoulder.

"I hate you" she said to him.

"*Arrey*, why?"

"Because I had to write that stupid program and you gave some *gyaan* and escaped" she replied.

"Alright forget that... tell me how did your HR round pan out?" he asked.

"It was fine, unlike you I was not in awe of the HR and gave well thought out answers to all her questions. How was your interaction with the so called hot HR? I bet you have some story about that as well" she replied.

"No not really. It was all a blur, all that I remember is looking at her Angelina Jolie lips moving as she spoke and I remember a few words here and there..."

"Words such as?" she asked.

"I only remember the seductive ones. I remember that she used the word '*pha-kij*' a lot and then she said something about 'rewarding loyalty' and 'late nights'..."

"Enough. You're insane" she said to him.

He could see the irritated expression on her face and found it very funny. She let him laugh for a bit before giving him yet another punch on his shoulder.

"Any idea when the results will be out?" he asked.

"The interviews will go on for another couple of hours and then they'll take time to select and reject people. So I think around seven or eight at night is when we can expect the results to be declared" she replied.

"Damn! I have to get back to the hospital way before that" he said to her.

"Don't worry, I'll be here till the results are declared, I'll call you and tell you whether we made it" she said to him.

"We'll make it" he said to her.

"Hey you know the crazy interview story regarding Vijayendra?" she asked him.

"Who? Rathore?"

"Yeah dude. Vijayendra Rathore" she answered.

"What about him?" he asked.

"So the story is that during the course of his HR round, he accidentally let slip the fact that he has given the GRE and secured a kick ass score. So the HR asked him why they should consider him for the job when they already know he'll leave for his MS. So he tells her that he is a Rajput and that Rajputs are very loyal and if she gives him the job, he will never leave the company!"

"What? That's insane!" he said as he burst out laughing.

"I hope he gets the job, random answers like that shouldn't lead to a rejection" she said.

They spent the rest of the afternoon talking about their interview moments until he left for the hospital.

At the hospital he narrated every detail of the first ever job interview of his life. He no longer felt bad about the fact that his mother did not respond. Somehow, his state of mind had become a lot more positive ever since he had resumed his friendship with the girl he now had feelings for. For some reason, he had a lot of hope that things would work out for him in life. The times when he'd despair about being all alone were over. *She* was with him, there hadn't been a single day in recent weeks when he hadn't spent hours and hours with her. Before she came into his life, all he did was survive; she had made him rediscover what it meant to be alive.

Just as he was thinking about her, he received a phone call from her.

"Hello" he said as he answered the call.

"Duuuuuuuude! We're not *berozgaar* anymore!" she yelled into the cell phone.

"Awesome, congrats" he said to her.

"Congratulations to you too! We are so going to party tonight and get drunk" she said to him excitedly.

He remembered the deal they had struck a week ago.

"Let's do it" he replied.

"Eight o'clock sharp, I'll pick you up from the hospital. Bye" she said to him and hung up.

He felt a mix of happiness and excitement. He had a job in his hand and soon he'd get drunk for the first time in his life.

He touched his mother's feet as he sought her blessings and felt a little guilty about having thoughts of drinking alcohol.

"Just this one time *maa*, never again I promise" he said to his mother.

When Dr. Roy arrived at the ward for the daily round, he informed the doctor about his placement. Dr. Roy patted him on the back and congratulated him. He signalled to the doctor that he wanted to talk to him outside the ward; something that was becoming a daily routine.

"I think I know what you want to say. You're planning to ask her out tonight, right?" said the neurologist.

"No. I've decided not to tell her for a while, I'll try and find out from her best friend if she has feelings for me" he replied.

"Not a bad idea, but the best friend will surely tell her about your questions."

"It'll be a comparatively smaller risk than a direct ask out" he said. "True."

"I wanted to ask you something else."

"Go ahead."

"I am planning to get drunk tonight. It's part of a pact I made with her... any tips so I don't end up making a fool of myself. I have never touched alcohol before" he said to the doctor.

The doctor had a smile on his face; he found these conversations with the young man very refreshing. They always brought back memories of his younger days.

"Sure, I think I can help you there. First tip, don't drink on an empty stomach. Second tip, drink loads of water between drinks. Third tip, don't drink after getting drunk."

"How will I know that I'm drunk?" he asked Dr. Roy.

"Believe me you will know" said the doctor with a smile on his face.

"Alright. Wish me luck."

"Good luck, have fun" said the doctor before walking off to the next ward.

He looked at his watch, he had almost an hour and a half to spare. He decided to rush back to his hostel room and get dressed for the night and then take a *rickshaw* to the hospital. He did not want to spend his energy tonight, travelling by his cycle. He wanted to save it up for all the dancing.

He was back at the hospital, where he waited at the reception. Close to eight o'clock, he got a call from her asking him to meet her outside the hospital entrance. He did as told and saw her car from afar as she made her way to the hospital gate.

She parked the car next to him and he opened the door to

get in. As soon as he opened the door he was stunned by what he saw. She was wearing a dark blue polo neck top and a black pencil skirt, that had a hemline which ended an inch above her knees. He had never seen her wearing a skirt before. The sight of her legs was breathtaking.

"Are you going to sit down or do you plan to just stand outside my car all night?" she said to him with a straight face, even though she was enjoying watching the effect her looks were having on him.

He got into the car and did not say a word. He was so conscious of the fact that she was wearing a skirt that he was completely focused on making sure he did not stare at her legs.

"Did you notice something special about me tonight?" she asked him.

He did not know how to respond. Is she looking for a compliment? I should've complimented her, what a fool I am! Alright, give her an answer before she thinks you're a jackass.

"Uh, you're wearing a skirt?" he replied and held his breath, wondering whether he had given the answer she had expected.

She laughed.

"Not that dude. Look at my feet, I'm wearing heels!" she said to him.

"Oh wow! You're wearing heels" he said nervously, not exactly sure of how she wanted him to respond.

"*Arrey*, you still haven't noticed the special thing. Look down" she said to him and pointed towards her feet.

He looked at her feet, she was wearing black colored high heels.

"You're driving the car, wearing heels?" he said in surprise.

"Now you got it. I am driving with heels on. It's an art, not every girl can do this" she replied.

"And no man would openly admit it, even if he could" he added, making her laugh.

He looked at her as she skillfully managed to use the accelerator, brakes and the clutch despite wearing heels.

"This looks really difficult, you should've put this on your resume" he said to her in jest.

"Maybe in phase two of placements I will" she replied.

She concentrated on driving as they got closer to Hiccups; she had to look for a decent parking spot. She found one close to the entrance.

"Hey I did not tell you the plan for tonight" she said to him.

"I thought it'll be pretty straightforward, get in, get drunk, get out" he replied.

"Not really. I can drive with heels when I am normal, not when I am drunk. In fact I don't know what I can or can not do when I'm drunk, it'll be the first time for me as well. Remember?" she said to him.

"OK. So what's the plan?" he asked.

"It's fairly simple. We have a couple of cocktails, here at Hiccups. Then we dance like crazy. Then we buy some alcohol from a shop and take it to my place, where it will be safe to get drunk, since the house is basically all mine for the next two days" she said to him.

"As of now the plan sounds fine. Obviously I will be the one picking up the alcohol from the shop?" he asked.

"Obviously. A man's got to do what a man's got to do" she said to him as they got out of the car and headed straight inside Hiccups.

He let her walk a step ahead of him so he could admire her beauty as she walked into the club. The combination dress she wore clung to her body, revealing how perfect her figure was. The pencil skirt accentuated her thin waist and statuesque legs; while the polo neck added to the beauty of her long, slender neck. As always, he was blown away by her flowing hair as he watched it bounce with each step she took.

They occupied a table and began talking.

"Hey I forgot to tell you one thing" he said to her.

"What?" she asked.

"You're looking beautiful" he said to her looking straight into her eyes, making her blush.

"Thank you, you're looking pretty handsome yourself" she replied, making him smile.

"Another thing. I have never had alcohol before in my life and in case I act like a complete fool or misbehave at all, apologies in advance and I give you permission to slap me" he said to her as she laughed.

"Chill dude. I don't think it'll come to that. I think we're the good kind of drunkards, not the pukey or misbehaving types. Just relax and have fun" she said to him.

"So what'll be your first drink, by which you lose your alcohol virginity" she said to him with a wink.

"I guess, the best way to lose one's virginity of any kind would be by having 'Sex On The Beach'" he replied with a naughty smile.

"Well said! Man, I wonder who came up with a name like that for a cocktail?" she asked.

"A very experienced man" he replied.

"Or woman" she added with a hint of a smile.

"Hey, how do we order two cocktails? What's the nomenclature? Do I tell the waiter, 'I'll have two sexes on the beach or 'I'll have sex on two beaches'?" he asked.

She had a confused look on her face and laughed only when she realized he was kidding.

"You forget it, I'll give the order" she said to him.

"As you wish" he replied.

The waiter arrived to take their orders.

"We'll have a non-veg platter" he said to the waiter, remembering Dr. Roy's advice about not having alcohol on an empty stomach.

"Anything to drink?" asked the waiter.

"Yes. I'll have a sex on the beach and so will he" she said to the waiter.

The waiter concealed a smile and then left.

She heard him laugh.

"Why are you laughing?" she asked him.

"That was too funny. 'I'll have sex on the beach and so will he'" he repeated her words in a voice that mimicked hers.

"Grow up!" she said to him with a roll of her eyes.

"Alright sorry" he said.

"It's cool, that was kinda funny" she said to him.

The waiter arrived soon with the platter and the two cocktails.

She held the cocktail glass aloft and gently struck it against his glass as they said cheers and took the first sip.

"Do you like it?" she asked him.

"It's nothing like I've ever tasted before. The taste is like you said, sweet and tangy. I like it" he said to her.

She felt thrilled that his first brush with alcohol had been to his liking. When they were close to finishing the first cocktail, they called for the waiter again.

"I'll have a Strawberry Daiquiri" she said to the waiter.

"Anything for you sir?" asked the waiter.

"What other cocktails do you serve?" he asked the waiter.

"Sir we have many cocktails for men, like Hole In One, Dirty Martini etc, but the bartender's specialty is Kamikaze. Would you like to try that?"

"What does it have?" he asked.

"Sir it's made of vodka, Curaçao triple sec and lemon juice" the waiter replied.

"I'll take it" he said to the waiter, after which the waiter walked away towards the bar.

"Do you even know what Curaçao triple sec is?" she asked him.

"I haven't got a clue" he answered.

"It's an alcohol extract made of orange peels. But why did you order it without knowing what it means?" she asked.

"I liked the name, Kamikaze"

"That's insane. Ordering a cocktail because of the name" she commented.

"Oh madam! Why do you think half the world orders 'sex on the beach'?" he said in his defence.

"Hm... good point!"

The second set of cocktails arrived in no time. He liked the

Kamikaze as much as the first cocktail even though the taste of the two cocktails differed quite a bit. Kamikaze was a little more bitter as compared to Sex On The Beach.

All the while as he sipped on the cocktails, he tried to check if he was getting drunk. But he wasn't feeling any different. After they finished the second cocktail, she asked him if he wanted to dance. He got up instantaneously, grabbed her by the hand and took her to the dance-floor. His enthusiastic demeanour took her by surprise.

They danced with a lot more freedom and energy that night. There were several reasons for it. One was that they had finished phase one of placements on day one itself. Another reason was that they were excited about their plan to get drunk and finally it was the first time that both of them had consumed alcohol together. It added an element of thrill to their mindsets.

For the first time ever, he initiated physical contact with her on the dance-floor when he rested his hands on her shoulders as they danced to a song with moderately slow beats. It wasn't a weekend night and the music was a little less intense than usual, but they were having fun. Towards the last few songs, the DJ started playing soft romance songs. Most of the couples in the disco began to slow dance.

She looked at him and said, "Do you know how to do the slow dance?"

"Not really" he replied.

"Just follow my lead, it's very simple" she said to him.

"OK" he said.

She held his left hand and placed it on her waist; she then placed her left hand on his shoulder and held his left hand with her right hand. She moved from side to side and looked into his eyes with a smile. She could feel the tension in his right hand which was on her waist. His face was blank. She felt like laughing but did not, she knew that in a few minutes he would get used to it and start to relax. Meanwhile his brain was working overtime.

My hand is on her waist! What the hell am I supposed to do? Do I rest my hand on her waist, am I supposed to hold her a little tighter or do I loosen my grip? I can't loosen my grip any more, my hand will slip off and touch her hips. Don't let that happen at any cost! She'll think you're drunk! You'll be like those drunk people you threw your cycle on! Oh damn! I can feel the warmth of her skin through the fabric of her dress. Am I holding her too tight? Someone help me, please!

"Relax" she said to him, almost as if she could hear his thoughts.

"OK" he said to her, putting up a calm expression, even though he was going crazy.

When the hell will this song end? Why is this the longest song?

Just then, she started to sway her hips from side to side as the tempo of the song increased a little. Each time she swayed to the right, it caused his hand to press harder against her waist. He looked at her face, her eyes were closed. That was when he had a thought.

If she's relaxed, why the heck am I getting so tense? Chill out and have fun.

With his mind finally at ease, he moved with a lot of freedom and got over his inhibition of physical contact with her. She immediately felt his grip on her waist tighten a bit and the rest of his body relax. She opened her eyes and smiled.

"This is fun *naa*?" she asked him.

"Yes it is" he replied as they danced until the last song for the night was played.

As soon as the music was over, they had a quick dinner and then headed off towards her house. On the way she stopped her car in front of a shop that went by the name of '*Black Dog – Wine Shop*'.

"What do you want me to get?" he asked her.

"Get four cans of beer and one small bottle of vodka along with some soda. That should do the trick" she told him.

A few minutes later, he was back inside the car with a black plastic bag in his hand with the alcohol and soda.

"I don't know why they even bother with these black bags.

Everyone knows that any guy carrying a black plastic bag at night is carrying alcohol. It's so dumb" he said to her.

"I agree" she said as she turned on the ignition and headed towards her house. They reached her building in no time and she brought him up to her apartment.

She unlocked the door to the apartment and took him straight to her bedroom. He observed the setting of her room.

"You're a Clint Eastwood fan too?" he asked her after he saw the poster on her wall.

"I love him. He's the handsomest man ever. Just look at him. If there was a time machine, I would go back in time and marry him" she replied, making him laugh.

"*Oye* control *yaar*" he said to her imitating Govinda from Jodi No. 1, now it was her turn to laugh.

"What I meant was that I am a huge fan of Clint Eastwood. That look of his from *The Good, The Bad and The Ugly* is so awesome. If a guy proposes to me in that getup, I will say yes" she said to him.

He pulled out his mobile phone and made a pretend call.

"Hello, Just Dial – *yeh Clint Eastwood ka* getup *kahaan milega?*"

She burst out laughing and then punched his right arm.

They settled down in the room and decided to have the beer first. They drank up both the beer cans in a hurry to get drunk. Within minutes of finishing the second beer can, they felt a little light headed.

"*Arrey* I almost forgot, we need to record our behaviour for all times to come" she said as she pulled out her mobile phone and placed it at a vantage point on top of her study table and started the video recorder.

"What do we do now?" he asked.

"I don't know" she replied.

"Damn! We should do something *naa* to show that we are drunk. Let's do one thing, you sing a song and then I'll sing a song and the one who screws up the lyrics more is the one who is drunk or rather more drunk.

What say?" he suggested.

"No way! I'm not singing, even if I am totally sloshed, which I am not" she said.

"Then what?"

"Let's do one thing, let's finish the vodka and then decide" she said.

"How did they come up with a name like vodka?" he asked.

"I don't know" she said as she mixed some vodka with soda in two glasses and handed one over to him. He looked at the glass in his hand for a while and then said out loud.

"Damn you vodka. Who did your *naamkaran*? Who?"

"I think you're finally getting drunk, I know I am. I can feel it, my head is spinning a bit" she said to him.

"Finally! Now sing a song" he said to her.

"You sing first, then I will sing" she said.

"No, it's ladies first" he replied.

"That is bull shit. Men just came up with that phrase so that they could make women stand ahead of them in queues and stare at their asses" she said, the alcohol finally talking in place of her.

"Men are smart, *saala*" he replied.

"Nothing like that, even women are smart. Women just go ahead in the queues, men can keep watching their asses, who cares" she said to him.

"Everyone is smart, *saala*" he responded as they both burst out laughing.

"Why are you saying *saala saala* all the time?" she asked him.

"It's the most accepted bad word that can be uttered in a sentence. Better than using the F word" he answered.

"Hm... Tell me one thing. Why do men use the F word so often?" she asked.

"To make up for the lack of it in real life. They get to do it so few times that they compensate for it by saying it all the time" he replied.

They laughed about that for a long time. There was silence for a while as they drank the vodka and she poured out another glass, leaving only half the amount of vodka in the bottle.

"Now you sing a song *naa*" she said to him.

"OK. I will sing one of my favourite songs. *Bulla Ki Jaana.*
Here goes. *Ting ting tididing – Ting ting tididing.*

Bulla ki jaana main kaun hoon
Bulla kiii jaana main kaun hoon

Naa main something naa something
Naa main something naa something
Naa main something naa mein paun

Bulla ki jaana main kaun
Bulla kiii jaana main kaun

Thank you" he said after his rendition of a very popular song
by Rabbi.

She laughed all the while when he was singing, right from the
beginning with his start of *'ting ting tididing'* and when he was
done, she clapped and hooted like crazy.

"Thank you" he said repeatedly.

"Now your turn" he said to her.

"I can't sing" she said.

"Not fair *yaar*, I sang, without background music and lyrics;
but I sang. You can't backtrack" he said to her.

"OK. I will do something better than sing..."

"What?" he asked her.

"I'll tell you a dirty joke. What say?" she said.

"Dirty joke? As in toilet joke or non-veg joke?" he asked.

"Obviously non-veg" she clarified.

"*Arrey*, what is so obvious about that. Toilet jokes are dirtier
than non-veg jokes" he said to her.

"Whatever! I'll tell a non-veg joke. OK?" she said.

"*Irshaad*" he replied.

"What do you call a maid servant, who gives blow jobs?" she
asked.

"I don't know. I've never met one" he replied and the two of
them burst out laughing.

"No no. That is not the joke" she said after controlling her laughter.

"I know that's not the joke... that's the tragedy of my life" he said and fell off his chair laughing.

"Wait *naa*, let me finish the joke" she said to him.

"OK. OK. *Irshaad* again"

"What do you call a maid servant, who gives blow jobs? The answer is – *Sakkubai*" she said.

There was a loud roar of laughter as she competed the joke, with both of them ending up with tears in their eyes.

"That was too good. Best joke ever" he said to her.

"Let's drink to that" she said as she poured out the remainder of the vodka into their glasses.

They were drunk to such an extent that neither of them realized how little soda had been added to the drink they were just having.

"Hey, I just thought of a nice game we can play. It's called *'One thing you didn't know about me.'* I read about it on the net sometime ago" she said to him.

"How do we play it?" he asked her.

"It's simple. Let me explain with an example – I will tell you one fact about me that you didn't know and then you have to tell me a fact that I didn't know about you. The person who tells a fact that was already known to the other, loses the game. Got it?" she said to him, explaining the rules of the game.

"Yeah got it. You start, ladies first" he said to her with a chuckle.

"OK. One thing you didn't know about me is.... wait, let me think.... got it. I know the entire song *'tum toh thehrey pardesi'* by heart. And by that I do not mean the initial few verses, I mean the full nine minute song" she said to him.

"That is an achievement. You should put that also on your resume" he said to her.

"Shut up! Now your turn"

"OK. One thing you didn't know about me is that I can actually move my ears" he said to her.

"What? Seriously? Show me how you do it" she said excitedly.

He concentrated hard, since his brain was pretty scrambled thanks to the alcohol and then moved the muscles that lie right behind the ear. Initially the movement of his ears was so slight that she could barely see it, but in a few seconds he started to wiggle his ears quite noticeably.

"Holy crap! That is awesome" she said to him and tried to see if she could move her own ears. She couldn't.

"Yeah I know. I used to freak out my classmates initially. During the seventh and eighth standard, when you know guys start getting interested in girls, I started a rumor that women are attracted to guys who can move their ears" he said to her.

"What? That's insane!" she exclaimed.

"*Arrey* I was in a boys' school back then. At that age, guys used to believe all kinds of random stuff. Like once a guy told me that women get turned on by raindrops and he quoted movie songs as evidence."

"Raindrops, seriously?"

"Yeah. Just think about it *naa*, *tip tip barsa paani* and so many other songs are there where heroines make all these seductive expressions simply because it's raining and the lyrics are also sorta suggestive with the whole *bheega tan, jaage armaan* routine" he said to her as she laughed.

Now that the two of them were properly drunk, they were laughing for extended periods of time and often for no reason. His mind was only alert about one thing – that he should not throw up at any cost. Every time he felt a burp coming up, he got tense but fortunately for him he did not face the embarrassment of throwing up at a girl's house after drinks.

They played the game for quite a while as each round of divulging unknown facts about each other, got crazier and crazier.

"Your turn" she said to him, starting another round of the game.

"OK. One thing you don't know about me is... that if I built a time machine... I would go to the early 90s and beg Pamela

Anderson to marry me or at least go out with me for a date."

"You really have the hots for Pamela *naa*?" she asked him.

"She was my first crush and David Hasselhoff was my life's first villain" he said to her making her laugh.

"I don't know why all you guys fantasize about her" she said to him.

"Ever wondered why the word fantasize, has the word size in it?" he said, making her laugh.

"You're totally drunk" she said to him.

"You're drunk too. And it's your turn now and... new rule... we have to make disclosures that are more *sansanikhez* than the previous ones. OK?" he suggested.

"Alright. By the way let, me warn you, I am feeling super tired now and might just drop off to sleep on my bed anytime. You're comfortable *naa* on that chair?" she asked.

"*Haan*, don't worry about me. You tell me one *sansanikhez* thing I don't know about you" he replied.

"Alright, just remember the only reason I am telling you this is because I am drunk. When I am sober I will disown this statement."

"Yeah fine. What is it?" he said with anticipation.

"OK. Here goes... I have seen porn" she said with a touch of embarrassment.

"That's it?"

"What that's it? Did you already know that?" she asked him, disappointed with his lack of excitement.

"No, but it's sort of expected *naa*. If you would've told me that you have never seen porn, that would've been *sansanikhez*" he said to her.

"Wait then. I have something better. I have a collection of Japanese porn."

"Now *that* is *sansanikhez*!" he said with a wink.

"Thank you" she replied.

"No. I should... I should be the one to thank you. You have done so much for me... I should be the one to say thank you and

I am saying it. Thank you" he said in an emotional tone, a sudden change from the humorous one he had a few seconds ago. The drastic change in mood was a result of him being completely high.

"You don't have to thank me" she said to him.

"No, I have to. Without you, I would've been sitting alone in my hostel room, looking out from my window at this time of the night, writing some sad poem... waiting for the morning to arrive and fill some hope in my life. But you... you've changed everything.

I didn't know I could have so much fun despite everything that's going on in my life. You did not give up on me... even when I tried to walk away" he said to her.

"Why are you saying all this now?" she asked him.

"Because I'll never be able to tell you this under normal circumstances. I'm too scared of offending you. But, now that I am completely devoid of any inhibitions, I'll tell you one thing you didn't know about me.

I think you're the most beautiful girl I've ever seen, not just physically but in a more pure sense. Everything about you is beautiful. Even my vocabulary is drunk right now, so I can't come up with the right words to describe how beautiful you are and how everything about you is simply amazing.

The one thing you didn't know about me is that I like you... I like you a lot, more than you can imagine and I've wanted to tell you that for so long, but every time I see you or hear your voice... it's breathtaking and words fail me. That's about it" he said to her and waited for her to respond.

She looked at the stuffed toy that he had gifted her on her birthday, which lay on her bed next to the pillow. She thought about what he had said and felt glad about the fact that he had finally confessed his feelings to her. She looked at him with drooping eyes and savoured the look of anxiousness on his face. He looks so cute right now that I could kiss him, she thought to herself.

"You lost the game" she said to him finally.

"What?" he replied, bewildered.

"You were supposed to tell me one thing about yourself that I didn't know and you lost" she said.

"I'm sorry if I'm too drunk to understand what you just said. But I just gave this long speech about how I feel about you, please can you forget about the game for a second and tell me what you think about what I said?" he said to her in a pleading tone.

She let out a small chuckle.

"I know how you feel about me, I've known for some time now but I was waiting for you to get comfortable enough to say it" she responded.

"Really?"

"Yeah. Had I known that all I needed to do was to get you drunk, I would've done it last week itself" she said to him with a smile.

But he still had the same look of anticipation on his face, which reminded her that she was yet to tell him about her feelings.

"I am not that good with words, so I'll just tell you in plain and simple terms, I think you're an amazing guy. Ever since we've been hanging out for the past few months, you have become a big part of my life to an extent that I've almost stopped spending time with anyone else. That says a lot about how I feel about you.

So if you want me to say it explicitly, then here you go. I have feelings for you and I think we should start calling our outings and trips what they really are – dates" she felt goosebumps all over her body as she said those words.

"You know, I thought about this moment so many times with the fear of you rejecting me that I did not think about how I would react if you said yes" he said to her, honestly; making her laugh softly.

"You can react however you want" she said to him.

"Alright then. Let me thank the ones who are responsible for making this moment come true. Thank you whoever invented beer and vodka and kamikaze and most of all – the guy who made Sex On The Beach" he said out loud, as they both cracked up laughing together.

"Hey, after we wake up tomorrow, will we forget that this happened?" he asked her.

"Will we forget that you asked me out? No, plus we have it all on video" she said.

"I'm not taking any chances" he said, pulling out his cell phone.

"What are you doing?" she asked him.

"Couple photo, as proof" he replied, making her laugh.

He walked towards her as she stood up. When he was next to her, she put her hands around his shoulders as he took a picture of them, smiling together with their cheeks in contact. He then sent an sms to her cell phone which said –

Don't forget to check out the video in the morning, I asked you out and you said yes :)

"You're crazy" she said to him as she fell onto her bed once again.

"You're beautiful" he said, returning to his chair.

He closed his eyes, which were begging him to go to sleep. When he next opened them, fifteen minutes had passed and she was fast asleep on the bed. He saw her sleeping calmly on the bed, wearing her blue polo neck top and pencil skirt. Her long flowing hair extended over the edge of the bed and stopped short of the floor, almost as if they had a will of their own and did not want to get sullied. He observed how the fabric of her dress clung to her skin, accentuating her curves. Her face almost looked like it had a calm smile, with her lips parted just slightly. She reminded him of a delicate flower. What he had done to deserve a girl like her, he did not know.

He wanted to reach out and touch her just to make sure he wasn't dreaming, but he stayed in his seat, resting his head against the wall behind him. He closed his eyes once again and was overcome by sleep.

The next day, she was the first one to wake up. Her head was very heavy but she did not have a headache. She got upset by the fact that she had fallen asleep with her party dress on and hadn't changed her clothes for the night. That was when the memories came flooding back to her. The dancing, the drinking, the silly antics in her bedroom and then him confessing his feelings for her – she remembered everything. She looked at him as he slept, with his hands folded over his chest. How did he manage to sleep all night long on a chair in that pose?

She smiled as she remembered how he had suddenly become emotional, just before telling her what he felt for her. Alcohol makes men unpredictable, she thought to herself.

She got up and stood right next to him, watching him as he slept, oblivious to the fact that she had woken up. She did not feel like waking him up, but decided that it was time. She tapped him gently on the shoulder a few times. He woke up, feeling a little disoriented as he tried to come to terms with the unfamiliar location. Moments after he came to his senses, the memories of the night gone by returned to him in bits and pieces. Is she my *girlfriend* now? Have I just woken up in my *girlfriend's* bedroom? Am I looking like a fool, right after waking up?

"Hi, Good morning" she said to him with a smile.

"Hey" he said to her, feeling a little embarrassed about what had happened last night.

She waited for him to say something, but he just stared at her blankly.

"So? Anything you want to talk about?" she asked him, hoping to kick off the discussion on the events of the previous night.

"Can you tell me where the washroom is?" he asked her.

She was a little taken aback by his response but did not let it show on her face. She directed him towards the washroom in her uncle's room.

A brief while later, she emerged out of the attached bathroom in her own room and wiped her face dry with a towel. She heard a knock on her bedroom door, she let him in. He looked refreshed and a lot more awake than he had been a while back. He asked her to sit down on the bed and sat down on the chair in front of the bed.

"Do you remember what happened last night?" he asked her. She nodded.

"Alright, but just to recap, we got drunk and I think I sang a song which was the second most unexpected thing I did last night. The most unexpected thing being what happened towards the end. I sort of asked you out and you said yes. Do you remember that?" he said to her, looking at her with an expression that was serious but did not give away too much.

"Yes I remember that pretty well" she replied, unsure of which way the conversation was going to go.

"OK. All I want to tell you is that I was drunk and I don't remember my exact words, all I know is that when I woke up this morning, a lot of things did not feel right. This room is unfamiliar, I spent the whole night sleeping on a chair and my back is killing me, I think I still am a little hungover and my head is splitting with pain. However, there is one thing that does feel right – the memory of last night and the fact that I finally had the courage to tell you how I felt.

You have no idea how difficult it can get for a guy to tell a girl that he likes her. There are so many fears that engulf one's mind. Will she reciprocate my feelings or will it drive her away? How can I possibly find the right words to tell her how much she means to me? Is it not enough that I get to spend so much time with her? Why should I risk losing it all? What for?

But you know what... that risk is definitely worth taking. We've come so close to each other just being friends... imagine where we can reach if we're together. I am glad that I told you how I felt and I have no words to describe the feeling when you said you felt the same way.

There are some moments that will remain with us forever, etched into our memories for us to revisit in the future. That was one such moment and you know what... I believe that together we will have many such moments" he said to her.

"How do you do that? she asked him.

"Do what?"

"Find the right words at the right time" she said to him with a smile.

"All I need to do is look into your eyes, everything else falls into place" he replied to her.

"Don't you think we're getting too mushy?" she asked him with a smirk.

"A little bit of mush is allowed *yaar*, we can't just crack jokes and give each other *gyaan* all the time *naa*?" he said, making her laugh.

"Dude, you want to check out the video from last night?"

"Yeah, totally" he replied.

She asked him to sit beside her on the bed as she held her cell phone at an angle that allowed both of them to watch the video from the previous night. They watched the video in silence and she was the first to speak once it was over.

"I can't believe you sang *Bulla Ki Jaana* and without knowing the lyrics" she said as she started to laugh.

"I can't believe you have a collection of Japanese porn! You are a Goddess" he asked her.

"Shut up!" she said, feigning offence and raising her hand to punch him on the shoulder.

"OK. Sorry" he said, asking her to stop.

"I still can't believe it. I'll have to watch this video again and again to let it sink in. You actually asked me out. What made you do that?" she asked him.

"I think it was the dirty joke. The moment I heard that, I was like – this chic is awesome, I have to date her" he replied, making her laugh once again.

"Yeah, right" she said, rolling her eyes over.

"What made you say yes?" he asked her after a brief pause.

"Everything about you" she replied.

There was a brief period of silence. She looked into his eyes; he returned her gaze as neither of them blinked. He knew what was going to happen next. He broke the gaze to look at her lips.

Her luscious lips looked rosy and tender. She parted them just a bit as she moved closer towards him, inviting him to do the same. Both of them bent forward, bringing their faces very close to each other and kept moving even closer. Her lips were so close to his that she could feel the warmth of his lips. He gazed into her eyes once again, with a look that sought her permission. She closed her eyes signalling her consent. He looked at her lips once again as she parted them further. Each breath of hers, encouraging his lips to caress hers.

As he moved forward, he felt the first alluring touch of her lips. With his eyes now closed, he felt her hands reach his shoulders and then the back of his head. She ran her hands through his hair. Emboldened, he cupped her face with his hands; feeling her soft, flawless skin as she pressed against him and brought herself closer.

With each passing second his heart started to race faster. He savoured the taste of her lips while she probed him further. They lost track of time and space; it seemed to them like they had entered a whole new world, undiscovered, untamed, a world where there were no limits and no constraints – just their desire and their curiosity.

They finally broke the kiss when they were close to getting out of breath. His hands retreated as she moved away from him. Her hands passed over his shoulders and arms before she lay them over her lap. They opened their eyes but did not look at each other. She closed her eyes again to let the feeling linger on, he looked at her blushing face with a faint smile. They were breathing heavily to catch their breath.

She finally opened her eyes and saw him looking at her. He had a calm look on his face. She could see how moist his lips were, because of her kiss. It made her smile.

"So, how did it feel?" she asked him, with a look of anticipation.

He closed his eyes to relive the moment.

"It felt like... your lips were meant to be kissed by me" he replied, opening his eyes.

Her face turned red as another blush followed his reply.

"You just earned yourself another kiss" she said to him and moved closer to him. This time she moved the entire distance and kissed him, placing her hands on his shoulders for support.

Their second kiss was more comfortable and passionate as compared to the first. This time he was the one running his hands through her hair. He felt the long strands of her dense, silken hair and it almost distracted him from the kiss. He marvelled at the perfection of her body as she once again, pressed against him. All the while, he did not let his hands reach down below her shoulder. He made sure that he held himself back to just touching her face and her hair.

It was the first intimate experience of his life and he wanted it to be perfect. He let her guide the second kiss and allowed her to take over completely. All he did was follow her lead. She broke the kiss again. But only momentarily to take a quick breath, getting back into position and taking over from where she left when breaking the kiss. He tried to ensure he took in as much of the experience as he could. So many things were happening at the same time. His brain had so many new sensations to go through. He tried to keep track of all those sensations – her hands running through his hair and moving across his back, her body pressing against his, his own hands cupping her face. There was so much going on all at once.

They stopped kissing after what seemed to them like an eternity. Both of them took some time to get their breaths back and wipe their lips dry. He did not know what to say to her. Should I say something romantic or should I say something funny or should I just stay silent? He had no clue.

"You're a good kisser" she said to him with a smile, ending his dilemma.

"I swear I have no prior experience" he said to her cheekily, it made her laugh.

"Are you hungry?" she asked him.

"For?"

"Food! Obviously!" she said to him.

"*Arrey* what's so obvious about that. One could be hungry for so many things given our current situation.

Haven't you read Mills and Boons?" he said with a wink as she laughed.

"You've read Mills and Boons?" she asked him.

"Of course not. I was just messing around. But I have seen a lot of them around, including one on your study table *ka* shelf " he replied.

"Thank God. I can't date a guy who reads Mills and Boons" she said to him.

"And I know why!" he added.

"Why?"

"Because he wouldn't know what to do in bed, ever! There is more sex on the cover of a Mills and Boons than in the whole book" he said to her.

"What? So you have read Mills and Boons!" she exclaimed, having fun.

"*Arrey* I was a school kid back then, I flicked it from a girl who used to travel in my school bus. The cover had this sultry, hot woman and some dude in a very seductive pose. I was blown away. I did a guy scan of the book and..."

"Wait! What's a guy scan?" she asked.

"It's what we do when we get a book that we expect will have some action in it. We run through the pages at the speed of light and look out for keywords on each page. When we find the keyword, we read the rest of the page in the hope of reading some stuff about 'stuff'.

But that book did not have a single full length scene. Every time something was about to happen, some random emotional conversation would start. For example:

In the heat of their passions, Roger and Emily lay down on the bed. Roger caressed her body, making her purr with anticipation. Just then, Emily looked into his eyes and said "Roger, will you love me this way when I am old and frail. Will you be my savior?"

"Yes darling. Only if you'll be my savior" said Roger as they got lost in an embrace and went to sleep with their arms around each other.

That's the kind of crap I've read..." he stopped his rant against Mills and Boons because of her uncontrollable laughter.

"I'm sorry. Go on... don't stop now" she said to him.

"That was exactly what I wanted to tell Roger and Emily" he replied as she fell onto her bed laughing.

"It was the most frustrating experience of my life and I swore never to waste my time on another Mills and Boons book no matter how sexy the cover girl looked" he said, concluding his Mills and Boons experience.

"That is not what Mills and Boons books are about. You just had some bad luck, they're quite raunchy at times" she said, defending one of her favourite book genres.

"Well, I hope you have some of those in your collection" he said to her with a naughty smirk on her face.

"Alright, now enough of your jokes. I need some food, will you be OK with corn flakes?" she asked.

"Totally" he said to her as they got up and made their way to her kitchen.

After having a simple and quickly conjured breakfast of milk and corn flakes, the two started a conversation as they sat on chairs that were part of the dining table set. "So now, you re my boyfriend. I like the sound of that" she said to him as she rested her face on her hands kept on the table.

"Me too. But I have one question, now that you are my girlfriend, am I allowed to look at you '*us nazar se*'?" he asked her, making her smile and blush at the same time.

"You're not only allowed to, you're encouraged to do so. I've been doing it for weeks" she said to him.

"You've been ogling me without letting me know... how could you... *havas ki pujarin*" he said loudly, covering his chest with his hands in a very filmy gesture that made her laugh hysterically.

"You're completely crazy, do you know that?" she said to him.

"Yeah, I think you've mentioned it before" he replied.

He spent some more time with her at the apartment before leaving for the hostel. When she got back to her room after seeing him off, she received a message on her cell phone from him.

Today I totally get what Katy Perry meant when she said – I kissed a girl and I liked it ;) Haha... brilliant! – she replied as she had a quiet laugh about the whole thing.

Who would've predicted that things would move so quickly in just one night? She thought to herself. One night ago, they were friends celebrating a job offer and now, they were a couple who had just experienced their first kiss. Her first kiss... it finally happened to her, at the fag end of third year. She had finally found a man who she wanted to be with... a man she wanted to kiss.

9

The Award

It had been a few months since the first kiss and the two of them were having the time of their lives. They were now in the Final Year of their engineering course and college had become just another one of their hang outs. They spent all their time in college, together and were inseparable. Along with Suparna, they formed a three member project group and ensured that they maximised the time they could spend with each other during weekdays. Weekends were spent watching movies and hanging out at various cafes and restaurants all around the city.

As a couple, they were discovering new facets of each other's personalities. Both of them opened up a lot towards each other than they had during their 'single' days. He still never spoke of his mother and father, but did allow her to join him on his hospital visits whenever she felt like. He introduced her to Dr. Roy during one such visit. Dr. Roy was extremely happy for him and even she took a liking to the neurologist, finding him to be a very humble and modest human being, despite having the stature of a renowned doctor.

That day *he* had travelled to the hospital in her car. The couple reached the neurology ward, and like every occasion when he was accompanied by his girlfriend in front of his mother, he felt very nervous and tense. His girlfriend always found it amusing.

Dr. Roy arrived at his usual time and was surprised to find a girl in the ward along with the patient's son.

"Hi Dr. Roy, this is my friend..." he said to the doctor, introducing his girlfriend.

"Hi, nice to finally meet you" said the neurologist as he shook hands with her.

"*Friend*, you say?" the doctor asked, teasing the young man.

He pointed towards his mother and then made a hush sign, as the doctor and his girlfriend had a quiet laugh about the whole thing. The doctor then went on with his business and checked the patient's reports. The doctor informed the patient's son that there was no improvement in his mother's condition. The young man shrugged off the expected news and thanked the doctor. Dr. Roy asked the couple to step out of the ward since he wanted to have a word with them. Once they were outside, the doctor addressed the young woman.

"I have heard a lot about you from him and now that I have finally met you, all I can say is whatever he said was not nearly enough" said the doctor, making him feel embarrassed but in a nice way.

"Thank you doctor and I must tell you that he has a lot of faith in you and always has the nicest things to say about you" she replied.

"Does he? Well then I must tell you something about him. This man is the most determined human being I have ever met, and will achieve great things in life. No other person can go through so much hardship all by himself and still have a smile on his face that is genuine" said the neurologist.

"I swear this wasn't prearranged, I didn't ask him to say all that" he said to his girlfriend, as all three of them shared a laugh.

The three of them spoke for a little while longer and then the couple made their way back to the ward as the doctor moved along to complete his round.

"Dr. Roy is such a nice guy" she said to him.

"He's married" he whispered to her, as she elbowed him.

They spent some time at the hospital before leaving for the day.

Even though the two of them did not change their public behaviour ever since they began their relationship, word had spread in college that the two of them were a couple. They didn't really care about their relationship becoming public knowledge and went about their college lives as usual. But their classmates had changed their behaviour towards them a little. Guys did not try and approach her anymore and her interactions with most people barring Suparna were minimal.

All engineering college couples get celebrity status with people staring at them as they walked about. This one aspect irritated her the most.

"Why do people stare so much at couples in college?" she asked him.

"I think it's in the hope that someday they'll spot the couple making out in college and they don't want to miss out on it" he replied, making her chuckle.

Final Year was turning out to be a pretty laid back affair as compared to the previous three years; all they had to deal with was one theoretical subject and an internship. They spent a majority of their time in the office premises of a major IT firm, working on an R&D project. With him being really good at coding and she being fairly good at presentations, the person to benefit the most from their partnership was Suparna. Suparna did nothing but read books during the compulsory time they had to spend in office. The steady flow of cash continued in their lives thanks to the stipend amount they got as payment for the internship.

The internship experience offered the trio, the best of both worlds – the chilled out atmosphere of college and the only thing that corporate life could offer normal human beings – money! There were other benefits in being interns, they did not have the responsibilities of employees, their managers were not too bothered about what they did as long as they made progress as per plan but the biggest benefit was getting a glimpse of corporate life.

During the initial weeks, they were thrilled about the free coffee vending machine and wondered why the employees chose to walk a brief distance to the nearest *chai ki dukaan*. Everything seemed so classy and polished on the surface. But somehow the employees working there did not have the kind of enthusiasm that the interns had. There was a visible sense of frustration amongst some of them, almost as if they hated the place and

were working there just because they had no other choice. A lot
of them had CAT or GATE preparations books inside their
drawers, which could be seen whenever they opened or closed
them. Another aspect of corporate life that was new to the
couple was the *sutta* break.

Since he did not smoke he found it quite amusing to watch
male employees head out repeatedly for their *sutta* breaks. The
sutta masters would signal their intent to take a break by flashing
the two fingered *sutta* sign. One day he followed the *sutta* masters
to see what the *sutta* break was all about.

A bunch of smoke loving men would walk out of the office
door and make their way to the 'smoking section' where they'd sit
along with their colleagues and complain about corporate life.
The bad quality food in the cafeteria, the printer that stopped
working, the micro managing boss, the AC duct that made their
cubicles too cold for comfort and then the eternal complaint of
all engineers and male corporate employees – the lack of hot
women. During those ten minutes, he got a glimpse of how
those people probably behaved in college. These men now
showed their real selves only during the *sutta* break and returned
into their corporate forms the moment they entered the office
again.

When he reported this to her, she had quite a lot to say.

"I don't understand this complaint that all guys have about
the lack of hot women. If they wanted to work in an environment filled with phoenix raising hot women, they should've
become photographers for Fashion TV or something. Why the
hell did they do engineering? And look, I agree that there are
very few women in engineering colleges and most of them are
not exactly Miss India candidates, but then neither are most guys
Pierce Brosnan or Clint Eastwood equivalents.

Where do you think all those not-hot women from engineering colleges go? They get placed in these same companies. What
do these guys expect that every IT company will have some
special profile created just to recruit hot women for their ogling

needs?" she said in a rant against corporate men and their complaints.

"You know what, that's not such a bad idea! It'll lead to increased productivity" he commented cheekily.

"Shut up! Loser!"

"*Arrey* why are you getting so riled up?" he said, clearing his stance on the subject.

"I'm not getting riled up. I'm just wondering why men are so immature even after college and carry on their insane expectations into their work life. I mean, why do men keep such insanely high expectations?"

"It's not just men, even women have some crazy expectations. Look at the stuff written in some of the books that women read. Every guy has a broad chest and dense hair and owns a horse..."

"Owns a horse? Where'd you get that from?" she interjected.

"I don't know, I think it was there in that Mills and Boons book that I skimmed through" he said, making her laugh.

"Anyway, back to corporate life. It's not easy for women either. Have you noticed that pretty girl who sits in the corner?" she asked.

"I don't think I have" he lied.

"Yes you have, anyway that's not the point. She's pretty and attractive and every day she gets approached by some random guy or the other, who doesn't have the courage or skill to ask her out properly, so he'll do it under the garb of a tea break. Had they not been in the same office, some of those guys wouldn't have had the guts to go talk to her, but because they're colleagues, she has to put up with their advances, which are mostly lame.

Guys keep complaining about the lack of hot women, while women have to put up with an excess of pathetic men."

"Are you OK?"

"Of course I am OK. Why are you asking me that?" she replied.

"You seem to be in a ranting mode today" he said.

"I guess I am. I'll tell you the truth, I have started to despise corporate life. It's all so fake. One day we're in college wearing jeans and t-shirts, the next day we're in an office wearing boring formals and calling every other document a 'deliverable'.

Half the time in office is spent in meetings which end up going nowhere. And everyone starts to talk weirdly. Since when did Indians start saying 'hey how you doin' to each other? Every Monday, I hear people ask each other, 'how was your weekend'. As if they give a damn about each others weekends. But they still go ahead and ask. Then comes the thing that pisses me off the most – someone who comes to me and says the words: 'can I ask you a quick question'.

What the heck is a 'quick question?' What the hell is wrong with these people? What happened to them? How did they go from being normal to becoming fake corporate jerks?"

"And you are afraid you'll turn into one of them?" he asked.

"I guess that's what will happen to all of us. We'll all turn into people living our lives just for two days every week" she sighed.

"No. That will not happen to us. I assure you. You know why? Because some people escape the shackles of a monotonous life. Every company has exceptions; those people whose smiles are still genuine, who don't speak with a fake accent and who don't pretend to be *firangs* in an Indian body. So relax, no one can make you into something you are not, so just be yourself" he said to her.

From her expression he could make out that she appreciated his efforts to boost her morale. But just the other day, she had overheard a conversation between two employees at the cafeteria, where one of them said to the other – The corporate world is a shiny prison and the employees are prisoners who've been sentenced for life.

The sincerity with which those words had been said had freaked her out a bit. As it is, she was always afraid of living a life of boredom and monotony. And having tasted a bit of corporate life, she had started to dread the end of college life.

While she had her apprehensions regarding corporate life, he couldn't wait to enter it. He realized that there were quite a few pretentious people in the corporate world. But that to him was no reflection on the entire system. He was looking forward to the challenges of working in an environment like that. There were so many mini-games going on in the battlefield of office. Battles that ranged from getting the attention of the office hottie to getting the attention of the management.

While she looked at the negatives of corporate world and brooded over them, he observed the nuances and intricacies of day-to-day office life. How the ones who surged ahead of their peers were almost always people who spoke well and came across as enthusiastic workers as against those who were laid back in their approach. He knew that doing well in the corporate world was all about playing the game and he was eager to start. Just one semester lay between him and the next phase of life.

By the start of the last semester, they had reached a steady routine. Four days of the week were spent in the company as they went about completing their internship, while Fridays were spent in college. The weekends meant their usual routine of movies, dancing and spending time at the hill. The routine was broken when she suggested something unexpected.

"A double date?" he asked her.

"Yeah. It'll be so much fun" she said excitedly.

He had an amused look on his face.

"Whats with the weird look? Suparna had told me that you'll give me some crazy look after I asked you to go for a double date."

"Not just me, every guy will give his chic the look if she asks him to go for a double date."

"Why? What is the deal with you guys and double dates?"

"Because somewhere deep inside we have this fantasy that the other guy will get ditched and the night will end up in a threesome!"

"I am flabbergasted by male stupidity!" she exclaimed.

"Woah! I think this is the first time I've heard you use the word flabbergasted. It sounds really hot when you say it" he said to her with a naughty smile.

His words resulted in him getting yet another punch from his girlfriend.

Over the next few days, despite a lot of discussion and planning, the double date did not materialize. But something else came up in college that made for an excellent distraction.

Their college was preparing for it's centenary celebrations and she was all set to perform a group dance during the ceremony. The occasion was to be followed by the presentation of some specially created awards, one of which was for Academic Excellence, that was to be given to him. The award was a specially designed silver shield with the college emblem embossed on it.

The day he got the news, he went to the hospital to speak to his mother.

"*Maa*, you won't believe this but I'm going to receive an award during the centenary celebrations of our college. The President of India is the Chief Guest. It's going to be awesome"

"What is going to be awesome?" asked Dr. Roy, who had stepped into the ward for his daily round as the young man was speaking to his comatose mother.

"It's the 100th anniversary of my college's foundation and I'm being given a special award; to be presented by the President" he answered.

"Congratulations. What is the award for?"

"For Academic Excellence. By some fluke I somehow managed to top my branch across seven semesters" he said to the doctor with as much modesty as he could.

"Seven times is no fluke. I've seen how hard you've worked and it is a commendable achievement. Well done."

"Thanks Dr. Roy, for everything."

The neurologist went on with the job of checking on the patient and then left the ward. He then continued to talk to his mother about the award for a while before leaving for the day.

That night as he lay down on his bed at the hostel, he looked back at his entire journey in college. Those troubled first two years now seemed like a distant memory. He had very few good memories from that dark period of his life. Those times had been filled with struggle and pain.

Then came the phase when she entered his life. He smiled as he thought about the misunderstandings that had taken place between them during the early stages of their friendship. But the phase after that had been almost perfect. Ever since her birthday party, they had grown steadily closer. They did not have to do anything special to keep their relationship interesting, they simply had great chemistry, all they had to do was spend time together. But there was an important development on the horizon. Phase two of placements.

By virtue of their GPAs, both of them were eligible for the interview process of all the dream companies. He had a restriction of applying to companies that were based within his city, while she was free to go wherever she wanted.

He desperately wanted her to remain in the same city as him after college. But he did not tell her this. He did not want to bury her dreams under the burden of his responsibilities. Neither did he want to part ways with her. He wondered what fate had in store for him and how the story of his relationship with her would pan out.

The day of the centenary celebration arrived at last. She woke up very early and rushed to the airport to pick up her parents who had flown in to watch their daughter perform at the event. She was glad that her parents, especially her father had taken the time to attend the ceremony. It was nice of the college authorities to invite all the parents, she thought.

She arrived in college with her parents and found a huge crowd of media persons and security officials at the premises. That was when she realized that the President was actually present at her college. She felt proud of the institution where she was studying. She led the way to the auditorium and ensured that her parents got aisle seats and could see the stage clearly. She asked them to save a seat next to theirs, which she planned to occupy after the stage performance.

She saw him enter the auditorium and acknowledged his presence with a discreet wave of her hand, which she intentionally hid from her parents. Her parents were unaware of her relationship with him, she had decided to inform them at a later time when things got serious between them. To her it was no longer a matter of 'if'; she knew that it was going to happen. It was just a question of 'when'.

She saw him take a seat in the second row of the auditorium that had been reserved for prize winners, and knew that he would be able to see her clearly when she danced on stage. The dance was scheduled to take place an hour into the ceremony, after all the customary speeches had been delivered.

He was keen on watching her perform on stage and waited with baited breath as the stage lights went out, signalling the arrival of the dancers on the stage. When the lights came back on, the dancers could be seen sitting on their haunches in a V shaped formation. She was at the centre of the V. He focused his attention on her. The music began to play; it was a fusion music track overlaid with a voice-over depicting the changing face of India over the past century. He expected the voice-over to be cheesy and lame, but the creative team had done a good job. The first seven minutes of the performance was a group dance that was executed almost perfectly by all the members of the dance team but then came another period of darkness on the stage and when the lights came back on, she was standing alone on stage in a different wardrobe than what she was using for the group dance. He wondered how she had managed to change so quickly during the few seconds of stage darkness.

The music then changed all of a sudden, the voice-over was replaced by a sample from the 70s song 'Dum *Maaro* Dum', where the words *'duniya se humne liya kya, duniya ne humko diya kya'* were played to a scorching beat, on which she danced with all her skill and style. Her dance moves were not meant to elicit hoots and whistles, but the *tapori* crowd amongst the student audience went ahead and whistled and hooted away to glory. They did not care that the President of the country was present in the auditorium. He could see from her facial expression that she did not appreciate the hooting at all, but she did not let it affect her performance.

After her performance was over, she got a great ovation from the crowd. She ensured that she made eye contact with him. She smiled as she saw him applaud with a lot of enthusiasm. She bowed before the audience once she was joined by the rest of the dance group. A few minutes later, he saw her make her way from back stage to the aisle seat next to her parents. He looked on as they hugged and congratulated their daughter. They were so happy about the fact that she had performed a dance performance in front of the President of the country.

That was when he looked around the auditorium, the place was filled with proud parents. Every award winner had brought his parents along. Every a ward winner but him. He had no one to look at him with the kind of pride that only a parent can feel. He was still alone, nothing had changed for him over nearly four years. This was probably the greatest moment of his career thus far and his mother was going to miss it. Was he fooling himself by believing that his achievements and accolades would make up for the time that had been lost? No matter how many awards he won, no matter how many shields and medals he won; nothing could change the fact that his mother was at a hospital, lost somewhere between life and death.

A sinking feeling started to overcome him. His name was announced. He walked onto the stage.

She looked on and struggled to control her loud cheers as she saw him climb the steps to the stage. She saw him walk up to the President and collect his shield. The shield looked spectacular, almost as though he was holding a large silver flame in his hand. But there was something wrong. She noticed it at first when he looked towards the cameras and posed for the photograph. He was smiling, but it was an empty smile. There was a certain sadness in his eyes as he walked past the President after bowing his head and got off stage. He did not return to his seat and quietly exited the auditorium. She knew that something was wrong, but couldn't figure out what it was.

She dialled his cell phone number, he did not answer. She tried it again, it was switched off. She was very concerned but there was nothing she could do; her parents were sitting right beside her and it would seem very odd if she was to leave for no apparent reason. She decided to wait till she was back home and alone in her room. But that time came too late in the day, several relatives kept dropping by her uncle's house to meet her parents. Once at home, she kept trying his cell phone number, but it was either switched off or he wasn't answering. Her anxiety was finally reduced when he sent her an sms late in the evening:

hi... sorry for not answering your calls... i'm going through a bit of a rough patch... will be off the radar for a couple of days... don't mind p.s. – u were great on stage!

She wondered what rough patch he was going through. She looked at the time, it was close to eight o'clock, it was too late for her to get to the hospital and talk to him there. She knew that he stayed in a boy's hostel and she'd never be able to get to his room. There was no way that she could speak to him unless he decided to use his cell phone, which she knew he would not do. She realized that there was nothing she could do and decided to wait for the next day.

It was an overcast Sunday morning and she dropped her parents off at the airport, well in time for their noon flight to Bangalore. As soon as she was done with that, she rushed to the hospital. She parked her car and quickly reached 'Neurology Ward 7'. She did not enter the ward and simply peeked inside through the square window on the door. She could not see him inside. She cursed a few expletives under her breath. Now what? She thought to herself. She thought about her options for a while and decided to try and see if she could have a word with Dr. Roy.

She found the way to the neurologist's office by inquiring at the reception. It was lunchtime and Dr. Roy was not in the office.

She decided to wait near the office to have a word with the doctor.

Dr. Roy did not take too long and looked surprised as he saw her standing outside his office.

"Hello" he said to her politely.

"Hi Dr. Roy. I'm sorry to bother you like this..." she explained the situation to him as best as she could "...so do you have any idea what's going on?"

"Not really. I met him last evening; he had brought a shield to show his mother. I thought he was looking a little tired. But now that you make me think of it, he did look a little down. Anyway, don't worry too much, he's been through a lot of tough times, he'll be fine" said the doctor, in a bid to comfort her.

"Alright. Doctor, if it is not too much to ask, can you give me your phone number and let me know if you hear from him. I am a little worried about what happened, it was very odd... the way he behaved."

Dr. Roy gave her his number and took hers so that he could call her and inform her if he saw her boyfriend. She thanked the doctor for his time and left the hospital.

She reached her car and was thinking of places that he could have gone to. He wasn't in college for sure, she had checked before reaching the hospital, now that he wasn't at the hospital either, it left only one probable option. The hill.

She drove swiftly and found herself at the foot of the hill within an hour. She then drove the car up the hill and reached as far as the hill road went. Parking the car in a hurry, she walked up the remainder of the distance to his plot with quick steps. Rain threatened to come down any moment. She thanked her stars that she had a raincoat on, not to guard against the rain, but more to protect her from the gusts of cold wind.

She breathed a sigh of relief when she saw his cycle near the banyan tree, but she still couldn't see him. She walked closer towards the edge and finally saw him sitting right on the edge of the hill with his legs dangling over the edge. She could see him staring down blankly at the steep drop below.

She called out his name, he turned around to look at her. He did not smile or get up from his position, he just signalled to her to come and sit next to him. She was very unsure of what to expect given his detached behaviour. She sat down on the ground, close to him but with no part of her body over the edge. She saw the pained expression on his face, he looked tired, almost as if he hadn't slept the night.

"What's wrong?" she asked him in a concerned voice. He did not respond.

"Please tell me what happened?" she asked again. He continued to stare into the emptiness below him.

"Talk to me... please" she implored him.

"I've never really told you what happened to my mother right?" he said, looking into her eyes.

She shook her head in silence.

"It's almost been four years to that day. I woke up because of a phone call, it was from the police. They informed me that my mother had been found seriously injured and bleeding on a roadside, that was on the way to a temple she visited every morning. They asked me to arrive at the hospital where she had been admitted.

By the time I reached the hospital, she was undergoing a surgery. The only other person with me at the hospital was my maternal uncle, who was there just because the police had found my mother's cell phone and dialled the first number on it, which was his before they reached me on the phone. He waited for about an hour, barely saying a word to me and then left after handing over an envelope with a cheque in it.

The surgery went on for four hours. My mother had suffered severe head trauma and even though the doctors did not tell me at the time, her life was in grave danger. During the surgery, the police informed me that she had been struck by a car, but there were no eye witnesses. My mother used to go to the temple very early in the morning, at about five thirty. I got the phone call at seven. No one knows when exactly she was struck by the car or how long she lay injured before some passerby called the police.

The police told me that they had filed an FIR and would investigate the case. None of that mattered to me, all I knew was that my mother was hurt very badly and I wanted to do something to help her. But there was nothing I could do. Nothing.

The worst kind of helplessness... is what you feel... when all you can do is watch while your mother struggles for every breath.

After the marathon surgery, they kept her in the ICU. She was in a coma. The doctors told me that she had very slim chances of surviving. I could scarcely believe what was happening.

We had just picked up the pieces of our lives after my father's death. We were living simple lives with some simple joys. Just my mother and me in our little world. I had just given my engineering entrance exam, I knew I had done well. She was so proud that I was going to become an engineer. A mother never has to say a word to tell her son how proud she is of him; one can see it in her eyes. I saw it in her eyes every day. We had never harmed anyone or done anything to deserve the kind of punishment we were going through.

And yet, there I was, all alone, standing guard in front of the doors to the ICU. Naively thinking that somehow my presence would stop her from dying. That night was the first time I really hoped that God existed.

You see this *rudraksh* that I wear around my neck all the time. It is sacred to me, because it has my mother's blessings in it. A few days before my mother's accident, she had given it to me – saying that it would protect me. I don't know why she had given it to me, but that became the one source of strength for me during the days that followed her accident.

Those initial few days after her accident were the toughest; I did not know whether or not she would survive. In addition to that, I faced the pressure of coughing up the money for the surgery and treatment. My uncle, my mother's brother, abandoned her when she needed him the most. All he did was hand over a cheque with a figure on it. He did not come to the hospital even once after the first day..."

"Why?" she asked him.

"You know those families where everyone stands by one another in their times of need? Well, my family isn't like that. There's a decade long property dispute going on amongst my mother's generation. It's a bitter, bitter dispute that has turned brothers and sisters against each other. My father's side did not really give a damn about my mother because my father was long gone. All I received was some sympathetic words. That was when I came to understand the harsh reality of life. Good things don't always happen to good people. Sometimes the worst of things happen to the best of people.

I sold the house that I lived in with my mother, it helped in paying off the surgery costs. I then sold every piece of jewellery my mother owned, every single possession of ours that could sell, I sold. I had ripped apart the cheque that my uncle gave to me in a fit of rage, but I did not have to regret it. Despite everything, I managed to stay afloat during those stormy tides.

I found a place to stay at a very cheap hostel, the same one where I stay right now. Fortune finally smiled and the engineering entrance results and the state board exam results were declared. I won a couple of scholarships that took care of my college expenses. I cut out all my expenditures; all I did was go to college, the hospital and back to my room. I was under so much pressure and I got so used to facing it all alone that I stopped meeting old friends or making new ones. Until you came along.

You have no idea, how much you have changed my life in the past one year. For a while, I actually thought I had recovered from the scars of those dark times. But yesterday at the presentation ceremony. I looked around and saw all those students with their parents. Even your parents had come to watch you perform on stage. I saw the joy and pride on their faces when you were dancing.

I then made my way on the stage to take the award from the President of India… a man whom I respect a lot. And I really missed my mother and my father. My father was gone; my mother was in a hospital fighting for her life. Even after four years of doing everything I could to set things right, things were just the same. My mother is still lying in hospital, not having spoken a word and not having opened her eyes in four long years. I go there every evening and I sit down and talk to her as though she is listening. But she isn't, is she? If she could hear me, she would have returned. For some reason she is in front of me but is still lost. And what can I do about it? Nothing. I am powerless. My success and achievements are all meaningless. Like stars in the sky on a dark moonless night, they shine but give no light!

My mother should have been there watching me get that award. After everything I have done, I deserved to have her in front of me at what was one of the greatest moments of my life. But she wasn't there. She's lost... gone somewhere I can't find her. And all I can do is wait. How long will I have to wait? How long can I wait?"

"As long as it takes" she said to him.

She moved closer to him and put her arms around him. He continued looking at the slope of the hill with his eyes downcast. She knew that she had to say something to get him to cast away the shadow of negativity that had taken over him.

"Look, I will not say that I can understand what you are going through. I can't. Only you know what you've been through. But you are not alone. Your mother is alive and I know that she will return. If she had to leave you, she would've gone long back.

But you need to understand that you are not alone anymore and I am here for you. Being in a relationship is not just about parties and dates; it's about making each other a part of our lives. You do not have to go through this alone."

"Why should you bear the burden of my misery? I am better off going through this part of my life alone" he said to her.

"I won't let you. Wherever you disappear to find solitude I will find you and we'll see this through together.

But I'll appreciate it if the next time you just tell me where you're going, petrol has become expensive you know!" she said to him, making him smile.

Just then it started to drizzle, she got up and tugged at his hands until he relented and got up to take shelter under the shade of the banyan tree. Pretty soon it was pouring, but the thick foliage of the banyan tree protected them from the rain. Meanwhile, she told him about how she went looking for him to college and the hospital before landing up at the hill.

"How did you know I'd be here?" he asked.

"A girlfriend's hunch" she said to him and flashed her lovely smile.

"How do you do this?"

"Do what?" she asked.

"Come to my rescue each time I'm about to give up."

"That's part of a girlfriend's job description" she said to him with a wink.

He looked at the scene around him, the dark overcast weather and the pouring rain made everything seem so gloomy and amongst that gloom, she stood in front of him, smiling and bringing cheer into his world. What made her search for him, despite him telling her that he wanted to stay away for a while? Why did she care so much about him? What had he possibly done for her to deserve such love?

That was the first time the word love entered his thoughts. Was she in love with him? The moment he asked himself the question, he realized that he did not really care, he knew he was in love with her. He took a step back to look at her. She was innocently wiping off a few drops of rain from her raincoat. He touched her chin with his fingers and looked into her eyes. He moved a step closer to her, clasped her hands in his and kissed her. It was an intense kiss that took her by surprise.

When he finally broke the kiss, it seemed to her to be their longest kiss. She kept her eyes closed for a few seconds after the kiss, like she always did, to allow the feeling to linger on. At last when she opened her eyes, she saw him looking at her with an anxious look on his face, as though he was debating something in his thoughts. She did not say a word for a while and waited for him to speak. But he was silent for too long.

She held his face in her palms and said "What is it?"

He took a deep breath before speaking.

"I don't know if this is the right moment to say it, but I have to tell you something..."

"What?"

"I love you" he said to her slowly, with a lot of sincerity.

As soon as she heard those words, she could feel herself blushing. She looked away from him for a second to look at the rain, the clouds, the lush green hill side; she wanted to capture this moment in her memory forever. She then studied his expression. He had an expectant look on his face. She thought he looked adorable as he was trying to hide his nervousness. She knew that his heart was racing twice as fast as hers. She kept him waiting for a little while longer, enjoying his vulnerability that increased with each moment.

"I love you too" she finally told him with a smile and watched his ears turn red.

She found it very cute. She wanted to kiss him, but before she could do that, he held her at her waist and lifted her up in the air. He carried her away from the shade of the banyan tree and into the rain. He swung her around a couple of times as if they were the lead pair of a Bollywood movie dancing in the rain. While he carried her in his arms, the rain poured over both of them. He faced the direction of the distant fort and yelled:

"You heard that? She loves me! You heard that... king of the ancient fort? My queen has arrived and she's better than all your thirty queens combined!"

She couldn't help but laugh at his boyish celebration as he carried her around for a while before returning to the cover of the banyan tree. After he calmed down a little, he looked a little embarrassed.

"Sorry... I got a little overexcited" he said to her sheepishly.

"*Naah*, I had fun" she said to him, putting her arms around him again. This time, she initiated the kiss and carried on for a longer time; she figured out how to breathe without breaking the kiss. He learnt the trick from her soon enough and he stopped kissing for a second to look at her and give her an appreciative glance for figuring out one of the finer nuances of kissing.

They finally stopped kissing and just looked at each other and smiled. A drop of rain fell from one of the leaves of the banyan tree and landed on her cheek. She saw him follow the drop with his eyes as it traced a path along her smooth skin, moving along her cheek and flowing down the side of her slender neck and finally settling down at the base of her neck. She looked at his eyes as they were fixated on the raindrop.

"Relax and trust me" he said as he bent forward and planted a kiss on her neck, at the exact spot where the raindrop lay. He planted short kisses on her neck and cheek as he retraced the path of the raindrop. She could sense that there was something different about the way he was kissing her. There was a lot of emotion and passion in his demeanour.

She had been taken by surprise when he kissed her on the neck but that was nothing compared to how she felt when he slipped his right hand under her cotton t-shirt. The feeling of his warm hand on her waist sent a shiver through her body. Very soon he was kissing her lips passionately, his left hand supported her head as she rested her body against the tree, while with his right hand, he slowly explored her body; marvelling at how perfect she was while doing so. After the initial surprise, she began to enjoy the sensations all over her body as she felt him discover her body as his hand moved from her waist upwards, stopping every now and then to feel her bare skin with his palm and fingers. This show of passion from him stirred feelings that were deep within her as she pressed her body against him and gave him complete freedom to discover her body as he wished.

The two lovers spent the entire afternoon exploring and probing each other under the cloudy skies, with the rain dripping through the leaves and branches of the tree as they forgot about everything else except each other's presence.

They finally controlled their rising passions as the rains abated and let go of each other. They settled their clothing a bit before making eye contact. She was still blushing. He held her in an affectionate embrace. She loved him a little more for doing that.

They started a conversation that had nothing to do with their recent physical intimacy, but it went nowhere. That was followed by another failed conversation about the weather. He finally decided to stop pretending like nothing had happened.

"Look, I don't know if you're comfortable discussing what happened. But I just want to tell you that it'll be awkward if we don't" he said to her, matter-of-factly.

"Yeah, I guess you're right" she replied.

"So... what are your thoughts on what happened?" he asked.

"It was unexpected to be honest. I totally did not foresee that we'd go as far as we did."

"But did you like it or not?"

"I did, it felt... right! And now that I think of it, I'm glad that it happened the way it did, unplanned.

Everything was natural, almost as if we were going with the flow. It was fun. Relax you did well" she said, giving him a pat on his back. He found that funny.

"How was it for you?" she asked him.

"It was perfect... you are perfect... I can't believe how amazing you are. Your clothes should feel honoured that you are wearing them."

"*Bas* enough... over-actor!" she said, laughing at his description of her physical beauty.

"Alright, but seriously. I am in awe of how stunningly beautiful and perfect you are" he said.

"You aren't all that bad either. I was surprised to see how muscular your arms and shoulders are! Good stuff" she said with an approving glance at his body.

"Wait till you see the rest of it" he replied with a naughty smile.

"Shut up!"

"I'm telling you, just wait till I get me a six pack; you'll be ripping my clothes off" he said and they burst out laughing.

They were over the initial bouts of embarrassment after having crossed a certain threshold of intimacy. Now they were back to their normal selves and had become comfortable with the new developments. The rain started to come down heavily once more.

"Dude, get into the car. This time it's very heavy" she said to him.

"But I need to get on and leave for the city; it'll take me time to ride the cycle back in the rain."

"No. Listen, we can put your cycle in the back of the car" she suggested.

"What? No way, the cycle won't fit inside the back of your car."

"It's a big car! It'll fit" she insisted.

She was right, they managed to adjust things and fit the cycle inside her uncle's car. They quickly settled down on the front seats of the car. She switched on the AC and turned on the 'heater mode' so that they'd avoid catching a cold. In a very short span of time the car was heated to a very cozy temperature. The windows quickly got covered by a layer of moisture.

"Dude, you remember the scene from Titanic?" she said to him.

"Which one?"

"*Arrey*, the one in the car where Kate Winslet slides her hand on the window, making an imprint because of the moisture."

"Woah! So that was your real intention to get me inside your car... you are a *havas ki pujarin!*"

His remark earned him a hard punch from his girlfriend.

"Shall we make a move then?" she asked him.

"Yep, I am all set."

"Put on your seat-belt and we'll be off to the city" she said as she tugged at her own seat-belt and fastened it around herself.

She saw that he had a very naughty smile on his face.

"What's cooking in that brain of yours?" she inquired.

"You promise not to punch me?"

"Alright, I promise."

"OK. I just saw you put on your seat-belt and I had a random thought in my head."

"Which is?"

"In my next *janam*, I want to be your seat-belt. I'll get to base two every day!" he said to her and after she pretended to be offended for a second, both of them burst out laughing.

"You are a total pervert!" she exclaimed.

"No. I'm an honest man with an imagination and a hot girlfriend" he replied.

She smiled, ruffled his hair and then started the journey back to the city.

The last few months of engineering were fairly hectic – with Phase Two of placements taking place and the rush to complete their final year projects. But they got done with it without too much trouble. The only concern was that he had been placed in a company located in the same city while she had secured a job in Bangalore. The companies that they had been placed in, were to their liking, since they offered the exact profiles they were looking for.

Even before Phase Two of placements had begun, they had decided what their strategies would be and how it would impact their relationship. He had a restriction of joining a company that offered a job within the same city, whereas she faced the dilemma of choosing to stay in the same city or returning to Bangalore where her parents lived.

Back in the days when she had just started her engineering studies, she planned to return back to her home town to start her professional career. But now that she had fallen in love with him, she was in two minds. She confided in him and he was very understanding. He encouraged her to get the Bangalore job without bothering about their relationship. She cracked the interview and got the job she had wanted.

They had helped each other in preparing for their respective interviews and had a lot of fun along the way. She remembered one such instance before his interview with a major software firm. She pretended to be the interviewer while he answered her questions. To make it more interesting, he pretended to apply for the position of a porn-star instead of the actual job profile.

"So, why is this your dream job?" she asked him, trying her best to sound senior and serious.

"I have always aspired to be a porn-star and no other company has the kind of expertise that this firm has. You have operations all over the world, with offices in Europe, Asia and America. I would love to work in a company with such diversity and high quality talent" he replied.

"Where do you see yourself, five years from now?"

"In an orgy!" he answered, making her laugh a bit, before she asked him the next question.

"What are some of the qualities you possess that would help you succeed as a porn-star?"

"Let's se... I'm a quick learner and a team player. I am flexible and would be suited for several positions and I don't mind working late nights as long as the work is challenging and satisfying."

She lost it completely after his last answer and couldn't help but laugh uncontrollably.

"What is wrong with you? How do you come up with such stuff?"

"It's a disease that can only be cured by constantly making out with my girlfriend."

"Shut up!" she said as he felt her land yet another punch on his shoulder.

As college drew to a close, they spent more and more time with each other. They knew that moving away to different cities would affect their relationship, but he was very sure that they would be able to see things through.

It was their last date before she left for Bangalore and all through the evening she was in a pensive mood. She barely had any food, refused to dance and did not feel like talking too much. They left Hiccups an hour after entering it and for the first time ever without dancing at all.

When they sat down inside her car, she felt bad about ruining the evening.

"Hey listen. I'm sorry about tonight. I know we had planned to have a kick ass time and all that, but I just can't get over the fact that in less than twelve hours I will be far far away from you and I don't even know when we would meet next. That sounds so scary! I don't know when we will meet next. How did we let it come to this? How could you let me give that interview? Why didn't you stop me?" she said in a choked voice.

"You think I didn't want you to stay? You're going back to your family, I'm going to be left all alone here. But that is what we need to do right now. We entered engineering college to start our careers and nothing else. Along the way we found each other, but that doesn't mean that we forget about our original intent. Even if I asked you to stay here, what about the future?

Won't there come a time when you or I feel like studying some more, maybe go abroad. Maybe a time will come when my mother will return and I can travel to different places. It would be a mistake to act short sighted and to miss out on our careers just because we're afraid of losing each other by staying away. And that's not going to happen..."

"How can you be so sure?"

"Because I won't find any girl who can possibly be as awesome as you and if you manage to meet someone better than me, I will kill him by crushing him under my cycle."

His goofy sense of humour once again brought the smile back on her face.

"Plus long distance relationships have a lot of benefits" he said to her.

"Oh really! For example?"

"Well, the first thing that comes to mind is phone sex, which I've heard is a 100% safe and a lot of fun..."

She raised her fist, threatening to give him her trademark punch, but then reached out and gave him a hug.

"I'll miss you" she said looking at him with tears welling up in her eyes.

"I won't let you miss me" he replied, as they kissed each other.

"I almost forgot... I have something for you" she said to him, breaking their kiss.

"What?" he asked her.

She opened the glove-box and pulled out a gift-wrapped item and handed it over to him. It felt like a photo frame. He unwrapped it in a hurry and smiled as he saw what it was – a framed collage of their photographs together over the past two years. It had their photograph from the Fastermind victory, one from her birthday party which kicked off their romance, one from the hill and the last one was their drunk couple pic taken minutes after he had asked her out.

"I got two of these made, one will remain with me in Bangalore and this one is for you to look at when you miss me" she said to him with a smile. He looked into her eyes, said nothing and moved forward to kiss her again.

After she got back home, she lay down on her bed thinking about him and what would be the fate of their relationship once she moved to Bangalore. The more she thought about it, the more confident she grew of their chances of surviving the long distance curse. He was very mature and focused, especially for his young age. And she knew that he loved her. She could see it in his eyes. She had faith that he'd find a way to make it work.

Her thoughts were broken by the sound of her cell phone ringing. It was him.

"Hi, wassup?" she said to him as soon as she answered the call.

"Nothing much. I thought that it'd be a good idea to get some long distance relationship practice even before you go"

"Alright, how do we do this?" she asked him.

"Well, I did some research on long distance relationships and this is how the drill works. Apparently couples give each other a call every night or at least every alternate night to keep the bonding strong. They then tell each other about how their day went and how they miss each other a lot.

Once that formality is done with, the guy gets to the part of the conversation that he is truly interested in... dirty talk..."

"*Accha?* And I bet you would like to practice some of that as well tonight" she said to him.

"Why not? I love your proactiveness, it's very healthy for a relationship. But before we begin, we need to decide what language we shall use for the dirty talk. Any chance you speak French? It's supposed to be the sexiest language, perfect for a long distance relationship."

"Alas I don't. You'll have to make do with Hindi and English."

"Then it has to be English, obviously."

"Why obviously? Why can't it be Hindi?" she asked.

"Are you kidding me? English is the better language for dirty talk, Hindi is probably the worst language for this purpose. Think of it, even a simple line like – let's move onto base two will sound so weird in Hindi – *chalo doosrey padhaav par chalte hain!* Yikes, not hot at all!"

He heard the sound of her laughter and stopped talking so he could hear it.

"Well, I have a different opinion. Hindi can be a great for dirty talk and it can be really sexy too" she said to him.

"Oh yeah, I challenge you to say something sexy in Hindi right now" he said to her.

"Alright, here goes..." she put on a seductive tone and said in soft slow words – "*ab main apne vastra utaarne jaa rahi hoon...* was that sexy enough?" she asked him.

For a few seconds he was stunned, he had never heard her speak in 'seduce mode' before. It blew him away.

"Can I call you back in ten minutes?"

"Shut up!" she said to him before they both burst into laughter.

They continued to talk to each other till the early hours of the morning. By the time she hung up the phone, she was convinced that they would make it work. They were just right for each other and they knew it.

10

The Happiest Day of His Life

The first year at work for both of them was a blur, filled with orientations, training sessions, late nights at office, team dinners, office parties and several other aspects that were a part of corporate life. They spoke every weekend for a few hours and stayed in touch via chat on weekdays. They met just once when she had come down to the city for the convocation ceremony.

He was a driven man at work, finding himself well ahead of his peers at the end of a year at work. His performance reviews were excellent and so were the financial incentives that were a result of his hard work. He got a major salary hike and a fat bonus cheque. But there was no time to celebrate; he was beginning to understand the cardinal rule of corporate life: the only reward for good work was more work. He started off working on a single project and by the end of one year he was staffed on three. He liked the intensity, there were days when he was in office from eight in the morning till three at night, but he did not mind it.

Meanwhile she had settled down into a busy but comfortable rhythm at work. She was enjoying the stay with her parents. After four years of being away, she liked coming home to her parents. She had a lot of school friends whom she was now back in touch with, having returned full time to Bangalore. The city had changed a lot over the past few years and she liked most of the things that had changed.

This phase of routine work carried on until the day he got a phone call from Dr. Roy. The neurologist wanted to discuss something important with him. The next day, he took sick leave from work and went to meet Dr. Roy at his office. When he entered the neurologist's office, he saw another doctor there – a lady doctor called Dr. Maria Fischer. Dr. Fischer was a very senior doctor from Germany, she had a medium height, pale white skin, piercing blue eyes and shoulder length hair that had greyed completely.

He wished both the doctors and then took a seat in front of Dr. Roy's table. Dr. Roy introduced him to Dr. Fischer and informed him that she was a leading brain surgeon from Germany and that she had some thoughts on his mother's case. Dr. Fischer then took over the conversation. She told him about a breakthrough procedure that would involve surgical intervention on the patient's brain-stem. The procedure sounded complex and risky.

"What are the chances of success?" he asked the two doctors.

"About forty percent patients have recovered" replied Dr. Fischer in a heavy German accent.

"What happens to the rest? Do they continue to remain in a coma..."

"A very high majority of failed cases end up as fatalities during the surgical procedure itself" said the German doctor.

A cold fear replaced the glimmer of hope that he felt before Dr. Fischer's statement about the fatalities. Dr. Roy then spoke about why the procedure was a worthwhile risk to take. The neurologist spoke at length about how despite the patient's condition remaining stable, there had been no improvement in brain function and how in the years to come there would be a rapid decline in his mother's condition if no intervention was to take place.

At the end of a very detailed discussion, he walked out of Dr. Roy's office and to his mother's ward. He stood next to her bed and looked at her, lying still. Her breathing and the beeping of the heart monitor being the only signs that she was alive. What do I do, *maa*? He said to her in silent words. How do I take this decision? I want you to return, but how can I risk your life? Can you even hear me? Do you know what all I've been through since you've been lost? This cruel trick that life is playing on me...

when will it end, *maa*? I don't know what decision I will take, but I want your blessings.

He touched his mother's feet and then walked out of the ward to a quiet corner of the hospital corridor. He dialled the number of the only person he wanted to speak to. She answered the phone with the kind of affection and love that drove away the fear in his heart for a brief while. She could sense from his tone that what he had to say was important. She was in office, she asked him to hold the line while she walked into an empty meeting room and then carried on the conversation with him.

In a long and detailed conversation, he told her about the dilemma he faced. She wished she was in his city in front of him at that time instead of being a thousand miles away in Bangalore. She could sense how badly he needed her.

"How much time do you have... to come to a decision?" she asked him.

"Two days at the most, Dr. Fischer will leave the country, three days from now. Dr. Roy wants her to be there for the procedure. But I don't know what to do. Forty percent is such a low rate of success."

"But at least there is some chance of success. You've waited patiently for five long years, nothing has changed has it? Maybe this is the chance at last! Right?"

There was a long pause, he was thinking very hard about the decision. He knew that by the end of the phone call his mind would be made. But it had to be the right decision. She decided to prod him a little further. She told him about how long he had waited and now the chance was there in front of him, all he had to do was seize it. She asked him to go ahead with the surgery.

"But how do I know this is the right decision?" he asked in despair.

"There is no way you can know if you're decision is right or wrong. It's a chance that you have to take. If I were you, I would go for it."

"It's easy for you to take a decision, she's not your mother" he said to her, without sounding bitter. She understood the emotion behind his words.

"You are right, but... maybe that's what is needed right now. To think a little objectively. I know this is not easy for you, but you have a choice to make. A choice that could potentially bring your mother back. I know there is a risk, a huge risk that something bad may happen. But if the risk is great, then so are the gains if this succeeds. Imagine hearing your mother's voice again. Isn't that worth the risk?

It has been five long years of struggle, you have taken risks earlier; you tore up your uncle's cheque because you backed yourself, you sold off your house... weren't those risks you took? But somehow you pulled it off because you believed in yourself. All I ask of you, is to do the same again. I don't know Dr. Roy too well, but I do know that he is a well-wisher of yours and your mother. He would not have suggested this procedure unless he thought there was merit in it. Have faith in him, if nothing else" she said to him with the hope that her words would convince him.

Once again, there was silence. She had said what she wanted to, there was nothing more that she could say to him on the matter. It was his turn to speak; it was time for him to take a decision. All the while that he was thinking, he looked at the *rudraksh* his mother had given him all those years ago. Almost hoping that it would magically speak to him and tell him what he must do. After thinking for a long time in silence, he took a deep breath, and finally spoke.

"No son should be asked to decide the fate of his mother's life... and I wish this decision wasn't mine to take. My mother always asked me to be brave and I'll use that thought as the foundation of my decision... the surgery will be performed."

She couldn't see him, but she knew that he had said those words with a fiery belief in his eyes. She had seen that look before and was glad that he was clear in his mind about the decision.

"I'll ask Dr. Roy and Dr. Fischer to perform the surgery tomorrow itself" he said to her.

"What time would it take place? I'm booking flight tickets" she said.

"No. Don't"

"Why?" she asked, puzzled.

"I don't know, I'm just good at facing pressure alone. And tomorrow will be a difficult time for me, I don't want you to see me like that."

"But... what will I do sitting all the way here. If I'm with you at least I can help a little bit."

"You can do something very important... pray... please, that's all I ask of you" he said to her.

Pray, because that's the one thing I can't do. He thought to himself.

"Alright" she said, knowing fully well that there was no arguing with him on some aspects.

"Thanks."

"Hey, what about the money for the surgery. At least let me help out over there" she said to him.

"No, I've got that covered. I'll get a medical loan with the hospital's help. It's not a big deal" he said to her.

"Are you sure? I almost feel like I'm doing nothing over here."

"Don't worry, if I ever default on the loan and get sent to jail, you can come down here to bail me out" he said to her with a small chuckle.

She was glad that he could afford a smile given the circumstances. They spoke for a while longer and before hanging up, he thanked her with all his heart and asked her once again to pray.

The next day, he was at the hospital early in the morning, despite the surgery being scheduled at noon. There were some formalities that he had to take care of – things like getting blood from a blood bank, in exchange he had to donate some of his own blood. Thanks to Dr. Roy and the Dean, the loan request had been fast tracked to a large extent and all he had to do was a bit of running around to get some signatures. Once the formalities were over, he waited in his mother's ward. He looked at his mother and whispered.

"It's been five long years... filled with countless tears. I've been left all alone... to face my fears. I don't know if you can hear me, but if you can... then know this... our time is here and when you're awake, you will see what I have done in the past five years. You will see what your son has become, despite everything we have endured. The wait has been long and hard but it's time to end it. Please come back *maa*... for me... please come back for your son"

He held out his *rudraksh* and gently held it against his mother's forehead. Just then, a nurse and ward boy entered the room along with Dr. Roy.

"It's time" said the neurologist.

He looked at the doctor and nodded his head. The nurse and the ward boy shifted the patient onto a stretcher and headed off towards the operation theatre. With each step that he took towards the OT, he felt the tension mount. This was it. His mother's fate was going to be decided inside a room that he would not be allowed to enter.

Everyone but him disappeared behind the doors of the OT, where they conducted the pre-surgery cleaning and other procedures. Dr. Roy came out one last time from the doors of the OT with the surgical gloves and mask on and told him that the surgery would be a long one. Shortly after Dr. Roy entered the OT, a small red bulb above the OT door came on. The surgery had begun.

He sent a quick sms to the love of his life: *the surgery has started.*

Within a minute he received her reply: *so have my prayers.*

She knew he did not want to be spoken to while the surgery was on. She prayed sincerely for his mother's return. She knew how much this meant to him and that he would never forgive himself should something go wrong. She felt her palms wet with nervous sweat and wondered how he was coping all alone.

For two hours he stood in front of the OT door, waiting to hear from Dr. Roy. Finally the door opened, but it was Dr. Fischer and not Dr. Roy who walked towards him. She had a worried look on her face.

"What's the matter?" he asked the surgeon.

"There have been some complications, she's bleeding internally. We're trying our best. The procedure will take more time, I just came to tell you that" said Dr. Fischer as she turned around to get back into the OT.

"Is her life in danger?" he asked the doctor, desperately.

"We're trying our best" came the reply as Dr. Fischer disappeared into the OT.

This can't happen. I won't let this happen. He thought to himself as he turned away from the OT and moved towards the staircase. He ran down the steps to reach the floor where the temple was located. In hurried steps he walked towards the temple and stopped a few steps away from the idol kept inside.

"It has been five long years since I last spoke to You. I gave You a promise the last time I stood in front of You. Ever since, I have kept my promise. It's time You lived up to Your end of the bargain. I am not here to pray to You, I am here to remind You that a son has spent five years waiting for his mother to return and during those five years, not once has he asked You for help and that today is the day when You have to come good on Your title of God and show me that the promise I made to You and stuck by, was not in vain... that there is more to my life than just sorrow and pain... let my mother return to me... please... I want to hear her voice again... I want to see her smile again" he beseeched the idol with his hands folded in reverence and his head bowed low.

He stood there, completely still and barely breathing; with his mind focused on the image of his mother as she was before the accident. A little while later, he opened his eyes and looked one last time at the idol in the temple before turning around and walking back to the OT. The red bulb was still lit as he waited patiently. There was nothing more that he could do, other than wait.

Another hour went by before he sensed some movement from the OT. The light bulb was turned off and Dr. Roy emerged from the door. The neurologist's face mask was on and he could not make out any expression on the doctor's face. Dr. Roy walked to the patient's son and gave him a hug.

"The operation was a success" whispered the doctor into the young man's ears.

He wanted to speak, but he was choked; tears had welled up in his eyes, blurring his vision.

"When will she gain consciousness?" he finally managed to ask.

"It'll take time, about half a day. We've kept her heavily sedated. Even when she awakens, it'll only be for a short while before we sedate her again. It will be a week before she'll be slightly functional. But she will make a full recovery" said the doctor.

Dr. Fischer then made her way towards the two men. She was beaming.

"I told you it'll work" she said, pointing towards Dr. Roy. Dr. Roy nodded with a knowing smile.

Actually, the neurologist wasn't totally convinced when Dr. Fischer had suggested the procedure and in the middle of the surgery when things had taken a turn for the worse, it was Dr. Fischer who pushed on to complete the procedure and did not give up.

"I cannot thank you enough Dr. Fischer and Dr. Roy. You have no idea what this means to me" he said to the senior doctors.

"Not many come back from the kind of internal bleeding she faced. Your mother is a fighter" said Dr. Fischer with a smile on her face.

"So is her son" remarked Dr. Roy.

The two doctors then made their way to the ICU where his mother had been shifted for post-op procedures.

After keeping his mother under observation for several hours, she was shifted to the neurology ward. He sat down on a chair next to her bed and rested his elbows on the edge of the bed. He looked at her, waiting for some sign of her waking.

Hours passed by and he kept waiting patiently, but towards midnight he started to tire. The day had been emotionally and physically draining. His eyes were heavy, he wanted to fall asleep. You have waited for five years, what's a few more hours – he thought to himself as he rested his head on the edge of his mother's bed. He closed his eyes and thought of the days gone by when he and his mother lived a simple and a happy life.

Just then, he felt a hand on his head, ruffling his hair gently. He recognized his mother's touch, even though her fingers were now frail. His heart skipped a beat. He slowly looked up, his mother had her eyes half open and there was a hint of a smile on her face.

"*Maa*, you're awake!" he whispered with teary eyes.

"Look at you... you've grown taller... but your hair is so dry... you haven't been oiling your hair, have you?" she whispered, reprimanding him about the state of his hair, in her faint voice.

He let out a short chuckle before breaking down and crying his heart out. He could hardly believe it, his mother was with him again!

"How long has it been?" she asked him in a feeble voice, once he controlled himself a little.

"Five years" he answered.

"Last I saw you, you were still a boy and now when I see you... you're a grown man. You look so much like your father" she said to him as a teardrop fell from her eye.

"I became an engineer *maa*..." he said to her as he filled her up on the significant events that she missed out on during the half a decade long coma she was in.

A nurse then walked into the room and administered a dose of sedatives to his mother. Before drifting off into the induced sleep, his mother whispered the words, "I'm proud of you" to him.

Just like that, all his burdens were gone. He felt the kind of freedom and joy that he had not known for years. His labours had at last borne fruit. He walked out of the ward and dialled the phone number of the woman he loved.

She had been waiting eagerly for him to call all day. But ever since the sms he had sent when the surgery started, there had been no further communication from him. She did not want to call him up and disturb him, in case he was busy looking after his mother. But she was anxiously waiting to find out what happened. At a half past midnight, she heard her cell phone ring. Her heart started to beat faster as she lifted her phone to answer his call.

"Hello" she said apprehensively.

"Hello... can you hear me?" he said.

From his voice she could make out that he was emotional. She started to get very worried.

"Yes I can hear you... how is your mother?" she asked him, speaking loud and clear so he could hear her clearly.

"It's a miracle. She's back! My mother is back... I heard her voice, she recognized me... everything will be alright now" he said to her as his voice cracked with emotion.

As soon as she heard those words, she started to cry. She remembered the sadness in his voice when he spoke about his mother in the past and the sacrifices he had made for her and now that it had all turned out to be for good, she could not hold back her tears.

When they finally calmed down enough to have a conversation, she told him that she wanted to meet him and that she would travel to his city on the weekend. He requested her not to and told her that there were a lot of things he had to arrange. When she insisted on visiting him, he asked her to wait for just a few weeks. She agreed eventually.

Over the next three months, he helped his mother with her recovery, rented a nice apartment in a large residential colony and bought a car on EMI. The day his mother was to be discharged, he drove her to their apartment in his own car. The pride on her face was worth all the world's riches to him.

When his mother reached home, she was filled with more

pride as she saw the display cabinet in the drawing room, filled with trophies, a silver shield and a photograph of him receiving the shield from the President of India. Right next to that photo was an old photograph of their once whole family. It brought a tear to her eye, but she did not let her son see it.

In a few days his mother had settled into the new house and had even started to take short evening walks within the colony premises. He got busy with work and was filled with immense joy when he came home to see his mother waiting for him. He cherished those moments... moments that he had waited to experience for five long and hard years. And they had come at last.

One such day when he returned from work, his mother had an amused smile on her face.

"What's going on *maa*?" he inquired.

"You know, till today I never realized how much you have grown in the last five years" said his mother.

"Oh yeah... and what brought about this sudden realization? Was it my receding hairline?"

"*Oh hoo... no baba...* I was cleaning up your room today and saw a very lovely collage of photos of you and a beautiful girl. That's when I realized how much you've grown. My son has a girlfriend" she said, smiling as she saw him blush with embarrassment.

"*Maa*, you're not supposed to do that."

"Alright, I'm sorry. I won't enter your room without asking you again. I sometimes forget that you are not a school going boy anymore..." she said before he interrupted.

"No, that's not what I meant. I meant that you're not supposed to be exerting yourself in cleaning and all. As it is you refuse to let me order food for lunch and dinner and waste your energy cooking and now you're doing stuff like cleaning. You know we're two days away from the review with Dr. Roy. You know how much he'll yell at me if he finds out you've been needlessly straining yourself."

"Good attempt at diverting the topic, but I'm your mother

and you can't fool me. Who is she?" she asked with a knowing smile.

He reluctantly sat down on the drawing room sofa and told his mother all about his relationship with the woman he loved. His mother heard his story with rapt attention as he went about telling her all the major events that took place between him and his girlfriend. Starting with Fastermind to their misunderstandings and then the parties at Hiccups. He even confessed to having alcohol the night when he disclosed his feelings to her and then their subsequent romance till she left for Bangalore.

"She was very insistent on coming here during your surgery, but I asked her not to come" he explained to his mother.

"Well, now you can call her here; that way I get to meet my future *bahu*" said his mother, expecting his shocked facial expression.

"Oh please *maa*, that sounds scary" he said to her as his mother had a laugh at his expense.

"Alright, fine. I won't talk about those things. As it is, your generation is getting used to marrying late. In our time if you liked a girl and she liked you, you married her. I don't know what you people keep waiting for."

"Enough enough. I'll call her here, you can see her... if you approve I'll run to the temple with her and come back married and in time for lunch. *Theek hai?*" he said to her mischievously as his mother laughed.

That night he spoke to his girlfriend and asked her if she wanted to come over to the city.

"So you told your mother everything about us?" she asked him.

"Well almost everything. I skipped out the parts where you physically assaulted me with your punches and forced me into making out with you."

"*Haha*, very funny! So it's decided, I am coming over this Saturday itself. I'll stay over at my uncle's and now that you have a car, you can drive me around for a change" she said to him.

"It would be my pleasure ma'am."

"Hey one question. When I meet your mom... what do I call her? *Sasu maa?*" she said, laughing as she imagined his expression. She loved teasing him.

"What is wrong with you women? Marriage related jokes are not funny for guys! It freaks us out" he said in an irritated voice, adding to her delight.

They continued their conversation, late into the night and once they finished, he lay down on his bed thinking about her visit.

On Saturday morning when she rang the doorbell of his flat, he opened the door and the sight of her, brought a smile to his face. She was wearing a beautiful embroidered cyan coloured *salwaar kameez*, her flowing hair and the matching *dupatta* added to her majestic beauty. She enjoyed the look on his face.

"*Ahem...* may I come in" she said, once she realized he was too engrossed in admiring her beauty.

"Oh yeah. Sorry!" he said, quickly recovering after getting caught off guard.

"It's so nice to finally meet you *beti*" said his mother as she saw the beautiful young woman enter the house.

Beti? What the heck? He thought to himself.

"Hello aunty, how are you now?"

He looked on as his girlfriend greeted her mother and touched her feet. He was stunned by this development. First my mother calls her *beti*... then my girlfriend touches her feet. What the hell is happening today!

"Nice house" she remarked to her boyfriend, bringing a genuine smile of pride to his face.

"Thank you!"

The three of them got talking and after some refreshments, made their way to his car. He felt a weird sense of fulfilment as he drove the two most important women in his life to the one place on Earth which he could call his own... the site at the top of the hill.

All through the journey, the two women were busy conversing and almost seemed oblivious to his presence. He chuckled at the thought of being reduced to a mere chauffeur. When he intervened with a complaint about feeling ignored, his mother responded by narrating an embarrassing story from his childhood. He did not interrupt the conversation between them again.

At the hill, the two women continued their bonding session as he tried to find ways of making himself useful. His mother and his girlfriend found the weather so amazing that they decided not to go to the restaurant, so he kept dashing between the restaurant at the other side of the hill and his own plot to get refreshments and snacks. When he was gone to get lunch, the two women got into discussing slightly serious topics.

"Aunty, can I ask you something? You come across as someone who has no complaints about what happened to you. How do you do that?" she asked his mother.

The elder lady smiled lovingly before answering.

"When people face some misfortune in life, they usually despair and complain to God about their fate. They ask questions like, why did this happen to me or what have I done to deserve this etc. But they never get an answer, do they?

Do you know why they get no answers? Because we are not here, in this world, to ask questions to God and our fate. We are here to find out what happens next. Time does not wait for those who question their fate. All we can and must do is move on and strive to see better days. And if those better days do come, it makes all the suffering and pain seem like a distant memory.

Besides, I have no complaints. My son has grown up to become a man who any mother would feel proud of. He has faced the worst kinds of situations in life and come out with his head held high. He could have fallen by the wayside and withered away, but he did not. He fought hard and saw through the tough times and now I see a beautiful future ahead for him" said his mother, running her hands gently over the young woman's cheeks.

"I can see where he gets his profoundness from" remarked his girlfriend.

"What do you mean by that?" asked the mother.

"So many times I have spoken to him and he comes up with these wonderful little monologues. I now know where he gets that ability from."

The mother smiled.

"And you like that about him?"

"Yes, it's part of his charm. That and his sense of humour" replied the young woman.

"He gets that from his father. His father always had a joke or a funny story to tell. There was never a dull moment at home. He also gets his eyes and his smile from his father" his mother said to his girlfriend.

He arrived with lunch and the three of them spent the rest of the day at the hill. In the evening, they returned to the city, where he dropped his mother home and then left for Hiccups with his girlfriend.

At the disco, they noticed that nothing had changed in a year. The music, the food and the ambience were just as good. It took them back to their college days and they danced together for a long time, before settling down on a table for dinner. After a quick dinner, he drove her to her uncle's apartment and parked the car near the building.

"I had a great time today, I swear. Your mom is awesome" she said to him.

"You both are made for each other, the perfect *saas bahu*; chit-chatting all day while I run around arranging food and transport" he remarked.

"Whatever!"

"But I'll tell you what. Today was a dream come true for me. Spending the whole day with the two people who matter the most to me. My mother and the woman I am deeply in love with. It was the happiest day of my life" he said to her, with a lot of conviction behind each word that he spoke.

She leaned in to kiss him. It was their first kiss in months and they took their time and enjoyed it.

"I never told you how beautiful you look in this dress" he said to her as they broke the kiss.

"You didn't need to, your reaction when you opened the door today morning was enough" she said to him and then kissed him again before getting out of his car.

It had been a month since her visit and he had begun to really miss her. There came an opportunity to meet her soon. Her birthday was a few weeks away and he wondered whether he should pay her a visit. But he was concerned about her family situation; while his mother knew about the two of them, her family did not. They had discussed it once and she had told him that when the right time came to inform her parents about their relationship, she would let him know. Thus far she had not told him anything about disclosing their relationship to her parents and he hadn't asked again. He did not want to pressure her in any way. Everyone had a way to deal with their family and he trusted her to figure out the best way to handle things.

One night, he got a call from her.

"Hey, wassup?" he said upon answering the phone.

"Sadness!"

"What happened?"

"Suparna is ditching me on my birthday and my parents have to attend some stupid marriage during that week. I will be all alone on my birthday" she complained to him.

"Damn! That sucks!"

"I know! What do I do?"

"Trust me" he said to her.

"What?"

"Just apply for a leave that day, I will drop by Bangalore and you can give me a tour of the Garden City and we'll celebrate your birthday together."

"Really! That sounds awesome" she said excitedly.

They planned it out, he was to reach Bangalore by the morning flight and spend the entire day with her and return the next afternoon. He spoke to his mother about it and his mother was glad that he was going to meet her in Bangalore for the first time ever.

"I wonder what gift I should give to her? She had been talking about a couple of books recently, *The Finkler Question* and *The Great Indian Novel*. Maybe I'll get her one of them. What do you think?" he asked his mother.

"There was this movie on TV yesterday afternoon, called Finding Forrester. Have you seen it?" his mother asked him.

"No" he said, wondering what it had to do with his gifting dilemma.

"Well, it had an excellent quote spoken by Sean Connery, where he says: the key to a woman's heart is an unexpected gift at an unexpected time" his mother said to him.

"*Maa*, it's her birthday. Neither would a gift be unexpected nor the time."

"Maybe you should think about how you can change that? It would make her birthday more special" his mother told him.

For the next couple of days, he kept thinking about conversations he had with her, hoping to spot a hint at what would make for a special gift. But he got nowhere. Then, one day, he looked at a status message that she put up on her chat profile.

You see in this world there's two kinds of people, my friend. Those with loaded guns, and those who dig.
— Love you Clint Eastwood!

As soon as he read that message, he smiled. He knew what he was going to do to make her birthday a memorable one.

She waited with anticipation as the clock struck twelve. The first birthday phone call she got was from her parents, up next was Suparna. She spoke for a long time with Suparna, checking all the incoming calls to see if it was *him* and rejecting them when she realized he hadn't called. After speaking to Suparna, for next hour or so, she spoke to several of her friends. Lying to them that she was with her family, cutting her birthday cake. The fact was that for the first time ever, she was alone on her birthday.

It was close to two thirty at night and he still hadn't called. She felt a little upset. So what if he's coming and visiting me in the morning, he still should've called. She thought to herself as she lay down on her bed. Feeling a hint of disappointment, she wondered if she should give him a phone call to reprimand him. I'll do it in person when I see him, she said to herself.

Just then, she heard the doorbell ring. Who could it be at this time? She thought to herself. She got up from her bed and walked to the drawing room, keeping her cell phone handy just in case something was amiss.

"Who is it?" she asked as she approached the door.

"You see in this world there's two kinds of women, my friend. Those with loving boyfriends, and those without" said a voice from the other side of the door.

She recognized the voice. But how could it be? He was supposed to reach Bangalore in the morning... she thought. Just to be completely sure, she looked through the peep hole on the door. It was blocked by a hand.

"Is it really you?" she asked once again.

"Why don't you open the door to find out" he said to her.

She clasped her hands in excitement before unlocking the door. The moment she opened the door, she was stunned into silence by the sight in front of her eyes.

He was standing in front of her, with his hands resting against the edges of the door-frame; wearing the Clint Eastwood costume from *The Good, The Bad and The Ugly*. She looked at his feet and then upwards – he had worn brown leather shoes, a pair of blue jeans, the trademark dusty green poncho with white markings on it and on his head, he wore a dark brown felt cap. She smiled as she watched him flick a toothpick held between his lips from one corner of his mouth to the other – mimicking the flick that Clint Eastwood performed with a cigarette.

"Happy Birthday, my lady" he said to her, taking off his hat and placing it on her head.

She took a quick step towards him and held him in a tight

embrace, which he returned. She just stood there with her arms around him, not wanting to let go of the moment.

He felt an immense sense of joy, he had taken the risk of looking like a complete fool in front of her; but it had worked out perfectly. Her reaction said it all to him. The look of amazement and wonder in her eyes was a pleasure for him to see. He ran his hands through her hair as she held him in an embrace and refused to let go. There was no better feeling in the world than to hold the love of your life in your arms, he thought to himself.

Finally, she let go of him and pulled him inside the apartment, shutting the door behind them. She placed the hat back on his head and looked at him with an amused smile.

"You're absolutely crazy, you know that?" she remarked.

"And you are the reason for it" he replied.

"How the hell did you get hold of this costume?" she asked him.

"It was no big deal. I just gave a call to Clint Eastwood... told him that my girlfriend was a big fan of his and it would really help me make her birthday special... so Clint asks me if my girlfriend was hot... I told him that she's so hot, if you brought a piece of bread and held it close to her, it'd turn into toast! That's all it took, he just sent over his hat and poncho and here I am."

She couldn't help but laugh at his crazy explanation and realized that he wasn't going to tell her how he actually got it. When she finally caught her breath after laughing, she continued her questioning.

"But weren't you supposed to come here later in the morning?"

"I wanted to surprise you."

"And you have" she said to him as she slung her arms around him once again and kissed him.

They had been away from each other for months and as they kissed each other passionately, he held himself back from getting carried away. He did not want her to feel that he had visited her just to get physically intimate with her.

She could sense his apprehensions and smiled to herself as she held him in an embrace. She felt the tense feeling in his arms as he held her but with the gentlest of grips. She knew him so well that she had read his thoughts. She wondered how strong his power of restraint was, to hold himself back even as she was clearly willing to allow him all the freedom he needed.

"This is the best birthday gift you could have ever given me." she said to him as she broke another one of their long and intense kisses.

"What birthday gift?"

"You know... the whole thing where my boyfriend surprises me by landing up here in a fantasy costume" she said to him.

"But that's not the gift."

"Then what is?" she asked him.

"Wait a second" he said to her as he walked towards the door, where he had kept a bag that he was carrying when she let him into the apartment.

She sat down on the drawing room sofa, waiting expectantly for the next surprise that he had planned for her. He carried the bag with him as he sat down on the sofa, right next to her. She watched as he pulled out a gift wrapped item and handed it over. As soon as she touched it, she knew it was a book. She ripped through the gift wrapping and had a smile on her face as she saw the title of the book *'The Finkler Question'*, it was a book she had wanted to read for months and simply hadn't found the time to buy it. She looked at him to thank him but he held up his hand in a gesture asking her to wait and then dug into the bag once again. This time he pulled out another gift wrapped book and placed it in her waiting hands. She had a big smile on her face when she saw the title of the book – *'The Great Indian Novel'*.

Once again, she realized, he had picked out gifts that she really wanted by listening carefully to their conversations. She looked at him with a look which said that she had fallen in love with him all over again. All of a sudden, she got up from the sofa and started to walk away towards the kitchen.

"Where are you going?" he asked, bewildered.

"I'm making coffee for us" she replied.

"Why?"

"Neither of us will get any sleep tonight" she said to him with a wink and a naughty smile on her face.

"I always knew that books were a man's best friend" he replied to her with a smirk, making her chuckle as she disappeared into the kitchen.

As he waited for her to return with the coffee, he felt a sense of elation as he thought of her reaction when she saw him in the Hollywood attire. He wasn't going to tell her that he had arranged for an office colleague in the US to buy it and send it over. Those were unnecessary details that took away from the mystery of a surprise.

He also regretted the fact that he was seeing her after so long. She was looking beautiful. Over the past one year, she had turned into more of a woman than the girl she was in college. There was a sense of maturity about her now, which enhanced her beauty. Her mannerisms had turned even more graceful. She exuded a sense of independence that showed in every action of hers, right from the way she walked to the way she kissed.

She returned with two mugs of coffee, they updated each other on the recent happenings in their lives. After they were done drinking their coffee, they had a quick photo session. She couldn't get enough of him and the fantasy attire he was wearing.

"Let's get more comfortable" she said to him as she held his hand and led him into her bedroom.

As soon as they were inside, she shut the door behind her and pushed him against a wall and started to kiss him passionately. She broke the kiss to take a step back and look at him in the getup once again.

"I still can't get over this look of yours. It is incredible" she said to him.

"I am glad that you like it. I was wondering whether I could pull it off."

"Well, I don't know about you... but I surely intend to pull it off you in less than a minute" she said, with a very naughty tone.

She kicked off the slip-ons she was wearing and took a step towards him. She stood up on her toes and kissed him. She could feel the apprehension in his touch as he held her waist in a light grip. She broke the kiss again and looked at his eyes. She could sense how vulnerable he was, fighting his own desire to hold her tight while she encouraged him in every way she could. She held his right hand by the wrist and brought his fingers to her lips and kissed each one of them. She then guided his hand and ran his fingers over her cheeks to her slender neck and then finally let his hand rest below her neck. They were both breathing a little heavily.

"Are you ready?" she asked him, looking into his eyes.

"We shouldn't rush into this" he said, fighting against every natural instinct of his.

"What are you afraid of?" she whispered to him.

"We don't have any protection" he replied.

She moved a step away towards a drawer next to her bed and opened it to reveal a blue box.

"Is that what I think it is?" he asked.

"Durability, reliability and excellence" she said to him with a wink as they both began to laugh.

"I can't believe you actually bought a pack of..."

"You're not the only one capable of springing surprises" she said to him with a wink.

He reached out... grabbed her by the hand and pulled her towards himself. He held her in a tight embrace, planting kisses on her lips and neck. As soon as she felt his touch she knew that he had gotten over his inhibitions and that he would now unleash all his passion for her. He took off his hat and flung it to a corner of the room; as she pulled off the Mexican costume he had put on to surprise her. They both looked into each other's eyes and smiled in anticipation of what was to follow.

A few hours later as the sun finally rose; the two of them lay on her bed, catching their breath. He ran his hands through her hair as she rested her head on his arm.

"So, how was it?" he asked her.

She laughed after hearing his question.

"You're asking me now, after going at it three times?"

"Well, you know how much I value your feedback. It will help me serve you better in the future. I assure you, your responses will remain anonymous" he said to her in a tone used by some customer care rep of a telecom company.

"So what kind of feedback are you looking for" she said to him with an amused look on her face.

"A simple question where you need to respond by selecting one of the given options to describe your experience" he said to her, continuing with his customer care voice.

"Alright, let's start" she said.

"How would you describe the performance of the representative that was sent over to your house last night? Good, Very Good, Excellent, Outstanding or Oh My God Please Don't Stop."

She burst out laughing as soon as he completed his question.

"We are still waiting for your answer ma'am" he said to her as she controlled her laughter.

"Oh My God Please Don't Stop" she replied.

"As you wish" he said to her as he leaned in closer to her face and started kissing her.

Once again, the young couple got lost in each other.

Later that day, they had lunch at a fancy restaurant called *Samarkand*. He was mighty pleased with the succulent *kebabs* and the *biryani*. She watched as he ate furiously, digging into his plate like there was no tomorrow.

"I have never seen you eat so much before" she remarked.

"Well, I had a very busy night. My boss rode me very hard and I need some energy" he replied to her with a wink.

"Shut up" she said to him and kicked him lightly under the table.

"Alright, sorry."

"I was thinking about one thing. You asked me how I felt about last night; you never told me what your thoughts were. So, what did you think about what happened?"

"I was just happy that I did not malfunction" he said to her matter-of-factly.

She laughed.

"You're insane" she said to him.

"Actually, it felt like I was in heaven and you were an angel."

"Thank you" she said with a smile.

"... a very naughty angel" he added.

"Ow... sorry" he said as he felt another kick on his ankle.

They finished their lunch and then moved towards the parking lot.

"Where to now?" he asked her.

"One of my favourite places in Bangalore since my childhood... Cubbon Park. It's beautiful and in this weather it will be perfect for an afternoon walk, but beware of overtly romantic couples" she said to him.

"Actually, I don't mind them as long as they're not ugly" he remarked.

She drove him in her father's car to Cubbon Park, where they quickly went through all the landscaped gardens and historical buildings. Walking on the soft green grass under the winter sun was a welcome change from the snazzy city distractions.

"For some reason, this place reminds me of the times we spent at the hill" she said to him as she stood under the shade of a banyan tree.

He smiled as he thought of the memorable afternoons he had with her at the hill, a thousand miles away from where they stood.

"It's been more than a year since I last went to the hill. How is it now?" she asked him.

"It's still just as it was. The swing you used to sit on, it's gotten wider as expected. The grass is thicker now and the flower bed has spread to the edge of the plot" he said to her.

"It must be so beautiful" she said.

"Not without you" he replied.

"Next time I come to your city, it's the first place we'll visit. OK?" she said to him.

"Fine" he said to her with a smile.

The couple spent an hour together at Cubbon Park. She took him to all her favourite spots at the park and after clicking a few photographs they were back in her car.

"Now we go to UB City" she said to him.

Having no real clue about Bangalore city, he thought that it would take time to reach their next destination, but within a couple of minutes they were standing in front of a tower that looked like it belonged to a different world altogether. Bang in the middle of the city, right next to one of the oldest gardens of the Garden City, was one of the most majestic and stylish complexes he had ever seen. The evening sky reflected on the glass panels on the sides of the building, displaying a wonderful mixture of natural and manmade beauty.

She gave him a quick tour of the tower after which they sat down on the steps of the picturesque amphitheatre; talking to each other with the sound of flowing water from the nearby fountain.

"How's your mother doing, health wise?" she asked him.

"She just had a check-up last week, the doctors say that she's doing very well. In fact just the other day she was telling me that she was planning to restart her career."

"Wow! That is great news."

"Yes it is."

"I wanted to tell you something serious."

"What?" he asked.

"I think it's time I tell my dad about us" she said to him and waited to see his reaction.

He looked up at the sky and had a thoughtful look on his face. She was glad that he did not seem tense or worried or put off by the idea.

"Do you think he'll have any issues with me?" he asked her frankly.

"No, not at all. He is pretty open minded and has no issues

about caste or community and all that. As it is, I just want to tell him that we're seeing each other, it's nothing more than that" she said to him.

"I'm fine with whatever you decide. Just let me know in advance, what I should wear when your dad wants to meet me" he said to her.

His response brought a smile of relief to her face. Ever since she had met his mother, she wanted to inform her family about her relationship with him. It would make things a lot simpler for her and it would also strengthen her relationship with him. They had never spoken about the future and she didn't want to think too far ahead about marriage. But the fact was that they had kept their relationship going strong despite the long distance between them. Their relationship was stronger than ever and now that he was mentally a lot more at ease, she thought it would be the best time for her father to know about their relationship.

As they both spoke to each other, the sun set completely and the lights started to take effect. Bangalore looked beautiful at night, every corner sparkling with colour and brightness. She took him to the top of the tower at UB City, showing him a beautiful panoramic view of the city. He admired the sight of the city adorned with lights and took a few photographs. After spending some time over there, she told him the name of their next destination for the night.

"We're going to Athena" she said to him.

"And what's that?"

"It's the best disco in the city" she replied.

"I knew you'd have a dance place in your list" he said to her with a smile on his face.

They reached Athena in no time and the moment they walked inside, he was blown away with the lighting and music. Athena was at least twice as big as Hiccups was. It was jam packed that night, despite it being a weekday and they started dancing as soon as they were on the dance floor. The music was louder than what he was accustomed to at Hiccups and the lighting was completely different. Athena had a lot of laser lights as compared to Hiccups which had more of the shiny disco balls that gave it a unique feel. But in a matter of minutes, he realized that the lighting and the location barely mattered. All he could see was the love of his life dancing next to him and all he could hear was the music that played.

They danced together till ten o'clock that night. After dancing, they had their dinner and left the club. She drove him back to her home and as soon as she shut the apartment door, they were locked in each other's arms as they began kissing each other. For the second night in a row, they kept each other awake.

The next morning as he boarded his flight back home, he had a pleasant smile on his face. The two nights he had spent with the woman he loved had been magical. The story of his life had finally turned around. He was happy at last. Genuinely happy.

11

The Stalemate

It had been a week since she celebrated her birthday. Her parents were back home and for the past few days, she had been thinking of how to approach her father to tell him about her relationship. Even though she was confident that her father would approve of him, she still felt very tense. She spoke to her boyfriend every night, telling him about how she had almost broached the topic with her parents during dinner and then bailed out at the last minute. He told her that instead of telling both her parents at once, maybe she could try sounding out her mother before telling her father. She liked the idea. Her mother had always been fairly relaxed about the choices she made in her life. It was her father who was very concerned about her career choices and other decisions in life. She decided to speak to her mother in the absence of her father.

It was a Monday; she took another sick leave from work. As soon as her father left home for work, she asked her mother to sit down and took a deep breath before telling her mother about him. After the initial bouts of shock, her mother came to terms with what she had to say. The mother asked her a lot of questions about him and how serious the couple were about a future together. She assured her mother that he was very serious about a future with her and that he was a thorough gentleman and a trustworthy man. She then gave her mother a crash course on his background and achievements. She felt like a *rishta* hawk, running through his resume and all his personality traits and talents.

After an hour long discussion, she was confident that her mother was convinced. However, her mother did caution her by telling her that her father would not get convinced so easily. She nodded her head in agreement and then embraced her mother. Her joy knew no bounds.

She sent an sms to her boyfriend:
just told mom about us... she's cool with it... super happy :)
Within seconds she got his reply:
gr8... hope you told her about my one and only demand...
She was surprised with his response and replied:
what demand?
She laughed as soon as she read his message:
ghabraiye mat... humein kuch nahin chahiye... hum toh bas itna chahtey hain ki baaratiyon ka swagat... ;)
She sent him another sms:
don't get too happy yet... still need to get dad to approve
best of luck – was his reply
same to you ;) – she responded.

That evening, after dinner, her mother retired to the bedroom while her father watched the news on TV. She sat down next to her father on the drawing room sofa.

"Anything on TV that you want to watch?" asked her father, wondering what she was doing in the drawing room instead of her usual practice of going to her room after dinner.

She felt very nervous and spoke in pauses without looking directly at her father.

"Papa... actually, the thing is... I want to talk to you about something important" she said to her father.

"Is everything OK?" her father asked with a concerned look on his face.

"Yeah. There's nothing to be worried about" she said hurriedly, trying to allay her father's concern.

"Alright. Then just go ahead and tell me. I'm your father, you don't have to be scared" her father said in a calm voice.

"There's someone in my life" she said to her father after taking a deep breath.

Her palms were sweating, her fists were clenched and her heart was racing. Her father's expression had not changed at all on hearing her last statement.

"He's from my college. My classmate. We've known each

other for more than four years. He's a really nice guy and..."

"Do I know him?" interrupted her father.

"Sort of. You remember the guy who got the award from the President in Final Year. I'm talking about him" she said, glad that she mentioned the President in the introduction.

Her father closed his eyes for a second, trying to picture the young man who his daughter was referring to.

"Go on. Tell me everything you can about this person" said her father.

She was relieved by her father's response. At least he wanted to know more about the man she loved. At least he had not reacted negatively at the outset. She started telling her father everything about *him*, right from the times in First Year when she wasn't friends with him and about how they became friends due to Fastermind. She mentioned every single achievement of his and when her father asked questions about his background, she told him whatever she knew. She did not try to smoothen out the rough edges of his dark past.

"... now his mother is fine and he's doing really well in his job. I really like him a lot Papa and I think we really have a chance to be together in the long-term" she said to her father.

"Has he asked you to marry him?" inquired her father.

"No."

"Do you want to marry him?" asked her father.

"Not right now. But definitely sometime in the future" she responded.

Her father took a deep breath and sighed. He closed his eyes and was lost in thought. She waited for him to respond for a while but then could not bear the uncomfortable silence.

"Papa, please say something" she pleaded to her father.

"I have to go to your friend's city next Saturday for a conference. I want to meet him. After I have met him I will tell you what I think" he said to her in an emotionless voice.

"That's it?" she asked her father.

"Yes. I have heard your part of the story, now I want to meet him and speak to him before I form an opinion. It's getting late now, I need to go to sleep" her father said to her and got up from the sofa. Before he walked off to his bedroom, he gently tapped her head, which brought her some relief and meant that her father was not upset.

She went to her room and immediately gave a call to her boyfriend, informing him about the latest development. She was very surprised to see how relaxed he was on hearing the news that her father wanted to meet him. She wondered why she was so tense, when her father and boyfriend seemed so relaxed. He tried to calm her down and asked her not to worry too much.

During the next few days, her father asked her quite a few questions about him, especially regarding his financial situation. She answered all the questions with complete honesty and with each passing day got more and more worried. She kept her boyfriend informed about her father's questions on a daily basis and soon it was Saturday.

He got up early that morning and prepared himself for the meeting with her father. He took his time, combing his hair carefully and making sure he looked as good as he possibly could. She had given him strict instructions on what to wear based on the likes and dislikes of her father. She specifically asked him to wear formals and put on a tie. He felt like he was getting ready for an interview. He did as he was told. This was important.

He reached the hotel ahead of time and went straight to the restaurant where he was to meet her father. He took his place on a table at the far end of the restaurant, one which would offer some privacy. A few minutes later, he saw her father. It was the first time he was seeing her father up close. Her father was wearing a brown tweed coat and looked very sophisticated.

"Hello, sir" he said, as he got up and shook hands with her father.

"Please sit" her father said to him.

Her father ordered a cup of coffee and a French toast, the younger man ordered just a cup of coffee. He guessed from the order that her father did not intend to spend too much time talking.

"Let's get straight to the point. My daughter says that the two of you are in love with each other. She has also told me what she claims to know about you. She wants me to approve of her relationship with you but I cannot simply do that based on what she has told me. I want you to tell me everything that I need to know about you. Once you have done so, I will tell you what I think of your future with her" said the older man.

Her father had an expressionless face and a very calm voice. He could not judge the mood that her father was in. He decided to start his monologue, one that he had worked on for the past few days. He started off by telling her father what he was doing with his life currently and what plans he had for the future. He then moved back into flashback mode and told him about his family history. Her father kept stabbing him with pointed questions, especially about his family's financial position, without ever getting into details.

"... and that's about it" he said in conclusion, as he wrapped up the brief narration of his life story.

Her father looked at him with a piercing gaze; which he confidently returned. After a few seconds of silence, the older man finally spoke.

"Everything you told me today was already known to me, based on what my daughter told me. Which means that she knows whatever there is to know about you. It also means that there has been no real revelation here and thus I hold the same opinion of you as I did before we met today.

Look, I do not want to stretch the suspense for you any more. So, I will tell you in plain words that I do not really support my daughter's relationship with you."

Her father's words, knocked the wind out of his lungs. He had to make a real effort to breathe.

"May I know why?" he asked her father.

"Sure. I'll tell you my reasons. But before I do, I want you to know that I have nothing against you. For all I know you are as perfect for her as she believes you to be. But I do have my apprehensions. Now, please do not take offence to what I have to say and instead try and understand why I am saying it.

The first real issue I have is with your financial position. You just started your career and within a year had to take a loan. The reason for it may be genuine, but the fact of the matter is, you do have major financial liabilities at this young age. The other concern I have is, that despite two generations of your family living in this city, you do not have a house to call your own. You may be doing really well in your job and you may be drawing a great salary, but we all know that a job in the corporate world is no lifetime guarantee of financial safety.

The second issue I have is regarding something that is not as tangible as financial security. It has more to do with your background. You seem to have led a life riddled with misfortunes: your father's unfortunate death, followed by your mother's accident and then the subsequent medical problems. While I do empathise with your situation, the fact is that you have been subjected to a lot of hardships. I've known a few people who have spent their formative years facing the brunt of misfortune. Even if they survive the rough tides, they remain forever scarred. Later in life, those scars manifest themselves into frustration and several other negative emotions. Emotions that you and my daughter are too young to understand. But I do hope you understand what I mean when I say that men, who lead tough lives, do not usually make for good husbands. I have only one daughter and I love her more than anything in this world. She is young and so are you and in today's times, kids are in such a tearing hurry to take big decisions. Decisions that can make or break their life. I have put in a lot of thought behind this matter and in my judgment I do not think that the two of you should think of a long-term future together. Marriage must be between equals..."

"... but shouldn't the measure be that of love. Why measure me against my financial position or my past misfortunes? Why not give me a chance? Why not give me some time to turn things around?" he said to her father, in a concerned but calm voice.

"I am no one to give you time. This is not about me. Please

do not misunderstand. This is not the generation where a daughter would abandon her love based on her father's concerns. I will not stop her from continuing her relationship with you. She is free to do as she wishes. It's just that this relationship does not have my blessings. I say this with no ill will towards you, but I simply do not think my daughter should think about entering a household whose past has been filled with struggles and setbacks. She comes from a different world; not too many college students could have afforded the kind of lifestyle she followed. She is too young to understand what she has and what she could lose by making the wrong choices in life" said the older man.

"But you know that she will not go against your wishes" he said.

"Yes I do. Which is why I ask you to think very hard about what I said. You are young but from what I have heard about you, you are also very mature. Please try and understand what I am saying. Think about what you really are without my daughter. Think about what she has done for you and what you have done for her. Do you want her to spend the rest of her life healing your scars? I am not a man who believes in astrology, but don't you think you have a greater share of sorrow and misfortune in your life than most others? I for one, would not willingly give my daughter away, to a man, who seems to be destined to fight against the odds for his entire life.

Right now we've reached a stalemate. I am not in favour of this relationship. My daughter will not go against my wishes and neither will she leave your side. The only person who can break this deadlock is you. I ask you to consider what I have just told you and even though it goes against you, you will realize that my decision would be the best for my daughter, who you claim to be in love with" said her father as he got up, kept enough money on the table to pay the bill and put his hand on the young man's shoulder once before leaving.

He stayed on at the table for an hour after her father had left; thinking about what he had been told. He had no argument against anything that her father had said. Her father had said a lot of things that were rational and made a lot of sense. But he knew that he was the right man for her. He loved her. He couldn't bear the thought of not being with her. She meant so much to him. He knew that there was only one person who could help him. He left the restaurant to go and speak with his mother.

As soon as he was home and his mother saw his face, she knew that something had gone wrong. He narrated the entire incident to his mother.

"Don't worry *beta*, I will speak to her father and convince him" she said to her son.

"Not yet *maa*. Let me address some of his concerns. He thinks we're poor and homeless. I'll pile up a mountain of money and buy a brand new house. Then you can speak to him" he said with his trademark determination.

"That will take time. Don't make this an ego issue. Think about her. This will be a tough phase for her. She has to balance two relationships. You must not make matters worse by taking on more challenges right now.

Think about ways by which you can convince her father" his mother said to him.

"I've thought about it *maa*. This is not an ego issue. Her father has two issues with me, my finances and my fate. There is nothing I can do to allay her father's concerns about my fate and destiny. That is not in my hands. It's my finances that I can work on improving. It will take time, I know. But during that time, even his mind-set may change a little in my favour."

"And how will you magically improve your finances?" asked his mother.

"I'll figure it out" he replied.

In his mind he had already started to think of ways by which he could get rid of the loan as soon as possible. An early promotion at work would help him out a great deal. From the very next day, he started to work with double his normal effort. He did not waste a single second in office. He worked hard and he worked smart. He played the corporate game: got close to his managers, said the right things at the right time, made sure every module of work he did, small or large, was noticed by his managers and volunteered for hiring and recruitment activities. His work had always been immaculate, but now that he was working with all his determination, the results were beyond the expectations of his peers and seniors. He got a lot of appreciation for going the extra mile at work. During the performance review cycle at his office, it had become clear that he would get promoted. He got word of it, but did not celebrate till he saw the official pronouncement.

During those months of extra hard work, he spent almost all his time in office. He'd reach office by nine in the morning and leave the next morning at three. His mother was concerned about his health but did not say anything to him, she knew why he was doing it. In the same period, his girlfriend made all the efforts she could to try and convince her father. But it was to no avail. Her father countered that effort by sending word out to all the *rishta* hawks to gather the finest catch from their community for her to choose from. Even though her father knew that there was a very slim chance of her choosing anyone else at that stage, he wanted to give her the message that she should start looking out for other options.

"Papa, he got a promotion" she said to her father with a hint of pride in her voice, the day she found out about her boyfriend's career progress.

"Let me know when he becomes the MD of the company" her father responded coldly.

The stalemate did not seem like it would come to an end soon. A few more months passed by and he saved every penny he could to repay the debt he owed to the bank. He was making steady progress, he had already paid back half the amount.

She waited patiently during those months, not pressurizing him to do anything in haste. She enrolled her mother to add to the lobbying efforts in convincing her father. But her father was adamant and refused to budge. She felt very frustrated with the whole situation. She wondered how long the stalemate was going to last.

Despite getting the promotion he was looking for, he did not let up on his efforts. He immersed himself in his work and it helped him stay away from any negative thoughts about the situation he faced. He had faith that somehow he would be able to pull things through and reach a stage where her father would give his consent to their relationship. He wondered how crazy his situation with his girlfriend had become. They were working so hard to convince her father to allow them to have a future together, even though the two of them had never discussed marriage with each other. It was almost as if it was something they had both taken for granted. He wanted to change that. He wanted to formally propose to her in a memorable way, once he had secured her father's consent. Every once in a while when he was alone and had time to think, he planned out how he would propose to her. He went through the monologue he had thought of in his mind and imagined her reaction once he asked her to marry him. It always brought a smile to her face.

The only minor event that took place during the interim was when his mother had a fall in the kitchen, causing a fracture in her right leg. Fortunately, she recovered completely in a few weeks, the only impact of the incident being a complete ban on his mother working in the kitchen, enforced strictly by him.

Meanwhile, the *rishta* hawks were doing a fine job, hunting down candidate after candidate for her. She wondered how matrimonial websites survived when community referrals were doing so well. Every week she rejected a resume. One day her father got upset, after she rejected a man who worked as a manager at a leading FMCG firm. The candidate's resume was impeccable and his salary was the kind that you hear of in the newspapers, offered to the top graduates of leading B-schools. Her father argued with her, asking her for a valid reason to reject the FMCG manager.

"Because you know that I love someone else" she said in a raised voice, losing her temper.

"And why do you love him? What has he done for you? What can he do for you?" asked her father in anger.

She looked away from her father for a second and pictured herself at the hill with her boyfriend and then at the club a thousand miles away dancing with the same man, the man she loved.

"He allows me to be myself... and that's all I need" she replied before walking off to her room.

A few weeks later, on a Sunday afternoon, he was busy accounting for his finances. He realized that he was just a few months away from paying off the medical loan he had taken. He felt relieved by that thought. Things were moving slowly but in the right direction. The moment he got rid of the loan, he would start building up his finances and then go to her father once again, to try and convince him to change his mind. If that didn't work, he'd bring out the heavy artillery and let his mother speak to her father.

He realized that his initial plan had been a little too optimistic. There was no way he could buy a house without resigning his fate to paying back a loan for the rest of his life. The house would have to wait for a while. But his relationship with her could not. They had already been away from each other for more than half a year. He missed her a lot. Just as he was busy pondering his future, he heard a faint knock on his bedroom door.

He opened the door to his room and found his mother resting herself against the wall next to the door. She was breathing hard. Her face looked pale.

"What happened *maa*?" he asked her, helping her to sit down on the bed in his room.

"I don't know *beta*, something is wrong. I woke up today morning and felt a little light headed for a while. Then it went away. But for the last hour or so I've been having an increasing pain in my chest and now I'm finding it hard to breathe" she said in a faint voice.

Without wasting a second, he picked up his cell phone and gave a call to Dr. Roy, who asked him to rush to the hospital. Despite it being a Sunday afternoon, Dr. Roy reached the hospital to take care of the young man's mother.

Dr. Roy conducted the preliminary check-up and referred the case to Dr. Chitnis, a senior cardiologist. The cardiologist asked for a few full body CT scans to be conducted immediately. Dr. Roy stayed with him all the while even though it was clear that the issue had nothing to do with the patient's brain. Once the CT scan results were out, Dr. Chitnis called Dr. Roy and the patient's son inside a room.

"It looks like she has a pulmonary embolism, but we need to conduct a few tests to confirm. Meanwhile I suggest we go ahead and place the patient in the ICU" said Dr. Chitnis.

As soon as Dr. Roy heard that statement, his face lost its colour.

"What is a pulmonary embolism?" asked the young man.

"It is a blood clot in the veins that reaches the lungs and triggers a massive cardiac arrest" said Dr. Roy covering his face with his hands.

"But how could that be? She was fine till last night. We just had a full body check-up done a couple of months back, nothing showed up then" said the young man, unable to understand why the doctors had such a worried look on their face.

"The trigger could be anything, an injury to a bone causing a tiny amount of marrow to leak out into the blood stream or it could even be a result of..." said Dr. Chitnis before he was interrupted by Dr. Roy.

"That is immaterial. Let's confirm the diagnosis quickly" said Dr. Roy with urgency in his voice.

"What if it is an embolism? How do we treat it?" he asked the doctors.

"There is no treatment for a pulmonary embolism that has reached such an advanced stage. It will be fatal" said Dr. Chitnis.

His heart sank. He could not believe what he was hearing. How could it be? Everything was fine today morning? There had to be a mistake. He thought to himself. How could a simple fracture lead to a fatal condition? He asked the doctors the same question, they gave him a reply that reminded him of what he had heard more than a decade ago: it was a one in a million chance.

How could his destiny be so cruel to him? He had already lost his father to a one in a million medical condition and now he was being told that his mother was going to suffer the same fate.

"This cannot happen" he said aloud and asked the doctors to conduct the confirmation test immediately. He waited near the test lab along with Dr. Roy. Both men did not speak a word to each other. The test was going to take close to an hour to be performed. Finally Dr. Roy spoke to the young man.

"Listen, there's still a small hope that the confirmation test results in a negative, but if it does not; no one can say how much time your mother has. If it is an embolism, you may be looking at just a few hours before it becomes fatal. Don't stand here, go to your mother. I will let you know when the results are out" said the neurologist.

After six years, the young man walked once again, with dread filling his heart, towards the hospital ICU. His mind was blank. He still had not come to terms with what the doctors had said. How could things take a turn for the worst so suddenly?

Before he knew it, he was in front of the ICU door. He looked at his mother through the glass panel. Her breathing was laboured, but she was conscious. He walked in, putting on a smile to cheer his mother up.

"What did the doctors say beta?" she asked him, innocently.

There is no treatment for a pulmonary embolism that has reached such an advanced stage. It will be fatal – the cardiologist's words echoed in his mind.

"They're still doing some tests" he replied, wishing that his voice hadn't cracked.

His mother looked at him with concern.

"Why are you crying?" she asked him.

That was when he realized that he had tears running down his face. He wiped them off, but they were quickly replaced by more tears. His mother asked him to tell her what the doctors had really said. He told her the truth and then burst into tears. She consoled him and asked him not to cry. He wanted to talk to her, but all he could do was cry. He was helpless and hoped against hope that the results of the tests turned out to be negative. Before he could regain his composure, he got a call on his phone from Dr. Roy asking him to come to his office.

"I'll be back soon *maa*, I promise" he said to his mother, fighting back more tears.

"I will be here when you are back, I promise" said his mother in a calm voice.

She watched her son leave. She called for the nurse and asked for a pen and a piece of paper. She hurriedly wrote down something on the page and asked the nurse to make sure that she posted that piece of paper in an envelope to an address that she wrote down on a separate page. She asked the nurse to do it immediately. The nurse complied. The hospital reception had a postal section. The nurse was back in five minutes. The patient felt a great sense of relief when she was told by the nurse that the letter had been submitted for posting.

He was at Dr. Roy's office, where Dr. Chitnis confirmed the presence of an embolism that was fast approaching the patient's lung. The cardiologist estimated that his mother had a couple of hours left before she died of a massive cardiac arrest the moment the embolism reached her lung.

"Is there nothing we can do?" he said to the doctors in the hope of a miracle.

"I'm afraid not. I'm really sorry" said Dr. Chitnis as Dr. Roy put his hand on the young man's shoulders to comfort him.

Only Dr. Roy knew what the young man was going through. The neurologist had seen how he had devoted five years of his life to bringing his mother back from a coma and now barely a year later, she was going to leave him forever.

"You should spend this time with your mother" Dr. Roy said to him.

He nodded and made his way back to the ICU – to speak to his mother for the last time.

As he took each step towards the ICU, a flurry of thoughts flooded his mind. There were so many things he wanted to say to his mother, so many things he wanted her to see, so many more years that he wanted to spend in her presence. How could he possibly do all those things in a couple of hours? Life was playing the most cruel joke on him. Making a son watch his mother die in front of him.

He reached the ICU door and took a quick glance from the glass panel once again to check if his mother was still alive – she was. He opened the door and walked in. She had a serene smile on her face. He broke down the moment he sat down beside his mother. She held him in a tight embrace, patting him gently on his back.

She knew that her time was over, he did not have to tell her what the doctors had said. Every breath she took made her feel like a thousand knives were piercing her, but she did not want her son to know that she was in pain. For several minutes the mother and son just held onto each other not saying a word.

"Why... are we so unlucky *maa*? Why us?" he whispered into her ears in broken words.

"We are not unlucky *beta*. How many mothers get a chance to say farewell to their sons? How many sons get to say goodbye to their mothers? I don't know how much time I have left now, so listen carefully. I want you to know that I am very proud of you and what you have done with your life. I am the most fortunate mother in the world to have a son like you. A son who has given nothing but pride to his parents. Your father was gone when you were little, for the best part of your teenage I was not there; but look at what you have made of your life.

And you know why I am proud of you, not just because of everything you have achieved in your career, but more so because you steered yourself in the right direction in life despite having no one but yourself as a guide. You worked hard and blossomed when you could so easily have withered away. You fought against all odds when you could so easily have given up and despite all the hardships you faced, your smile is still so full of life. Always remain like this. It is your greatest strength" said the mother to her son.

"You are the best mother in the whole world *maa*... and I want you to know that even when you were not there in front of me, I always thought of you when I was in trouble. And without your blessings I would not have survived for a single day and I love you... so much" he said to his mother with tears welling up in his eyes despite his best efforts to stop them.

"I love you too *beta* and my blessings and your father's blessings will always be there with you. You must never worry about anything in life. *Iske baad sab kuch theek ho jayega.* Nothing and no one will be able to harm you or stop you from getting what you want. I promise you..."

She could feel her heart racing. She knew that she had just a few breaths left in her.

"Listen to me... don't ever feel that you are alone. You are not and you will never be alone. Be brave... like you have been. I love you... God bless you" she said with her last few breaths.

He looked at her as she said those words. She was not crying, she had a smile on her face as she said her last words. And then as she exhaled for the last time, he saw her eyes close. Dr. Roy who had been watching from outside the ICU, walked in and embraced the young man who cried inconsolably.

The light from the young man's life was gone. He did not know what he would do now, with fate having snatched away both his parents from him in the cruellest of ways. He looked at his mother and held her hand, wishing that she'd return his touch. Wishing that he would once again see her eyes light up the way they did when she saw him. Wishing that she would once again hold him in her arms and give him courage. Wishing that once again she'd speak to him so that he could hear her voice again. But he knew that was not going to happen again. She was gone, forever.

"Goodbye *maa*" he whispered tearfully.

Three days later...

She woke up in the morning and checked her mobile phone. It had several missed calls, all of them from Dr. Roy. Surprised, she called him back immediately. Dr. Roy answered the phone and asked her if she knew where he was. The neurologist sounded worried.

"What's the matter?" she asked the doctor.

"Oh. Don't you know?" the doctor replied with a surprised tone.

"Don't I know what?"

"I am afraid there is some bad news. His mother passed away three days ago" said the neurologist in a sombre tone.

She could not believe the words she was hearing.

"What? Oh my God. How did this happen?" she asked him, stunned.

"Well, she had a rare medical condition called an embolism caused due to a blood clot. The clot was triggered by a fracture, the blood clot reached her lungs and then caused a massive cardiac arrest" the neurologist informed her.

She was speechless. She could barely grasp what the doctor had told her.

"It's been two days since I saw him. I met him during the funeral and after that I tried speaking to him. But his cell phone was switched off and today when I went to his house, he wasn't there. So I thought of calling you up. But I guess, even you don't know where he is" said the doctor, dejectedly.

"I'll find him" she replied and then hung up the phone.

She found it hard to breathe. His mother was no more. That very thought sent a shiver down her spine. Why didn't he tell her about it? She felt a tear running down her cheek. She thought about the afternoon she had spent with his mother on the hill. She was such a nice woman. Even though she had met her for just one day, she felt a strong connection with her. She could not believe that his mother was gone.

But she knew where she could find him. She was sure of it. She knew what she had to do. She packed her travel bag and then booked a ticket on the earliest flight out of Bangalore to his city.

Half an hour after she got the call from Dr. Roy, she was in the drawing room of her house, ready to go to *him*. Her father was having his breakfast and saw her with her bag packed to leave.

"Where are you going?" asked her father, confused by what he saw.

"His mother passed away" she said to her father.

"Oh, no. I'm sorry to hear that" her father replied in a serious tone.

"I am going to see him. He needs me right now" she said to her father in a determined voice.

"I understand, I'll drop you to the airport" her father said to her as he got up to help her carry the bag to the car.

The drive to the airport was filled with silence, occasionally broken by sounds of sniffing as she cried softly.

They reached the airport and as she left the car to walk inside the airport, her father held her hand and looked into her eyes.

"Listen, promise me you won't do anything in haste" he said to his daughter.

"Relax, I am just going there to comfort him. I won't get carried away. Trust me" she said to her father.

As soon as she reached the city, she went to her uncle's house and borrowed his car. She drove swiftly but with caution and reached the hill in a hurry. She walked the last portion towards the edge in hurried steps. She finally saw him. Sitting on the edge of the hill, staring into the nothingness below with downcast eyes. She felt a sense of relief once she saw him.

Once she was close to him, she called out his name. He did not respond. She took another step towards him and called out his name again. He turned around to look at her. He looked tired, almost as if he hadn't slept for days. He stood up and walked towards her, his face was expressionless. As though he was too exhausted to change the expression on his face. She walked up to him and held him in an embrace.

"I am so sorry" she said to him.

"Why did you come here?" he asked her in a sombre voice.

"What do you mean?" she asked, confused by his question.

"I mean why have you come here? Why can't you let me be alone?" he repeated.

"I can't let you be alone. Especially at this time. Why are you speaking to me like this?" she asked him.

"Because I am tired... tired of being abandoned... tired of fighting desperately only to feel miserable in defeat. And it's always defeat for me. No victory... not when it matters the most. My father was taken away from me... I could do nothing, I was too little. But my mother asked me to be brave and I did as I was told. I was brave.

A few years later, my mother was on her way to a temple when she met with an accident. I watched my mother's life hang in the balance between life and death for years. For five years. I gave a promise to God that I would never pray, in exchange for her life. In the absence of my mother and father, the one Being who we all turn to... I told that one last Hope that I would never pray to Him again, all He had to do was bring my mother back.

For five long years I waited for my mother to return and she did. For a while I thought that maybe my luck had turned at last. But just when I had put together the broken pieces of my life, destiny shattered everything.

One morning, my mother was with me... by evening she was dead. Gone. Forever. No chance of return. This time destiny did not even care to give me the small mercy of hope.

Everything I have really wanted has been taken away from me. That's why I asked you, why you were here... because, I could bear the loss of my father, I was too small back then anyway. I somehow fought back when my mother was lost for five years.

But now I am broken, I cannot take it anymore. My mother has gone away forever and I am all alone. And I can somehow learn to live that way. But what I cannot do, is live with the hope that you will be a part of my life and watch that final hope get destroyed. If that happens, it will drive me over that edge" he said, pointing towards the edge of the hill.

She held him in a tight embrace.

"Shhh... Don't say such things. I am right here. I will never leave you. And you are not alone. I am here for you... right now and always" she said to him with tears in her eyes.

He cried on her shoulder and returned her embrace.

"Why did this happen? Why did destiny choose me to face all this misery? Wasn't the punishment during those five years enough?" he asked her in despair.

"On this very hill, your mother told me something that I think you need to hear right now. Do you know what she told me? She said that whenever something unfortunate happens... we should not ask such questions. These questions have no answers. Because it is not our duty to ask questions of God or our Destiny. All we have to do is move on and live our lives. And that life is all about finding out what happens next.

That's what your mother told me and I think it was for a purpose. She could've told me so many things that day, but that was what she told me. And I think you need to follow what she said" she said to the man she loved.

"My mother said that to you?"

"Yes. That day when we were here at the hill and you had gone to get us lunch. We talked about a lot of things. She was a really nice woman... but why didn't you tell me when it happened? I found out from Dr. Roy" she said to him, with tears in her eyes.

"Everything happened so fast that day. I couldn't think straight. The next day when I thought of calling you, I remembered what your father had said to me about misfortune being a part of my life and I thought that maybe he was right. I did not want to burden you with my life's tragedy" he explained to her.

"Forget about what my father said. Your life is not all about misfortune. If that was the case, then your mother would never have returned. She would never have seen how much you have achieved. She would never have spent a year with you. A beautiful year that not all mothers get to spend with their sons..."

"... and she got a chance to meet you" he said with a faint smile.

"She had the nicest things to say about you, you know that?" he said to her, as she embraced him once again with a fresh set of tears flowing down her face.

"I'm here now. Everything will be alright" she whispered into his ear.

Later that evening, they had a simple dinner together at his house. After which they got talking again.

"I'm sorry about the way I spoke to you earlier today" he said to her.

"You have nothing to be sorry about. In fact I am sorry that you had to go through everything, all by yourself" she said as she held his hand.

He held out his *rudraksh* and looked at it.

"This is all that my mother left behind" he said to her, staring at the sacred bead that he had kept with himself for almost seven years, since the day his mother had given it to him.

She could see how exhausted he was and asked him to go to sleep. The moment he lay down on his bed, he fell into a tired and dreamless sleep. She watched as the calm returned to his face. She could see how badly he needed her. She also realized how much she wanted to be with him. It was time for her to take a decision and in her heart she knew she already had. She was going to stay with him for a few more days and then return to Bangalore to inform her father that she wanted to be with *him* and no one else. She hoped that her father would understand.

At that very moment, her cell phone started to ring. It was a phone call from her father.

"Papa?"

"Hi. Listen, where are you right now?" her father asked.

"I'm at his house. He's resting. What's the matter?" she asked.

"I am in your city. Please tell me the address of his house."

"What? Why are you here? I promised you *naa* that I wouldn't do anything stupid. Don't you trust me" she remarked angrily.

"Listen to me, this is important. You can yell at me later, just tell me your address" her father said to her.

She gave her father the address and waited for him to arrive. As she waited for her father, she kept guessing why he had travelled all the way from Bangalore to the city. It made no sense. She heard a knock on the door. She looked through the peep-hole in the door. It was her father. She opened the door.

"Papa, what are you doing here?" she said to him as soon as he entered.

"Where is he?" asked her father.

"Sleeping in his room. What's the matter, will you at least say something instead of asking me questions?" she said to her father.

Her father held out an envelope.

"After dropping you off at the airport, I returned home. An hour or so later, I received this envelope. It has a letter inside, addressed to me. I want you to read it" her father said as he handed over the envelope to her.

She opened the envelope carefully and pulled out the letter it contained. She read the words slowly and by the time she finished reading the letter, she had tears in her eyes. She grabbed her father's arm and started sobbing. Her father consoled her for a while.

"I want to speak to him" said her father.

"But he's sleeping."

"I am sure he'd like to read this letter immediately. Go. Wake him up. Tell him I'm here to see him and I have something he needs to have a look at."

She walked to his room and called his name out a few times. He woke up with a start.

"Relax... it's just me" she said to him.

He took a while to snap out of his drowsiness. When he was finally awake and in his senses, she spoke to him.

"My father is here..."

"What?"

"Don't worry. Everything is fine... he just needs to talk to you... immediately" she said to him in as calm as voice as she could put up.

He did not understand what was going on. He was very tired and decided to find out what the matter was and walked to the drawing room sofa where her father was sitting with a letter in his hand.

"Hello sir" he said to her father.

Her father shook his hand.

"I am really sorry for your loss" her father said to him.

He nodded his head.

"I want to have a word with you alone" her father said.

"As you wish" he replied.

She disappeared into his room but kept her ear on the door to hear the conversation between her father and her boyfriend.

"I received a letter today afternoon. It was from your mother and I think you should read it" her father said as he handed over the letter to the young man.

He held the letter as if it was a holy book. He could recognize his mother's hand writing. He read the date on the letter, it was written on the day of her death. He skipped through the salutations and read the body of the letter. It read:

I will be dead before this letter reaches you. I wanted to have a conversation with you in person, but fate has other plans for me. I do not have much time left so I will keep this short. I am the mother of the young man who is in love with your daughter.

And I believe that you have met my son. I also know that you do not approve of my son's relationship with your daughter. Your reasons, I have been told, are my son's financial situation and your belief that his life is going to be filled with misfortune. I am writing this letter with the hope to convince you to change your mind.

My son does not own a house of his own as of this moment. But a few years ago, he did. He had to sell it to pay for the expenses that kept me alive after my accident. He lived all by himself and paid for his engineering expenses with nothing but his scholarships and awards. There aren't too many eighteen year olds who will be able to face life the way my son did. He was brave enough to take tough decisions at that young age. He chose to live without a roof over his head just so that he could save his mother. Houses can be made whole again, families cannot. He realized this at a very young age.

My son does have a loan that he will soon repay completely. Once again, that is something he could not avoid. He took a loan to bring his mother back. It's a price that any son would be willing to pay for his mother's life. It would be a travesty of justice if he was punished for doing his duty as a son.

My son does not have a cloud of misfortune hanging over his head, I do. It was my husband who died of a rare disorder. It is I who met with an accident while visiting a temple. I was the one who spent five years in a coma. And today, I am the one dying of a condition as rare as the one that took my husband's life.

My son is the man who topped his college in each year of his engineering degree. My son is the man who brought his mother back from the brink of death. My son is the man who met the most beautiful woman in this world and fell in love with her. My son is the man who that very woman loves. For all these reasons and more, my son is the most fortunate man in the world.

And as my dying wish, I take away with me, all the clouds of misfortune that could ever come in the way of my son or in the way of those he loves.

Please allow my son and your daughter to go wherever their love takes them. I assure you that my son will treat her like the princess that she is and will give her every joy in the world.

A teardrop made its way down his face as he finished reading the letter. He couldn't believe the words that he had just read. Even moments before dying, his mother was doing all she could to secure her son's future. He broke down as he had that thought. Her father gently patted him on his shoulder, to console him. After a couple of minutes, he had regained his composure.

Her father spoke first.

"I came here to give you this letter and to tell you how sorry I am for the way I treated you. This may not be the best time to talk about such things, but I want you to know that henceforth I will not stand in the way of your relationship with my daughter. I was wrong to have judged you the way I did and I admire your mother for the courage with which she wrote that letter. I will always regret never having met a woman as brave as her in person. As far as I am concerned, you have my blessings" her father said to him in a choked voice.

As soon as she heard her father's words, she ran out towards the drawing room and gave her father a big hug. *He* walked to her father and touched his feet. Her father then gave him a gentle hug. The bereaved young man looked up at her father and then at her... he then closed his eyes and pictured the smiling face of his dear, departed mother. When he opened his eyes, there was a gleam in his eyes and a serene, faint smile on his lips...

The Calm after the Storm

One Year Later...

It was a night bathed in the light of a bright, full moon. They stepped out of the car and walked towards the edge of the hill. She was wearing a flowing white gown that had a layer of embroidery with silver and golden thread on it. The embroidered flowers and stars on her gown shone under the moonlight. A pearl necklace adorned her long, slender neck and he loved the soft sound that emanated from the pearls as they gently bounced with each step that she took.

She stood next to the *banyan* tree and waited for him to speak. She looked at him as he stood motionless in front of her, admiring her beauty. He was wearing a black tuxedo and a dark grey tie that seemed to blend in perfectly with the suit, under the moonlight. She smiled as she thought about how different he looked from the time when she had first seen him in college. He used to ride a cycle, wear the plainest of clothes every day and live a simple life. And now, he drove his own car, wore the best suits that money could buy and was all set to live the good life. But deep down, in his heart, he was still the same man whom she had met in college. A man who could sacrifice everything he had for those he loved. And she knew that he loved her.

That night he'd asked her to travel with him to the hill, so that he could ask her something important. She already knew what he was going to ask her and he already knew what her answer would be. All that she wanted to see was how he would ask her the question.

So far, he hadn't disappointed her. The moment he had seen her at her uncle's apartment, he had given her a bouquet of twenty one roses. It was the most beautiful thing she had ever seen. The roses were of different colours – red, pink, orange, blue, white, peach and yellow. The blue roses had an enchanting aura about them. She had never seen blue roses before and they turned out to be her favourite amongst all the others. She held the bouquet in her right hand as she stood on the soft grass, near the edge of the hill.

She looked into his gleaming eyes as he stood in front of her. She looked so beautiful that he was afraid he'd forget what he wanted to say to her. She had an expectant look in her eyes that made him a little nervous. A cool breeze started to drift along the hill top, making her hair flow in the wind. That sight blew him away and she could see the amazement on his face. She fought a smile as she wondered how, even after five years together, he still got distracted by her looks.

For a while, neither of them spoke. She waited for him to start and he waited to collect his thoughts. He closed his eyes for a few seconds and when he opened them, he had a solemn look on his face. She knew he was going to speak soon and found her heart beating faster in anticipation of what she hoped would be one of the most memorable moments of her life.

He looked into her loving eyes and took a deep breath before speaking.

"We both know why we are here tonight. On top of this hill... away from the rest of the world. Just the two of us... standing at a place that has been witness to so many moments that brought us closer. Well, I brought you here to tell you something and to ask you a question at the end of it. And I really hope it turns out like I had imagined, because you look so beautiful that I am afraid I will forget half the things I wanted to say to you. But I will try my best not to let that happen. So here goes..." he paused for a while and took another deep breath before continuing.

"... do you know when a man realizes that he is truly in love with a woman? When he starts picturing the moment when he asks her to spend the rest of her life with him. And I have been thinking of that very moment, for so many months that I have lost count. And I always wondered, what would be the most perfect place for me to have this conversation with you... and I thought and thought for several nights until I realized a simple truth. Any place on this Earth, where you are with me is the perfect place. All I need to do is look at you and I feel like I'm in heaven... and at times I wonder whether you even know how truly beautiful you are. Your beauty is every woman's envy and every man's desire.

We've been together for just about five years and sometimes when I look back at the times before we met... I wonder how I even existed without knowing you. You came into my life and changed everything... forever. Before you walked into my life, all I did was survive... you made me rediscover what it means to be alive. And I cannot bear to imagine a life without you. Without you, the morning would have no meaning and there would be no beauty in any evening.

You rescued me from a life full of darkness and turned it into a beautiful dream. A dream where I could see you smile, hear you laugh and dance the night away with you. And somewhere along the way, as the dream unravelled itself... I fell in love with you.

You mean more to me than you can imagine. In my life, you are the light at the end of the tunnel. You are like the calm after the storm. And every day I fall a little more in love with you. And I know that I have said a lot tonight... but the truth is that... words simply cannot convey how much I love you."

He paused once again as his hand reached inside his coat pocket. He pulled out a red velvet box and held it gently in his right hand. He got down on one knee and looked into her eyes again and continued in the same gentle, loving tone in which he was speaking.

"And now that I have told you what I really feel about you. I arrive at the question that I wished to ask you... will you marry me?"

He opened the velvet box to reveal a beautiful ring. It was made of platinum with seven diamonds engraved in it. It was shaped like a crown, with a large diamond encircled by six smaller ones along the surface of the platinum ring. He could see the reflection of the ring in her eyes, with the diamonds shining bright under the moon light.

She could not believe what was happening. Even though she knew that he was going to propose to her, never did she imagine that he would do it so perfectly. The words he had said to her were more precious to her than the diamonds on the ring. She knew that she would remember each moment of that night for the rest of her life. He had made it that memorable!

She had a smile on her face and a tear in her eye as she held out her left hand for him to hold.

"Yes... of course I will" she said in a whisper.

He gently slipped the ring over her finger, kissed her hand and stood up. She put her arms around him and looked into his eyes once before he leaned in to kiss her. It was the first kiss of their new life... a life that they had decided to spend together. The cascading moonlight shimmered through the leaves of the banyan tree blessing this union and the stars twinkled as if in a distant applause. That night, marked the beginning of their new journey. A journey that would last a lifetime. A lifetime that they would spend together.

About the Author

Harsh Pande was born and educated at Pune. In spite of suffering from complex orthopedic disorders by birth, which entailed a battle for rehabilitation through several surgeries, he displayed an unusually resilient spirit and a remarkable lust for life. He topped the Maharashtra State Board Examinations both in the 10th and 12th Standards while studying at St. Vincent's High School and Junior College. He also represented the West Zone in the popular and televised Bournvita Quiz Contest while at school. He then graduated with a distinction from the prestigious College of Engineering Pune winning a Gold Medal at the Tata Research Development and Design Centre during his internship.

A successful Computer Engineer, he was selected into one of the leading consulting firms in the world. Through all these years, writing had remained a consistent passion. He wrote actively for the school and college magazines, posted regularly on his widely popular blog and also found time to launch a very mischievous 'Project Breakup' on Facebook. Those who came in contact with him were fascinated by his wit and indomitable cheerful attitude towards life.

The book you now hold in your hands is his first; the inspiration for which was "an epiphany" he experienced while holidaying in Goa.

Harsh Pande, sadly, passed away on 23rd April 2012. He was 24 years, 3 months and 16 days old.

About the Author

HARSH PANDE was born and educated at Pune. In spite of suffering from complex orthopedic disorders by birth, which entailed a battle for rehabilitation through several surgeries, he displayed an unusually resilient spirit and a remarkable lust for life. He topped the Maharashtra State Board Examinations both in the 10th and 12th Standards while studying at St. Vincent's High School and Junior College. He also represented the West Zone in the popular and televised Bournvita Quiz Contest while at school. He then graduated with a distinction from the prestigious College of Engineering Pune winning a Gold Medal at the Tata Research Development and Design Centre during his internship.

A successful Computer Engineer, he was selected into one of the leading consulting firms in the world. Through all these years, writing had remained a consistent passion. He wrote actively for the school and college magazines, posted regularly on his widely popular blog and also found time to launch a very mischievous 'Project Breakup' on Facebook. Those who came in contact with him were fascinated by his wit and indomitable cheerful attitude towards life.

The book you now hold in your hands is his first; the inspiration for which was "an epiphany" he experienced while holidaying in Goa.

Harsh Pande, sadly, passed away on 23rd April 2012. He was 24 years, 3 months and 16 days old.